SPITTING FEATHERS

MARTYN SMITH

Copyright © 2015 Martyn Smith
Spitting Feathers

Published 2015.

Book cover and design by artist Christine Southworth – see her cover artwork on "You're Not Alone: An Indie Author Anthology".

All rights reserved. No part of this book may be reproduced or transmitted in any form or by any means, electronic or mechanical, including photocopying, recording, or by any information storage and retrieval system without the written permission of the author, except where permitted by law.

First printing: 2015.
ISBN-13: 978-1519737359
ISBN-10: 1519737351

British Cataloguing Publication Data
A catalogue record of this book is available from
The British Library.

Also available on Kindle from Amazon

Contents

Chapter 1: Turkey Poo, Politicians and Circling Supermarkets....... 5
Chapter 2: The Cold War, Sporrans and Sweet Talk 14
Chapter 3: Mad Professors, Grey Children and Cesspits............ 25
Chapter 4: Dolly Mixtures, Directions and Armageddon 29
Chapter 5: Family Honour and Unbuttoned Shirts.................. 35
Chapter 6: The Twilight Zone 42
Chapter 7: Ollie and Kenneth Come In from the Cold 48
Chapter 8: Cucumbers, Doughnuts and Other Surprises............. 54
Chapter 9: Love and Hate 64
Chapter 10: Apollo 13 and Indian Rain Dances 70
Chapter 11: Locals, Lawyers and Charm Offensives................. 81
Chapter 12: Placards Meet the Implacable 90
Chapter 13: Bitter Sweet and Career Confetti 99
Chapter 14: Cold War Concrete and Coded Messages................ 110
Chapter 15: Suspenders and the Death Penalty 126
Chapter 16: Doggy Dust-up and Bite-sized Chunks 141
Chapter 17: Brigadiers, Briefs and Boxes of Joy................. 151
Chapter 18: Big Slips and Slip Ups 169
Chapter 19: Mopeds, Managers and Ski Lifts...................... 181
Chapter 20: Elevenses, Mischief and the Medieval................ 193
Chapter 21: Stumpy, Scorn and Swinging Doors.................... 202
Chapter 22: Doo-Wops and Dodgy Directions 215
Chapter 23: A Tale of Two 'Fetes'............................... 226
Chapter 24: Shamed and Stumped 242
Chapter 25: Good Things Come in Threes 256
Chapter 26: Completed and Deleted 268
Chapter 27: Explosive Stuff 281
Chapter 28: A Watershed Moment.................................. 288

A Note from the Author 292
About the Author 293
Acknowledgements 294

Chapter 1:
Turkey Poo, Politicians and Circling Supermarkets

Attila looked across the farmyard at the taut, Harris Tweed-covered posterior bending over invitingly like a partially filled hot air balloon. It was Fred Gooley preparing the morning's feed. He should have known something was up. Of all the Wirral White turkeys he had bred for Christmas over the years, Attila, who arrived at Feathers Farm as a poult three years previously, had evaded the festive feast. Fred had a quiet and quizzical respect for her cunning and, despite her wicked side, had grown to understand her moves and actions. It was as if she was trying to communicate, and this kept him intrigued.

Attila lowered her head and stretched out her neck, her eyes squinting yet sharply focused on the invitingly ample posterior. In respect to their leader, the gaggle parted slowly in knowing anticipation as Attila emerged in proud defiance from a mass of white feathers. She slowly moved forward towards her target, her spiked feet purposefully strident, gathering speed as her wings unfolded. In seconds she was airborne, at speed, legs trailing, neck fully extended and eyes focused. Years of dust and turkey poo were sucked skyward as the wind whooshed through her outstretched wings, their tips just brushing the ground. At that moment, Fred suddenly raised his head in knowing recognition of the sound. But it was too late.

At turkey supersonic speed, Attila shut her eyes and a nano second later embedded her sharp beak into what appeared to be just the slightest of slackness where Fred's ample posterior cheeks met. Attila sunk to the ground in exhaustion, the result of another direct hit. A faint chuckle followed, suggesting gleeful satisfaction.

Fred let out an enormous broad Cornish howl. "Ahhhhh! You little bugger, you – just you wait till Christmas!" Fred screamed unconvincingly as Attila, still chuckling, quickly scrambled to her feet and made a hasty retreat back into the mass of feathers, who closed ranks as their leader returned to the anonymity of the fold. As had happened so often, Fred would just have to put up with this, the latest of pranks only Attila could muster.

***

Attila had been christened by Fred's youngest grandchild, Dan, who would often stand by the farm's courtyard fence to spot and name the cheekiest of the Wirral Whites; not a good idea given their intended fate in the festive season. One morning, in his haste to get a closer look at the Whites, Dan approached a little too close and the pecking altercation that followed left the poor child in tears with what looked like a cheap tattoo on each foot and a grey pullover so full of holes that it would have looked good on any dead gangster. Gordon, the older grandchild, watched the entire fracas from the other side of the fence with mild amusement and suddenly a name for the errant Wirral White became clear. Gordon was, at the time, grappling at school with famous fifth century Hungarian warmongers and 'Attila the Hen' seemed entirely appropriate for the fearsome fowl. It was some time later that Grandpa Fred told Gordon that Attila was not in fact a hen but a turkey, albeit a turkey hen, but by then it was too late. And so it was that Attila came to be.

On arrival in 2004, Attila soon realised that, although she and the thousands of other poults were growing up fast at Feathers Farm and having the time of their lives, it seemed a bit excessive for her master to have that many birds as pets. After all, they only had one cat. The turkeys' living conditions were luxurious: they were kept warm at night, had lots of food and water, were all healthy and nobody fought. She noticed that she and her other feathered friends were starting to put on weight and every now and again Fred would put one of his 'pets' on an antique-looking spring-loaded contraption and then write something down. Oddly though, he never put the family cat on the gadget. Something wasn't quite right. It was all too good to be true.

The old stone barn opposite Attila's barn 'home' in the courtyard behind the farmhouse fascinated her as it never seemed to be used, so one day she hopped on the window ledge to peer through the dusty glass. An eerie beam of light shone through a skylight to illuminate sinister-looking hooks suspended from a ceiling gantry, a table with a neatly laid out selection of knives of all shapes and sizes and a large pile of canvas bags in the corner covered with white feathers. Attila looked down at her protruding chest and gulped. The white feathers on those bags were the same as hers. This was not a happy place. It was a building of darkness. Her friends weren't pets at all – and neither was she. Something nasty was going to happen to them all. Her master was a smiling assassin.

By late November her worst fears were realised when the gaggle started to reduce in numbers. They would go into the building of darkness but not come out and by Christmas, they had all gone. Attila's survival instincts kicked in as she dodged the daily round up. She regularly sneaked back into the upper levels of her two-storey barn home to hide but she knew that, if she was to survive, it was time to take matters into her own claws.

The post-Christmas period was a natural lull in turkey farming. Fred was outside taking a breather when Attila decided it was time to reveal herself and hopped onto the wall at the end of the courtyard to attract his attention. She looked over to Fred who, motionless, couldn't believe his eyes. He was truly astonished. "Bloody hell. You little bugger, you. How did you escape? Where have you been hiding?"

This cat and mouse game went on for weeks but by the end of February, the distance between Attila and Fred had slowly reduced to just a few feet as she instinctively and more confidently felt that her life was no longer in danger. Fred just wouldn't do that sort of thing for fun. She wasn't to know that as a Christmas turkey, it was now a bit late and anyway, she was probably a bit on the tough side. There was only one thing for it: after another day of sizing each other up, she stayed motionless and closed her eyes, hoping she had made the right decision.

Fred picked her up and carried her to a stone seat in the courtyard, where he sat down. And so they had formed a bond, an unholy alliance which, with the exception of Fred's wife Grace, no one would ever understand nor believe. Attila became Fred's living 'weathercock' in relation to all things. His wise owl, his counsellor, his sounding board. Only the Nubians had a more secret language than Fred had with Attila.

***

Fred and Grace Gooley had been in the Christmas turkey business at Feathers Farm for over 35 years but it was hard to make a living and, now in their 60s, they deserved a well-earned rest and retirement. Fred was a large man, prone to wearing Harris Tweed and always immediately recognisable in his signature flat hat. Although stern in appearance, he was also a gentle man, a gentle giant who respected the sanctity of all life – including his Wirral White turkeys, which he cared for well in their short life. He had a trusting demeanour and would take advice when necessary. Fred was never one to throw his weight around but he had an instinctive sense of right, which his Cornish accent was adept at communicating.

Fred and Grace were well matched. Childhood sweethearts in the harsh world of farming on Bodmin Moor, their families went back many generations. Grace too was large and, at one time, a voluptuous shapely woman, her size contributed to in no small way by her fanatical desire to cook. Age had caught up with her and many of her youthful physical attractions were heading south. She had great respect for animals – which extended to her willingness to nestle orphaned and runt turkey chicks in her ample bosom. Fred was never surprised to find turkey feed in their bed following a bout of poult nurturing. Grace developed a penchant for clay pipe smoking from her mother, an austere woman who could easily have passed for a wrestler and who, forty-five years earlier, famously and single-handedly dispatched a much thinner Fred into the farm's dung heap when she thought he had been taking advantage of her daughter's pneumatic body.

Grace was Fred's anchor. She had faith in everything he did, which cemented their strong and lengthy bond together. She could easily be forgiven for being just a dutiful housewife, partly because she was regularly found in the kitchen and partly because she was a woman of few words. But she undoubtedly had a presence in standing proudly alongside her husband. She had a liking for floral dresses, which were made by her sister, Gwenifer, and bore more than a passing resemblance to the curtains bedecking the inside of Feathers Farm. As Gwenifer had also made all the curtains, Grace knew that her sister's 'decimal dyslexia' often resulted in the purchase of too much curtain material at the local market and, to avoid the embarrassment of owning up, she would regularly knock up a dress or two out of the leftovers. Grace never complained.

Their daughter Rozen had fled the Feathers Farm nest some years earlier and was now married with two children, Dan and Gordon.

The Gooleys had served the area for years and they were very popular stalwarts of the local community. They firmly believed that free range tasted better than intensively produced meat and that the Cornish were a discerning people who would be prepared to pay more for all the benefits of organic food.

Perhaps 'Let the Gooleys make your Christmas' was not the best hook line for their annual Christmas turkey advertising campaign but it was well embedded in local tradition and the locals had just got used to it.

In addition to his large posterior, Fred was sitting on his other main asset, the attractive Feathers Farm and its stone barns, which he felt had potential for residential conversion to meet the market for thrusting executives or perhaps second home owners in this pretty part of Cornwall. None of the locals would begrudge them the opportunity to capitalise on their assets in a changing world, where the big supermarkets were circling like vultures and scooping up the Christmas turkey market. Fred had tried to compete with them to save his organic business but his local campaign, 'Don't let the supermarkets ruin the Gooleys', had got him into trouble with both the supermarkets and the Advertising Standards Office.

The Gooleys' Christmas turkey days were numbered and it was now time to plan for change. Conversion of the farm buildings would support Fred and Grace's happy and well-earned retirement. It was their pension. A move to their little cottage on the edge of Bodmin, which had been in the family for decades, beckoned.

***

The front door of Feathers Farm rattled with the pounding of its sheep's head knocker. As Fred opened it, their cat Flossie scuttled out between his legs and headed to the nearest undergrowth to find some wildlife to catch. Fred was confronted by a large rotund man, upper torso protruding arrogantly, Hitchcock-style, a drinker's nose, ruby cheeks and the wispy grey remnants of what was at one time a full head of hair. A country 'uniform' comprising red trousers, checked shirt and green tweed jacket completed the picture.

The man opened his mouth and a foghorn delivery followed. "Morning Fred, my name is Trevelyan Trelyon. I'm your Trefriggit district councillor. You left a message with my secretary a few days ago. Something about getting planning permission to convert your farm buildings into housing. Not a problem, Fred. I have always been in local politics – like my father, and his father, and his father, and his father, and his father. The Trelyon family get things done. My campaign banner is 'You can Rely-on Trelyon'. That's me, Rely-on Trelyon. Now how can I help?"

Generations of Trelyons had been popular with the local community in running local politics in an altruistic style. Later generations inherited that political legacy more as a duty but in the cut and thrust cynical world of modern politics, past public service held little relevance. Sadly Trevelyan's reputation was tarnished and even he had heard on the grapevine that he had become known locally as 'Unrely-on Trelyon' because he had been tempted to portray the three worst attributes of a modern politician: an unending ability to transmit and not receive, a blind willingness to agree to vote on catchy populist actions and a failure to stand up and be counted if things got tricky. In the odd moment when he wasn't living in denial, Trevelyan showed a genuine keenness to shed himself of such cynical political traits.

Without another word, Trevelyan squeezed past Fred and strode down the well-worn eighteenth century flagstone corridor, adorned with family paraphernalia, into the parlour, only to be confronted at the door by an enormous cloud of blue smoke. "Fred, I think you ought to come quickly. The curtains have caught fire," he said, looking somewhat alarmed as Fred nonchalantly walked down the corridor, a knowing look on his face. He pointed his waggling finger at the ghostly outline of a woman in a curtain-matching dress sitting by the window. Wafts of blue smoke drifted from her clay pipe as the motionless, smoky figure slowly came into view.

"Shag," Fred said.

"What?!" Trevelyan spluttered.

"Burley Blend Budget Shag. It's Grace's favourite pipe tobacco, you know."

"Oh!"

Grace was sitting in her favourite chair, her smoking chair in the parlour. She took another three puffs, smoke obscuring her face again, before looking at Trevelyan. "And who are you?"

"Good morning. I'm your district councillor, Trevelyan. I understand that you and Fred want to retire. Don't you worry about a thing, Mrs Gooley, it will be a mere formality. You can rely on Trelyon." The party political broadcast seemed to go on and on as Trevelyan explained at length how he could help Fred and Grace achieve their goal.

Just then Attila, who had found a vantage point on a water trough just outside the window to take in the proceedings, flapped her wings to distract Fred. Trevelyan poked his ruddy face between Fred and Grace. "What's that?"

Trelyon's privileged upbringing and irrelevant family history touched a raw nerve with Fred, who sarcastically retorted: "It's a large turkey. They're white things with feathers. This is what they look like before you eat them at Christmas!"

"Why is it looking at me? It looks a little menacing."

"That's because it is a little menacing."

"Really? Oh look, it's turning around and ... Oh! It's waving its bottom feathers at me!"

Attila's bottom waving was a sure sign that she didn't like what she saw. Fred decided that he wasn't going to reveal her secret ways and pondered whether her dissent was a sign that maybe the planning permission to convert his farm buildings might not be quite as easy as Trevelyan had indicated. Fred decided to stir things up a little. "Look, I think she is coming in to see you. That should be interesting."

Trelyon wasn't convinced that waving bottom feathers was a term of endearment and felt that a frenzied pecking attack was imminent. He quickly straightened up and, with blood rushing to his neck to join his already glowing cheeks, prepared himself for a rapid exit. "Well, I must be going. It was nice to meet you both. What I will do now is pop into the Trefriggit district council planning office and have a quick word with the chief planning officer, Jim Stern. I'll give you a ring about what to do next but I can't see a problem. Where's the front door?"

Trelyon, showing all the relief of a sceptical attendee escaping from a timeshare seminar, hastily followed Fred back down the corridor to the front door but by the time they got there, Attila had scrambled onto the farmhouse roof. She started to squawk loudly as the door opened. Trelyon's ears pricked up as he poked his head out and looked around the porch, only to see the turkey looking down at him menacingly. Fearing he was about to appear as an expendable extra in a remake of Hitchcock's *The Birds*, he scurried back to his car, head down, one arm flailing behind him like a windmill in some sort of frantic farewell.

Fred could see that Attila was giving another warning sign to treat

Trelyon's optimism with caution. Flossie the cat scurried back through the rapidly closing front door with the tail of what was once a living creature hanging out of her mouth. The security and warmth of the kitchen range beckoned.

Chapter 2:
The Cold War, Sporrans and Sweet Talk

Barely a week had passed since Trevelyan Trelyon's meeting at Feathers Farm when Fred received a phone call from the councillor who, surprisingly, turned out to be as good as his word. Sensing that Fred was not receptive to another 'Unrely-on' Trelyon party political broadcast, he got straight to the point.

"Mr Gooley, I spoke yesterday with the chief planning officer at the district council, Jim Stern, and he can't see any issues with your development proposals at Feathers Farm. In principle, the conversion of the farm buildings to housing meets the council's planning policy as long as you can show that it's not economically viable to continue with the business – which he accepted it was highly unlikely to be given its size, remote location and the sad way farming is going these days. A housing conversion development would therefore be an acceptable alternative use for the farm buildings. He's on side."

It was a good start, which buoyed Fred up no end. Trevelyan continued. "Yes, but Jim made it clear that you will need professional planning advice because your barns are old and there is also environmental and planning policy stuff you need to take advice on. Lots of box ticking, I'm afraid. Planning's a bloody minefield these days."

"Did he give you any names of advisors?"

"Not allowed to, I'm afraid. He can't show favouritism to any business. Something to do with transparency. What's the world coming to! I know a firm called Ashley Sweet Associates in Truro. They are architects but I am sure they can help with the planning as well."

Attila was perched near Fred on the water trough, in earshot of Trevelyan's foghorn delivery booming over the phone. Fred noticed her cocking her head attentively to one side. They looked at each other. A sharp squawk soon sounded as a warning to beware. Fred acknowledged her with a nod and immediately challenged Trevelyan. "This is an important step for my future retirement plans, but wouldn't I need someone who knows about planning, given Jim Stern's remarks? You said it yourself. I need professional planning advice. Doesn't an architect just design things? I don't want to appoint the wrong person."

"Oh, I'm sure Ashley will sort all that out for you. It's not going to be controversial. Just a load of box ticking. Anyway, Jim did say that design is also very important because Feathers Farm is historically interesting. I think Ashley Sweet is the right person. Give him a try."

Fred was astute enough to realise that he was about to delve into the rarefied and bureaucratic world of town planning, which was as familiar to him as the offside rule, but he decided to see what Ashley Sweet had to say for himself before he took any decisions. With thoughts of "nothing ventured, nothing gained" at the back of his mind and forewarned by Attila's guarded response, he was soon on the phone to the Truro architect.

A few days later, the sheep's head knocker gave a resounding thud once again. Fred opened the door to be confronted by a short, dapper man, immaculately groomed, with swept back hair, in a blue linen sports jacket, black corduroys, a black open neck shirt and carrying a red plastic briefcase. It was late afternoon and it was Ashley Sweet, precisely on time, to talk about Fred's old barns. As a traditional man, Fred felt slightly uneasy about the gold necklace and wisps of chest hair poking through the top of Ashley's shirt, not to mention the red plastic briefcase, but he put his doubts aside. After all, this was an architect, an artist, someone creative. Flamboyance seemed to fit the job description perfectly.

Flossie spotted a beam of light at the end of the dark corridor and headed at pace to the open front door, only stopping to wrap herself around Ashley's legs. In no time the hairy tortoiseshell managed to deposit such a large mass of multi-coloured cat fluff onto his neat black corduroys that they quickly took on the appearance of yeti snow boots. Cats can instinctively sense a friend or foe and Flossie was no exception.

Ashley bent down to run his fingers behind the purring pussy's ears and, looking up at Fred, introduced himself in an effeminate but assertive voice. "Oh, hello Mr Gooley, I'm Ashley. Ashley Sweet. Ummm, I've got a Japanese bobtail." Not being familiar with cat breeds, Fred leaned forward to look at the back of Ashley's head, expecting to see a trendy pigtail which, to him, would have entirely complemented the rest of his artist's 'uniform'. Sweet soon realised that Fred hadn't quite got it. "No no, it's a type of cat. They're very friendly, you know. What's this one called? She's very purry, isn't she?"

Fred had more important things to do than outline Flossie's life story. "Good afternoon, Mr Sweet. It's Flossie; she's a tortoiseshell. Thank you for coming over. Shall we start by having a look around the farm?" Fred quickly turned and marched purposefully along the corridor to the waiting rear farm courtyard, outbuildings and paddocks. Ashley swiftly followed, bent over and hopping along as he continued to sweep tortoiseshell hair from the bottom of his trousers.

Ashley and his partner had owned a successful architects' practice in Yorkshire, Ashley Sweet Associates, which enabled them to subsidise a major change in their lifestyle when they relocated to Truro a few years earlier. Unfortunately, within only a few months of arriving in Cornwall, his temporary secretary at the time made a major faux pas. Faced with a ridiculously small address box on a Cornish planning application form, she entered the firm as "A Sweet Ass" and it wasn't long before the innuendos crept into the dialogue amongst the professionals during their regular Friday night after work drinks in the city. Ashley's sensitivity over his notoriety proved to be unfounded as the Celtic peninsula had long since embraced changing social attitudes and the moment soon passed. Paradoxically, the event helped to put Ashley Sweet Associates on the business map quicker than Ashley could have dreamt of, even if it wasn't quite in the way he would have preferred.

Fred guided Ashley on a tour of the property whilst it was still light. As it was still March, the Christmas turkey 'growing' season had yet to start so the buildings and land were empty – with the exception of Attila, who had moved from the water trough to take up a vantage point on the roof of the slaughterhouse, where she was weighing up the dapper dresser.

Ashley soon spotted Fred's 'spy in the camp'. "What's that up there? It looks like a turkey! Was it one that got away?"

Fred confirmed Ashley's astute conclusions and could see that he didn't need to defend Attila's special qualities as the architect was far too absorbed by the old buildings and their potential for conversion to housing. She sat motionless. The jury was out.

They headed back inside to the front room, where Grace arrived with some tea and a Victoria sponge, all presented in her best tea service. With his head cocked to one side and his hands clasped together, Ashley introduced himself and washed down the sponge with a sip of well-made Darjeeling. Carefully placing the teacup down to take out a red plastic pen from his jacket, he started to wave it about creatively like a conductor's baton. With his other hand acting in harmony, the music emerged from Ashley's mouth.

"Well, Mr and Mrs Gooley, I do think you have a fantastic opportunity to create one extra dwelling by converting the old two-storey stone barn, and extending the farmhouse by linking it to the slaughterhouse to increase and improve its living accommodation. I do think it will make a lovely little housing scheme. Removal of those old rusty steel Dutch barns beyond the courtyard will also improve views of the landscape and the ten acres of paddocks could be used by the new occupiers for orchards or keeping horses. I have a pretty good idea of what we need to do and I'll send you a quote for the work, a few sketch ideas of how it will look and information on what surveys are needed for the planning process."

Fred explained how important the whole issue was to their retirement plans and that he had limited savings to fund the scheme. He quickly focused on three critical questions: how long would it take to get planning permission, should he restock turkey poults for the coming Christmas season and would the nearby Ministry of Defence storage depot have any bearing on the proposals? He explained that breeding organic Christmas turkeys was his only business and source of income and therefore timing was absolutely critical.

"Well," Ashley said, raising his baton once more, "I need about two months to commission the surveys and prepare all the drawings and reports for submission to Trefriggit district council so, allowing for slippage, planning permission could be expected in August or September. As for the Ministry of Defence, I am not sure what you mean. You are not referring to that old cold war depot, are you? What's it called… Tre… Tre… something?"

"It's Tredyedeath Depot. Yes I am, Mr Sweet. It's an operating military storage depot just down the road, you know."

"Oh, it's been there for years, Mr Gooley. In my experience, I have never known the Ministry of Defence to get involved in anything in this area. They keep themselves to themselves, you know."

Ashley's suggested timeframe answered the first two of Fred's questions and would provide enough time to market and sell Feathers Farm before Christmas. With the increasing costs of breeding and processing organic turkeys, diminishing returns and margins that were continually squeezed by the supermarkets, Fred just didn't have the stomach to do it one final time.

He leaned forward. "Jim Stern wants the planning application to demonstrate that my business is not economically viable so you have to deal with that, Mr Sweet." He grabbed a copy of his local weekly paper, the *Trecarsick Trumpet*, from the sideboard. On the front page was a national supermarket advertising campaign. Grasping it tightly in his right hand, his demeanor visibly changed as he shook it in anger and sharpened his Cornish drawl. "You see, Mr Sweet, I buy in day old poults around late May, early June and my breeding season to dispatch is around twenty-two to twenty-six weeks of fresh air and care. By comparison, a processed, tasteless supermarket turkey will be ready to eat in just over twelve weeks.

Poor little buggers never see the light of day and are fed on animal protein and growth promoters. No life at all. Even their what they call specialty turkeys only get to about sixteen weeks. That's why they're cheap. How can I compete with that when everyone is counting their pennies?" Fred's grip on the tightly screwed up *Trumpet* slackened as he took a few moments to calm down, but before Ashley was able to stop him, a sermon on turkey husbandry and welfare soon followed unabated.

While Ashley was writing it all down for his viability report he hadn't noticed Flossie creep into the lounge, having arrived back into the farmhouse through the open kitchen window. She immediately saw the opportunity to launch herself onto the cat-friendly Yorkshireman for another love-in. Despite Ashley's best endeavours to gently extract her painfully kneading claws from his crotch, it was too late to avoid the deposit of a further mass of tortoiseshell hair, which took on the distinct appearance of a sporran to match the yeti boots.

Grace could see that Ashley was frantically struggling to return his smart trousers to something resembling their appearance when he arrived, and she rushed out of the lounge in search of one of Fred's less successful birthday presents: a pet hair removal roller. On her return to the lounge, she strode purposefully towards a worried-looking Ashley, arm outstretched as she lowered the sticky implement in the direction of his crotch. "Here, let me help."

Fearing that he was about to be molested in the nether regions by the large pet hair removal roller-wielding turkey farmer's wife, Ashley swiftly reached out and in one sweeping action, graciously removed it from her clutches and started to de-fur himself with the sticky cylinder. "Um, thank you so much, Mrs Gooley, that's very kind. Look, it's coming off quite quickly."

Undistracted and totally focused, Fred finally finished his turkey sermon. Ashley immediately grabbed the opportunity and sprang to his feet. "Well, Mr Gooley, that was all soooooo helpful. Free range, organic turkeys clearly require a lot of looking after and by all accounts, with the economy beginning to falter, I can make a good economic argument to demonstrate that the increasing impact of cheap food imports and the dominance of the big supermarkets has adversely impacted your business."

"So, Mr Sweet, there's nothing you have missed, nothing I need to worry about?" Fred said, his voice maintaining its urgency. "You don't need to discuss this proposal with the council or anything? You didn't answer my question about the Ministry of Defence's depot."

"Mr Gooley, the risk of failure is infinitesimal. I wouldn't restock. I would call it a day. The sale of the farm, with planning permission for the development I propose, will meet your retirement objectives. I don't need to see the council about the depot. It's benign."

It was now dusk. As Fred opened the front door for Ashley, the eerie glow of Tredyedeath Depot's security lighting could be seen in the distance. Ashley hesitated and stared at the discordant night sky but made no comment.

Fred received the formal contractual paperwork to sign a week later, which, despite Attila's misgivings and the costs involved, gave him the confidence to instruct Ashley to proceed with the project, including all the essential surveys. As a matter of courtesy, he also called Trevelyan Trelyon to let him know so that he could ensure Jim Stern monitored the application's progress.

On Ashley's advice, Fred cancelled his annual order for day old Wirral White turkey poults, taking what he saw as a very small calculated risk by closing the business before he had received planning permission.

Over the following four weeks Feathers Farm was surveyed to within an inch of its life. Specialists came and went armed with all manner of technology, from theodolites to bat detecting meters. Land and buildings were surveyed, drains were checked and ecologists hunted for any protected living thing that Flossie hadn't already consumed. Archaeologists looked for relics and traffic engineers counted anything on wheels. Fred could see where the money was going – and fast, all spent to support the box ticking planning application whose approval he believed to be a foregone conclusion. He felt instinctively uncomfortable that, after forty years of Christmas turkey farming, and despite all the hassles caused by the supermarkets and his declining profits, he now had nothing to do but wait. His life was on hold and he didn't like it. Sitting around was not in his DNA and Grace did her best to keep up his spirits.

***

It was April. Ordinarily, by now the land and buildings would have been prepared for the new poult arrivals. A waft of smoke caught Fred's nose as it floated past the open back door. Grace was sitting quietly in her favourite chair, puffing on the skinny shaft of one of her many clay pipes. Attila scurried out of the two-storey barn where she had made her home over the winter. She wasn't to know that the previous Christmas turkey-rearing season would be the last one at Feathers Farm, but she somehow felt, and could see in Fred's demeanor, that change was coming.

She trotted over to Fred, head bobbing in time with her clawed feet, and jumped onto the edge of the water trough. "Well Attila, my little girl, I'm afraid things are going to change around here. You won't be having any more friends to look after. And I don't know what I am going to do with you either." Attila looked at Fred, cocked her head to one side and gave a knowing chuckle. The moment was broken by the sound of a car pulling up outside. It was Ashley Sweet with some draft plans of the proposed development. Fred went inside to answer the front door.

Ashley was holding his signature red plastic briefcase to his chest with both arms like his life depended on it. "Good morning, Mr Gooley. Well, I have a set of the draft plans of the proposed development for you and Mrs Gooley to have a look at."

Fred turned around, his voice booming down the corridor. "Grace, it's Mr Sweet with some plans of the farm. Come and have a look – and can we have some tea please, darling?"

Ashley stepped inside hesitantly and in a stooping motion looked down around Fred's portly frame into the slightly smoky hallway. To his relief, Flossie was nowhere to be seen. She was upstairs, tucked up in the warmth of a mass of Grace's big cotton pants in an old wicker laundry basket, sleeping off another night of outdoor wildlife guerilla activity. Ashley was soon guided into the front room to once again sample the consuming comfort of the velvet sofa. As he extracted his drawings of the proposed development from his red briefcase, a pet hair removal roller dropped out but, with Flossie nowhere to be seen, he quickly put it away. Grace arrived with the tea.

"Well, I know that you have been visited by various surveyors and assessors, which I mentioned last time we met, and I am pleased to say that we have been given a clean bill of health by all of them."

"Just as well, Mr Sweet," Fred replied. "Those bloody surveys have cost me a hell of a lot of money, and I haven't even had your bill yet!"

Ashley characteristically put a hand on one knee and cocked his head. "Oh yes, I know, tell me about it. I'm afraid it's part of the planning process, which we can't avoid. We're all just slaves to the planning system. It's so awful. You wonder anything gets done. I hate being a slave. Well, most of the time."

Ashley's draft plans were well drawn and reflected much of what he had discussed with Fred and Grace at their previous meeting. They both commented positively on the scheme. "Well, it all seems to be in order, Mr Sweet," Fred said. "It looks an attractive scheme. You're in charge. What happens next?"

"Well, I will now get plans drawn up in detail, prepare my planning report, compile all the surveys and then submit the planning application. I have made a note to comment about the economic unviability of your business and I do think you made the right decision to take my advice and cease trading, which helps our case. Following the formal registration of the planning application by the district council, there is then a twenty-one day public consultation period for comment after which the application will be determined. It should all happen within about eight weeks. The chief planning officer, Jim Stern can determine it himself as it's too small a scheme for the planning committee to worry about."

"Thank you, Mr Sweet, that's all very helpful. What a palaver. I know I have asked you this before but do you need to speak to the council at all – and what about the Ministry of Defence?" Fred asked.

"Well, Mr Gooley, I spoke to Councillor Trevelyan Trelyon after we last met – given that you mentioned that he had spoken to Jim Stern, who said it was all likely to be acceptable. He repeated to me that everything would be fine."

Fred paused for a moment to think. "Well, okay, as long as you are happy about that. I don't want any cock ups, Mr Sweet."

Ashley bode his farewells. On leaving the farmhouse, he spotted Attila sitting on the fabric roof of his Volkswagen convertible and quickly turned to Fred, who was standing on the front door steps. "Isn't that…?"

"Yes, it's the same one you saw the last time you were here, Mr Sweet. If you remember I now only have one turkey left and that's her. She's a little bugger sometimes. She can go off people." Attila squinted intently at Ashley before turning in the direction of Tredyedeath Depot and, extending her neck, squawking loudly whilst simultaneously waving her bottom feathers. Fred read the signs and pointed in the same direction. "That's the Ministry's Tredyedeath Depot over there, Mr Sweet. Can you see? The turkey's pointing right at it."

Ashley was more concerned that Attila was going to do something nasty and uncleanable on his car's roof fabric and rushed over, waving his hands and red briefcase around, his swept back hair fighting to escape from its gelled straightjacket. "Shoo, shoo, off with you turkey, get off my roof!"

Attila was unimpressed. Nobody spoke to her like that. She turned around, pulled her neck in and prepared her beak and claws for a turkey dust up. Fred quickly rushed over to avoid the emerging fracas and with outstretched arms, picked up his 'weathercock' from the convertible's roof. Ashley flicked off a single white feather and, relieved to find no further evidence, jumped in the car.

Fred bore down on the wound down window. "Mr Sweet, she's her own bird, you know. You'll have to be polite to her in future. She won't stand for any nonsense, you know."

Ashley looked in the rear view mirror and repositioned his hair. "I'll be in touch, Mr Gooley. Bye."

Flossie, awoken from her slumbers by the kafuffle, wandered along the upstairs corridor, jumped onto the hallway window ledge and peered out to see the back of Ashley's car disappearing from view. With nothing going on, she returned to the warmth of the laundry basket.

The planning application for the development at Feathers Farm was submitted a month later. It was now the middle of May 2008. For Fred, it was the end of one era of his life and the beginning of a new one. What could go wrong?

Chapter 3:
Mad Professors, Grey Children and Cesspits

Feathers Farm lay just outside Trecarsick on Bodmin Moor, a 'Best Kept Cornish Village' well known on the Cornish tourist trail. With a strong and vehemently protective community, Trecarsick had it all: a village shop, parish church, primary school and a well-run pub, the Tinner's Whippet, all loosely arranged around an immaculately tended village green. Its relative remoteness yet invaluable role in serving nearby less well-off rural communities gave added support and protection to its much loved local facilities. The village was only accessible via tumbling, narrow, winding roads tightly bound by traditional Cornish hedges and many a time the tranquil atmosphere would be broken by the sound of a car's abrupt halt to empty its contents of grey-faced children desperate to be sick anywhere. The cast iron "Trecarsick Village Green - no dog fouling" sign, placed carefully to protect its reputation, would regularly receive a direct hit. The name of Trecarsick was firmly on the tourist map, but not always for the right reasons.

For any lover of the Cornish landscape, Bodmin Moor had all the attributes that characterised its endearing qualities and Feathers Farm's buildings just soaked into it as a historic remnant of the synergy between landscape and ancient rural farming practices. A beautiful, rugged, multi-faceted landscape comprising ancient and spiritual terrain contrasted boldly with the moorlands, hewn with polished granite boulders mixed with marshland, gorse and heather. It was a landscape to respect, a landscape to enjoy – and the Gooleys at Feathers Farm never took it for granted.

Feathers Farm had been in the Gooley family for many generations and started life as a sheep farm, ideally suited as they were to the harsh terrain, variable climate and beautiful ruggedness of Bodmin Moor. But it eventually became unsustainable and Fred's father Bert reluctantly decided that, if the family were to stay in farming, they would have to diversify. Bert's beloved flock of Moreland sheep and most of the rugged farmland were sold to leave a smallholding sufficient for a new venture, a Christmas turkey breeding business, which Bert felt confident would secure the future of the farm for him, his wife Morwenna and, ultimately, his son Fred.

The eighteenth century farmhouse was located on the roadside with two granite- and slate-roofed outbuildings on either side lying at right angles to the road. The one on the left was a large attractive two-storey barn whilst the other, single-storey building was used as the slaughterhouse. Both barns retained many original features, were in good condition and eminently suitable for conversion to housing. The barns and farmhouse formed a courtyard enclosed by a rear wall, which gave security from foxes after the free-roaming turkeys had returned from the paddocks for the night. Beyond the courtyard lay two old rusty steel-framed Dutch barns, a relic from Bert's sheep rearing days, which provided welcome shade for the free-range turkeys in the summer months. Ten acres of undulating land fell beyond the farm buildings, all divided neatly into paddocks for the turkeys to roam in.

The farmhouse layout was typical of its period with a central front door and corridor linking the front to the back, which contained the central staircase. At the front of the house, the formal dining room lay on one side of the corridor with the front room, which was used for special occasions, on the other side. At the rear, the kitchen, kept warm by the large coal-fired range cooker, lay on one side and the parlour, which Fred and Grace used daily, on the other. The parlour window enabled Fred to keep an eye over the rear courtyard and paddocks beyond, where he kept and bred his Wirral White turkeys.

Fred inherited the family business sooner than he had expected after Bert tripped and fell face first into the farmyard cesspit; not a good place to fall into in any position, face first being unquestionably the least attractive. Rumour had it that Bert had spotted local spinster and man hunter Chesten Chiverton, who was passing Feathers Farm at the time. Bert had a hopeless and unfulfilled crush on Chesten, who was some twenty-five years his junior, and in his haste to catch her by the farm gate for a chat, he took the short cut past the cesspit where some inappropriately parked farm machinery caught him out. In a move Fred Astaire would have been proud of, Bert picked up his left foot to release the bottom of his trousers from the tine of an old nine leg Ferguson grubber and proceeded to pirouette three times on the ball of his right foot. Loss of balance was inevitable, with the choice of direction limited to almost certain death or ignominy. In one direction lay the exposed sharp tentacles of a menacing-looking upturned Pierse raker which had been in the family for years whilst in the other was the cesspit. Bert wisely chose the cesspit.

Chiverton was Cornish for 'house on the unploughed grassland' but Bert was just another one of a long line of aging dreamers unlikely to ever plough and furrow Chesten's grassland, where many a tractor had been before. Bert never quite recovered from the sprained back, twisted knee and endless inoculations in his bottom, which left him unable to sit down for what seemed like months. The trauma also left his nose with a permanent twitch and a sense that all those around him had trodden in something nasty. It was Morwenna who suggested that retirement, hastened by his unfortunate cesspit accident, would give him the opportunity to hang everything up – and she meant everything. Fred took up the reins of the business and the cesspit was soon filled in, followed by the disposal of the ancient farm equipment to a National Trust agricultural museum. Chesten was not seen at the farm again and eventually ran off with a gynaecologist from Saltash.

The farm was located just over a quarter of a mile from the Ministry of Defence's storage facility Tredyedeath Depot, where the artificial glow of the security lights created a sinister and conspicuous backdrop in the night sky. An old disused nineteenth century tin mine initially adapted amid much secrecy in 1957 by the Ministry of Defence, it had a doomsday, sci-fi, mad professor feel about it. Although it was a locally unwelcome discordant feature at night, most people had got used to it over the years.

Local folklore and a sprinkling of parochialism led to wild streaks of fantasy about Tredyedeath Depot's role and purpose. Some were convinced it was in fact a secret breeding establishment for large wildcats as a more agile alternative to the Alsatian guard dog, and that the well documented Beast of Bodmin Moor was none other than an escaped trainee. Others suggested it was an experimental crop circle establishment, given the increasing numbers of these strange features appearing in the locality. However, the favoured and more logical opinion was that Tredyedeath Depot was simply a storage dump.

After all, with Trecarsick firmly on the Cornish tourist trail, the parish council were very keen not to stir up rumours that the sinister glow in the night sky might somehow be anything from a nuclear weapons depot to a 'Village of the Damned' experiment resulting in captured tourists being bred as zombies by aliens as part of a plan for Cornish and, ultimately, world domination. Even the more extreme local conspiracy theorists hadn't thought that one up.

Chapter 4:
Dolly Mixtures, Directions and Armageddon

Tredyedeath Depot lay about a mile from Trecarsick and just over a quarter of a mile from Feathers Farm. Following the onset of the Cold War, the Ministry created a network of dispersed storage facilities to enable the country to function in a doomsday scenario that no one wanted to think about: a nuclear holocaust. Tin mines were ideal for underground storage and Tredyedeath Mine's rapid acquisition as a depot was secured in late 1956 using the might of the Ministry's compulsory land acquisition legal machinery.

Tredyedeath Mine contained a single horizontal entrance at ground level, known as an adit, which ran many hundreds of yards into the hillside from a small cliff face and from which other adits had originally been created at the same level. These were subsequently widened and strengthened by the Ministry to increase underground storage capacity. The land immediately around the mine entrance was flat as a result of earlier eighteenth century surface mining activity and this provided the ideal opportunity for the Ministry to build a security gatehouse by Trecarsick Road, a two-storey office block, canteen, restroom and toilets. A separate kennel building and guard dog exercise yard lay nearby. A barrack block was also constructed to provide flexibility for security and operational personnel who might be stationed there depending on the scale and nature of the storage. The site was surrounded by a U-shaped perimeter security fence that joined the mine cliff face about 100 metres either side of the single mine entrance and was topped off by regularly spaced security lighting whose distinctive orange glow contributed to the depot's sinister appearance in the night sky.

The local community initially viewed Tredyedeath Depot with some suspicion because of its potential to store something nasty; the Trecarsick locals knew it was no coincidence that it was remote from inhabitants and mainly underground. It soon became enshrined in folklore that it was just used for storing military field rations.

Trecarsick's village shop was very popular with the locals and its early success was directly due to its commercially-minded owner, the busy, diminutive, industrious and not to be messed with Cordelia Craddock. Her entrepreneurial spirit came from her father, who was a leading light in the 1948 Berlin airlift and, with his help, she bought the shop in 1956 at the age of twenty-five. Cordelia worked tirelessly from dawn to dusk keeping the shop's shelves stocked and the vegetables fresh and her fleet of local village paperboys were at her beck and call on the promise of extra funds to supplement their meager pocket money at a time of post war austerity. She never missed an opportunity and in those early days, the army convoys heading for Tredyedeath Depot would regularly detour to stop off at the village shop for provisions after a long journey, knowing that the return trip would always begin well before even Cordelia's early morning start. She feared that such detours were probably not officially sanctioned by the Ministry of Defence and that one day it would come to an end, so she made the most of it.

The increasingly popular *Playboy* magazine, launched in 1953, was soon purchased by the market savvy Cordelia specifically for the convoy market and placed in an innocuous position at the end of the magazine rack a few shelves above the fresh vegetables. Unfortunately – and to her embarrassment – a copy of the semi-concealed men's magazine was dislodged by a village regular reaching for that month's edition of *Motor Cycling Magazine*. It fell ignominiously from the rack, wedging itself in the children's section just below Do-It-Yourself and above a box of cucumbers. A group of mothers who had just collected their little ones from Trecarsick Primary School arrived to find the errant magazine poking out between *The Beano* and that well-known schoolgirl comic, *Girl*. It wasn't the easiest thing in post war Britain for mothers to explain away pictures of exposed bits of the female anatomy to an unsuspecting, inquisitive and distracted six year old when all they were looking for was some Dolly Mixtures. Despite a mixture of hilarity, outrage and embarrassment, Cordelia knew that it was only a matter of time before a delegation from the staunchly parochial Trecarsick parish council would arrive on the shop doorstep to complain and, sure enough, two hours later they turned up. It was made clear by the chairman that they didn't much like the thought of their post-pubescent village daughters being interfered with by a bunch of aroused convoy squaddies, distracted by depraved material following their visit to the shop allegedly to buy some Murray Mints.

Cordelia made her apologies but in her quest for profit relocated the offending magazines under the counter to serve future convoy stop-offs. She finally decided to stop selling *Playboy* altogether when an errant paperboy deliberately slipped a copy inside the *Trecarsick Trumpet* for onward delivery by bicycle to the vicarage. By all accounts the sermon the following Sunday morning by the invigorated vicar, a family man with five children, was one of the best the parish church of St Piran had seen for some years. Despite that, he graciously had a quiet word with Cordelia on her way out of the service to the effect that, for the sake of her beloved village shop, the risk of further discretions was too great. *Playboy* never graced the village shop again.

Convoy visits to Cordelia's shop for essential supplies stopped not long after the *Playboy* incident and she just assumed that the security regulations had been more rigorously applied to the convoy drivers. But, unbeknown to the locals, the type of storage at Tredyedeath Depot had changed slowly over the years, though never to the extent that additional military personnel were required to be housed at the barracks, which might have given the game away. Vaccines for mass inoculation against germ warfare, ammunition, secret guidance system equipment and specialist medical supplies were all stored at one time or another, smuggled in by trucks still thought to be carrying field rations. Cordelia eventually passed the shop on to her equally industrious daughter Karensa but she still helped out from time to time.

In 2002, Tredyedeath Depot's isolated location, underground storage capability and improved communications brought it into focus under the Ministry of Defence's new rapid deployment explosives storage programme, unfortunately named ARCE: Army Regional Centre for Explosives. No one knew how long the ARCE programme was going to last as so much depended upon the ever-changing nature of warfare. However, the storage of explosives brought with it a bureaucratic regime of regulatory control designed to prevent new civilian development occurring anywhere within an explosion zone 500 metres from the relevant ARCE Depot. This military health and safety-derived explosion zone was depicted by a broadly circular yellow line on what was known as the Safeguarding Map. The extent of existing human habitation within the explosion zone then influenced the amount and type of explosives that could be stored. A safeguarding map boundary was thus created around Tredyedeath Depot under a government direction, explaining its purposes and the applicable controls. Trecarsick fell outside the safeguarding map explosion zone but fundamentally, Feathers Farm was located just within it.

Trefriggit district council had been informed by the Ministry of Defence about the safeguarding map. This required the council to consult the Ministry of Defence about any planning application for development submitted within the safeguarding map area which would increase the number of civilians within it. The safeguarding map and yellow line was added to the council planning department's public database, known as the plotting sheets, which was available to council planning officers and professional practitioners who needed to know about those sorts of things. The council was also required to create a planning policy to deal with planning applications within the safeguarding map area. The government's direction made it clear that the Ministry had extensive powers to call for a public inquiry if the district council was minded to approve a planning application in the safeguarding map area with which the Ministry of Defence disagreed. The direction was designed to prevent the Ministry from finding itself in the position of its ARCE facility being compromised by new civilian development being approved within the safeguarding map area, the consequence of which might force the Ministry into reducing explosive storage capability at the relevant facility in the interests of public safety.

In Trecarsick, life went on as usual even though Tredyedeath Depot's new ARCE status and direction were now in the public domain. But this was rarefied, bureaucratic planning mumbo jumbo that Joe Public had no hope of understanding. In any event, the direction and safeguarding map didn't actually say what nasty substances were being stored or their potential effect on humans, so no one was any the wiser. The number of convoys rumbling past the village didn't change that much, other than occurring at night, and of course not much could be seen in the landscape other than the eerie glow of the perimeter fence security lights, which continued to pollute the night sky. The Ministry was quite happy to keep it all under wraps as long as they could even though by the late 1990s 'transparency' and 'consultation' were becoming the buzz words affecting the way of life in modern Britain. The concept of public relations remained an anathema to the Ministry of Defence and something of a paradox for any military man whose basic training was to do harm to angry people, a category of enemy that certainly included public objectors.

The Ministry of Defence had a reputation for years of uncontrolled overspending and whilst this was always claimed to be justified by the threat of war and immediate annihilation by an out of control Red Army, the spending culture never changed despite the end of the Cold War having been officially declared in 1991. There had never been any great clarity between the Ministry of Defence's paymasters in the once smoke-filled corridors of Whitehall and the high ranking 'pips' on the ground who operated a 'mother knows best' attitude to procurement and defence of the realm. When it came to thinking about whether to order twenty-four Armageddon C83 Mk11 rockets, it certainly wouldn't be cost at the forefront of a military man's decision-making process. In reality, the only big hole the 'pips' were guaranteed to make from such a purchase was in the defence budget.

A recession was looming and with the politicians' desire to reduce public spending from all quarters, the only battle on the horizon was likely to be between the government's political mandarins and high ranking members of the military. Cutbacks were coming and the procurement culture had to change. Under the wide scope of the Defence Spending Review, a reduction in and disposal of all those 1950s Cold War property acquisitions – including those in the ARCE programme – was likely to be one of the many emerging battlegrounds in the Ministry's quest to bring spending under control. A sword of Damocles hung over Tredyedeath Depot.

Chapter 5:
Family Honour and Unbuttoned Shirts

Tredyedeath Depot's new ARCE status brought with it a change in personnel in 2002 with the arrival of the officious new base commander, Major Charles Fox-Thrasher, who managed what was initially a small storage facility with a skeleton security team. This continued until 2007 when a significant ARCE reorganisation to reflect heightened national security resulted in the appointment of a new second in charge, Captain Richard Lovely, along with a warrant officer, two staff sergeants and a number of security dog handlers to patrol the facility twenty-four hours a day. This reorganisation also resulted in an increase in explosives stored. The depot's enhanced status gave Major Fox-Thrasher the opportunity to secure funds to refurbish the barrack block, construct new kennels and exercise yard and improve the access into the mine for deliveries. Fox-Thrasher made sure that the office, canteen, restroom and toilet block were also refurbished to a high standard.

Fox-Thrasher was also required to install the very latest surveillance system within the mine, which included round-the-clock CCTV and an alarm system triggered by a range of detectors. These were all linked directly to the Ministry of Defence's centralised ARCE security and explosives procurement headquarters in Bromsgrove, where all ARCE depots could be monitored by a team of trained security officers able to direct the depot commander on how to manage a breach of security until reinforcements arrived. On a day-to-day basis, mine security was controlled by a transponder mounted just inside the entrance gate which, when triggered by a small fob, would switch off all the alarms. The mine entrance was protected by an open texture steel security gate, the theory being that the blast impact of an explosion could be controlled through the mine opening rather than being retained within a sealed space, which would have more devastating consequences.

As depot commander, Fox-Thrasher was in overall charge due to his technical explosives experience, but the day to day running of the depot was taken on by his second in charge, Captain Lovely, a logistics expert who had practical experience in managing other ARCE facilities to ensure that capability was being maintained. Fox-Thrasher and Lovely were two quite different people and from the moment they met it was clear that they weren't going to see eye to eye on any level.

Fox-Thrasher came from a military family that stretched back to the Boer War. The only boy of three children, he was beaten at the slightest opportunity by his stern father in the twisted Victorian belief that it would make a man of him. He was sent off to a strict public school at an early age for yet more beatings. A life in the military was therefore obligatory to uphold the family honour. The major's childhood experiences left him a scarred man, bereft of a sense of humour, and he regularly vented a deep seated and uncounselled anger on humans and inanimate things in equal measure. This upbringing gave Fox-Thrasher few endearing personal qualities and he simply got on with army life. Now in his fifties, the major was an upright man, six foot tall with a stiff backbone, lean frame and swept back grey hair, who was rarely seen out of his neatly pressed uniform and shiny shoes. With thirty years of army life behind him, including some front line experience, his rise through the ranks to major was more to do with the passage of time and family regimental connections than pure merit. However, over the years he developed a reputation for having a geek-like encyclopaedic knowledge of anything explosive related and he was a regular contributor to his favourite magazine, the Royal Artillery's *Bang!*. When it came to explosives, if Fox-Thrasher didn't know it, it wasn't worth knowing. A stickler for the rule book made him an ideal candidate to take charge of explosives, a solitary life chosen for him by his seniors, having found him to be totally devoid of social and man management skills. However, his obsession for explosives had not gone unnoticed by Captain Lovely in the short time they had been acquainted.

His private life was disjointed – one failed marriage yielding two daughters which, in the eyes of his enraged father, made him a reject, a defect incapable of maintaining the family's military bloodline, a task considered totally inappropriate for the opposite sex. Tredyedeath Depot was therefore a logical and isolated place for a posting and he was fortunate to have the opportunity to live nearby in his inherited cottage on Bodmin Moor, once used as a family holiday home for generations. Protecting Tredyedeath Depot's safeguarding map from all intruders became one of Major Charles Fox-Thrasher's tasks. The explosion zone yellow line was his front line. His Maginot Line.

Compared to Fox-Thrasher, Captain Richard Lovely was a soldier from the opposite end of the social and cultural spectrum. Dickie to his friends, Captain Lovely was Cornish and lucky enough to find himself posted to Tredyedeath Depot, not far from his family roots. Lovely came from a respectable hard-working farming family who were very proud of his achievements. He was smart enough to realise early on that getting paid to attend university and learn a commercial skill on an army scholarship was a good way to start a career, given that his parents were of limited means and had two other sons to support. A logistics degree allowed him to see the world with the army, but it was only ever a stop gap. Dickie never wanted a long-term military career.

A good-looking man with fair to blond hair and now in his late thirties, he was undoubtedly a catch for any girl, but so far his disjointed army life around the world had prevented any long-term relationships. He kept himself fit by playing rugby and maintained a just legal army haircut that graced his five foot ten frame. He had already served the minimum sixteen year term, which both repaid the army university investment in him and provided for a long-term pension. He was still enjoying army life, but beginning to feel that Tredyedeath Depot may be his last posting. Lovely lived 'on camp' in the comfortable, refurbished barracks. His family upbringing gave him the common touch, a social skill that enabled him to mix with all ranks in the military, but he felt more comfortable in the presence of non-commissioned officers and security guards. Lovely was a well-rounded, decent man, one who both listened and respected other people's views whilst commanding respect himself. Logistics suited his character; he would never have made a front line soldier.

In the early months following the reorganisation at Tredyedeath Depot, the major, captain and the explosives protection team stayed on camp to ensure all systems were working properly but by early 2008, things were more relaxed and Captain Lovely had started to explore the beautiful Cornish landscape on his days off. As a farmer's son he loved animals and had become friendly, on camp, with guard dog handler Private Jimmy Johnston and his ferocious-looking German Shepherd, Bismarck. Bismarck had for some reason taken a shining to the captain and Jimmy was more than happy to allow Dickie to take the fearsome Sheppy for a walk along the pretty local footpaths on those days when they were both off duty. It gave Bismarck some variety from the monotony of repeatedly walking along the depot's security fence.

One day Dickie and his canine companion arrived at Trecarsick and decided to have a look around the village. Seeing the village shop, he was suddenly reminded of the need for some urgent provisions and he stopped to call in. By now the attractive Karensa Craddock had taken over the shop from her feisty mother Cordelia, who, at seventy-seven, was well into her retirement but still popped in from time to time to help out. Cordelia's desire for success with the shop had kept her family plans on hold and she'd had her daughter late in life. Karensa was now in her late thirties and, like her mother, running the shop left her little time to think about a family of her own. In the sheltered world of Trecarsick, the local village 'talent' was limited to a few unmarried locals with dubious habits who'd been left on the shelf and could usually be found at the Tinner's Whippet playing dominoes. That only left some 'second time arounders' who invariably came with an assortment of baggage, most of it unwanted.

Cordelia instilled in Karensa the need to be patient and wait for her knight in shining armour to burst into the shop but she was beginning to think that he and his steed had long since vanished down a derelict mine shaft. Karensa was very attractive and had those 'girl next door' looks. She was taller than her mother, which gave her shapely figure proportions she could not quite contain within her village shop 'uniform' of jeans or leggings and an open, loose-fitting shirt. The villagers were never quite sure whether her tendency to keep her range of shirts too unbuttoned was just her view on fashion or a psychological attempt to keep alive her hopes of catching her man. Whatever the reason, arrival of the popular weekly *Trecarsick Trumpet* on Thursday mornings, the busiest day of the week, was all the excuse the village menfolk needed to check out the lovely Karensa and she took full advantage of it. Their ritual queuing outside the shop at 8am had become an almost exclusively male event and the subsequent lingering in the shop to catch a glimpse of the lovely Karensa invariably resulted in totally unnecessary household purchases. Karensa's occasional and unpredictable undoing of one extra button ensured that she made Thursday a 'value added' day and the womenfolk cruelly coined it 'Trumpet Thursday' to denote what they saw as a bunch of sad village men having a gawp.

So when Captain Lovely, with Bismarck in tow, breezed into Trecarsick village shop in his smart uniform, looking to find something powerful to unblock the now quite smelly barrack block toilet, to Karensa it was like a breath of fresh air. Their eyes met across the counter over some boxes of crumpets at the end of their 'sell by' date. Dickie was left momentarily speechless by the figure of loveliness before him. He had to say something to break the lengthening, staring, silence.

"Hello. Old crumpet?!"

Karensa, looking indignant, flicked back her flowing blonde hair. "I beg your pardon?"

"There, err, yes, there on the counter, crumpets. The shelf life is today, isn't it? I'll have a box. Yes, I'll have a box," Lovely mumbled.

"Oh. Oh yes, right, ok. Just one box? They are on special offer, you know."

"Yes, I see. Thank you. Oh, ok, I'll have another one. I'll have two. Just going to have a look around the shop." The captain gathered himself together after not such a great start. There were plenty of better chat-up lines he could have used than 'Old crumpet'. What was he thinking? He wandered aimlessly around the shop with Bismarck in tow, his swinging tail just brushing the cornflake packets that wobbled from side to side in unison with the beast's hind quarters as he moved gracefully along the aisle.

Lovely recomposed himself and returned to the counter. "I've got a bad smell."

"Pardon?" Karensa asked.

"The barrack toilet. It's blocked. I need something to clear it."

"Oh! So where do you work then?"

"Tredyedeath Depot. I was posted there late last year."

"What? That old mine used by the Ministry of Defence to store stuff?"

"Yes. Sorry, I should have introduced myself. I'm Lovely."

"I'll be the judge of that," Karensa said.

"No, no. Captain Richard Lovely. Dickie to my friends. Please call me Dickie. This is Bismarck, one of our guard dogs."

By this time a few young mums with children in tow had arrived in the shop and were taking the opportunity to give Dickie the once over. Karensa was too focused on him to notice. She leaned over the counter towards Dickie and said softly: "Bend-it-Bang!"

"Sorry!?"

"This will get rid of the bad smell in your barrack. It's called Bend-it-Bang. If this doesn't get rid of whatever is blocking your toilet U-bend, I would use some of the explosives allegedly being stored at your mine. By the way, I'm Karensa Craddock, shop owner. Very pleased to meet you."

It was a bit of a bumpy start but there was no denying that there was a spark between them. Slowly they both dropped their guard. A bottle of Bend-it-Bang and two boxes of out of date crumpets were duly purchased and, in between sales to waiting villagers, they started to develop a rapport.

By this stage, Bismarck was getting bored and starting to lick the ankles of a four-year-old girl who was having great fun tugging his tail. Her mother was far too distracted to notice as she and some other mums had gathered around the magazine rack to compare fantasies about the handsome Dickie. Suddenly she looked down in horror and, fearing that giant guard dogs were trained to lick first before consuming an arm or leg, swooped up the distracted child from a disappointed-looking Bismarck.

Now in deep eye-to-eye conversation with Dickie, Karensa didn't notice the subsequent murmurings about dogs not being allowed in shops as the other mothers started to gather up their children, along with their shopping, in order to avoid a bloodbath. Unfortunately, in their quest to avoid the inquisitive Bismarck biting off dangling appendages, assorted shop items started to spill from bags as they hurried out of the front door and down the steps. Bismarck cocked his head to one side in amazement as he wondered what all the fuss was about, whilst scanning the scattered provisions for something edible. The lamp chops and mince lasted just a few seconds.

It wasn't long before Dickie was back at Trecarsick in one of the depot's army Land Rovers to take Karensa out on their first date. She would always wear a dress for Dickie on her days off, the village shop 'uniform' being consigned to the wardrobe. Bismarck would sometimes come along for the ride.

Chapter 6:
The Twilight Zone

The phone rang in Jim Stern's office. It was Councillor Trevelyan Trelyon. With the Gooleys' planning application now registered, he was keen to ensure that Jim was going to personally oversee it, given their popularity as pillars of the local community. Trelyon was also not going to miss the opportunity to gain some political capital from the process to restore his patchy reputation.

Jim quickly explained that he would have to consult all the usual statutory organisations, the parish council and neighbours in the normal way, and as he was passing Tredyedeath Depot on his way home that night, he would deposit a copy of the application with the Ministry of Defence for their comments.

Alarm bells rang in Trevelyan's ears. "Why do you have to consult the Ministry of Defence, Jim? What have they got to do with it?"

"Well, Trevelyan, the Gooleys' planning application site falls inside the Tredyedeath Depot explosion zone and the council has a lawful obligation to consult the Ministry. Mind you, it's only just inside by a few metres."

"What explosion zone? What lawful obligation?" Trelyon asked. Jim went into more detail about Tredyedeath Depot's ARCE programme and the government's direction, which obliged the district council, on receipt of a planning application inside the explosion zone, to consult the Ministry of Defence. Trevelyan knew that Fred had ceased trading. He was worried. "Jim, have we consulted them before?"

"Well, no. Actually, we haven't, Trevelyan, because agricultural operations are excluded from the direction consultation procedure and we have never before had any planning applications in the explosion zone for non-agricultural development." Jim continued to explain that, although not exactly bedtime reading, the safeguarding map and accompanying direction were not secret but available for the public to view in the council's offices on its plotting sheet database. "Funnily enough, I noticed that Ashley Sweet has not indicated in his documentation that he had spoken to the Ministry to get their views before he lodged the Gooleys' planning application. Of course that's up to him but we have a statutory duty to consult them. Period."

This was all news to Trelyon, who agreed with Jim Stern to await the end of the usual twenty-one day consultation period and see what came out in the wash.

***

Dickie was at his desk at the depot early when the phone rang. "Captain Lovely, it's gatehouse security here. Last night we were handed an envelope from someone claiming to be the chief planning officer and he asked that it be given to the person in charge. We have checked that it's nothing sinister and I'll drop it over now. He said it was something about a planning application."

The envelope duly arrived and Dickie opened it to reveal a copy of the Gooleys' planning application. It was accompanied by an official request from the Trefriggit district council planning department under the Town and Country Planning Act 1990 that the Ministry of Defence send its comments on the application to the council within twenty-one days of the date on the letter. The letter explained that the Ministry's consultation was triggered by the location of the application site within the Tredyedeath Depot explosion zone and to assist, the council had included an extract of the safeguarding map showing the Feathers Farm planning application site marked in red.

Major Fox-Thrasher was due in the office at his regular time of 10am, which gave Lovely enough time to look through the application in detail before discussing it with him. The major's office was next to the captain's, just along the corridor on the first floor of the office block, and his daily routine would include liaising with Dickie on the day's work programme, which often included the delivery and collection of explosives. The major's day always included a walk around the inside of the mine to check the general environment and condition of the explosives, something he seemed increasingly to enjoy. Modern technology and his explosives background enabled him and his warrant officer to carry out specific stability checks, which they always did together. Explosives of different types were also shared with other ARCE facilities and some were 'retired' after fixed 'shelf life' periods so convoy inventory checks were regularly required prior to arrival and departure. Dickie could always hear the major approaching as the corridor would resonate with the sound of his army issue leather steel-tipped shoes. The major rarely knocked on Dickie's door or tried to make small talk.

The major arrived on time, stormed in and immediately started to go through the day's programme. "Morning, Lovely. What have you got for me today?"

"Morning, sir. Sir, we have received details of a planning application within the yellow line. Within the safeguarding map explosion zone."

"Yes, Lovely, I do know the purpose of the yellow line. What's the planning application for?"

"It's for the conversion of an old two-storey barn to a dwelling and the enlargement of an adjacent farmhouse by linking it to an existing single-storey barn. The applicants are turkey farmers, a Mr and Mrs Gooley. It's right on the edge of the safeguarding map, but within it by just a few metres," Lovely explained.

The major's lingering delight from another morning's trip around his beloved explosives rapidly faded as he struggled to control the contortions of discontent written all over his face. "What? What?!! We can't have that, Lovely. You'd better object to it. It's going to mean more people in the explosion zone. More people means fewer explosives. Lovely, we can't have that. If it's in the explosion zone, we object. I don't care if it's one inch inside the zone or right outside our front door. If it's in the zone, we object."

Fox-Thrasher snatched the application material from Lovely's desk and flicked through the pages, barely stopping to look at the details. He wasn't prepared to listen to Lovely's suggestion that they should first find out a bit more about the application so they could make an informed judgment. He also rejected his captain's suggestion that the application proposal's location on the very edge of the explosion zone should be considered by applying the Ministry's explosives storage capacity 'formula', given that it was also such a small-scale development scheme.

Dickie could see that there was a possibility that the risk to human habitation from an explosion would be so small that it wouldn't be worth bothering about. He went on to point out that any objection the Ministry submitted would have to be justified and that to make sense of it, he felt he should look behind the safeguarding map direction and its purposes to explain the Ministry's position to the district council. It was a typically measured response from the captain.

Fox-Thrasher's face contorted further. "You are not getting it, Lovely. Not getting it at all. Look, Captain, it's pretty straightforward to me. I'm no expert in planning but I do know what the purpose of the safeguarding map is and that's to prevent the increase in humans in the explosion zone, which might reduce our explosives storage capacity. That's it. What could be simpler, Captain? I am ordering you to object to it. It's only a bloody farm, for Christ's sake. Anyway, we are hardly likely to get any grief from the farmer if we get it wrong. What's his name – Gooley? What sort of stupid name is that? Bloody farmers."

At that point Fox-Thrasher, his ruddy face and neck now somewhat similar to the top of a thermometer, swivelled sharply and walked out, leaving Dickie feeling more than a little abused, not to mention irritated, at having received such an unnecessary order. In the months since his arrival, Dickie was still trying to uncover Fox-Thrasher's soft side, a side that might show compassion, one that would enable them to find some middle ground and ease their working relationship, but to date it had all been to no avail. He was rapidly coming to the conclusion that no such personality trait existed. His instincts told him to look into the application further. He had some time before the council's response was required so he decided to send a copy of the application to the Ministry's Property and Protection Division for its views.

Division, as it had become known, were in charge of all matters when it came to the production and management of the safeguarding map and arguably should have been the organisation to which the district council should have consulted directly, so Dickie felt it right to inform them straight away. He would explain to the rule-obsessed major, when he calmed down, that it was a requirement of the direction that Division be consulted.

Just after Fox-Thrasher's purposeful exit from Dickie's office, the phone rang. It was Karensa. With a few more beats of his heart to add to those irritatingly generated by the major, Dickie's ears pricked up and his voice softened. "Hi Kar, how are you, darling? Great to hear from you. What's that, you can't make our date next Tuesday because you want to go to the Trecarsick parish council meeting?"

Karensa explained that she wanted to support Cordelia, who was being honoured for forty years of service as a parish councillor, particularly as this was to be her last attendance. To commemorate her stoic public service, she was going to receive a special lifetime achievement award at the end of the council meeting.

"How lovely for your mum, Kar," Dickie said. "Tell you what, why don't we watch it together at the village hall and we can have a bite to eat at the Tinner's Whippet afterwards? I'll bring Bismarck. He's off duty that night."

Karensa was impressed by Dickie's patience and went on to explain that the meeting shouldn't take long because there were only a few matters on the agenda and just one planning application to be considered. One by local turkey farmers Mr and Mrs Gooley.

"Mr and Mrs Gooley!?" Dickie exclaimed, his voice revealing just a hint of nervousness.

"Yes, Dickie, the Gooleys," Karensa replied. "Do you know them? They're friends of the family, you know. The Gooleys and the Craddocks go back years. They're a very popular couple who have decided to retire and they are selling up. The big supermarkets were slowly putting them out of business, you know. We used to sell their organic turkeys in the shop. It's sad really; they were always excellent, very tasty. The parish is bound to support their planning application. We all wish them well. I think the Gooleys are going to be there. See you then, bye."

Dickie put the phone down and lowered his head in his hands. He was just beginning to feel a bond developing with Karensa and now she might slip through his hands over some bloody planning application which he, as Ministry of Defence consultee, had been ordered to object to by the major. All he could do was keep quiet and find out more about the Gooleys' application. But he knew he was going to have to tell Karensa the bad news at some point – and it probably wouldn't be too long. He needed a plan to save his relationship and save his job.

Chapter 7:
Ollie and Kenneth Come In from the Cold

Dickie enjoyed his days off, when he had the chance to take Bismarck for a walk around the beautiful Cornish countryside, but he was beginning to doubt the beast's effectiveness. He just seemed too nice to be a guard dog. It all started with that first trip to the village shop when a local child, fearing no malice and exercising her childlike sixth sense, had enormous fun pulling Bismarck's tail, to his obvious enjoyment. Karensa had suggested that next time he came to the shop, it would be better to tie Bismarck to a lamppost just outside by the village green. This would avoid a repeat of the events the first time they met – although she blamed the jealous mums for ogling him and abandoning their children in the process. Nevertheless, she wanted to retain the goodwill of her customers and avoid the wrath of the council's health and safety officers so the lamppost solution seemed the best idea.

Dickie obliged but regularly found, during 'after school' hours, Bismarck flat on his back with his legs in the air having his tummy tickled by groups of small children, their bicycles abandoned on the village green in their haste to give the hairy monster a cuddle. They were having great fun. No child, or anyone else for that matter, had been bitten, chewed or lost an appendage and Bismark would just make the odd warning growl if the rough and tumble got too much. In the wilds of the countryside on their days off, Dickie would notice other dogs happily approaching Bismarck with no fear and becoming the best of friends within a few sniffs. In doggy language they seemed to be saying: "Hey Bizzy, how are you doin', you great big softie. Check out the sheep shit over there! Have a good walk."

***

It was late at the depot, and Dickie was still working in the office under the faint glow of his military issue Anglepoise, preparing for the arrival of a convoy the next day, when he heard some activity outside. Someone was shuffling about and whispering. He switched the lamp off and crept over to the office window, which was slightly ajar. It was dark outside, with just the orange glow of the security lights casting long shadows over the kennels, which he could see from his office.

He heard a voice, which seemed to be coming from near the kennels. "Fluffy, Fluffy? For God's sake come here. Fluffy, come here. Bring Ollie here, bring Ollie here. Fluffy – come here now!"

The four security guard dog patrols worked in paired shifts with two dogs and their handlers on duty at any one time. When they were off duty, two guard dogs would normally return to their individual covered kennels, each with its own exercise yard. Dickie noticed that Bismarck's gate was open and he wasn't inside. He then glimpsed out of the corner of his eye what appeared to be a man walking about like an ape with what looked like a cuddly toy in his hand. Dickie took his torch and went outside to investigate. Shielded by a parked Land Rover, he raised the torch to his chest, pointed it in the direction of the ape-like, cuddly toy-bearing human and flicked on the switch. A beam of white light pierced the faint orange glow and landed on the slowly straightening shape of a uniformed human being. It was Private Jimmy Johnston.

"Private Johnston. Jimmy. What on earth are you doing? What's that in your hand? Why is Bismarck's exercise yard gate open? Who is Fluffy? Who is Ollie? And why are you whispering?"

Just then Bismarck came around the corner, very happy to see his friends Dickie and Jimmy. His tail was wagging full pelt and he sidled up to Jimmy, head down in a submissive manner, and proceeded to wrap himself around the private's legs. He held a well-slobbered cuddly toy firmly in his mouth, dangly bits of damp fabric hanging out at the sides.

Johnston looked a bit sheepish. "Err, Bismarck got out, sir, and I was trying to get him back in his kennel. Honest I was."

"So what is that in his mouth?" Dickie asked.

"That's Ollie, sir."

"Ollie?"

"Yessir. Ollie the Octopus."

"And in your hand?"

"Kenneth, sir."

"Kenneth!?"

"Yessir, Kenneth the Killer Whale, sir."

"Guard dogs with cuddly toys, eh? That's a new one on me, Johnston. And what or who is Fluffy? Another cuddly toy, I suppose?"

At the mention of 'Fluffy', Bismarck moved through Johnston's legs and put his paw on Dickie's right knee. Dickie looked down and repeated the word. Bismarck gave a little bark. By now suspicious, Dickie tried out a few more dog commands prefixed by the word 'Fluffy'. Bismarck obeyed. Dickie slowly and knowingly raised his head and looked at Private Johnston's worried face. He felt his earlier suspicions about Bismarck's dodgy guard dog credentials might have some truth in them. Johnston looked away and then down at his feet to avoid eye contact. He was crestfallen.

"Jimmy, I think you'd better come into the office. I want to know everything. And bring Bismarck and his toys with you. I don't want any evidence left outside when the dog patrol shift changes."

Back in the office, Jimmy sat down opposite Dickie and Bismarck lay down beside him. Dickie made it clear that he wanted just one explanation – and it had better be the truth. Private Johnston was a trained dog handler from the 1st Military Working Dog Regiment, 101 Military Working Dog Squadron based in Aldershot. Of that there was no doubt. He had been in the army for twelve years and dog handling was what he had always wanted to do. The only thing he wanted to do. Animals were his life. But he didn't see his long-term career in the army. He saw it with an animal charity, or perhaps a dogs' home. The Sheppy was his favourite breed, so much so that he had managed to persuade his loving parents to have one as a pet. A six-month-old rescue dog was soon acquired. That was when the trouble started.

Johnston began his explanation. "Well sir, when I had the opportunity to apply for the Tredyedeath Depot posting I jumped at it. I think you know that my girlfriend lives in Wadebridge and it was just fantastic for me. I see her when I'm off duty. She's the one for me, you know, sir. She's the one for me."

Dickie pointed at the now comatose Bismarck, who was surrounded by a semi-chewed Ollie and a damp-looking Kenneth. The 'guard' dog's ear flicked to indicate that he was still alive and partially listening to the discussions. "Jimmy, I am not interested in your sex life. It's that big hairy thing down there that we are here to talk about. Keep going."

"Well sir, the fact is that two days before I was due to be posted to Tredyedeath Depot, Bismarck got a terrible virus. I mean, he was such a healthy dog. I had him and trained him all his life." Tears started to well up in Jimmy's eyes. "And, well sir, well, he… he just died in my arms in the back of my Land Rover. No one knew."

Dickie reached forward and put his hand on Johnston's knee to calm him. "Go on, Jimmy."

"It would take months for me to retrain another Sheppy and that would put paid to any chance of being with my girlfriend. I might lose her. I was desperate. I had to get the Tredyedeath Depot posting somehow. Well sir, it just happened to be that, at the same time, my parents were struggling to look after, err err….." Johnston gazed down at the now sparked-out Alsatian.

Dickie interrupted. "Oh no, Johnston, tell me it's not Fluffy?"

Johnston continued. "Yes sir. It's Fluffy. He was just getting too big for them. It was all my fault in the first place. I should never have persuaded them to buy him. My sister's five-year-old daughter called him Fluffy and that's when she bought Ollie and Kenneth for him to play with. Kenneth is my dad's middle name. Of the two he prefers Ollie, you know, but he also plays with Kenneth. Don't know why really, I think…"

Dickie butted in again. "Jimmy, please! I am not interested in Fluffy's cuddly toy preference. Just get to the point."

Jimmy went on to explain that as he got larger, Fluffy was so pleased to see visitors to his parents' house that his vigorously wagging tail was in the habit of swiping the tea service clean off the coffee table and into a thousand irreparable pieces. Amusing though that was to visitors, his parents were now on their fifteenth tea service and Jimmy's mum was at her wits' end. When an inconsolable Jimmy phoned his parents to say that Bismarck had died, and that he was going to miss out on the Tredyedeath Depot posting and the chance to be with his girlfriend, his mum immediately jumped at the opportunity. She suggested that he take Fluffy off their hands. After all, he looked the same as Bismarck and of course to Fluffy, Jimmy was part of the family so no one would realise that he had been swapped. It was a win win situation – apart from the little issue that Jimmy had conveniently forgotten. He was in charge of defending the realm and Fluffy was clearly not only not up to the job but was an unlawful interloper. It was a high-risk strategy and a rapid exit from the army for Jimmy and Fluffy might be the consequence if his deception was exposed.

"Jimmy! What the hell were you thinking? Even if no one spotted that Bismarck is Fluffy, what about dog handling refresher days? I think your commanding officer would spot the difference between fetching a cuddly toy and ripping someone's arm off. And what about just the tiniest little issue of a real life situation?"

"Ah, but the terrorists won't know his identity, sir," Jimmy replied.

"Excuse me if sixteen years of experience counts for nothing, Johnston, but guard dogs are trained to attack, bring down and immobilize anyone who breaches security. What would you do in defending the realm, Johnston? Order 'Bismarck' to lick them to death?!"

"I see what you mean, sir. I hadn't thought of that, sir. Actually sir, he doesn't like people in black. He barks at them, you know. Terrorists wear black. Would that help?"

"Oh please, Johnston. You are trying my patience. I thought you were brighter than that. Dogs and women have gone to your head. You are in serious trouble. Get out and take your living and stuffed entourage with you. You'd better get him back in his kennel, the shift is about to change – and if I were you I would hide those... those cuddly things. I'll be in touch. Oh, and just more one thing. Don't mention this to anyone whilst I think about what to do about you."

Jimmy picked up Kenneth, tucked it under his arm and pulled on Fluffy's chain. The dozing dog slowly rose to his feet and grabbed Ollie in his mouth. As they left Dickie's office, Fluffy look back at Dickie, now with his head in his hands, pondering what to do. Once outside, Johnston's head re-emerged around the door. "You know sir, he can catch Frisbees in flight and my nieces taught him to put Jenga blocks neatly back in their box, which he loves doing. Now that's a real skill. I have got an old explosive storage box in my room in the barracks and Mum and Dad gave me the Jenga blocks when the nieces got bored with them. I am quite good at Jenga now and as soon as they topple over Fluffy picks them up and puts them back neatly in the box. You're smart, aren't you, Fluffy?"

Dickie, head still down but now shaking in dismay, just pointed silently at the door.

Chapter 8:
Cucumbers, Doughnuts and Other Surprises

It was Tuesday, Trecarsick parish council meeting day. Parish council meetings were always held in the evenings in Trecarsick village hall and this gave Dickie the opportunity to work a full day before he met Karensa. Major Fox-Thrasher was not due in the office which, for Dickie, was good news as he had decided to find out a bit more about the Gooleys' planning application, which the council were to debate as part of the public consultation process. Karensa had mentioned that the Gooleys would be there so it would give him a chance to have a chat with them and do some surreptitious fact finding. He decided he wouldn't mention to Karensa the major's 'shoot first and ask questions later' order to object to the planning application or mention that he had been given the task of submitting the Ministry's official response to Trefriggit district council. Despite his misgivings, he decided to take Fluffy, aka Bismarck, with him on his usual mile-long walk across the beautiful moorland to Trecarsick. They had become a regular feature of the local scene and it wasn't Bismarck's fault that his guard dog skills were at the poodle end of the killer instinct scale.

Dickie arrived with Bismarck in tow at the attractive granite and slate village hall, adjacent to the village green. Karensa was inside, waiting expectantly, wearing a pretty dress to impress her beau. She had arrived early to find a seat at the end of the row in the middle of the hall by the front door. This was her usual spot at parish council meetings, which she regularly attended. She had been well trained by Cordelia, for the sake of the village shop, to show her face at the meetings as a gesture of goodwill and to show local solidarity. Attendance would also keep her in tune with local issues, not that the village shop wasn't already a hive of activity when it came to local gossip. The seat position was strategically chosen by Cordelia, as it gave Karensa the chance to slip away if the evening's proceedings got too parochial. When it came to discussing the annual village green maintenance contract, it would often take three times as long to agree on the height of the grass as it would to actually cut it. Anyone stilll left in the hall by this time would probably have given up the will to live. This, however, was a special night.

The *Trecarsick Trumpet* hack Trevedic Penhaligon struck a pose at the back of the hall in his usual place. The tall journalist had become well known over the years, his characteristic long coat and fedora striking a distinctive chord in a rural area more noted for its jeans and agricultural overalls. He rued missed career opportunities in his early professional life and the *Trumpet* was now his home. It was going to see him out. He never did manage to find that elusive scoop that would elevate his status from being just another hack, but he never gave up trying. Although now part of the furniture, he still imagined himself, in a Walter Mitty sort of way, as a Carl Bernstein/Bob Woodward type. However, he knew inwardly that his Watergate scoop was, at best, more likely to relate to a stolen gate. He was, however, diligent, always poised with his trusty pen, notebook and pocket camera, ready to extract the flavour of the events before him, whatever they were. His snappy *Trumpet* headlines, though not up to Fleet Street standards, gave him some local notoriety.

It was a quarter to seven and the village hall was already filling up. Dickie walked in with Bismarck in tow and in an instant the once chatty seated congregation fell silent. The reaction to the large people-eating Sheppy was immediate and swiftly followed by what could only be described as a stampede as the locals scrambled to their feet, terror on their faces as the rows of chairs parted like the Red Sea with a clattering sound of wood on wood. Karensa found the sight quite amusing as locals jostled to take up all the spare seats on the other side of the hall, as far away as possible from the beast. She had got to know Bismarck well and although had yet to discover his true identity, she already suspected that he was pretty harmless.

Dickie maintained a dignified pose in his attempt to ensure that the fearsome guard dog lived up to his name. He looked across the hall at worried onlookers and raised his voice as he patted Bismarck on the head. "Don't worry, everyone. He's only trained to kill when he's on duty, you know. He's off duty now so there is nothing to worry about. Isn't that right, Bismarck?"

Bismarck's ears pricked up and he looked at Dickie expectantly, waiting for one of the doggie snacks he normally carried in case he needed to attract the dog's attention. As the amassed locals sat down, a neat semi-circle of empty chairs started to emerge around Dickie and Karensa like a fallout zone. The later arrivals had no choice but to slowly and reluctantly fill up the empty 'cordon sanitaire'. Karensa asked Dickie how he was and how everything was going at the depot.

"Not good, Kar. Not good," he replied.

"Oh Dickie, why not?"

"Bismarck here, the fearsome guard dog trained to kill and maim at the mention of the word terrorist, is not Bismarck at all but Fluffy, a rescue dog smuggled into the base by one of the guard dog handlers. It was his parents' pet. The real Bismarck died and his handler didn't want to lose the posting as he is madly in love with his girlfriend in Wadebridge. It's left me in a difficult position, Kar. Private Johnston is very loyal. Fluffy here is totally useless. You may as well patrol the security fence with a Chihuahua for all the good he is going to do. He has even got two cuddly toys, for God's sake, and he likes playing with Frisbees and Jenga blocks. The best he can do is to bark at anyone wearing black!"

Karensa smiled wryly. "Oh, that explains everything – particularly the endless cuddles Fluffy here gets from the local kids outside the shop. I always said kids can sense a friendly dog. At least I won't need to keep an eye on him sniffing some 'nursery fodder' in the future. Still, the good news is that he looks like a guard dog so the terrorists won't know his real identity."

"That's precisely what Private Johnston said!" Dickie spluttered. "If that was the case the army could save a lot of money in the cutbacks by disbanding the dog handling regiment altogether and using a load of rescue dogs instead! Kar, when it comes to the crunch, or maybe I should say 'bite', I don't think just looking fierce is good enough."

"Sorry." Karensa patted Fluffy on the head. He looked up. "You naughty boy, Fluffy. I bet you are loving it here. Where are your cuddly toys then?"

Dickie decided to change the subject. "Also, Fox-Thrasher has ordered me to deal with the…" He stopped.

"The what?"

"Oh nothing, just some boring explosive stuff on base that's taking time to sort out."

Just then the Gooleys arrived at the hall and were immediately welcomed by the many locals, who were keen to show their support for the popular farmers. The Gooleys had mainly come to see Cordelia receive her long service award but knew their planning application was also being considered at the meeting so it would give them the opportunity to answer any questions about the proposals. They immediately recognised Karensa and sat down in the 'fallout zone' at the end of the row in front of Karensa and Dickie. Big dogs didn't worry them and it gave Fred the opportunity to chat to Karensa whilst Grace squashed down her voluminous colourful dress and gave Bismarck a bit of love. Karensa introduced them to Dickie and explained about his role at Tredyedeath Depot. Grace looked over, her X-ray eyes scanning Dickie for any faults. Seemingly impressed, she raised her eyebrows and gave a knowing nod to Karensa to signify her approval.

Dickie looked at the honesty in Fred and Grace and decided there and then that he may as well dive in head first. If nothing else it might at least gain him Karensa's respect. "Your planning application at Feathers Farm, Mr Gooley. It looks interesting."

"How did you know about that? What's that got to do with Tredyedeath Depot?" Fred immediately retorted.

"Well sir, we have been sent a copy of the application by Trefriggit district council, who have asked us to comment on it."

"What? Why?"

"Because it's within the explosion zone of the depot. Within the safeguarding map area. The Ministry of Defence has to comply with some regulatory matters when a planning application falls inside an explosion zone."

Fred looked surprised and turned to attract Grace's attention. "I didn't know that! What safeguarding map? How long has it been there?"

Dickie explained that explosives were being stored under the ARCE programme but decided not to go into great detail as he wanted more information from Fred. It was clearly news to Karensa as well and she, Fred and Grace sat attentively as Dickie explained a little of the background. He tried to defuse the situation by explaining that Feathers Farm was only just inside the explosion zone by a matter of a few metres but Grace, a normally quiet and determined supporter of her loving husband, was implacable. She uncharacteristically and perceptively snapped back. "I bet you a pound to a penny it makes absolutely no difference to the Ministry of Defence whether Feathers Farm is two inches inside your whatsit map or sitting on top of the bloody mine. Who is dealing with it at the Ministry?"

Fearing the worst and not wishing to ruin the evening – or his burgeoning relationship with the lovely Karensa – Dickie felt the need for a delaying tactic. He needed a white lie. "It's not been decided yet, Mrs Gooley. Would you mind if I spent a little more time with you both up at the farm rather than here?"

Fred, now with his large arms folded in front of his protruding chest, his flat hat having worked its way down his forehead, leaned purposefully towards Dickie. "I think that's a bloody good idea, Dickie. Eight thirty Thursday morning then."

Dickie could see that he had no choice and agreed to the time there and then. The room fell quiet as the parish council meeting formalities started with a report on dog fouling, which gave Karensa just enough time to gently squeeze Dickie's thigh and whisper in his ear, "You kept that quiet. Their planning application is going to be ok, isn't it?"

"Kar, I have no idea, it's all a bit soon. I didn't mention it to you because there was nothing to say. It only came in a few days ago," he replied.

"Well, if the application is inside some sort of explosion zone, it strikes me that there might be an issue. I know you will be able to help them, Dickie. You're a good man. They are good people."

"Kar, you have to understand. I am not in overall charge. Fox-Thrasher is and you know what he's like. I have never got involved in planning applications before. I don't even know what the regulations say about these things. I will speak to the Gooleys on Thursday and find out a bit more. Anyway, this is your mum's night tonight."

The evening's events got going and the Gooleys' planning application sailed through with unanimous support from the parish, mixed with a spatter of applause. From the brief discussions that had taken place, Dickie picked up on the fact that the Gooleys' business had once been a successful working turkey farm that employed around half a dozen people and that despite the village shop doing its best to promote the sale of Fred's Christmas turkeys, the business had been declining.

Cordelia stepped up to receive her parish council long service award, to the rapturous applause of the hall. It sat proudly covered, awaiting its highly anticipated unveiling. There was a moment of silence, a sort of quiet shock, when the cover was theatrically whisked away by the council chairman to expose a contemporary interpretation of that Cornish megalithic structure from the Penwith peninsula, Men-an-Tol. Made rather badly by a local sculptor and mounted on a wooden plinth with a brass plaque, it looked not dissimilar to a doughnut with erect half cucumbers placed suggestively on either side. The parish council came up with the idea as Cordelia's ancient family roots hailed from the Penwith area, but they probably weren't aware that folklore suggested that Men-an-Tol had a ritualistic fertility significance. Now 76 years old, it wasn't going to have any effect on Cordelia but it certainly caught the eye of Karensa, who was by now gripping tightly onto Dickie's arm and quietly giggling at the salacious sculpture. However, in typically gracious fashion Cordelia was delighted to accept it, suggesting that it would look good in the village shop for all to see. Although she didn't say it, she certainly didn't want it displayed at home and as the shop did indeed sell cucumbers and doughnuts, it seemed entirely appropriate. Everyone retired afterwards to the Tinner's Whippet for a celebratory drink.

***

It was eight o'clock on 'Trumpet Thursday'. Dickie was in one of the depot's Land Rovers, on his way to meet the Gooleys. Wearing full army dress, he called in to the village shop to see Karensa. She always had goosebumps when she saw her Captain Lovely in uniform and although she didn't realise it, being Trumpet Thursday, that undone extra shirt button did something for Dickie too. The slow moving queue of male *Trumpet* readers extended outside the shop as they waited patiently to be served by Karensa whilst inside, men hovered for unwanted purchase opportunities, just to be served again. The *Trumpet*'s front page story reported on Fred and Grace's planning application and it was clear that Trevedic Penhaligon had been up all Tuesday night to maintain his notoriety. 'Gallant Gooleys' Golden Goose: parish council gives local farmers' housing scheme the nod' was certainly up to his standards. After a quick chat with Karensa, Dickie bought a copy of the paper for his office files and headed off along the winding lanes to Feathers Farm.

Fred and Grace were waiting patiently for the captain, who arrived on time to be ushered into the front room for the important business of the morning. Attila was on the roof looking down with interest and she dropped down onto the window sill to get a closer look. She could see from the expression on Fred and Grace's faces that they were worried about something. The Gooleys' body language gave a purposeful air. This was their pension they were going to be talking about and they looked like they had more questions than Dickie.

Once in the lounge, the obligatory china tea service soon appeared with some home-made apple strudel and Dickie's first thought was that he was glad he hadn't brought Fluffy in. With fifteen tea service 'kills' to his name, a sixteenth would certainly have been on the cards in his delight at meeting the welcoming Fred and Grace.

"Mr Gooley, can I start by saying that I am not here in an official capacity and have no authority to see you. I am in charge of the depot on a daily basis but Major Charles Fox-Thrasher is the commander. I have taken it upon myself to understand a little more about your planning application, what your business is and the scale of the operation. I have masters to deal with and there is a separate division within the Defence Estates which also looks into these matters and sets the rules. I know that you are popular locally and I want to see if I can help. I can then put all this information into our file and take it into account when the Ministry considers its response to your application. I would particularly like to know what existed here when the explosion zone safeguarding map was drawn up in 2002."

Dickie's frank approach and background explanation seemed to calm down Fred and Grace a little and after an hour of discussion, with Attila looking on from outside, Dickie accepted an invitation to have a look at the two farm buildings, courtyard, paddocks and the old steel framed barns, all of which just fell within the explosion zone Major Fox-Thrasher was so jealously guarding.

Attila had scrambled her way back into the rear courtyard and initially wandered cautiously, if a little bravely, up to Dickie to have a closer look. She then followed a few paces behind whilst Fred and Dickie viewed the scene, with Fred pointing out various locations and their relevance to his turkey business.

Dickie turned around, looked down at Attila and smiled. "I guess you kept one as a pet, did you, Mr Gooley? My dad used to keep a few.

Turkeys are surprisingly sociable animals but I guess as a turkey farmer for forty years you must know their characters inside out. Correct me if I'm wrong but he looks like a Wirral White to me?"

Fred was impressed. "You must be a farmer's son?"

Dickie nodded and talked a little about his background. It wasn't long before Attila started to nod vigorously, which indicated to Fred that the captain was a friendly face, someone he could do business with. Attila then followed it up with a subsequent cock of the head from side to side, which indicated the need to also be cautious. Seeming to be satisfied, she turned and wandered off to the comfort and safety of the barn.

The meeting took over an hour and a half and Dickie said that whilst he couldn't promise anything, he would report his findings to the specialists and his commander at the base. On walking Dickie back to the front door, Fred had one last question. "Tell me, Captain Lovely. It's about the explosion zone. I vaguely recall that there was an advert in the *Trumpet* about it when it was created in 2002. A few locals around here mentioned it but it soon got forgotten about because it was just seen as a continuation of the storage that's taken place at the mine since the 1950s. However, I am now being professionally advised and I am concerned that my advisor was not more diligent in finding out about the safeguarding map before he advised me to cease my turkey business. Did anyone approach you or the major about my proposals before the planning application was submitted?"

"No, Mr Gooley, nobody contacted us at all," Dickie said. "The first the major and I heard about the application was when we received a copy from the district council's chief planning officer, Jim Stern, asking for comment. It's not like we get a lot of these applications. We're just too remote."

"Thank you, Captain. Well let me tell you this for the record. Grace and I won't get mucked about by anyone and if we have to fight to get what we want, we will. You – I mean the Ministry – will have to put up a bloody good reason why my proposal shouldn't be allowed. You have been frank with me and I hope I have also made myself clear. My business is gone but it could legitimately return, although that's not my intention. I expect to get planning permission so I can sell up and retire. We're not made of money, you know."

Dickie nodded. "I fully understand, Mr Gooley. We will be scrupulously fair and fully justify our decisions."

Dickie had barely jumped back into the Land Rover to leave when Fred picked up the phone to call Ashley Sweet. "Mr Sweet, it's Fred Gooley here. It's about the planning application. I have had Captain Lovely from the Ministry of Defence's Tredyedeath Depot here wanting information about our business. He's just left. The Ministry of Defence has been consulted by the district council. Were you aware that the Ministry would be consulted because Feathers Farm falls within its explosion zone? Were you? Were you?"

On the other end of the phone, a hesitant and shocked Ashley sat back in his yellow plastic chair. "Well, err, no Mr Gooley. That's news to me."

"Well, they have and as far as I can see it shouldn't have been news to you if you had done your job properly. There's nothing we can do now. They'd better be happy with it. I am sure you will let me know what you propose to do. Good day."

It was a short sharp call to put Ashley on notice. A worried and uneasy Fred made a note of the call on his notepad by the phone.

Chapter 9:
Love and Hate

On his arrival back at Tredyedeath Depot, Dickie immediately made up an official Ministry file on the Gooleys' planning application, which would contain evidence relating to aspects of the turkey farmer's business along with the planning application proposals. Dickie had many reasons for doing this, not least because he was going on leave for a break with Karensa for a few days and he didn't trust the major not to take matters into his own hands. Experience of dealing with the major told him it was always best to be forearmed. The first item he put in the file was Trevedic's snappy *Trumpet* headline article about the parish's support for the application, which provided a lot of background information about the Gooleys and their turkey business. He also prepared a file note under the heading 'local information' from his discussions that morning with Fred and Grace – but didn't mention that he had actually met them. He also printed off his email to Division asking for its feedback, a request which he still hadn't yet told the major about.

A few barks disturbed the peace as the major's Land Rover pulled into the car park near the kennels. In seemingly just a few seconds he was standing in the captain's office doorway. "Morning, Lovely. Just seen a strange thing. Looks like one of the guard dogs has caught something. Brightly coloured, and he's got green things hanging from his mouth. Sent that Farmer Gooley application objection to the council yet?"

Dickie realised Fox-Thrasher was talking about Fluffy. He had to think fast. Quickly, he brought his birding skills to the fore. "Oh, oh err, yes sir, it's those damned ring-necked parakeets. They are getting everywhere, you know. Did you know that they are migrating from the south east of the country? Very green they are, sir. Pretty impressive catch for Bismarck. He can catch birds in mid-air, you know."

"Parakeets, eh? Well done Bismarck. Good to see he's on the ball.

We've got some damn good guard dogs here, Lovely. Should have brought my gun. Haven't shot any birds for a while. Bloody things. Waste of space. Would have made good practice too. What about that Gooley farmer application objection? Gone in, has it?"

"Well sir, as this is a planning issue, I decided to contact Division in the Defence Estates section for their comments and I am still waiting to hear from them."

"What? What?!" Fox-Thrasher exclaimed. "That's not what I told you to do, Lovely. I am the explosives expert around here, not you. You are just a logistics officer, whatever that job description means. Can't you do a simple job, Lovely? You are managing this base under my control and don't you forget it."

Dickie refused to be flustered and aimed for the major's weakness – his penchant for rules. "Well sir, I looked at the internal rules appended to the safeguarding map direction. It's quite clear that when planning applications are submitted within a safeguarding map explosion zone, Division has to be consulted. Now you wouldn't want to breach the Ministry's rules, would you, sir?"

"Rules? Oh well, that's quite different, Lovely. Why didn't you mention it before? Got to stick by the rules, Lovely. In that case it looks like you had no option. Get them to pull their finger out. I want it sorted."

With that, the major turned and goose-stepped out of the office, leaving Dickie with the job of chasing Division, who promised to respond on the application in four days – which fitted in very nicely with Dickie's planned trip away with Karensa, as he would be back in time to receive their comments and recommendations.

He knocked on the major's office door and stepped inside to relay the information to the major, who was by now at his desk furiously writing an article for his beloved *Bang!* magazine. "Sir, I will leave the blue application file I have created by my desk. It's clearly marked and has got some useful information in it if you want to have a look." Fox-Thrasher, head down, just nodded briefly to acknowledge Dickie's message. He was still clearly irritated that he hadn't got the answer he was hoping for.

Before Dickie left, he warned Private Johnston to keep Fluffy out of Fox-Thrasher's way; he might not be so lucky next time Ollie made an appearance disguised as a dead ring-necked parakeet. Dickie couldn't guarantee that the major wouldn't want a closer look and said he would decide what he was going to do about Bismarck/Fluffy when he got back. Johnston was clearly thankful that he had a stay of execution and told Dickie that he had decided to see out his remaining term in the army, which had barely two years to run, and then leave for a life in civvy street, hopefully working in an animal rescue centre near his girlfriend in Wadebridge. He thought that might help Dickie in his deliberations. However, neither of them had thought about what would happen to Fluffy/Bismarck, who was technically 'owned' by the army. When Dickie raised this future dillema, they just looked at each other with raised eyebrows.

The major looked down from his office to see the captain's army Land Rover drive out of the base for his break away with Karensa. He immediately picked up the phone to Division. Wally Dinsmore, a civilian surveyor working within Division, took the call. "Mr Dinsmore, it's Major Fox-Thrasher, commander at Tredyedeath Depot. Captain Lovely should have sent you details of a planning application within our explosion zone. I want some answers." Fox-Thrasher just couldn't resist taking over control of the Gooleys' application as soon as Dickie's back was turned. Despite the advice in the regulations, he didn't like the idea of a bunch of civil servants hundreds of miles away telling him what to do.

"Yes, Mr Dinsmore," he continued, "I appreciate that you told Captain Lovely you would get back to him in a few days but that's not good enough. I am being pressured by the council to provide the Ministry's comments – which I am happy to do – but I want an answer from you today on the technical stuff. If it helps you, the application site was an illegal turkey business which is not an agricultural operation but a factory, and it doesn't have planning permission. It has now closed. I understand that the Health and Safety Executive also object to the proposals on public health grounds because of the extra people living in the explosion zone generated by this application. Please get back to me with your views. It's not rocket science, Dinsmore." Having given his direct phone number, Fox-Thrasher hung up and carried on with his *Bang!* article.

A matter of a few hours went by before Fox-Thrasher's phone rang. It was Wally Dinsmore at Division. The major listened carefully before replying. "Thank you very much for all that, Mr Dinsmore. So just to be clear, on the basis of the information I gave you, there are grounds to object because housing created by the application proposals will permanently bring extra people into the explosion zone and adversely impact on the explosives capability of the Ministry's Tredyedeath Depot ARCE facility contrary to the national defence interests. Leave it up to me. What's that? The regulations say that the Ministry can't force the district council to refuse the planning application but if it's going to ignore the Ministry's objection, the Secretary of State for Planning can prevent the council determining it and hold a public inquiry so he can decide it himself? That's very helpful. That should be enough to put the council buggers off!"

Fox-Thrasher immediately stopped writing his article and eagerly started to prepare the Ministry's objection to the planning application. It was soon completed and, post haste, on its journey to the district council. Fox-Thrasher was a happy man and immediately went into the mine for an evening's therapeutic solitary wander amongst the explosives.

***

Dickie and Karensa had chosen St Ives and the Penwith peninsula for their three-day break, their first and much anticipated trip away together. It enabled Karensa to look up some Craddock family relatives and for both of them to walk the rugged moor and coastline and share some quality time without the distractions of the village shop or Tredyedeath Depot. It also gave them time to visit the now infamous ancient monument Men-an-Tol, which had caused much amusement at Cordelia's parish council presentation. It wasn't long before Karensa quickly crawled through the stone ring when Dickie's back was turned. Only time would tell if its mystical fertility powers would bear fruit so, ironically, she decided to keep mum for the time being. In the meantime, a few judicious photographs of the Neolithic monument would bring some resonance for Cordelia, who suggested later that their appropriate placement in the shop alongside her long service award would avoid any embarrassing misinterpretation of what it was actually supposed to resemble.

***

On Dickie's return to the depot, the major decided to take the initiative and bring the captain up to speed, at least the way he saw it. In his usual fashion, he came barging straight into Dickie's office even before the captain had the chance to sit down. Clumsily, the awkward major attempted some small talk. "Morning, Captain. How was your little break with Cornelia in Devon? Did you have a good time?"

"It's Cordelia and she's seventy-six. My break was with her daughter Karensa in Cornwall. Yes thank you, Major, it was lovely sampling the sights of the Penwith peninsula. I see that my file on the Gooleys' application hasn't moved. I assume that Defence Estates haven't come back yet with their comments?"

"Oh yes indeed they have. They certainly have," the major boasted. "They were able to deal with it a little earlier than anticipated. Jolly efficient of them, I thought. They have very clearly objected and I have sent off the objection to the council requesting that they refuse the application forthwith. Nothing for you to do, Captain Lovely. It's all done. Glad you had a good break in Devon."

As Fox-Thrasher started to walk out of the office, the captain quickly picked up the blue file and opened it. The major looked round. "Sir,"

Dickie said, "there is nothing on file as far as I can see from Division. What was the basis of their objection?"

"Oh, lots of reasons. I won't bore you with it all. They didn't put it in writing so I just took it down over the phone. All about more people in the explosion zone prejudicing our explosive storage capability here – and we don't want that. We just don't want it. It will be refused by the council and that will be the end of it. Bloody farmers."

Dickie decided he wasn't going to get any sense out of the major, who clearly hadn't looked at the contents of the blue file. Neither was he convinced that the major had told him the whole story, or that his dialogue with Division was anything other than one sided to suit his rigid agenda. The only saving grace as far as Dickie was concerned was that it wasn't his signature on the objection to the council so hopefully his burgeoning relationship with Karensa wouldn't be too tarnished.

But he nevertheless felt undermined and saddened that a sense of right had not prevailed. In the short term, it was going to be difficult for him to deal with the Gooleys and the local community, who he saw regularly on his frequent trips to the village shop. He was now part of the problem, not the solution. But he naturally suspected from his discussions with the Gooleys that once the 'truth will out', a quite different picture would emerge – and when it did he was going to make damned sure that it would be the major in the firing line and not him..

Chapter 10:
Apollo 13 and Indian Rain Dances

The district council's twenty-one day consultation period for the Gooleys' planning application soon expired and all the relevant consultees had responded. The parish council's wholehearted support for the proposal was welcome, as was support from the local community including the Craddock family. All the technical departments gave the planning application a clean bill of health including the council's own important policy planners, who were satisfied that the alternative use of one barn for a house and the extension of the farmhouse into the old slaughterhouse would be acceptable.

The objection to the planning application from the Ministry of Defence was about as popular as a Bodmin Moor wind farm proposal and unquestionably unwelcome news to Chief Planning Officer Jim Stern. He immediately called Trevelyan Trelyon to break the news. "Trevelyan. We've had a problem."

"Jim. So nice to hear from you. What a great film Apollo 13 was – and hasn't that iconic quote gone down in history? You bought the video, did you?" Trevelyan had a dubious intellectual propensity for unintentionally going 'off piste' at the strangest of occasions, by no means an unusual characteristic for a councillor, particularly during council meetings. He wouldn't have realised that the hard-working chief planning officer didn't have the time for tittle-tattle, even with his political masters.

"No, Trevelyan. We have a problem with the Gooleys' planning application. The Ministry of Defence have objected to it on the basis that the application site falls within the Tredyedeath Depot explosion zone on the safeguarding map. They want the council – or, more to the point, me – to refuse it."

"What?! That's absurd. They're tossers! Can we ignore it? What do the regulations say, Jim? I need to be briefed!" Trelyon spluttered.

In anticipation, Jim had already taken the trouble to dust off and examine the legal direction that created the safeguarding map for the depot, which had been sitting quietly in the darkness of a bottom drawer, undisturbed for many years. The council hadn't received a planning application within the explosion zone since it was created in 2002 other than for minor agricultural operations, which the regulations treated as 'exempt works'. Although the district was littered with former tin mines like Swiss cheese, this was the only one being used by the Ministry.

"Trevelyan, I don't think I can just ignore the objection unless there are very good reasons to do so. I do think the Ministry has gone totally over the top but of course the Gooleys' agent should have tried to anticipate the Ministry's position before he submitted the application by checking out the information on our plotting sheets. It's all there. If there is good news, it's that the Ministry cannot force the district council to refuse the application. The bad news is that if I ignore this objection and recommend approval, the Ministry has a right to ask the Secretary of State for Planning to hold a public inquiry to enable its objection to be heard. This would be in front of an independently appointed planning inspector. The application is then determined by the Secretary of State for Planning on the basis of the inspector's recommendation. It's heavyweight stuff, Trevelyan. As chief planning officer I cannot unilaterally place the council in that position and to that expense even if I wanted to. If you and your fellow councillors want to fight the Ministry, it has to be on the basis of a decision democratically made by the council, not by me using the powers of determination vested in me. At the moment, therefore, I will have to use my delegated powers to recommend the application be refused."

"Bloody hell, Jim," Trelyon moaned, "this is a disaster for me... errrr, I mean the Gooleys. What do you think we should do? What can I do?"

"Well, in the first instance, as Mr Gooley's elected councillor, you can of course remove my powers of determination. This would force me to present the planning application to the planning committee for it to make the democratic decision, whatever my recommendation is. I think that's the best way to go at the moment." The phone went quiet. Jim could see that Trevelyan was struggling and hadn't quite got it. "Trevelyan, can I assume you have removed my determination powers? A 'yes' would be the right answer."

"Err, oh, yes. Err, yes. Done. What's next?"

"Now, I am happy to just sit on the application for the time being but the Gooleys' agent, Mr Sweet, needs to know the position – and so does Fred Gooley. I want to meet the commander at Tredyedeath Depot to understand the background to the Ministry's objection. I need more information anyway for my report on the application to the planning committee. I would be happy for Mr Gooley's agent to attend as well. Of course it would be my intention to try and persuade the depot commander to change his mind," Jim explained.

"You'll be lucky, Jim. I met him once at some official function a few years ago. He's a snob and a total shit. I don't mind coming along."

"Trevelyan, at this live stage of the planning process I don't need to remind you that your rules of engagement as a councillor prohibit any interference. You will have to wait until the application is presented to the council's planning committee to determine to have your say. If I were you, if there's going to be a fight, I would galvanise your fellow councillors – but of course that's up to you and them. This application isn't going to be determined any time soon. You'd better call Mr and Mrs Gooley and I will call Mr Sweet. Let me have the meeting with the commander and we will see what happens."

Trevelyan agreed to Jim's eminently sensible strategy but knew that a call to the Gooleys was going to be difficult. He decided that it would be better to meet Fred and Grace face to face.

***

Jim Stern immediately called Ashley, who was sitting at his desk, dressed all in black with his cuffs rolled over, his hair in its usual neat place. A yellow linen jacket hung on the wall behind his yellow plastic chair. His desk was bedecked with three screens showing various drawings and photos, together with a smartphone in its holder, a tablet in another holder and a grey hard drive. Some silver 'techie' desk art complemented the scene, reinforcing Ashley the architect's membership of the twenty-first century and his dream working environment.

"Mr Sweet. Hello, it's Jim Stern here from the planning office. It's about the Gooleys' planning application, which you submitted on their behalf. I'll come straight to the point. We have received an objection from the Ministry of Defence. It's come from the commander at Tredyedeath Depot. They have requested that the application be refused because it falls within the explosion zone, as shown on the safeguarding map here in the planning office. All this information is shown on our plotting sheets."

The phone went quiet. It was clear that Ashley hadn't a clue about the council's plotting sheets, their relevance to the Ministry's objection or, more to the point, what role they had in his handling of Fred's application.

"Oh how awful," he said. "What a surprise. That's not very nice of them. Can they do that?"

"I am afraid they can, Mr Sweet," Jim replied. "It now leaves me in a difficult position. At the moment, I have no choice but to recommend refusal. Had it not been for this objection I would have supported it."

"Oh dear, what a shame. The Gooleys won't be very pleased."

"Mr Sweet, from what I know of the locally popular Mr and Mrs Gooley, I think that's an understatement. I am, however, prepared to attend a meeting with you and the Tredyedeath Depot commander as I have a number of questions I need to ask him about the explosion zone anyway – but I have to say that, in my view, you should have discussed this with the Ministry before the planning application was submitted."

"Oh. But they have never objected before," Ashley said.

"That's not really the point. Anyway, there has not been a planning application in the explosion zone before for the Ministry to object to. I can say that the district councillor, Trevelyan Trelyon, is going to do what he can to retrieve the situation but I am not hopeful. In all likelihood this could end up at a public inquiry."

"Oh dear me. I have never done one of those before," Ashley bleated. "They sound quite frightening events. Don't you get yelled at by a high powered barrister? I wouldn't like that."

"Mr Sweet, I think you'd better have a word with Mr and Mrs Gooley," Jim said. "Meanwhile, I will try and arrange a meeting with the commander and get back to you."

Ashley sat back in his chair and pondered the news. Initially he hadn't quite taken in the enormity of the situation and the implications for him professionally but Jim's message soon began to sink in. It was no good. He couldn't just phone up the Gooleys with the bad news. He was not going to shy away from his responsibilities. He had to pay them a visit there and then, explain his position and, if necessary, face the consequences.

***

Attila was resting in the barn when she suddenly stirred. Her sixth sense felt that something was about to happen so, embodying her role as protector, she decided to warn Fred and Grace. Grace was in the kitchen surrounded by pastry whilst Fred was sorting some paperwork in the parlour. Flossie had taken up residence curled up on the top of the hot range, her pink nose indicating that spontaneous combustion was probably just a few degrees away. One eye was shut and the other focused on various spare pie bits, both sweet and savoury. Attila scrambled out of the barn and jumped onto the wide parlour windowsill, spotted Fred, and pecked at the window to indicate that someone was about to arrive. Fred looked up. At that point the approaching sound of car engines broke the peace and a few seconds later, two cars pulled up. It was Trevelyan and Ashley who had, coincidentally, arrived at the same time to bring Fred and Grace the bad news. Attila knew immediately something wasn't right and, unusually for her, she hopped off the windowsill and waddled through the open back door and into the farmhouse to be met by Fred who, by now, was already on his feet.

"Now you know you are not allowed in here, Attila," he said. "I don't want another one of your altercations with Flossie. I know you both get on and like a bit of rough and tumble but Grace can't be doing with lumps of cat hair and feathers all over the place, particularly not on pie day. The last time you two had a dust up, it took her an hour to unblock the vacuum cleaner. She's still picking feathers out of the curtains, you know."

The animated Attila looked up at Fred, squawked and cocked her head from side to side: Beware, something's not quite right. Fred nodded in recognition, gently ushered Attila out into the yard and walked down the corridor to the front door. Both Ashley and Trevelyan were by now out of their cars and, never having met before, made their introductions. Both then proceeded to perform different versions of what appeared to be a ritualistic Indian rain dance whilst wondering what on earth the other was doing. Ashley was bent over and looking skywards whilst moving his red plastic case from side to side above his head as he moved in a crab motion towards the front door. Trevelyan, looking at the ground, was hopping up and down with his arms flailing in the air, his large waistcoat-covered torso just about keeping in time with the rest of his body.

Fred looked on in astonishment at the performances. "Morning, gentlemen. Are you both all right? Have you just joined the Masonic Lodge? I thought they did all that stuff in private. It looks a bit bloody weird to me."

In an unchoreographed moment, Ashley and Trevelyan both opened the dialogue in unison. "Where's that turkey?"

It was clear that their last visit to Feathers Farm had left an indelible mark on their memories and thoughts of a lingering 'death by turkey' or worse were uppermost in their minds. As their weird moves continued in their quest to defend themselves from imminent turkey attack, they cast their eyes over the immediate scene in search of the errant feathered fowl, anticipating that her cunning might lead her to attack from the sun like a fighter pilot.

"Oh, she's around the back, out of the way," Fred said.

Trevelyan looked up at the ridge of the farmhouse and spotted something. "So what's that up there then?"

"Bloody thing. Attila, get down!" Fred shouted. "Sorry about that, gentlemen." The ancient rain dances subsided as they moved quickly towards the sanctity of the farmhouse, its welcoming front door already open, allowing them to scurry inside to the safety of the hallway where they both straightened up. "Well this is a surprise. Both of you at the same time. I guess you are here to tell Grace and me the good news, are you?"

There was a slight pause as Ashley and Trevelyan looked at each other, wondering who was going to deliver the bombshell news. Trevelyan nodded his head, indicating to Ashley that he would be the bearer of bad news. "Well Fred, I am afraid the news is bad. The Ministry of Defence has objected to your planning application because Feathers Farm falls within Tredyedeath Depot's explosion zone."

Trevelyan started to expand on the reasons for the objection but Fred, by now red faced, interrupted. He straightened up, folded his arms and looked intently at both of them. "I asked you, Mr Sweet, before the application was submitted, if that Ministry storage depot would have any bearing on my application and you said no. I stopped my business because of you, Mr Sweet. Trelyon, you recommended Mr Sweet to me and you said Mr Stern at the planning office said it would be all right. I trusted you both. This is a bloody disaster." He covered his face with his large rough hands. "I have no income and what savings we had have all but gone on this bloody planning application. On all those bloody surveys. Bloody hell." He looked up. "Someone's going to pay for this – and it's not going to be me and Grace." Fred would have said more but, incandescent, he couldn't think straight. He needed to take stock. He needed to calm down.

Ashley felt his right hand run out of blood as it gripped his red plastic briefcase ever tighter. He felt it was the right time for him to say something. "Well, the good news is that we have only the one objection. Everyone else is in support. Can we go into the front room and talk this over? There is more we need to explain." He paused. "Is that cat in there?"

"Mr Sweet, unless you are telling me that you just add up all support and objection and see who wins, the good news, as you put it, is totally meaningless to me. An objection is an objection, and in this case a powerful one at that. Don't you think? Well?" Fred shouted.

"Err no, I mean yes, Mr Gooley. Planning doesn't work like that. We have to deal with each objection."

"Exactly. If you haven't got anything positive to say, Mr Sweet, I would shut up if I were you!"

Fred was about to send them packing out of the farmhouse when Grace, having heard raised voices, appeared from the kitchen and walked down the hallway. "Hello. What's all the fuss? Are we all happy or sad then?" Fred explained the situation to Grace and, visibly shaken, she bundled everyone into the front room, turned around and headed back to the kitchen. She needed to keep busy. She needed to think. She made a pot of tea.

Once everyone was seated, Fred remained motionless as Trevelyan explained the discussions he'd had with Jim Stern. In classic politician speak, he hyped up his role and influence. "What I can say, Fred, here and now, is that I have personally instructed Jim Stern to present the planning application to the planning committee rather than determine it himself. This means that whatever Jim's professional recommendation is, the planning committee will determine your application. I am glad I have been so influential in the matter."

Trevelyan made it clear that with no other objections, he felt confident he would get the support of his fellow councillors on the planning committee. He didn't refer to Jim Stern's likely recommendation as chief planning officer that if the Ministry stuck to their guns and even with the planning committee's support for Fred's proposal, the council might be stopped in its tracks to allow the Secretary of State for Planning to hold a public inquiry, with all the resulting delay that would entail. If Trevelyan had learnt one thing as a politician it was to manage fallout. Bad news in bite size chunks was the order of the day.

Ashley didn't seek to defend his advice and, looking down, remained largely silent. Once Trevelyan had said as much as he felt he could, Ashley grabbed the opportunity to extract any positivity by indicating that, at the insistence of Jim Stern, he and Jim would be meeting the commander at the depot with two objectives: to better understand the nature of the Ministry's objection and to persuade it to withdraw its objection. He remained optimistic that the situation could be retrieved but Trevelyan kept quiet, knowing from the personalities involved that this would be a tall order.

Fred remained curiously calm. "I'm coming to that bloody meeting. I want to see what this Tredyedeath Depot is like. What this commander is like. I appreciate that you are my agent, Mr Sweet but I want to be there as your client. It's just a great pity you haven't been there before. If we don't persuade the Ministry to back down, I guess we take our chances with the planning committee. It's far from ideal."

Ashley willingly agreed to Fred's attendance at the meeting. He had no choice. Grace arrived with the tea, which was quickly consumed in almost total silence. She decided to let Fred tell her the full story later but what she had heard was more than enough to let her know that they could be in for a rough time.

Trevelyan was sensitive enough to see that Fred and Grace were having difficulty taking it all in and he decided that it was time to go. He explained that political protocol prevented him from attending the meeting at Tredyedeath Depot, but that he would take stock of the whole situation afterwards, as Jim Stern had agreed to maintain close contact and keep him briefed. He assured the Gooleys that everyone was rooting for them and he would keep them posted. Then, having bid his farewells, he performed another strange Indian rain dance on the way to his car and roared off. Ashley had also taken the opportunity to make his excuses and followed Trevelyan out of the farmhouse to his convertible.

Attila was still sitting on the ridge of the farmhouse. She didn't need to sit on the lounge window sill to see that these messengers had brought bad news. Somehow she already knew. Ashley became the focus of her outstretched neck, and she flicked around to wave her bottom feathers up and down at him, signifying a personal dislike for what he had got Fred into. She flicked around again and started to run down the roof, which gave her just enough speed to allow her short wings to get her airborne. Her target was Ashley's convertible. Fred knew what was coming. The wind started to whistle through her wings as the silver machine came into range. Ashley froze in horror and looked on, powerless, as his cries of "Oh no, please, please no!" fell on Attila's not-so-deaf ears. It was an impressive poo. The nasty mess left on the fabric roof and windscreen would take more than a team of hard-working Romanian car washers to remove. Fred's ashen face momentarily twitched to reveal a wry smile as Attila gathered herself up in the field and started to walk back. She hopped through the fence past Ashley, who was scrambling about inside the car looking for a box of tissues. Then she stopped in front of Fred and started to lift one leg and then the other. This went on for about thirty seconds. It was a message Fred recognised. It meant he needed to do something, take charge, take control.

He looked over at Ashley, who had given up on the tissues and was about to drive off, windscreen washers and wipers at full tilt as he tried to clear the rapidly drying guano as it smeared across the windscreen like the remains of a melting ice cream. "Let me know when the meeting at Tredyedeath Depot is, Mr Sweet. By the way, it may be your last one on this job. Good day." With that, Fred shut the front door and retired to think about the consequences. It had been a bad day.

Attila was back in the courtyard and she hopped onto the water trough within sight of the parlour window, still hopping from one leg to the other to reinforce to Fred that he had to take control. She felt she had made a worthwhile contribution, but not the sort you would put in a church collection box.

Chapter 11:
Locals, Lawyers and Charm Offensives

Fred and Grace had a bad night's sleep. Fred knew that with his natural fighting instincts and Attila's sixth sense, he was going to have to take matters to another level. The family solicitors and successful Truro-based law firm Steel, Cash and Scamper had served the Gooleys well over the years and Fred felt it was now time to call on their services despite his diminishing funds. With Ashley Sweet so ineffective, one thing was certain: Fred and Grace needed independent advice. If Ashley's contract was to be terminated, which was the way Fred was feeling, he needed to know when, what the consequences would be, what recompense he could expect and who would replace him. He made an appointment to see his advisor, Penelope Breakage, a respected partner in the practice who the Gooleys held in high regard.

Steel, Cash and Scamper had just moved into their swanky new premises in Truro, a twenty-first century glass and steel structure located in the middle of the cathedral city that made a confident statement of the business's commercial success and standing in the legal profession. Fred had seen the firm grow over the years and would be the first person to recognise and applaud its success.

Penelope had been a partner for three years. She was a rising star in the firm and living in a county she loved. Now thirty-five, she had thrown herself into her career to the extent that those difficult decisions on balancing career needs with partners and children had just not presented themselves. But she wasn't concerned that some of her university peer group colleagues were ahead of her in the marriage and kiddy stakes. A high achiever, Penelope had a forceful personality and a wry sense of humour, and her first class university law degree had projected her into the world of land and property, including town planning, in a top ranking country practice. She was a keen sportswoman, five foot five tall, with a slim figure, long brown hair and a certain tomboy attraction that proved to be no hindrance in attracting boyfriends. But it would always be on her terms. She was certainly in control of her destiny and that's the way she liked it. She was, however, accident prone, which didn't sit well with her leisure pursuits but it certainly never held her back. She angrily rejected her parents' claim that it was caused by undiagnosed mild dyspraxia, a condition affecting physical co-ordination, though she would often be seen around Truro with a bandage wrapped around something or other – which came as no surprise to those who knew her.

Fred had briefed Penelope well, enabling her to digest his planning application and consultation comments from the district council's website. She noted the groundswell of local support, which didn't surprise her as she and her business colleagues knew just how popular the Gooleys were. Fred had also mentioned that Trevelyan 'Rely-on' Trelyon was doing what he could at the political level although he was less enamoured with his recommended consultant, Ashley Sweet, who he definitely couldn't rely on.

Although the boundary of the Tredyedeath Depot safeguarding map was not available on the council's website, the direction and accompanying explanation were. Penelope knew from her property experience that the detailed wording of the Ministry's direction applied to the whole country and its purpose was to protect human life. Each safeguarding map was specific to the local depot in question. She and the chief planning officer, Jim Stern knew each other well, so much so that she could pick up the phone to him at any time if she needed to. Her firm represented the district council from time to time when the council's own legal services department was overstretched. From her discussions with Fred, she could see he was not fully conversant with the full implications of the Ministry's objection and in her view, this was Ashley Sweet's fault. That Trevelyan had clearly not been totally frank either given his detailed discussions with Jim Stern indicated to Penelope that it was now time to lay all the cards on the table.

Fred and Grace arrived early and took their seats in the smart, minimalistic waiting area. Fred was bedecked in his Sunday best green Harris Tweed three piece suit and Grace had chosen another one of Gwenifer's colourful creations. They made a striking contrast as they sat back in the plush black leather and chrome seats, which complemented the Cornish slate floor.

Penelope soon arrived and gave them a warm welcome, whilst concealing a red stained bandage on her little finger. She looked businesslike in her black attire, in preparedness for an impending Truro County Court appearance later that day. Her office was on the third floor at the end of a curved glazed corridor which contained four meeting room suites, each one named to reflect the firm's professional ethical standards: Honesty, Integrity, Sincerity and Morality. Fred and Grace were clearly impressed with the whole set up, even more so when they entered her office to find a freshly brewed cup of tea waiting for them. They sat down on some uncomfortable trendy clear plastic chairs and looked at Penelope attentively.

"Well Fred and Grace, I have read all the background material and spoken to Jim Stern. I won't beat about the bush but we do have an issue here and this may not be one which will be resolved easily or quickly. We know that the district council is, in principle, supportive of your application at professional planning and political levels but the Ministry of Defence holds all the cards. Unless we can find a flaw in their arguments we may not succeed. Explosion zones are an important part of the nation's defence strategy and protected by law."

Fred was quick to retort: "And what about the advice I received? I closed my business on the high expectation of receiving planning permission!"

"That's another issue, and here I do feel you have good grounds to make a claim against your advisors, who clearly have not been diligent," Penelope said. "However, what we need to do in the short term is to identify the veracity of the Ministry's objection to your application. I certainly think the Ministry's position is flawed given the labour-intensive nature of your business compared to what you are now proposing. I understand that Jim Stern has arranged to meet the commanding officer at Tredyedeath Depot, a Major Fox-Thrasher I believe, and you, Fred, and Mr Sweet are to attend. It seems to me that you should have this meeting and then we need to speak again. We can then see if you need a new planning advisor and what we should do about making a claim against your existing consultant."

It all made eminent sense to Fred, who agreed before listening intently as Penelope explained the background to the whole explosion zone issue. She handed him a copy of the direction and highlighted its important parts – including the one that allowed the Ministry of Defence to request the Secretary of State for Planning to intervene. She explained that the matter could rumble on for another year to eighteen months, possibly longer.

Fred was aghast but stayed lucid. "Penelope, I was not aware of any of that. I now have no income and most of our savings have gone into this planning application. I could go bankrupt. Attila and I agree that we are moving into a recession. Not only will the value of my assets go down but my costs in fighting this ridiculous objection, which Attila thinks I should do, will only increase the longer it goes on. A delay of a year or eighteen months, or longer, could be disastrous. I could lose everything."

With Grace vigorously nodding in silent agreement, Penelope could see the strained look on the couple's faces. "Fred, Grace. There is nothing I can do about that other than to give you robust support and advice. My firm – I – will be fully behind you. We should be able to get some recompense if you sue your advisors over the cost of the application and your loss in earnings, plus interest – all, of course, incurred by you as a result of bad advice. But who is Attila? A friend of the family? A wise owl?"

"She's just… well, just a friend. I suppose you could call her a wise owl. I hadn't thought of her like that," Fred said.

Fred and Grace were now in full command of all the unpleasant facts and it was clear that the meeting with the commander would be a critical one for the Gooleys' finances. It was now the end of June and six weeks had passed since Fred's application had been submitted. Disconsolate, Fred and Grace arrived back at Feathers Farm to be met by Attila sitting on the roof, her sharp hearing recognising their aging, rattling Land Rover approaching some miles away. She gave a familiar nod to welcome them home. A message was waiting on their phone from Ashley, confirming that Jim Stern's meeting with the commander had been arranged for early August – a disappointing five weeks' time. It was just more delay.

***

'Trumpet Thursday' had come around again at the Trecarsick village shop and Trevedic Penhaligon had excelled himself with the week's headline. He was well ahead of the locals this time, having diligently waded through the Gooleys' planning application on the council's website to find the Ministry's objection, robustly written by Major Fox-Thrasher. This was big news. In his zealous attempt to repel the Gooleys' proposals as wholly inappropriate, Fox-Thrasher had naively and unwittingly elevated Tredyedeath Depot from a sleepy local Ministry of Defence backwater to a major explosives facility that had more than enough destructive force to put Trecarsick on the moon. The headline on the newspaper board outside the shop stood out conspicuously, like Fluffy on a training exercise. The punchy headline said it all: 'Defence Depot 'Direction' Dashes Development Dream'. The strapline read 'Ministry Missive calls foul on Feathers Farm's future'. This was Trevedic's best yet. The shop soon became rife with rumour. Just how much explosives was stored at the mine? How had it been kept under wraps for so long? What was an explosion zone, or a safeguarding map? And why pick on the Gooleys anyway?

Cordelia had been helping in the shop and had heard enough. She immediately booked the village hall for a local meeting to crank up the community and Karensa was duly instructed to start a petition: 'Support your Gooleys'. The Craddocks were going to be the first names on the list.

With matters gathering apace, Dickie was going to have to face hostile questioning when he next came to see Karensa so she decided to give him a call. "Dickie. Have you seen the *Trumpet*? All hell's broken loose here. Why didn't you tell me the Ministry objected to Fred and Grace's application? I'm disappointed with you. Mum has called a local meeting to form an action group. Have you read what Fox-Thrasher has written about the proposals? It's pretty scary stuff."

"Hold on, Kar," Dickie said defensively. "I can't speak for what Fox-Thrasher has said because I haven't actually read it. He just told me that he was going to object on instruction from Defence Estates and not to worry. Anyway, there is a meeting here in a few weeks' time. I took the call from Jim Stern, the chief planning officer. He wants some answers and he made it clear that the district council is supportive. The major tried to stall it, tried to delay, but he eventually agreed when Jim insisted. I am attending and so are Fred and his advisor, Mr Sweet. It's put me in a difficult position, Kar, as I have already seen Fred, as you know – and Fox-Thrasher doesn't know that. There's a lot to play for yet. Tell your mum to cancel the village hall and wait to see what comes out at the meeting."

Karensa laughed, some sympathy in her voice. She knew her mother better than that. "Dickie, I think there's more chance of Fluffy ripping someone's arm off than my mother cancelling the booking. She's got her head down. Anyway, it's not just about the Gooleys. It's also about what's stored in that mine. Fox-Thrasher's let the cat out of the bag. What's the date of your meeting?"

"Kar, I can't tell you that. It's private."

"Oh! Well, I'm sure Fox-Thrasher would be interested to know all about Bismarck – or should I say Fluffy!!"

"Kar, you can't do that. It's blackmail!" Dickie cried.

"Look Dickie, I know you. Really, we're both on the same side, aren't we? I'm sure a few locals with placards at the gate on the day of the meeting won't do any harm. What's the date then?"

Reluctantly, and suspecting that Fred would have told Cordelia anyway, Dickie revealed the meeting date and reaffirmed to his love that he would do what he could to find out how much Division really knew about the whole affair.

A placated and persuasive Karensa rang off. Dickie pulled out the blue file on the Gooleys' application and looked at precisely what the major had written. It was naively candid 'explosive' stuff and he could see from the major's language why the locals might have cause for concern. But there was no indication from the Defence's bureaucratic system of 'copy boxes' that a copy of the objection had been sent to Division, as the rules required. This was predictably consistent with the so-called 'verbal instruction' to object the major claimed to have been given by Division. Dickie sat upright and reflected for a moment. He had a possible lever.

***

The village hall meeting soon came around and the building quickly filled up with inquisitive locals. Cordelia hadn't given them much to go on other than that it was about Tredyedeath Depot and what Trevedic had written in the *Trumpet*, so she knew she had her work cut out. Fred decided to make an appearance but he didn't want to court favours, so he sat at the back whilst Cordelia opened the proceedings.

"Thank you all for coming along tonight and I am glad to see that our friend Fred Gooley is here too. Welcome, Fred. As you know, Fred's planning application, which we all support, has been objected to by the Ministry of Defence. I have a copy of the Ministry's objection here which has been signed by a Major Fox-Thrasher at Tredyedeath Depot. It makes it clear that we are all living in close proximity to dangerous explosives – and that's news to me. It's probably news to you all as well. I remember all those years ago when the mine opened and then it was…"

Cordelia's voice dropped as she started to meander aimlessly into the Ministry's benign historic use of the mine, into times past when she used to serve the army convoys carrying 'field rations'. Mention of the *Playboy* incident might have rekindled interest but it was too late. She hadn't noticed that she was quickly losing the audience, whose initial silence had become quiet chatter now slowly increasing in volume.

Fred could see what was happening and came to her rescue. He walked onto the stage and started to articulate Cordelia's concerns, his back straight, stomach out and both arms waving like a giant puppet controlled from the rafters. "Err, well everyone, the point Cordelia is making is that we were all happy with the historic low level of storage activity at Tredyedeath Depot and welcomed those working there into the community on their days off. Some of us even guessed that there might have been some explosives at the mine more recently – but now the cat's out of the bag as a result of my planning application, we need to know more." Fred raised his voice in a rallying cry. "Should we have been consulted about the ARCE programme referred to in the major's objection letter? How much explosives are actually there? How does the safeguarding map, which I have never seen or heard of before, restrict our daily lives? We need answers from the major, the commander at the depot. Yes everyone, we need answers."

Fred's physical size and likable personality cut a striking pose on the stage, dwarfing the diminutive Cordelia, who stood proudly by his side, clearly motivated by Fred's short but stirring address. Immediately rejuvenated, the locals were in fighting mood. The aged Trecarsick demographic wasn't likely to start a major *Les Miserables*-style assault on the depot as most would struggle to climb a flight of stairs, but that wasn't going to put them off. Word had already got around, thanks to Karensa, that Fred was meeting the commander in a few weeks' time and quick as a flash, Beryl and her husband Harold, villagers of many years standing, stood up and suggested that they all produce their own campaign placards and turn up at the depot on the day of the meeting to support Fred and Grace and show their discontent about the explosives.

Mischief was in the air. Here was an opportunity to unleash their hidden being. This was 'Spirit of the Blitz' stuff. The suggestion received unanimous support and after some more stirring speeches from locals wanting to get something irrelevant off their chests about waste bin collection and the occasional late night noise from the Tinner's Whippet, everyone retired to the back of the hall for a cup of tea and some scones that Karensa had brought over from the shop, along with the 'Support your Gooleys' petition for some more signatures.

Karensa took out her mobile. She needed to bring Dickie up to speed. "Hi Dickie, it's Karensa. They are in fighting mood up here. Fox-Thrasher's opened up a right can of worms. They all know about the meeting with Jim Stern to talk about the application and a few have agreed to mount a peaceful protest outside the gates of the depot on the day. It's not just about the Gooleys now but about the whole issue of explosives storage. I think the major is going to have to go on the charm offensive to defuse the situation. The next time you come up here, you better be prepared for some barracking. I would bring Fluffy with you for protection, if you know what I mean, ha ha. Your secret is safe with me."

"Bloody hell, Kar, this is getting out of control," Dickie said, sounding worried. "Don't worry. I will make sure the major is in the firing line. Charm offensive? That's a laugh. Fox-Thrasher's got less charm than the contents of a Christmas cracker. Thanks, Kar. I think the time is approaching for me to speak to someone in Division."

Chapter 12:
Placards Meet the Implacable

It was early August and the time had flown since Fred and Grace met Trevelyan and Ashley at Feathers Farm to hear the bad news. Dickie, who'd woken up early at the depot to prepare for the meeting, had offered to take the minutes on the basis that he knew the major would want to do all the talking. This gave him the ideal opportunity to get some facts on record, in his own words and into the blue file, which was awaiting its launch to a higher place at an appropriate time. About half an hour before the meeting Dickie walked out of his office and looked out of the upstairs corridor window towards the gatehouse, half expecting to see, on the basis of what Karensa had told him, a couple of hardened grey-haired Trecarsick locals expressing their democratic right to protest. He had to look twice.

To his surprise, there were about fifty grey-haired sixty-somethings gripping tightly onto an assortment of neatly made placards. Someone had been busy in their garden shed, he thought. He could also see Trevedic Penhaligon's fedora poking well above the pack, a notebook in one hand as he juggled with his camera in the other, preparing to take some photographs of this locally momentous occasion to light up the next edition of the *Trumpet*. Dickie quickly retrieved a pair of binoculars from his desk and raised them to his face. His fingers worked frantically as he focused on the assembled mass and, more importantly, their placards, in anticipation of a few genteel slogans.

He lowered the binoculars for a moment, blinked and then fixed them again firmly in position whilst lowering an arm to extract his mobile phone to call Karensa at the village shop. "Well Kar, the village protestors you mentioned have certainly arrived. Yes, they are here all right – outside the gatehouse. I thought, on the basis of what you said after the village hall meeting, that there would be just a few of them. Actually, there's about forty-five more than just a few. I am just looking at a sea of placards right now."

"Really, Dickie? What a surprise! Did I say a few?" Karensa said, not letting on that she already had a hundred signatures on the Gooleys' petition and she knew local feeling was running high. "Never mind. I am sure they all mean well, bless them."

"Not so sure about that, Kar. Not sure at all. I don't think the major is going to be too impressed with 'Up your ARCE', 'Go blow yourself', 'Your ARCE is ruining the Gooleys', 'Mine your own business', 'Your ARCE is full of hot air', 'Hands off the Gooleys', 'Don't be a pain in the ARCE'. I could go on, Kar, but it's much the same message on another thirty placards. I can see Beryl, Harold, Betty, Albert, Dorothy, Gerald, Mary, Donald, Gertrude, Arthur, all your family friends and many more. I never thought they had it in them to come up with such creative messages. Still, they seem to be enjoying themselves. They look a bit like naughty school kids. Beryl's is particularly enlightening and wins the competition for the most inventive, or should I say invective, placard. It's 'Don't F*+^! with the Gooleys'. That'll take all of five seconds to work out! It will be interesting to see what the major makes of it all." Dickie paused. "Oh, he's just driving into the depot now. Got to go. Bye."

Dickie returned the mobile back to the safety of his jacket, walked back into his office and quickly returned the binoculars to his desk drawer. In a matter of seconds the major barged in in customary fashion, looking a little flustered. "Have you seen what's outside? What the hell's that all about? Bloody cruise missile objectors. They get everywhere. I thought they went back to their middle class lifestyle years ago. Why do they think we've got any missiles here? I'd shoot the lot of them. Nearly ran a few of the old buggers down!"

Dickie felt a little relieved that the major had totally missed the point. "No sir, they are not cruise missile objectors. They stopped campaigning twenty years ago. I thought you might have guessed but maybe you didn't manage to read the placards. They are local villagers who know about today's meeting with the chief planning officer concerning the Gooleys' application. They not only support the application but they are concerned about the storage of explosives here, which you stated in some detail in your objection letter to the council on the Ministry's behalf. It's all over the council's website."

"What meeting? I didn't agree to any meeting! I thought all Ministry of Defence letters to the council were confidential. What's the world coming to? Well they are all wasting their bloody time – objectors, chief planning officer, the lot of them. When is it?"

"In about ten minutes, sir and yes, sir, you did agree to have the meeting," Dickie said slightly smugly as he reached into the blue file. "Here is an email from the chief planning officer to you about the need for it and your, if I may say so, reluctant reply agreeing to hold it provided you didn't have to travel anywhere. These days all comments, emails and objections on planning applications are available for the public to see, even those from the Ministry of Defence. It's all about transparency in the public interest."

"Transparency? Transparency?! We'll be making tanks out of glass next to give the enemy an even chance. Public interest? Bloody ridiculous." With that, the major, showing enough rouge on his cheeks and neck to make a circus clown proud, turned around sharply and returned to his office.

The attendees arrived shortly afterwards and gathered in the downstairs entrance hall. Fred took the unusual step of bringing Attila with him and he left her in the back of his Land Rover with the canvas rear awning rolled up so he could see her inside. They were shown to the upstairs meeting room whereupon Fred put his papers down on a chair by a window in full view of the car park. He then rushed back to his Land Rover on the pretext that he had forgotten his pen, and quickly re-parked it so he could clearly see Attila from his upstairs seat.

The meeting room echoed to the sound of polite introductions. The major, sitting upright, was at the head of the table with the captain next to him. Ashley sat between Jim and Fred. In a rare moment of blunt sociability to get the meeting off to a good start, Fox-Thrasher introduced himself as Charles and the captain as Dick, a name Dickie never used. The major couldn't even get that right. It nevertheless had the effect of transporting Ashley to another place. He had already looked the captain up and down, resplendent in his uniform and barely army-legal blond locks, but Dickie had been warned by Karensa that he might get the once over, so he averted his eyes so as not to give any indication that he might be available for a kinky game of 'interrogation'.

Fred didn't let on that he had met the captain before at the farm; Cordelia Craddock had already warned him that he was potential son-in-law material but that he might just be a spy in the camp. In any event, Fred could see immediately from their strained body language that the captain and major had little in common.

Jim Stern was anxious to get to the point. "Well, Major, as I explained to Captain Lovely on the phone when we arranged this disappointingly delayed meeting, I, on behalf of the council, am minded to recommend approval of Mr Gooley's planning application and from informal feedback I have had at the political level, so are the district's councillors. Your objection to the application is the only one the council has received and ideally I would like to come out of the meeting with an agreement from you that, once you have heard my considered views on the proposals, the Ministry, which I understand in this case is you, will respectfully withdraw its objection. My reasoning is simple. I have read the actual wording of the direction to guide the council's consideration of a planning application to ensure that, and I quote, *'people may not remain for long periods of time'* inside the explosion zone. The application site falls right on the edge of the safeguarding map and the housing proposals will, from the evidence I have seen, generate fewer people than the turkey farm which it will replace. With that in mind, it seems to me that the purpose of the direction, which is to protect persons should there be an explosion, would not be prejudiced by this planning application."

Fox-Thrasher could see that Stern had briefed himself well and, for the first time, fleetingly saw a chink in his perceived impenetrable armour before his shutters of denial came down faster than a cruise missile. Dickie was writing away furiously. It all made sense to him but Fox-Thrasher wasn't going to budge and decided to go on the offensive. "That may be so, Mr Stern, but I had a look at the direction and understand that agricultural operations are exempt so if it is agricultural – which I doubt – it cannot be taken into account in any analysis. Anyway, the turkey business has ceased and was more than likely an illegal turkey factory and not an agricultural use at all. I would also object to it restarting which, of course, would require planning permission. My ARCE is more important to the defence of the realm than an illegal turkey factory. Oh, and the Health and Safety Executive also object to the proposals."

Jim and Fred looked visibly shocked at the major's arrogance and wayward arguments. Fred's feet drummed on the floor uncontrollably for a brief moment but he decided to keep quiet and let Jim do the talking. He was more interested in what Attila had sensed and might even hear. Turkeys have very sensitive hearing and the windows of the office were open to let some air in on what was a sunny, humid August day. He looked out of the window behind him at the animated Attila, who was whirling frantically around in the back of his Land Rover – which indicated only one thing. The major was talking absolute rubbish.

Jim continued. "Major, I am a little confused by your arguments, if these are the ones that have led to your objection. Just for the record, Major, as this meeting is being minuted, Mr Gooley's turkey business was not an illegal factory, and it never has been. It was a lawful agricultural operation and although it has ceased trading, it is capable of being started up again by him, or anyone else for that matter, without the need for new planning permission. The fact that it has ceased trading is a distraction and of no relevance to me."

There was a moment's silence whilst Jim took down a few notes. With the bit between his teeth, he looked up, straight at the major. "Major, you seem to want to have your cake and eat it. You seem to suggest that, in making any comparison of impact on human safety, it's not possible to count the number of humans in the explosion zone resulting from Mr Gooley's continued turkey business compared with the housing development he now proposes, because the direction stipulates that an agricultural operation is an exempt use and therefore cannot be taken into account. What you suggest therefore is that Mr Gooley's proposed housing will result in a net gain in the number of people within the explosion zone, contrary to the purposes of the direction." Jim paused and then continued.

"I am afraid your argument on this score also fails because, in planning parlance, I am entitled to take into account important 'material considerations' in considering whether or not the terms and the spirit of the direction would be met. Mr Gooley's planning application for housing will generate fewer people in your explosion zone than his continued use as a turkey farm. Period. The fact that it might be an exempt agricultural operation is of absolutely no concern to me. But I can see that it would be of considerable concern to someone in the Ministry who originally drafted the direction, who might not have considered the scenario we are now facing. It's clearly a mess but that's not my problem. I am a pragmatist. I have a planning application to determine and Mr Gooley here would expect me to take a professional view, as I have done. I would now like to see the Health and Safety Executive's objection which you claim exists. It's certainly not been sent to the council."

Dickie could see that Fox-Thrasher was in a corner. It was blindingly obvious to him that, while he was gallivanting around the Penwith peninsula with Karensa, Division's instructions to object to the application had been given on the basis of spurious and misleading information from the major, which it had blindly accepted.

The major decided on that classic of all outflanking military strategies: create a distraction. "Mr Stern, the Ministry of Defence technical team uses a very complicated tried and tested formula for determining the capacity of an ARCE site. The capability of my ARCE, and therefore its capacity, is directly related to the number of inhabitants within a safeguarding map. I am quite sure it would have taken into account all uses and inhabitants within the explosion zone, whether they were there illegally or not, when creating the Tredyedeath Depot safeguarding map in 2002. More inhabitants will reduce the capability of my ARCE. It's as simple as that. Did you look at my ARCE, Mr Sweet, before you submitted the application? I'm just not prepared to get caught with my trousers down if my ARCE isn't up to scratch. Mr Sweet, you are the consultant to Mr Gooley. I am sure you don't want to get caught with your trousers down in protecting the Gooleys, do you? But that's what's happened here. It's not my problem. It's yours. The objection stays."

Jim Stern knew that the major had a point about Ashley's incompetence but the fact remained that he was ducking the central issue. He could see that Ashley, already looking a little pink around the gills and struggling with the imagery created by the trouserless major with an exposed ARCE, was unable to bring anything new to the discussion.

Fred took another look out of the window at the still animated and continuously whirling Attila, and calmly waded in. "Major. You didn't mention the Health and Safety Executive objection. I know them quite well as they used to check my turkey business out from time to time when it was operating to make sure that it was up to scratch."

"Oh, it was a verbal discussion I had with them. They asked me to include reference to their concerns when I sent in my comments to Mr Stern's department. That's enough, isn't it?"

Jim joined in. "In that case I am sure you won't mind if I contact them directly. I do need their objection on their headed paper for it to be a formally logged objection. Who do I speak to?"

The major looked flushed, knowing that there had been no contact at all with the Executive. "I'll get the captain here to email you the details."

The meeting rumbled on with no progress as the major continued to skirt around the central issue. Jim had made his point, the major wasn't going to budge, Ashley just sat there dwarfed by two heavyweights and Fred had heard enough. Dickie had been too busy taking the minutes to contribute and he knew that there was always the possibility that he would be contradicted by the major anyway. In any event, he thought Jim was more than capable of putting his points forward, which had been carefully minuted.

The meeting slowed in pace and seemed to be moving to a natural end. Suddenly, Dickie had an idea. "Gentlemen, it seems to me that it would be best if I sent everyone a copy of the minutes, which sets out our respective positions on the matter."

Fred immediately leaned forward. He looked past the captain and stared straight at Major Fox-Thrasher. A Fred stare could be quite intimidating. "I think, and I am sure Mr Stern here agrees with me, that that's an excellent idea, Captain Lovely, but I just want to make one point, Major. If my planning application ends up at a public inquiry, my lawyers and their team will subpoena you, sir, to give evidence. I have never heard such rubbish before in the face of quite reasonable and unanswered questions by Mr Stern here. The truth will out, and you and your Ministry cronies are going to pay for it. Good day."

Fred quickly gathered up his belongings and walked purposefully out of the room, followed soon after by Jim. As Ashley frantically scrambled to put on his orange linen jacket, he turned around to face the major and captain, who were quietly rising from their seats. "Well, that didn't go too well, did it? Ummm. I will speak to Mr Gooley. I am sure he'll calm down. Mr Stern seems a nice person, doesn't he?" Ashley gushed.

Neither man responded but once Ashley was out of the room, the major also headed for the door, his head down. Even he could see that the matter was not going to go away as he hoped it would. He looked around at the captain. "Those bloody minutes are going nowhere. They stay here. Got that, Lovely?" The major was nothing if not consistent. An old school thinker. To him, the Ministry of Defence was a confidential organisation and as far as he was concerned, Joe Public was almost as bad as the enemy.

He was still living in a world where walls had ears and careless talk cost lives.

Dickie just nodded. He might have been prevented from circulating the minutes to the enemy but he was damned sure there was a rule somewhere which required him to send them to Division. Dickie's blue folder on the Gooleys' application beckoned.

He went over to the window and looked down at the car park. Ashley was walking to his convertible and momentarily stopped to look at the irritatingly steadfast white stain on its fabric roof, where Attila had left her mark. He shook his head before getting in. Jim had already left the depot and Fred was lowering the rear awning on his Land Rover. Dickie got a glimpse of a flash of white feathers that he recognised from his trip to Feathers Farm. He smiled as Fred patted Attila on the head and moved her backwards onto some straw before he buckled up the awning. Two guard dogs watched with curiosity from their exercise yard nearby. Attila had given all the signals Fred needed. Everything in that meeting had been made up by the major to protect his empire.

The gaggle of village protestors had long gone back to their allotments, garden sheds and other pastimes, having made their point. They had decided, however, to leave a few poignant placards against the fence to remind passers-by of local feeling. 'Defuse your Feathers Objection' and 'Don't make an ARCE of yourselves' seemed a little more dignified. Trevedic Penhaligon had left much earlier to digitally process his photos of the protest and think up his next riveting *Trumpet* headline on the Gooleys' planning saga.

Chapter 13:
Bitter Sweet and Career Confetti

Fred soon arrived back at Feathers Farm and let Attila out of the Land Rover and back into what had become her own personal exercise courtyard to stretch her legs. As he went inside to tell Grace how badly the meeting had gone, he could see, waiting on the hall table, a letter from their bank manager, Dennis Blackstaff. Fred's immediate suspicions about its contents proved to be correct as Dennis waffled on in 'bankspeak' about the Gooleys' 'financial negative buoyancy' and his need to provide an assurance that a 'fiscal strategy' was in place to 'reenergize his finances'. In 'Fredspeak' it was clear: he had the bank's money and it wanted it back.

Dennis' parsimonious letter continued with missives about the impact of emerging recessionary forces on the worsening state of the economy and his bank's need to be extra prudent in dealing with debts. As it was Dennis' bank which was the major contributor to the dire state of the economy, having blindly led the blind in the charge over the 'fiscal precipice' towards national bankruptcy, even Fred could muster a wry smile at the sad and bitter irony of it all. Nevertheless, it was just another worry for Fred and Grace over which, ultimately, they had little control.

To solve his problem, Fred pondered for a moment that perhaps he could chop Dennis up into small pieces and surreptitiously feed him to the turkeys of his competitors who had sold out to the big supermarkets. Apart from the immense satisfaction of it all, it would buy Fred some more time whilst Dennis was being replaced by another head office minion. But he soon realised that supermarket turkeys sell on price, not flavour, so it probably wouldn't have slowed their march towards world domination. Paradoxically, the demand for turkeys might actually increase if the populous knew they were eating turkeys fed on chopped-up bank managers. To Fred, it seemed that the supermarkets could just do no wrong.

Having broken the news about the meeting with the major and the bank's thinly veiled threat, Fred left Grace to relieve her stress in the kitchen while he phoned Penelope Breakage. "Penelope, I'm afraid the meeting with the commander went very badly. It's clear that he is the stumbling block. I can't even tell if he is being instructed from above but my guess, and Attila's, is that he's got his head in the sand. Jim Stern was very clear and measured and you might want to speak to him about what he is going to do next. Grace and I are now very worried about where the planning application is heading. I can tell you one thing though. We have to get rid of Mr Sweet and instruct someone else. He was useless. I also think we should sue him for bad advice. I want my costs and my loss of earnings back with interest. Mr Sweet advised me to close my business, you know. Funnily enough, I actually agree with the major that he should have been consulted about his ARCE before the application was submitted."

"His ARCE? That's a bit rude," Penelope replied. "What's the major's ARCE got to do with it?"

"Oh, it's short for Army Regional Centre for Explosives. ARCE. The major is an explosives expert and the Tredyedeath Depot ARCE is very clearly his baby – but he is full of crap."

"Oh, I see. Nothing worse than a baby with a big ARCE full of crap, is there, Fred!? Look Fred, I haven't been to Feathers Farm for quite a while so why don't I meet up with you and Grace at the farm – and if you would permit me, I will bring Johnny Smidgen along. He's a well-known local planning consultant with whom I have worked for a few years now and he would be really useful in assisting me with both your claim against Mr Sweet and in pursuing your planning application, particularly if it has to go to a public inquiry."

"Thanks, Penelope," Fred said. "I wish I'd sought your guidance in the first place rather than Trevelyan's. Mr Sweet was a bad choice for my proposals. I am more than happy to instruct Mr Smidgen on your advice but I should warn you that I am running out of money and my bank manager is starting to chase us. I am not prepared to give up though. I want the major's nose rubbed in the dirt."

Penelope could hear the faltering in Fred's angry voice. She decided to lighten the conversation. "Sounds like he needs his ARCE rubbed in the dirt as well, eh Fred! Fred, my firm goes back a long way with the Gooleys. I am sure we can sort something out on the finance side. I do have in mind that we might want to think about suing the Ministry of Defence if it turns out that they have been delaying your proposals deliberately and unnecessarily without good cause. There is a process for doing that – but let's take it step by step."

Penelope agreed to call Jim Stern for an update before her meeting at Feathers Farm whilst Fred would bring Trevelyan Trelyon up to speed. They also agreed to talk about the manner in which Ashley Sweet would be dis-instructed, the timing for any claim against his firm and how Johnny Smidgen might take over as the Gooleys' planning advisor.

***

Johnny Smidgen was a planning director of the Planet Planning Group, an established town planning consultancy in Cornwall. At thirty-seven, he had fifteen years' experience, a good professional reputation and came highly recommended by Penelope, with whom he had a good working relationship. A smartly dressed man, Johnny spoke as fast as he drove, had a roving eye for pretty girls, a good sense of humour, was a good listener and had the common touch in advising clients from all walks of life.

Town planning was not Johnny's first career choice though, as he was convinced that his professional life should have been in advertising. This was due to his absolute belief in his ability to think laterally in creating new brands, brand awareness and most importantly, building customer loyalty. He had the skill, aptitude and ability to make a difference in the world of advertising, or so he thought.

But Johnny had a profound weakness – an unpredictable, albeit harmless, split personality which could strike at any time with an indiscriminate use of the lethal combination of political incorrectness and humour, irrespective of who it would offend. He believed that a laugh at all costs was worth it and he saw humour, like music, as a form of classless communication. Perhaps that was why, at thirty-seven, he was still a bachelor. A failure to recognise the downsides of this potentially insulting trait meant that in his early adult life, it was only a matter of time before he would be faced with a few home truths. Indeed many around him, particularly his immediate family, felt that for his sake, the earlier the better.

At the age of eighteen he choose the trainee advertising manager apprentice path rather than university. He worked tirelessly to create, in his mind, a stunning CV with which he would take on the world. This secured three interviews; clearly a good start. His interview strategy was simple: he would demonstrate his advertising prowess by presenting a fictitious new product which the interviewer would find irresistible, landing him the job in advertising he yearned for. Bedecked in a new suit, shirt, tie, clean shoes and a cracking haircut, he was ready for corporate life. His mum and dad were very proud of their Johnny despite their inward misgivings about his chosen career path.

For his first interview, he arrived in eager anticipation at the hallowed doorways of a national institution: a confectionery business held in high affection by UK consumers. He entered the boardroom with a confident air. What could go wrong?

The abusive onslaught Johnny received from the head of advertising five minutes into the interview was, he felt, quite unnecessary and most eighteen year olds would have given up their intended career path there and then. His idea for a new chocolate bar called *Broadmoor*, bedecked with a wrapper showing a pair of hands tightly gripping the bars of a secure cell block window, with the strap line 'You'd be mad not to try one – may contain nuts' splashed across the front, went down badly. His hasty exit – head down and clutching presentation boards under both arms –

was ignominious as he rushed past five unsuspecting and nervous candidates in the smart waiting room, its walls bedecked with copy from famous advertising campaigns from days gone by. They clearly looked shocked at his premature departure, wondering which one of them would be next up for the corporate beheading. Johnny never did get an official rejection and in his world of denial, that was very unfortunate.

The next interview was with a pharmaceutical firm on the verge of a cure for dementia, where Johnny proudly presented his slogan: 'Don't forget your dementia mints: it's a no brainer'. Smidgen's physical ejection from the building was, he felt, a little harsh and the lack of any feedback from his interview, downright rude. Johnny finally recognised the writing was on the wall at his third attempt to break into the world of advertising, with an ethical condom manufacturer targeting third world countries. Although he could see that 'Shagger: It's a step in the right erection' might not be quite the right message for schools and local surgeries supported by foreign aid, he was disappointed to be forced to stand by and watch his CV and presentation boards ceremonially reduced to confetti by the corporate shredder, specially brought in for the occasion.

Reluctantly, Smidgen turned away from his first choice career path, much to the relief of his doubting parents. His father worked in the second oldest profession known to man, surveying, and he saw in Johnny many of his own professional attributes, which he felt could be used to good effect. He was almost relieved to therefore fund the four years of university study in town planning which soon followed and the resulting degree launched Johnny's career. The Planet Planning Group soon became a natural home for Johnny's talents and he relished every challenge. But that subversive uncontrollable personality trait was never far from the surface, always ready for him to launch on some unsuspecting victim. Even Johnny was never quite sure when that might happen next.

***

By the time Fred called Trevelyan, Jim Stern had already spoken to him and Fred could tell he was angry about the lack of progress made at the meeting. So much so that Trevelyan had immediately contacted Fred's local MP, Sir Michael Stride-Pecker, Member of Parliament for Bodmin Central. A man on a mission, Trevelyan felt that it was now time to take the issue to another level.

Sir Michael sat on the Treasury Select Committee and was an intelligent, articulate, respected and well-known figure in the House, having been a Member for the safe Bodmin Conservative seat for many years. He always made it his duty to attend his local constituency surgery on Saturday mornings despite the distance and difficulty in getting away from his busy work schedule in London. Making the time for his Bodmin surgery certainly endeared him to his constituents and this clearly contributed to the safeness of his seat in the House. He was one of the driving forces behind the campaign to 'Save our Sleeper', the popular and not hugely profitable but undoubtedly romantic overnight train known as the Night Riviera, which rumbled slowly from London to Penzance. It had not gone unnoticed that one of the biggest beneficiaries of the campaign would be Sir Michael himself, a regular user of public transport, who took full advantage of its convenient stop en route at Bodmin Parkway. Still, if it also helped him to keep in touch with his constituents at the Saturday morning surgery, no one would begrudge him a degree of self-interest. In any event, many supporters of the campaign, particularly train buffs, were persuaded by his eloquent arguments that the Night Riviera represented an economically important link to the far southwest of the country, where continued central government public investment was an important factor in growing the region's economy.

Sir Michael had a direct line to another career politician, fellow Conservative and personal friend, the Secretary of State for Defence, the Right Honourable Guy Gunston. Before he was made Secretary of State, 'Gunpowder Guy' had a reputation for 'shooting from the hip' to get things done and in that respect Sir Michael couldn't have had a better colleague with whom he could lobby on his constituents' behalf now that he had moved into a ministerial role in defence. Trevelyan was delighted that Sir Michael had agreed to take up the Gooleys' cause and use his influence with Gunpowder Guy at an appropriate time. The lines of communication to the highest level had been established and at last 'Relyon' Trelyon felt proud to be maintaining his and his family's tradition.

***

A few days later, Penelope arrived early at Feathers Farm, having collected the smartly dressed Johnny Smidgen from his Truro office so they could share information on the journey. She always preferred to drive, as she couldn't stand Johnny's ludicrously fast driving, which they would often joke about, even though he felt just a little miffed over her slight on this, of all masculine traits. Pen, as Johnny called her, much to her constant irritation, couldn't stomach the thought of arriving at Feathers Farm looking a similar shade to Trecarsick village green, only to be faced with something Grace had lovingly cooked for the occasion, to be washed down with copious cups of tea. Penelope and Johnny got on very well and despite their quite different backgrounds, she got Johnny's odd sense of humour, his off-the-wall approach to life and professional problem-solving skills. She knew him well enough to tell him when it was the right time to shut up and, inwardly recognising his own failings, he always obliged.

Johnny, ever diligent, had looked at the background to Fred's application following an earlier conversation with Penelope, so he was well briefed. "Pen, I see that good old Ashley Sweet is the consultant. Ashley and Fred, eh? What a contrast. Actually, he's not a bad architect – but he's just not a planner. With development in the countryside, it doesn't matter whether it looks simple or not. In my view it never is. It looks to me that Ashley has given poor old Fred a bum steer, ha ha!"

"Johnny – it's Penelope, by the way. And I wouldn't do any gay jokes about Ashley with Fred. He wouldn't find it funny. In fact, I'm not sure he even realises."

Johnny agreed. He'd noticed a bandage on Penelope's finger but as he had never seen her without a bandage on some part of her anatomy, he made no comment. They agreed that Penelope would lead the meeting with Johnny giving support whilst he checked out with his 'body language barometer' how best to approach Fred and Grace.

***

Fred was pleased to see Penelope and, following her introduction to Johnny, showed them both around the farm before they retired to the front room, quickly followed by Grace with the now obligatory tea service and some home-made stress-relieving shortcake. It wasn't long before Johnny felt able to contribute and a strategy soon appeared that all agreed upon. Johnny would visit the Trefriggit district council planning department to view the now infamous safeguarding map and, taking into account what Fred had told him, produce a report for Penelope on the apparent failings of Ashley's advice prior to the submission of the planning application. This would confirm precisely what the map contained and would be used to support Penelope's claim, on behalf of the Gooleys, against Ashley's firm. Separately, as the Gooleys' planning application was to be determined by the council's planning committee in early September, a matter of a few weeks away, Johnny would obtain an up to date position from Jim Stern on his recommendation to the committee now that the meeting with the major at Tredyedeath Depot had taken place. The outcome of those discussions would then inform how and whether Fred's planning application needed further political promotion, if necessary, involving Trevelyan Trelyon.

Johnny and Penelope could see that Fred was determined not to be beaten and warned that a public inquiry was probably inevitable unless the Ministry of Defence and, more to the point, the major, withdrew its objection – which seemed unlikely.

Johnny then went on to explain that if the council refused to grant planning permission in early September, Fred was entitled to appeal against the council's decision and the Ministry would have to explain its objection at a public inquiry. Alternatively, if the council resolved to approve the planning application by ignoring the Ministry of Defence's objection, the Secretary of State for Planning might be persuaded by the Ministry to suspend the council's decision and hold a public inquiry to allow the Ministry to explain its objection. Thus in either scenario the veracity of the Ministry's objection would be tested in front of an independent planning inspector who would recommend whether to permit or refuse the planning application. The decision would then rest with Secretary of State for Planning. Fred would have full opportunity to counter the Ministry's objection using evidence which Johnny would present on his behalf but this would require the assistance of a barrister instructed by Penelope to lead the charge against the Ministry. It would all take time and money.

It was also clear that, for Fred to secure a successful outcome, the Ministry's objection would have to be taken apart piece by piece, and it was obvious that the major either had something to hide or was just plain arrogant. This just reinforced to Fred that this was a fight worth having to get to the truth. He commented to Penelope that the minutes of the meeting had not appeared as promised, and she agreed to chase the major. She was also aware from her discussions with Jim Stern that the Health and Safety Executive objection continued to remain a mystery.

The full implications in terms of timing and costs were explained. It didn't make for happy news for Fred's overdraft, which was going to take a further hammering.

Fred led Penelope and Johnny down the corridor and into the courtyard, where Attila came out of her two-storey barn home to see what was going on. She wandered over to say hello, her head nodding in recognition that here were some friendly faces. To Fred's amazement and

Attila's total surprise, Johnny bent down and, without hesitation, collected up the feisty turkey with both hands to have a closer look. She didn't have the time to fight even if she wanted to, but any misgivings about her apparent fate soon faded. This was the first time anyone other than Fred had had the confidence to pick up the young lady, who was now a little coy cradled in Johnny's arms whilst he ran his hands over her feathers. He spoke to her quietly, as all animal lovers do, in the rather weird expectation of actually being understood. Penelope watched in amazement and stepped forward. She should have realised what was coming.

"Don't get too close, Pen. You don't want a cock in your face – or maybe you do, ha ha!"

Fred butted in, not grasping the innuendo. "Actually a male turkey is a gobbler, not a cock. But it's not a gobbler anyway but a 'she' turkey. She's a hen."

Johnny's ears pricked up to allow his brain to distil Fred's lecture on turkey genders as he prepared to deliver another insensitive remark. "Not sure if it makes that much difference, Pen. Gobbler or cock? Whatever takes your fancy. Still, as it's neither you're safe."

"Johnny, I think we are done with the turkey jokes," Penelope groaned. "Fred is keen to show us around the farm."

Fred turned around briefly. "She's called Attila and she's a Wirral White. She's very special to me. More than you will ever know. Mr Smidgen, she will attack if provoked."

Penelope suddenly realised that this was the same 'wise owl' that Fred had referred to at their meeting in her office and she began to understand their relationship. For Johnny, still holding Attila tightly in his arms as he looked around the farm, the significance of the bird had not yet become fully clear but he sensed the bond between bird and owner. He noticed that she never took her eyes off Fred during their wanderings and her head regularly moved to pick up his voice and intonations.

With the meeting over, Johnny gently put Attila back on her feet and dusted off his suit. She gave a little shake to make sure all her feathers were where they should be and wandered off back to the safety of her home, looking over to Fred as she waddled by. Fred felt that he'd finally received some good advice from sound consultants and had a sensible strategy to move the project along. He agreed with Penelope that it was right for him to relieve Ashley of his duties. Once Penelope had Johnny's report, she would, subject to its findings and recommendations, and with Fred's agreement, lodge an initial claim against Ashley's business for financial loss caused by his poor advice.

As they left the farmhouse, Penelope and Johnny noticed a copy of the *Trumpet* on the hall table. Trevedic Penhaligon was clearly revelling in his new-found notoriety with a full front page reporting on the protest at the gates of Tredyedeath Depot, along with a photo of the mass of placards. He'd clearly had some difficulty in taking a suitable photograph for the paper as nearly all of the placards were too offensive for the *Trumpet* but he managed to get the angle just right to accompany a historic headline: 'Pensioners Protest Against Plot to Prohibit Planning Proposals'. For Trevedic, it was the biggest local news for years and as far as Fred was concerned, all news was good news.

Fred phoned to give Ashley the bad news. The conversation was short and slightly bizzarre. Ashley would not be returning to Feathers Farm and litigation may follow. Yet Ashley seemed more delighted in being able to put his pet hair removal roller away – and the thought of not being accosted by Flossie or having his car 'bombed' by Attila was more than a small blessing.

Chapter 14:
Cold War Concrete and Coded Messages

Trefriggit district council's four-storey offices on the edge of Bodmin were set within a smartly manicured, landscaped setting, orientated to benefit from beautiful views of Bodmin Moor. A picturesque backdrop provided some consolation for those incarcerated within its working environment, for this early 1960s structure had suffered badly from the test of time. The judicious and thoughtful use of Cornish slate and granite to provide local identity to the 'new world' design couldn't disguise the domineering, copious volumes of shuttered concrete, a de rigour material seemingly mandatory in post-war public architecture. Money was no object in the quest to use 'statement' public buildings to reinforce an orderly society and escape the past. This two-dimensional design, which seemed so welcoming in the 1960s, resulted in a massive facade of almost totally windowless concrete defiantly facing the town, with all the thermal properties of an iceberg. This was post-modern architecture at its most brutal. The building now represented twenty-first century repression for cynics of political ethics, and sent the wrong messages to those with agendas convinced that the world was conspiring against them. Conveniently, the monolithic structure stood for everything they hated. Yet, paradoxically, incarcerated within its innards were hard-working public servants striving to make local people's lives better with only limited resources. For all its visual and physical failings, to some it was a mausoleum whilst to others it was a sanctuary.

However, despite the building's physical discordance and the lack of funds to replace it any time soon, the council worked hard with the internal layout to make visitors welcome, for, whether they liked it or not, this was where democracy played out at grass roots level. Internal refits over the years increasingly took on the need for inclusivity, nowhere more so than in the bowels of the building that contained the main council chamber, a gladiatorial circular debating room with curved terraces of desks dressed in rich Cornish oak, stepping down to a central chairman's podium where the politicians would do their thing. Pictures of past council leaders adorned the walls and the raised public gallery at the back of the chamber gave good views over democracy in action. Despite its good acoustics, an audio system had been installed, for the hard of hearing, for the quietly spoken and, as cynics would proclaim, for councillors like Trevelyan Trelyon who just liked to hear the sound of their own voice. It was here and in some smaller ante-chambers where the councillors, closely advised by their professional officers, sometimes struggled with their consciences in making decisions. This was where the harsh reality of the public interest came rudely face to face with individual constituents' needs and demands. Nirvana was reached when the decision pleased all parties, a rare occurrence. This was where the planning committee would decide the fate of the Gooleys' planning application.

Johnny took no time in picking up the mantle after his and Penelope's meeting with Fred and Grace. His first port of call was the district council's planning department, where the mysteries of the Tredyedeath Depot safeguarding map and now infamous yellow line defining the explosion zone could be found. Here were the plotting sheets that Jim had told Trevelyan about soon after Fred's planning application had been submitted. Smidgen was going to waste no time in getting to the nub of the issue.

It was mid-morning and a normal busy day in the council offices when the relative peace of its smartly landscaped surroundings was sharply interrupted by a wailing sound shortly followed by some screeching. A wildlife fan would have guessed it was foxes calling like startled babies, or perhaps a barn owl hunting by day. However, they would have struggled to explain the puffs of blue smoke that wafted up above the well-trimmed copper beech hedge separating the neatly laid out council car park from the wider world beyond. Birds dived into the hedge for cover whilst a few people appeared at the office windows, mug in one hand whilst they wiped away streams of condensation with the other to see where the noise was coming from. It was Johnny Smidgen arriving in usual style, his hot hatch protesting at being thrashed to within an inch of its life as it consumed another small slice of the earth's resources. Johnny shot into the car park at speed and immediately focused on the rare and sought after sole remaining visitor parking space. In the process he narrowly missed the slow-moving ancient mayoral black Daimler – once owned by the Duchy – being driven off by its diminutive grey-haired chauffeur for a wash and brush up. The two-tonne monster, like the chauffer, was from a bygone age and had all the handling qualities of a barge. Wrestling with the giant steering wheel to keep the megalith in a straight line and the occupants from being sick was part of the chauffer's job description but it didn't stipulate the driver's minimum height. From where Johnny was sitting, it looked like this dinosaur was being driven by a chauffer's hat.

Johnny, tieless yet resplendent in a blue suit and white shirt that would have caught Ashley Sweet's eye, breezed into the council offices as he had done on numerous occasions before, and proceeded straight up to the third floor: the home of the planning department. With one eye he caught sight of Jim Stern walking through reception whilst the other eye was momentarily distracted by a vision of prettiness at the counter who was trying bravely to placate an irate elderly gentleman. Johnny knew that planning applications tended to bring the worst out in people and the audible ranting about a neighbour's rear house extension was a classic example.

Jim and Johnny's professional paths had crossed from time to time and they had a mutual respect for each other as their careers progressed, despite their quite different public and private sector roles. Johnny, like Penelope, represented the council on occasions when Jim's department couldn't cope and both knew the game well. Jim had been at the council for many years and had worked his way up from a junior position to chief planning officer. A Londoner, cockney and family man from Millwall, Jim was originally attracted to the Duchy for work but it wasn't long before he was seduced by its lifestyle and culture. The decision to make Cornwall – and Trefriggit district council – his home didn't take long. As far as he was concerned, he wouldn't be going anywhere else. He had earned a reputation in the council for being hard working, fair, with a natural tendency for sound judgement and a sense of right rather than simply hiding behind rules and regulations. He knew from experience that, when it came to town planning matters, common sense sometimes got well and truly obscured and he was quite prepared to stand up and be counted. This made him a strong and respected leader amongst his professional peers and elected councillors, whose political longevity at the council varied hugely.

"Hello Johnny, what are you doing here?" Jim asked, noticing one of Johnny's eyes affixed on the vision of loviness. "And stop looking at Kylie over there. She only started on Monday. She's only twenty. Dirty dog."

"Is it that obvious? Sorry!" Johnny laughed. "Anyway, it's research on the Gooleys' planning application. I know you've spoken to Pen about it. Fred has given Ashley Sweet the bum's rush, so to speak, and I have been instructed to prepare a report on his handling of the planning application for a potential claim against his firm. I need to look at the council's plotting sheets to see what he missed on the Tredyedeath Depot explosion zone. We are also going to fight the Ministry of Defence as well – depending on the application's outcome at the planning committee meeting. I do need to speak to you about that."

"Plotting sheets, eh? Well, just so long as you are not plotting to get Kylie between the sheets!" Jim knew Johnny well enough to know that he had a hopeless roving eye for anything over eighteen in a skirt in the mistaken believe that, by acting cool and wearing something trendy, he still could cut it at thirty-seven. The reality was that when it came to women, Johnny, still a bachelor, was in all likelihood in the 'second time around' market and would have been better off chasing Kylie's mum. Not that Jim would suggest it. He knew that, when it came to Johnny and women, he would take any suggestion literally. Johnny's failure to make a career in advertising was blurted out by him at a drunken Christmas gathering of local public and private sector professionals so it came as no surprise to Jim that Johnny's 'target market' for a love partner was, at best, hopelessly optimistic. "When you've finished, Johnny, get Kylie to give me a call and I will bring you up to speed on the Gooleys' planning application. I am afraid it's not good news."

Smidgen could see that Kylie was still struggling with the agitated pensioner but he knew that he had more scope to help her out. After all, he was immune to the typical abusive onslaught regularly dished out at public servants by stressed and disrespectful customers; "Now look here jobsworth, my rates pay your salary."

Johnny saw his chance to jump in and impress the picture of loveliness. "Hello, sir. Can I help you? I am a planning consultant."

"Too bloody right you can. This…"

"Young lady? I could hear over there that she was trying ever so hard to help you with your problem. Isn't planning such a minefield? Now what's the problem?"

Johnny's few words and open body language seemed to take the steam out of the situation and the pensioner leaned back slightly in recognition. "Was she? Oh! Right then. She doesn't have an objection form so I can complain about my neighbour's proposed extension. Typical of the council. Bloody ridiculous."

"Ah yes. That's because there are no objection forms. If you write your letter of objection to the council, they will take it into account. It's really as simple as that. I see that you already have the planning application number written on a piece of paper. That's a very good start. Well done. Here's the council's contact details." With that, Johnny grabbed a compliment slip from the counter giving all the council's departmental addresses and handed him the slip. Placing one arm gently around the pensioner's shoulders, he swivelled him firmly in the direction of the exit door. The pensioner started to shuffle forwards like a nodding Swiss clock figurine at the strike of noon. Johnny opened the door and the pensioner, still grasping the compliment slip tightly, quietly edged outside towards the lifts. "There you are, sir. Hope that helps. Best of luck. Bye bye."

The delighted and clearly impressed Kylie looked on. "Thank you so much. He was just beginning to get difficult. How can I help you?"

Johnny stared momentarily at his 'Birth of Venus' but soon let the moment pass in his quest to extract the Tredyedeath Depot information. The plan chest behind Kylie contained the map-based plotting sheets for the whole district. This was the bible for any practitioner looking to establish what constraints existed that might affect how a planning application would be assessed by the council. A plotting sheet would show listed buildings, ancient monuments, tree preservation orders, Sites of Special Scientific Interest and a wealth of other relevant but prosaic information. It was meat and veg to most planners. The plotting sheets were available for the public to view but in the rarefied world of town planning it was just more indecipherable gobbledegook. As a result they were generally only used by the council's planning officers and planning practitioners – though sadly not by Ashley Sweet.

He quickly explained what he was after and after a few minutes Kylie returned with the evidence. "I think this is what you are looking for," she said, handing over the relevant map. "Just let me know if you want me to show you anything more."

Johnny hesitated and refrained from suggesting that she was, of course, only talking about the plotting sheet. He took the plan to a nearby desk to extract the information he was looking for. As he suspected, the boundary of the official safeguarding map explosion zone had been plotted as a yellow line and Tredyedeath Depot could be seen lying in the centre of the zone with Feathers Farm just on the edge but, very importantly, clearly within it. The plotting sheet also contained a written explanation in the border about the Ministry's 2002 explosion zone direction, its purposes and the required procedure for the council to consult with the Ministry.

Having checked the plotting sheet for any other related information, Johnny handed it back to Kylie and asked her to phone Jim. He came out straight away and they sat down in a small meeting room, where Jim took the lead. "Johnny, I will get straight to the point. You know I had a meeting with the major at Tredyedeath Depot. Well, he has not withdrawn the Ministry's objection and as a result, as I previously explained to Trevelyan Trelyon, I feel obliged to recommend refusal. However, I am pleased to say that Trevelyan used his prerogative as Mr Gooley's district councillor to remove my delegated powers of determination. This will enable the planning committee to make the decision and therefore set out the council's stance if this ends up at a public inquiry." Jim leaned forward towards Johnny. "I can, however, tell you off the record that my report to the planning committee will express my unhappiness with the Ministry's lack of reasoning in its objection, for the reasons I explained to the major. The smarter councillors will see this as a coded message that I want the application approved despite my recommendation. In short, Mr Gooley's application proposals will generate fewer people in the explosion zone than his legitimate turkey business and therefore there will be less danger to human life in the event of an explosion. It's as simple as that. The major hasn't had the courtesy to send me the minutes of our meeting and as for the alleged Health and Safety Executive objection, well, they confirmed to me that they have no jurisdiction over military related issues. They did not speak to the major or make a verbal objection to anyone else at the base so he is clearly lying as well. It's all very unsatisfactory – but public money is at stake. If this ends up at a public inquiry, I need a clear steer from the planning committee on what position the council will take. It's the only stumbling block to the application being approved. The battle is with that bastard major at the mine. Between you and me, Johnny, I might need your help."

Jim explained that he had spoken to Ashley and Penelope after the Ministry's objection had been received. As far as he was concerned, Fred had been badly advised by Ashley because of his failure to identify the depot as an obstacle to Fred's plans, which could have been tackled head on.

Johnny was grateful to Jim for being candid. The planning committee meeting was only a couple of weeks away and Jim knew that Johnny would orchestrate politicking to gain councillor support. He quietly hoped that his recommendation for refusal would be rejected as he didn't want to let the major get away with it – particularly as it involved such a popular member of the local community. Ironically, Ashley had produced quite a good design so he had no concerns about the scheme itself. They parted amicably and agreed to chat again at the planning committee meeting.

As he was leaving, Johnny noticed the lovely Kylie, who was now more confidently helping another frustrated customer. He looked back to see Jim staring at him, arms folded and eyebrows raised. Jim lowered his voice. "What did I say to you when you came in, eh? Dirty dog."

Kylie momentarily looked up and gave a wry smile, which Johnny interpreted as being a little suggestive. He smiled and couldn't resist giving a hopelessly optimistic wink as he left. Five minutes later, the peace of the car park was once again shattered by the wailing sound of a car engine and screeching as Johnny rocketed backwards out of his parking space, only to stop almost as quickly. The now gleaming black mayoral battleship, still under the vague control of the chauffer's hat, was rumbling back to its HQ to await its next official calling.

Johnny arrived back at his office and called Penelope and Fred to say that Jim was 'softly' recommending Fred's application for refusal. He agreed to meet Fred and Grace at Feathers Farm with Trevelyan Trelyon to discuss the committee meeting and what could be done.

***

A week later, and with only a week to go before the planning committee meeting, Johnny's report on Ashley's advice and his management of Fred's application was ready for Penelope to commence legal proceedings. He downloaded a copy of Jim's report for the committee and digested its coded messages. It was mid-morning on Trumpet Thursday and Johnny decided to call at Trecarsick village shop on his way to Feathers Farm; he knew the shop was spearheading the petition in support of Fred's proposals and he wanted to see how it was going. Trevedic Penhaligon had contacted Jim Stern a few days earlier for an update on his recommendation, which gave him all he needed for another memorable *Trumpet* headline, now displayed proudly on the newspaper board outside the shop: 'Planners Put Paid to Poultry Planning Proposals'.

Johnny arrived at the village shop to find a few mesmerised locals still hanging about inside looking vacantly at the shelves for something to prolong their weekly visit. The usual early morning rush of *Trumpet*-purchasing oglers keen to see 'top button' Karensa had now subsided and she was behind the counter in her usual attire, putting six jars of Marmite and four bags of sugar into a box for one captivated local who was wondering what on earth he was going to buy next. Johnny wasn't aware of this weekly ritual but, like most local men, his knees also went weak at the vision of the hard-working shop owner. He didn't need a roving eye this time; both were available for action. Here was someone more of his age and definitely worth a crack at.

He steadied himself, ready to launch a politically incorrect chat up line on the unsuspecting Karensa whilst using the opportunity to enquire about the petition, when he felt the bottom of his trousers moving upwards and something wet rubbing on his ankle, followed by a licking sensation. He looked down to see a large mass of brown and black hair. It was Fluffy, sans lead, tail wagging, giving a welcoming lick on Johnny's now noticeably trembling right leg. Fearful that his remaining years might be confined to crutches, Smidgen remained uncharacteristically motionless and quiet. Luckily his bladder held out – as did his other leg, which was now just about holding him up.

Unbeknown to Johnny, the event was being watched by a smiling Dickie, in civvies, quietly sitting in the corner of the shop. It was his day off and he had come up from the depot to see the love of his life. The corner came to life. "Hello, I'm Captain Richard Lovely from Tredyedeath

Depot and this is my girlfriend Karensa Craddock, who owns the shop. Call me Dickie. Don't worry about Bismarck. He is one of our guard dogs at the base, but he's off duty. He doesn't eat people when he's off duty. He likes you. Is your other leg available? Only joking!"

With Karensa seemingly protected by a good-looking army captain in charge of high explosives and in control of a giant man-eating dog, Johnny felt the odds were heavily stacked against asking her out on a date. The thought of being propelled in small bits over Bodmin Moor or losing an appendage or two seemed, on balance, a little too risky even for him. He mentally regrouped, focused on business and introduced himself. "Thank God for that. He seems friendly enough. Hello Dickie and Karensa. I'm Johnny Smidgen from the Planet Planning Group. I've taken over advising Fred Gooley on his planning application and I see the *Trumpet* has already got the story. Disappointing, isn't it? Anyway, I can tell you that Fred is up for a fight. A man after my own heart. The Ministry's objection has not gone down well anywhere. I see that a petition has been organised here in the shop in support of Fred! I guess you are keeping your head down, Captain, eh? Civvies is probably a good idea outside the depot – and I'm glad to see your pet lion here is under control."

"Err, well actually, it's Karensa's mum who's organised the petition," Dickie said, "but we don't really talk about it much. Off the record, it's a shame it has got this far really."

"Well, as far as I can see, Captain, it's all the Ministry's making. From what I have heard on the grapevine, I am not convinced that Jim's recommendation to refuse is going to be accepted by the councillors. If it is then Fred will appeal anyway. However, if it isn't accepted, what do you think the Ministry will do? Nothing? Call for an inquiry? If there is an inquiry, the Ministry will have to produce good evidence to substantiate its objection. Who would give the evidence? Your major? You? Who? If you ask me, I think the council are going to call the Ministry's bluff."

Dickie looked uneasy. He could see that Johnny's prediction, one from an experienced planning practitioner more than capable of reading the runes, might be right. In the rarefied world at Tredyedeath Depot, he hadn't thought of a possible alternative outcome despite the meeting with Jim Stern, who had expressed concern about the weakness of the Ministry's objection.

Although Dickie didn't like what the major had done, he had assumed, rightly or wrongly, that the Ministry's objection would be sustained by the council and that would be the end of it. After all, to Dickie, this was the Ministry of Defence, a government department wishing to protect military assets for the security of the nation. What councillor would stand up against that argument when the chief planning officer was supporting it? When they'd met with the major he'd felt that Fred's frustrated ranting and threatened appeal was an understandable 'spur of the moment' venting from an angry applicant who probably wouldn't go through with it. Even the petition that Cordelia had organised was more to do with Fred's popularity than some obvious miscarriage of justice.

But Johnny's assessment of the situation now brought a new perspective, particularly as the major was driven by his noticeably unhealthy love of explosives and blind faith that he was always right. The meeting with Jim Stern had quickly convinced Dickie that the Ministry's position was unsound and, it seemed, his view was shared by many locals tuned into the saga, locals who would regularly meet him on his off duty trips to see Karensa at the shop.

***

Johnny pulled up at Feathers Farm, acrid smoke pouring from his brakes after another roller coaster ride through the country lanes. Trevelyan was already inside having rain danced from his car to avoid 'attack by turkey'. The two had met before on a few occasions over the years; town planning issues often brought professional planners and politicians together in a sometimes uneasy alliance. Johnny knew of 'Unrely-on's' reputation and his sensitivity to it so it came as no surprise that the jolly councillor saw

Fred's proposals as a cause celebre to elevate his standing in the eyes of his constituents. Johnny also knew from experience that, when it came to dealing with local politicians, it was best to let them think any good idea was theirs.

Grace's pipe had long been extinguished along with most of the resultant haze; there was no sign of Flossie and Attila was inside her corner of the barn having a snooze. All was quiet on the western front. Once inside, the front room beckoned, along with the mandatory tea and cakes.

Fred and Grace looked strained. Their bank manager, Dennis Blackstaff, had insisted that he meet them to discuss their ever-increasing overdraft and he was due to arrive that afternoon. Fred knew it was going to be a difficult meeting. A proud man, he hinted only briefly to Johnny and Trevelyan of his financial worries. But they got the message. The application had to be approved and Trevelyan's fellow councillors had to get behind him. Johnny produced a copy of Jim Stern's intelligently written report, which he summarised before proceeding to explain how the planning committee meeting operated in allowing interested parties to address the committee in the council chamber. Johnny knew that the parish council would speak in favour and that Cordelia Craddock was planning a dramatic appearance as a result of her petition, which now had well over 150 signatures. Johnny was also permitted to speak as Fred's agent. With Jim Stern verbally highlighting his coded messages of support at the meeting, the ever upbeat and optimistic Johnny said that all the signs looked good despite Jim's adverse recommendation. This was just the fillip Fred and Grace needed. It was what they wanted to hear.

Trevelyan, who had been sitting on his hands, patiently waiting to reclaim any good ideas as his own, saw the moment and moved into transmit mode. Grace's bone china collection, housed in a glass-fronted dresser, began to vibrate in protest as he erupted into electioneering volume. "Fred, in all my years I have never come across such an appalling situation and I am sorry that you have been subjected to the Ministry's idiocy. They are all idiots. You know that. You have met the major. I am going to phone every member of the planning committee personally to express my position and seek their support. Strictly speaking, councillors have to keep an open mind until the meeting – but we all know the way the world goes around. Fred, leave it to me."

Johnny took some time to reflect. There were two matters he felt needed to be considered. "Trevelyan, I think it would be a good idea if you called your councillors before the chairman's briefing, which is normally two days before the committee meeting. It would be nice to think that the chair is also on side and can brief accordingly."

Trevelyan's response was predictable. "Yes, thank you Johnny for that but I had already thought of it."

Johnny moved on and looked at the councillor. "The other unanswered question is whether the major will be at the meeting. He is allowed to speak about his objection, you know. Now, it is inevitable that one or two of your fellow councillors are dyed in the wool doctrinarians so you won't be able to absolutely rely on all of them being on your side, will you, Trevelyan? Wouldn't it be nice to think that the major had so much confidence, so much arrogance, in the recommendation for refusal that he felt it unnecessary to turn up at the meeting and speak?"

Trevelyan was still musing over what 'doctrinarian' meant when Fred chipped in. "I get the drift, Smidgen. I will speak to Cordelia. She can tell Karensa, who can plant the idea in Dickie's ear."

Johnny immediately thought about planting something else in Karensa but he wisely kept it to himself. "I'll tell you what, Fred, I will call into the village shop myself after this meeting and let Karensa know. It will save you the trouble. Captain Lovely was there this morning and might still be now. I might be able to plant the idea with him. He's an intelligent man. I think he might be receptive."

Fred agreed and after some more inane ranting by Trevelyan about how his family had helped the Freds of this world over the decades, the meeting finished.

Johnny arrived back at the village shop, which by now was quite quiet, its peace only broken by the distant sound of his arrival accompanied by the customary puffs of white, blue and black smoke from a variety of his car's mechanical orifices. Once inside, he didn't notice Dickie, who was still sitting in the corner having a coffee, Fluffy sprawled out below him like a lumpy hearth rug. Dickie had been patiently waiting for Karensa to finish reordering products purchased unnecessarily that morning, as they always were on a Trumpet Thursday. Marmite, shoe polish, 'value' sherry, bin liners, stain remover, Bend-it-Bang. She often wondered where all the purchases were actually being stored. Once finished, Dickie and she could then have some valuable time together as the afternoon 'relief' had just arrived in the form of Cordelia.

Johnny caught Karensa's eye, looked up and pointed at the hideous Men-an-Tol sculpture sitting high on a shelf behind the counter, along with a few photos of the real thing. "Hello Karensa, it's Johnny again. Does that need batteries?"

"Oh, it's Mum's award for long service. Forty years, in fact," Karensa said.

"What, she's been selling sex aids for forty years? What a good idea. It's an intriguing looking thing. It looks a bit uncomfortable though."

Despite her shock at Johnny's rather brash but characteristically candid comments, Karensa saw some irony in his observations given her mother's commercial astuteness, which she had inherited. If the demand was there, it certainly wouldn't have stopped her mother selling sex aids – as the ill-fated 1957 *Playboy* incident demonstrated. She decided not to rise to the bait. "No, it was forty years of service to the parish council. She thought it would look good in the shop as a memento of when she was running it. It's an ancient fertility thing."

"Aha, so it is a sex aid then!" Johnny laughed raucously. "I didn't know they could be that old. Do you wind it up then?"

Karensa smiled but could see she needed to be more direct; Johnny was giving no signs of moving off the topic. Dickie, who had been watching the schoolboy humour with interest, stood up and came over. A rather sleepy looking Fluffy arose from her slumbers and soon followed. "It's just a bad sculpture," Dickie said. "I think we can all agree on that. I can see the funny side of it – as you clearly can too, Johnny – but Karensa is trying to finish up so we can go for a walk. Can I help you at all?"

Johnny's demeanour changed and he focused back on the task in hand. Karensa completed her final re-order of Bend-it-Bang and looked up, knowing that Johnny had been to Feathers Farm. "Yes. I've just come from a meeting with Fred and Trevelyan. If I could be candid, I realise from what I said to you both this morning that there is some confidence in our camp about the outcome of the application despite Jim Stern's recommendation. Anyway, I realise that I may have been a bit overconfident and certainly wouldn't wish you, Dickie, to feel that you have to suggest to the major that the Ministry's objection needs bolstering at the planning committee meeting. After all, it's up for refusal and I am sure the major will be more than happy with that. I can't imagine why he wouldn't be, would you?"

Dickie looked at Johnny and gave a knowing smile. He had clearly got the message. Karensa leaned over across the counter towards Johnny, her unfixed top buttons dangling suggestively to reveal just a shadowy glimpse of her underwear. She was now well and truly in Johnny's face. In his personal space. He started to look a little flushed, almost shy. She lowered her voice. "Johnny, my love, just you leave Dickie to me. He's putty in my hands. I am sure he and his commanding officer are quite happy with Jim Stern's recommendation. I mean, what could go wrong eh?"

The semi-distracted Johnny moved back a little and saw that there was nothing more he needed to say. The message had been well and truly understood. The strategy was set. He made his goodbyes and headed back to his office in his usual haste.

***

That afternoon, Dennis Blackstaff arrived at Feathers Farm. Grace produced a glass of water as tea and cakes were certainly not on the menu. He had brought some official-looking papers with him. The message was stark. The recession was getting worse, Feathers Farm was going down in value as it stood, and the housing market for barn conversions and second homes was on the wane so its value as a development site was also declining. And all the time Fred's unsupported costs were going up. The bank wanted some blood as surety if Fred was to continue fighting for his development against the Ministry, and now against Ashley's firm over poor advice. Fred was going to have to provide surety to support his overdraft – and Feathers Farm would be the bank's guarantee. Dennis, or more to the point, his masters, wouldn't settle for anything else.

The papers were reluctantly signed and Dennis went on his way, leaving Fred and Grace to ponder over the old days when the bank manager was someone genuinely there to help, someone who knew his business, someone who would take a big picture view, give advice, open up revenue avenues and, with the full knowledge of the situation, take some of the risk. In the twenty-first century, they were now dealing with automatons controlled by head office. Advice came out of a computer, calculated by graphs and targets and bonus-led profits. It was a world they had hoped to avoid in their retirement. All they could do was remain optimistic. Fred wandered outside to have a quiet chat with Attila whilst Grace went back to the kitchen to bake something.

Chapter 15:
Suspenders and the Death Penalty

It was early Thursday morning, the day the Trefriggit district council planning committee would determine Fred and Grace's future. A very important day for the popular turkey farmer and his family.

Aware of the impending committee meeting, Dickie arrived early at his office to contemplate the content of a memo he was preparing for the major regarding Jim Stern's recommendation. Uppermost in his mind was Johnny Smidgen's 'suggestion' that the recommendation for refusal ought to be enough to satisfy the major that his attendance at the meeting would be unnecessary. Dickie knew the major was too arrogant to attend off his own bat and certainly not if Dickie suggested it. To the major, the thought of a military man of his standing having to grovel in front of a ragbag of parochial local politicians would be akin to waving the white flag.

Dickie buckled down and decided to keep the memo short and sweet; he'd copy it to Division a little later in the day just in case some smartarse in officialdom might suggest that the major appear at the committee meeting 'belt and braces'.

'Major. I am sure you will be pleased to know that, following your meeting with Mr Stern, the chief planning officer, at this office – which I attended, along with Mr Gooley and his agent – the planning application for development at Feathers Farm has been recommended for refusal. The planning committee are considering the application tonight and I will report back tomorrow morning on the outcome once I have spoken to Mr Stern. Captain R Lovely.'

With the 'sent' button deployed, a copy was expeditiously bound into Dickie's 'get out of jail' blue folder.

About an hour later, the major breezed into Dickie's office in his customary fashion, showing no sign that a polite knock might, just for once, have been on the cards. Dickie remained seated, appearing disinterested that the memo, which he assumed the major wanted to speak to him about, was nothing more than a courteous update about a formality. He certainly didn't want to set any hares running that the planning committee might just decide to take a different view. The major was in an uncharacteristically good mood, one Dickie had never seen him in before. He clearly had other things on his mind. It was almost childlike.

"Lovely, Lovely. I can't tell you how excited I am. It's just so exciting. I have just had word from Bromsgrove that we have been chosen as the national ARCE storage facility for a top secret experimental explosive, SSPHE. It's wonderful stuff, you know. It was reported in last month's *Bang!*. I can't wait to see it. Of course we will have to put a dog patrol within the mine and the stuff has to be stored separately."

The major was practically slobbering, trembling with excitement at the thought of this, the latest type of explosive developed by the army's boffins, but still in its prototype stage of development. To Dickie it was just another explosive, another way to vent mass destruction, and he certainly wasn't going to get sucked into the major's state of euphoria.

"Well, Major, I am very pleased to hear that. What is SSPHE and why is it so wonderful?

"It stands for Super Sensitive Proximity High Explosive. SSPHE. It's an explosive stick made in two parts which, individually, have no explosive properties whatsoever. One stick is blue and one stick is red. They are always stored in separate boxes. The sticks are about the size of Jenga blocks. Do you play Jenga, Captain? Anyway, the secret is that they explode once they are tied or even just placed together side by side. The writing on the side of the stick tells you how long you have got before they explode. They don't need detonators, wires, electronics or any fancy technology. They just need to be placed together to explode. So if you want one to go off in 30 minutes you find one blue and one red stick each stating 30 minutes on the side, put them together and that's it. Bang. It's their proximity to each other and the sensitivity of the special chemical reaction between them when they are put together which is the secret, hence their name, SSPHE. It's brilliant! I just can't wait. Apparently they have a timing accuracy to within ten seconds of their stated time and can be made to explode any time from one minute to one day. Fantastic. Got to go. Must have a look in the mine to see where we can store them separately from the rest of the explosives. I think we are getting six boxes of each colour – and for safety, they are the twelve hour type. Oh, and thank you, Captain, for the memo on the planning committee meeting. Looks like a done deal to me. Bloody farmers."

With that the animated major left as fast as he had arrived, whistling proudly to himself as he walked down the corridor, down the stairs and out of the office towards the mine. Dickie looked out of his window, a little uneasy to see the major, who was now swinging his security key fob like a cheerleader, in this state of mind. But he was pleased that his mind was on other matters. Jenga blocks kept coming into Dickie's head but he couldn't remember why. Jenga blocks? Jenga blocks? Where had he heard that mentioned before?

***

It was like the changing of the guard at Trefriggit district council offices. By six o'clock most of the offices were empty, with just a few committed hard-working staff still at their desks grappling with mounting piles of paperwork. The once full staff car park, which had been momentarily empty, was beginning to fill up again, this time with members of the public eager to attend the seven o'clock planning committee meeting in the main council chamber, deep in the bowels of the post war concrete monolith.

Planning committee meetings in any council were rarely quiet events and often contained a mix of squabbling humanity driven by self-interest. Here was democracy in action, where decisions were made by elected councillors. Farmers, solicitors, housewives, failed insurance salesmen, shopkeepers, in fact anyone from any walk of life could be an elected councillor if he or she had the time. The job description didn't exclude those who liked the sound of their own voices, or require intelligence or fairness. One just had to be elected. But a believer in democracy who was prepared to stand up and be counted, who had the requisite elephantine thick-skinned persona and a short memory, also seemed to help. Men and women attempting to be 'straight and true' in the face of little comprehension of a hideous planning system thrust upon them following their appointment onto the planning committee; numerous acts of parliament, reams of constantly changing, sometimes conflicting and strange-sounding government guidance and oddly worded legal 'Instruments': these doctrines of democracy all hung over councillors like a dark force attempting to control their very thoughts and deeds, mysteriously cloaked in 'planning speak' about as decipherable as Esperanto.

But if there was any reason to sympathise with the councillors struggling to battle the planning forces of darkness, it was very quickly dispelled when it came to the council chamber debate. The public platform that so many councillors yearned for revealed frightening insights into politically driven agendas, poor briefing, laziness, or simply sheer ignorance. Even the vocal ones had a disconcerting habit of putting their head in the proverbial guillotine only to pull the lever themselves. Rarely would a debate provide any remotely interested member of the public with the vague hope that, when it came to the all important vote, democracy in action would demonstrate a semblance of common sense.

Yet despite turmoil, confusion, and sometimes total bedlam, most planning committee decisions strangely seemed to just end up being the right ones. No one could really fathom it out. Democracy somehow worked despite itself. Perhaps part of the reason was that force of numbers came to the rescue, with the silent majority ultimately steering, with a firm hand, the 'gumption' tiller through choppy waters. But it was also, in no small part, due to one important ingredient which, ultimately, councillors could and would fall back on: the advice of their professional officers. In Trefriggit district council, Jim Stern, as chief planning officer, sat at the side of the chairman, the experienced Gorlas Godolphin, and all professional reports to the chair would come through him. The buck stopped with Jim, a journeyed professional. Of course, not all his recommendations were accepted by the committee but he was a pragmatist. After all, it was a democratic system and if the councillors wanted to make a different decision, that was entirely up to them. All he could do was advise them of the potential unpalatable consequences – including the possibility of their decisions being challenged via a variety of external appeal processes, the outcome of which would be determined, heaven forbid, by an unelected 'outsider'. Such 'challenges' also had cost implications, which Jim knew the council was also sensitive about, particularly as the recession was increasingly reducing its finances. So the chief planning officer's recommendations were always taken very seriously.

It was going to be a busy meeting packed with a wide range of applications for the councillors to determine. Johnny arrived at the same time as Fred and Grace to find Trevelyan Trelyon and Jim Stern having a quiet chat. They both looked over and gave a knowing nod in recognition.

A small queue had already formed next to the committee clerk's desk by people registering their democratic right to speak to the committee for just three minutes. This public right was rigidly policed by the chair, who had a fearsome reputation for switching off the public microphone precisely at the end of the three minute period. Planning applications had a reputation for encouraging inane ramblings about matters little to do with the matter at hand and he always made it clear that democracy in action wasn't a soap box for members of the public to complain about a neighbour's cat doing something nasty in their back garden. The planning application agenda was typically varied, with a mix of schemes from house extensions to new shop fronts, various scales of housing developments to gypsy sites. New offices, hamburger joints, caravan parks, barn conversions; there was no letting up on the variety of uses sought by applicants all seeking approval which would generate that vital piece of paper: the Planning Permission.

The public auditorium was a microcosm of society waiting for their fate to be decided by the committee. It was their pension, their kids' school fees, their burgeoning business, their baby, their piece of Cornwall anxiously awaiting the committee's thumbs up or thumbs down. Johnny was a regular visitor to the committee meetings on behalf of his clients and used to pass his time reading the auditorium body language to guess which applicant fitted which application. The nervous, angry, optimistic, pessimistic, arrogant, argumentative, apprehensive, agitated, volatile, neurotic, hysterical, over confident, dismissive, composed and daunted were all there, scowling at each other as they wondered if that stranger's attendance 'over there' was anything to do with their application.

Jim decided to keep his distance despite agreeing to meet Johnny when they last discussed Fred's application at the council offices. He knew there were no objectors to Fred's application other than the major, who he predicted wasn't the sort to belittle himself at such an occasion. He wasn't aware that the major was still inside Tredyedeath Depot mine, distracted and salivating at the thought of the impending arrival of SSPHE. However, Jim didn't want to be seen speaking to any members of the public for fear that the more disgruntled ones would think his next trip up country to watch Millwall play at home was being funded by a successful applicant. An old hand, Jim had seen and heard it all before. Hopelessly optimistic and ultimately rejected, applicants often found it more palatable to suggest that Jim's planning department was sleeping with an objector than to withdraw from a world of denial and face the far more painful experience called reality.

However, Trevelyan confidently walked over and steered Fred, Grace and Johnny into a quiet part of the chamber. He proudly whispered that he had spoken to all his committee colleagues as well as the chairman, who was onside, and expressed his confidence that Jim's recommendation for refusal would be overturned. With ten minutes to go to the start of the meeting and just as he returned to mingle amongst his fellow councillors on the committee, Cordelia and Karensa breezed into the chamber, followed by a gang of supporters, some holding the offensive placards that had been saved from their earlier protest at Tredyedeath Depot. Hot on their heels was Trevedic Penhaligon, notebook in hand, ready to unleash the next chapter in Fred's sorry saga along with the obligatory Trevedic headline. He couldn't wait. Unbeknown to Fred and Grace, they had all been mingling outside the council offices giving Trevedic most of the copy he needed for next week's *Trumpet* along with a very nice photo of the placard-waving group for the front page. The committee meeting's decision would cap it off nicely.

The chairman, Gorlas Godolphin, caught sight of Cordelia, whom he knew of old, and immediately went over to greet her. He gently put his arm around her shoulders and took her over to one side. She could see he meant business as he lowered his voice. "Hello Cordelia my dear, how are you? You have a disruptive look about you and I see that you have brought reinforcements. I know – this is all about Fred Gooley, isn't it? Now, I have seen that look of yours on many occasions at the parish council meetings. You're not going to disrupt my meeting, are you, Cordelia? We have a lot of applications to get through, you know."

Cordelia was an old hand at local government procedures and knew that, on occasion, Gorlas would reorder the agenda's list of applications to bring forward a planning application for early determination if there was sufficient public interest. Committee meetings were known to run on for hours, well into the evening, and Gorlas had the sense to manage meetings, when the need arose, for the public's benefit. "Tell you what, Gorlas, you put Fred Gooley's planning application at the front of the queue and I and my team of aging agitators will be as good as gold. How about that?"

"That's blackmail!!" Gorlas exclaimed. "You are not the only applicant here, you know. However, as it's you, and as your friends are taking up a lot of the auditorium seats, I will put the application on first on the understanding that you and your entourage will vacate the council chamber once we have decided it. That should at least free up some seats for others. Is that a deal? Oh, and put those more offensive placards away, otherwise I might change my mind."

Cordelia got want she wanted and the placards were quickly placed outside in the hallway. Gorlas got down to business and opened the meeting with the usual committee formalities, which had a wonderful habit of anaesthetising those disgruntled members of the public whose tendency on arrival in the council chamber was to start a mass brawl.

Half an hour was taken up with formalities: signing in attending councillors, noting absentees, agreeing minutes of the last meeting and hearing general public questions. An hour was spent discussing a report from Jim's department on the announcement of the latest government guidance revealing that new council policies agreed over hours of diligent debate at the previous committee meeting were now immediately out of date. It recommended revised policies be prepared in a report for consideration and debate at the next committee meeting. A half hour lively debate then ensued on dog fouling in public parks, a seemingly recurrent favourite. A further fifteen minutes was wasted as maverick and slightly obsessive councillor Bert Sloggett 'moved' a motion calling for the willful damage to a statutory listed building to be treated as a capital offence. This unfortunate democratic right was unanimously rejected by the committee, the irritated Gorlas reminding the aging councillor that the death penalty had in fact been repealed by the government in 1965, the last vote on the issue being in 1969. Some of Cordelia's A-Team plus a few other agitators had started to doze off.

Finally, the agenda turned to planning applications and the public suddenly regained their animation like newly wound up dolls. Gorlas explained that the agenda had been reordered to allow Feathers Farm to be the first to be considered. Audible mumblings of discontent were heard within the auditorium followed by a shuffling of papers.

Jim Stern succinctly and eloquently summarised Fred's application, expressing his concern over what he saw as flaws in the Ministry's objection and referring to Trevelyan's insistence that it should be determined by the committee as it raised issues of sufficient local importance as to make a delegated decision inappropriate. He outlined the Ministry's lack of objectivity and explained that his meeting with the major at Tredyedeath Depot had produced no clarity of the Ministry's concerns whatsoever.

Following that initial introduction, Gorlas looked at a slip of paper provided by the committee clerk and invited the registered public speakers to have their say. This was standard practice on every planning application.

Both Trecarsick parish council and Cordelia's speeches focused on the human angle as they eloquently summarised the important contribution Fred and Grace's business had made to the local community for many years, how they bred the best tasting turkeys in Cornwall and that they deserved a well-earned retirement. Three minutes of speaking was a good discipline for Cordelia, who had a reputation for rambling on. Gorlas came to her rescue by occasionally interrupting to remind her that the seconds were counting down. But Cordelia had something up her sleeve to break the monotony. On cue, Karensa, wearing a fetching tight-fitting low cut dress, sauntered over to the chairman, grasping Cordelia's petition close to her ample chest. At one hundred and seventy signatures, Karensa had certainly used her persuasive powers at the village shop, particularly on Trumpet Thursdays. She bent forward suggestively and handed Gorlas the petition as the largely male committee of councillors looked on in envy at Karensa's shapely figure.

As she bore down down on the now slighted flustered chairman, a distinctive and recognisable shadow of her upper topography curves was cast invitingly across his committee papers from the ideally positioned overhead lighting. The temporary darkness was like a scene from the 1950s sci-fi flick *Attack of the 50 Foot Woman*. She turned her head, leaned towards Gorlas and spoke slowly and softly into his right ear. "I'm delighted to see the Gooleys with such support?"

With that she turned around sharply and walked back to her seat, her bottom momentarily pointing directly at Gorlas' glowing face. Her simple message had temporarily transported the now dazed chairman into a fantasy dream sequence where only he knew that under her tight fitting attire was a magnificent arrangement of underwear all held together with silk-covered contraptions for which only he had the tools to loosen.

Gorlas returned to reality with the intention of addressing his colleagues on one matter. But, still mesmerized by Karensa's star appearance, it wasn't long before he made a complete hash of it. "Just before I ask Mr Smidgen to speak, could I remind my fellow councillors in considering this application that the taste of the Gooleys' Christmas turkeys is not a planning issue… although I have to say the one I had last Christmas was particularly enjoyable with all the trimmings. Very nice it was too. Breasts! Oh! I mean the turkey breast and trimmings were very lickable, err …or should I say tender, err juicy… Yes, well, anyway, I just wanted, yes I just wanted all councillors to be clear about why we are here. Now. Mr Suspenders, err I mean Mr Stockings, oh err Mr Smidgen? Over to you."

Johnny found Karensa's intervention a rare and enjoyable distraction but even he felt the need to get going if for no other reason than to silence the still murmuring committee members. He had been working diligently on a plan to bury the Ministry's objection. It was designed to call the Ministry's bluff. An old hand in addressing the planning committee, Johnny was well known to most of the councillors so they knew he was going to be more focused on planning matters than the taste of Fred Gooley's turkeys or his popularity in the community. Dressed in his smartest suit, he moved towards the microphone, hands by his sides, and quickly introduced himself. With no notes and just his arms and hands to help him, Charades-style, he got down to business. Jim Stern watched on with interest, waiting to nod in agreement at any moment he thought might help.

"Mr Chairman, it's obvious from Mr Stern's excellent committee report that there is only one objection to Mr Gooley's application at Feathers Farm and that is from the Ministry of Defence. If it hadn't been for the Ministry, there is no question that Mr Stern would be recommending this application to you for approval. That's an obvious but important point you need to be aware of. If I may be so bold, I can see, as I am sure you can, that even Mr Stern is not convinced about the veracity of the Ministry's objection and you will know from his report that his meeting with the Ministry's representatives at Tredyedeath Depot gave him no comfort. No comfort whatsoever. However, I fully respect his desire to put this application to the planning committee to determine – given that any representation from the Ministry of Defence always has to be taken seriously.

"I would therefore like you to think carefully about the implications of two possible scenarios, of two outcomes. The first is that you accept Mr Stern's recommendation and refuse my client's application; the second is that you reject the recommendation and approve my client's application. In the first scenario, my client has a right of appeal to be heard at a public inquiry. I can tell you now that he will exercise that right and you can see him over there with his wife, nodding with me in agreement. In the circumstances I suspect you probably wouldn't blame him. I am not stating this as a threat: merely just a fact. In that circumstance, the onus would be on the council, not the Ministry of Defence, to defend its decision to refuse planning permission. If the council cannot do that – and we have already heard from Mr Stern that he feels the Ministry's objection is poor – then the council would be faced with paying my client's appeal costs. In those circumstances, you need to know that the Ministry would get off scot free. From what we have heard from Mr Stern, can you really afford to take that risk?"

Johnny paused for a moment and looked around the chamber before continuing. "And now, councillors, I come to the second scenario. If you decide to approve my client's application, Mr Stern will advise you that before you issue the planning permission, there is a legal obligation on the council to notify the Secretary of State for Planning of its decision. This is because the Ministry of Defence has a right to call for a public inquiry to explain its objection. Now, here's the rub. If, under scrutiny, the Ministry is not able to defend its position at the inquiry, as indeed Mr Stern feels, the council would not be liable for any costs. It would be the Ministry that would face the music. The other point I would like to make is that, of course, by adopting the second scenario, you would also be calling the Ministry's bluff as there is always the possibility that it may not, in the event, decide to request a public inquiry or, better still, persuade the Secretary of State for Planning that a public inquiry is actually justifiable.

"So, in summary, I am asking this committee to resolve to grant planning permission for Mr Gooley's development, which will throw the Ministry of Defence's unfounded objection back into their court. You have a lot more to lose if you don't and you know as well as I do that there are more deserving causes on which to spend scarce council funds in these times of impending austerity. Thank you very much."

Looking pleased with himself, Smidgen walked back to his seat to a warm round of applause from Cordelia, her troops, Karensa, Fred and Grace. He looked over at Jim, who gave him a smile and a surreptitious thumbs up, his right hand semi-concealed by his paperwork. The decision was now up to the committee. Johnny had planted the seeds; Jim just needed to get out the watering can. The councillors quickly took the bait and started firing questions at Jim about explosion zones, legal directions, the safeguarding map, what was stored at the mine, the legal obligation on the council that Johnny had alluded to and what sort of costs might the council incur under Johnny's different scenarios. It was clear that the councillors didn't have the stomach to refuse Fred's application and the cross section of local support in the auditorium, from the parochial to the professional, definitely struck the right chord, whether it was planning related or not.

Jim decided to cut to the chase. "Councillors, Mr Smidgen did quite rightly refer to the legal process which will have to take place if you vote to approve this application and, to a large extent, once that button had been pressed, what happens next is out of our hands. All I have to do is to send Mr Gooley's planning application, the Ministry's objection, your resolution to approve it and the reasons for your decision to the Secretary of State for Planning and he will confer directly with the Ministry of Defence. What I can tell you from my experience is that it is rare for the Secretary of State – who, by the way, has twenty-eight days to get back to me – to not allow the Ministry of Defence to have its day in court if it so chooses so unless the Ministry decides to back down, I think it likely that, in all likelihood, we will be faced with a public inquiry. Of course, the council would attend as supporters of the application so Mr Smidgen is correct in that we wouldn't be attending the inquiry to defend a rejection that we may find to be undefendable and as a result would not be liable for anyone else's costs. That could only happen if we were to refuse the application."

The cards were all on the table. It was time for the councillors to stand up and be counted. Trevelyan had, throughout the proceedings, been making a few notes. With a full auditorium in front of him and as Fred's councillor, Gorlas invited him to speak first. The rotund Trevelyan jumped to his feet and drew breath, the taut buttons on his waistcoat straightening up in anticipation that one more inhalation would result in their ejection like a machine gun, resulting in inevitable eye damage to anyone within range. The closest councillors leaned back cautiously.

"Thank you, Mr Chairman. For those who don't know me – and I am sure there's not many – I am Trevelyan Trelyon, Fred Gooley's district councillor. I'm better known as 'Rely-on Trelyon'. That's me all right, Rely-on Trelyon…" The public remained motionless at 'Rely-on's' theatrical opening and continued ramblings about himself and his forefathers. "Anyway, whilst I fully understand Mr Stern's reasoning for recommending this application for refusal, quite frankly, I think it should be approved because if you ask me the Ministry is an ass. Yes, they are an ass all right. They even know it themselves. Look! It's in Mr Stern's committee report. Apparently Tredyedeath Depot is an ARCE. Ha ha!"

Gorlas immediately interjected. "Very funny, Trevelyan. You may or may not be right but I need planning reasons if we are to approve this application – so can you keep to the point? I can see the Ministry challenging our decision to approve if it is based on the sole fact that we think it's an ass! If that happens, I think the council would be found to be the ass, wouldn't you? And by the way, you don't need to stand up."

Trelyon smiled wryly in defiance and remained on his feet as he rambled on for another fifteen minutes, not adding much to what the parish council or Cordelia had already and far more sincerely expressed. He hadn't really grasped the issue about the alleged threat to human life within the explosion zone and the flaws in the Ministry's objection that Jim had identified. Trevelyan sat down feeling smug that he had had his day in court, standing up for his constituent – even if most of what he had said was irrelevant. Thinking that he ought to take ownership of something technical to sound knowledgeable, he stood up again. "And another thing. Mr Smidgen is, of course, absolutely correct in what he told you. I was going to say exactly the same thing myself. We can't take the risk on paying out costs. I say we call the Ministry's bluff."

A few more speakers carried on with the same theme and eventually, Gorlas presented the motion that the application be refused in line with Jim's recommendation – which was seconded by the vice chairman. This would immediately flush out any supporters of the recommendation and confirm the chairman's suspicions that the committee was in no mood to acquiesce just because the objector was the Ministry of Defence.

Even Bert Sloggett seemed to be vaguely tuned in, although his only question to the chair asking whether there were any Churchill tanks still running and stored at Tredyedeath Depot was nothing if not consistent. Gorlas was happy to confirm that the last such tank was decommissioned in 1969, co-incidentally the same year in which the government had the final vote on capital punishment.

As predicted, the motion – and therefore Jim's recommendation – was unanimously rejected. A motion to approve the application was soon accepted and another half an hour was spent discussing and agreeing the reasons required by the direction, which would have to be sent to the Secretary of State for Planning. Jim was quietly pleased and looking forward to having a battle with the major if it became necessary.

A jubilant Fred and Grace knew that this probably wasn't going to be the end of it all, a view Johnny shared, but at least they had the district council on their side, not to mention the local community. Another twenty-eight days of delay seemed to be on the cards and with it more cost and worry. Fred, Grace and their supporting entourage left the council auditorium and as they slowly filed past the seats of semi-comatose public still waiting for their application to be heard, they glanced over to a watching Trevelyan and gave him a thankful smile and nod for his help. The auditorium was quite a solemn place after a few hours of typical council business and even those spoiling for a fight on arrival now appeared to be, at best, on Temazepam and at worst, candidates as extras for a remake of Night of the Living Dead.

The only animated soul appeared to be *Trumpet* hack Trevedic Penhaligon, who felt he had a public duty to stay for the duration to record the outcome of the remaining applications. If nothing else it might provide more copy for the *Trumpet* and who knew, there was still always the chance of some fireworks in the council chamber. The council's lengthy discussions over a planning application for an oversized dog kennel gave him just the spare time he needed to conjure up another stunning front page headline on Fred's proposals. From the look of satisfaction on his face, one had come to mind which would light up any village shop.

A week later the pile of *Trumpets* on Karensa's shop counter and on the pavement board outside gave the message. 'Committee Councillors Challenge Chief's Concerns.'

Chapter 16:
Doggy Dust-up and Bite-sized Chunks

Major Fox-Thrasher seemed to have a new lease of life. He had a new spring in his step. The mine had become his wife, his lover, his best and probably only friend. The impending arrival of SSPHE, his new babies, consummated the relationship. In addition to his daily checks of the mine with a warrant officer, he had taken to visiting his beloved explosives most nights after dark to check on what had become his private domain and he was now preparing for his babies' homecoming. Dickie thought it was all becoming a little unhealthy and decided not to follow him for fear that he might stumble across something weirdly distasteful. Karensa, in one of her mischievous moments, suggested to Dickie that the major might have formed a one man sect and was kneeling before the temple to pay homage to the god of mass destruction. Or perhaps it was a masochistic sexual ritual involving the strange and worrying insertion of sticks of explosive. As the major switched off the alarms and surveillance cameras, conveniently, no one outside the base knew what he was up to. As far as Dickie was concerned, one could only hazard a guess.

Still, if it kept the major happy and out of harm's way, it was fine by the captain – but he suspected the major's growing euphoria might be severely dented by the news, which he had received from Karensa the previous night, that Trefriggit district council had resolved to approve Fred and Grace's planning application and therefore reject the Ministry's, or more to the point, the major's objection. His discussions with Karensa about the previous night's committee meeting refreshed his memory about what was going to happen next – which he knew was not exactly in line with the major's strategy.

Dickie knew that managing the major's expectations would be the right approach and it would be best to deliver the bad news in bite size chunks, on the major's own territory, and with a few white lies thrown in to soften the blow. But he wouldn't be able to predict what the major might do or what the fall out would be once he had all the facts at his disposal. Dickie put his trepidation behind him, approached the major's office, straightened up and knocked confidently on the door.

"Come."

"Good morning, sir," Dickie began. "How are you this morning? I see you have the latest copy of *Bang!*; I noticed it in this morning's post. Anything new to report in the world of mass destruction? Do you have any date yet on the SSPHE delivery? It can't be long now. I am quite sure you are looking forward to seeing those red and blue 'Jenga' sticks. I just thought I would report on last night's district council planning committee meeting. Well sir, the committee have resolved to send Mr Gooley's application to the Secretary of State for Planning in case he wants to hold a public inquiry. So the decision has not been made yet. Division will be notified and they will probably contact us."

"What? What?!" Fox-Thrasher exploded. "So the council didn't refuse it then?"

"Well, err, actually no, sir, but the good news is that they are not allowed to approve it either until the Secretary of State for Planning has had a look and he's got twenty-eight days to make a decision on what to do. It's all set out in the legal direction."

"Captain, unless you take me for a complete fool, that means that if the council didn't refuse it, the bloody idiots must have agreed to grant it. That's right, isn't it, my man? That's right, isn't it?"

"Well, technically speaking yes, but the actual decision may not be up to the council anymore," Dickie hastily confirmed.

"Technically speaking, bollocks!" the major shouted. "It bloody well would have been if they had refused it. If they had, there wouldn't be any point in sending it to the Secretary of State for Planning, would there? This is a bloody disaster, Lovely. It's a bloody disaster!"

Being a 'rules' man, the major had recalled the procedure being explained to him when he originally spoke to Division about objecting and he'd very quickly seen straight through the captain's attempted subterfuge. He looked ugly. Dickie should have realised that the major was, after all, a strategist. His beloved explosives, his babies, were under threat from a new enemy, an enemy within, an enemy who were invisible and fought with pens and paper – and they were right on his doorstep and ready to attack.

"Get out, Lovely. I'll handle it."

With that Dickie made a sharp exit back to his office and shut the door. He made a quick call to Karensa to tell her that the major was on the warpath and to get the message to Fred and Johnny Smidgen. He could hear strange muffled sounds coming from the major's office followed by the sound of pacing up and down. It was all a bit ominous. Seconds later, the major's door was flung open, followed by the increasingly thunderous sound of footsteps in the corridor as they approached the captain's office. Dickie just managed to put the phone down before the major rattled the doorknob, stormed in and stood defiantly in the doorway with his arms folded.

"Just so you know, Lovely, I am going to phone Division now and tell them to expect an approach from the Secretary of State for Planning. I will insist that they tell the Secretary of State for Planning to refuse the application straight away and be done with it."

Dickie could see that, in the major's desperate attempt to get rid of the problem, he had either deliberately misinformed himself or had just decided to be obtuse about the direction procedure, about which he knew full well. Dickie needed to give him a quick reality check and set out some home truths at the same time. "Sir, from my reading and understanding of the direction rules, I don't think the Secretary of State for Planning has the legal powers to just refuse the Gooleys' planning application, even if he wanted to. The council's made its decision and it is simply asking the Secretary of State whether it can go ahead and issue it. The only alternative is for a public inquiry in which the Ministry's objection – the one which, of course, you so carefully prepared – will be forensically assessed under cross-examination in front of an independently appointed inspector. The public inquiry process takes decision making out of the council's hands and in those circumstances it would then be for the Secretary of State for Planning to determine the planning application on receipt of the inquiry inspector's report and recommendation."

Major Fox-Thrasher stiffened up. The thought of being interrogated like a prisoner of war by sharp-suited pen-waving lawyers was total anathema to him. An abomination – and he was going to have none of it. His head remained firmly buried in the sand of denial. "Lovely. Once the Secretary of State for Planning has read the bloody objection, I am sure he will see sense and change his mind. Anyway, what more would he need? It's all there. It's all there. It's bloody ridiculous. I'll phone Division to stop this nonsense now."

Dickie knew that it wasn't 'all there' and neither was the major, as Jim Stern had discovered at their now infamous meeting. But it seemed to the captain that the public inquiry process would make sure it would be all there. The major would be squeezed through the mangle of truth – and the result wouldn't be a pretty sight.

The major made a swift exit back to his office and was soon heard through its thin walls barking down the phone at the hapless Wally Dinsmore in the Division that he should do whatever he had to do to get the Secretary of State for Planning to exercise whatever powers he could muster, refuse the application, get rid of the problem and, for the sake of his ARCE, stand up for the defence of the realm.

***

The wheels of bureaucracy rumbled on slowly and it took a week for the district council's overstretched legal team to draw up, with Jim Stern's guidance, all the necessary paperwork on the Gooleys' application for dispatch to, and assessment by, the Secretary of State for Planning. An auto-generated acknowledgement soon followed and made it clear, like most government auto-acknowledgements, that it was going to take, at the very least, the maximum time allowable by the direction to make a decision on whether or not to allow the council to go ahead and issue the Gooleys' planning permission. Within two weeks Division were formally requested by the office for the Secretary of State for Planning to give its official position on the matter.

The Secretary of State's office knew that the technicalities of a Ministry of Defence objection on explosion issues was well outside the scope of the sort of planning referrals with which it normally dealt. Typically, those tended to be confined to dealing with hysteria whipped up by objectors fighting with all they could muster against the march of development for new and much needed housing; often well organised, but blindly hypocritical action groups seeking the respect of objectivity by supporting the need for new housing for their sons and daughters – but just not on their doorstep.

Because the Ministry's objection was all a bit technical, it was unlikely that the Secretary of State for Planning would simply overrule it, without first giving it a good airing through the public inquiry process. However, in the clamour to hold an inquiry to fuel the desire for public transparency, the fundamental question would often get left behind: is the issue really of such importance to justify the cost to the public purse, not to mention the poor old planning applicant? It was ironic, therefore, that the decision was made behind the walls of secrecy by civil servants grappling with all sorts of weird and conflicting politically driven agendas that they certainly wouldn't want to reveal in public. After all, the sight of government ministers brawling in the corridors of Westminster over the protection of their powerbase was not something the mandarins particularly welcomed. That was normally kept for the House of Commons Strangers' Bar.

In the event the decision was left in the hands of the Ministry and it wasn't long before Division reaffirmed its objection. The tirade of verbal abuse rained down by the major that the national defence of the realm was at stake was still in the mind of poor old Wally Dinsmore who, a few months earlier, had been given the job by his seniors of dealing with a pretty minor issue, one which the major should easily have sorted out himself without their involvement. There was no evidence to take any other view, and anyway, Wally couldn't read between the lines of Jim Stern's clever report on the application included within the paperwork. Its recommendation for refusal was clear enough and seemed more important than Jim's mumbo jumbo 'planning speak' that preceded it. Who would want to read all that stuff?

The Ministry of Defence – the major – had got its way and it all seemed a far cry to a Christmas turkey farmer who simply wanted to convert a barn to a dwelling and extend a farmhouse. To Fred and Grace, the idea that such a minor proposal might threaten the defence of the realm seemed as improbable as the major telling a joke.

***

As expected, on the twenty-eighth day of the twenty-eight day referral period the Secretary of State for Planning formally notified the district council legal department that it could not issue Fred and Grace with the planning permission the council had resolved to approve as the decision would now be made by the Secretary of State following consideration of all the issues at a public inquiry. Division were also notified. Another two weeks passed before the public inquiry date was set for early March 2009, five months away. A disappointed Jim Stern immediately called Trevelyan Trelyon to inform him of the news, which soon filtered back to Fred and Grace, Johnny Smidgen and Penelope. By the time of the public inquiry it would be a year since Fred had accepted Ashley Sweet's flawed advice to cease business and instructed him to draw up plans for Feathers Farm. Fred and Grace's financial position took yet another heavy blow.

Back at Tredyedeath Depot, Dickie had been kept up to speed of events by Division and he immediately informed the major. It was early evening and he managed to catch him at an opportune moment, crossing the car park in his usual upbeat mood in anticipation of visiting the mine for his nightly 'constitution'. Dickie felt mischievous, if not a little overconfident as he gripped the ever-growing blue folder under his left arm.

As he approached the major, he could hear some strange noises coming from the direction of the kennels but he remained focused. "Good evening, sir. Good news. The Gooleys' planning application is going to a public inquiry and you will have the opportunity to explain your – I mean, the Ministry's – objection to an inspector. The Secretary of State for Planning will make the decision. I am sure you will relish that, won't you, sir? The good reputation of Division and its support for you is now firmly resting on your shoulders. Do you want me to instruct a barrister to assist you?"

If Major Fox-Thrasher had any weaknesses, he wasn't going to show them, but his demeanour quickly changed as he started to morph into anger and resentment, as the Jekyll and Hyde in him took hold. How could the Secretary of State for Planning summarily ignore his demands that it should give the Gooleys' application short shrift, as of course the major had done from the beginning? How dare his civil servants rebuff a military man? He was now going to fight the faceless 'enemy from within' over the protection of his beloved explosives.

He looked straight at Captain Lovely, just managing to keep his seething anger under control. "Thank you, Lovely. Don't need to hide behind a barrister. Don't actually see why I should bother to turn up. The evidence is all there in my objection. It's all there."

Dickie maintained his composure. "Sir, the public inquiry will analyse your objection in detail and in context to assess the impact of the Gooleys' application on the safeguarding area, and our explosives capability. At the very least you will need to turn up. Division have sent us a handy little booklet prepared by the government agency running the public inquiry. They are called the Planning Inspectorate – PINS for short – and the public inquiry inspector is called a planning inspector. The booklet tells you what you need to do for the inquiry. I'll put it on your desk."

"Well, if you must, Lovely," Fox-Thrasher said. "I know a few expert explosives chaps who can help me out. Better to have military 'pips' to support me than some blood-sucking sharp-suited barrister in civvies. We need guns and bombs, Lovely, not pens and paper. Bloody acronym-ridden bureaucrats. Bloody paperwork. They're all wasters."

Dickie shrugged his shoulders, amazed at the major's continued denial, but his day in court – or, more to the point, his day of judgement – would come in five months' time. He was clearly far more focused on his regular, seemingly unhealthy trips to the temple of mass destruction, the only location on camp which could momentarily restore the major to the semblance of a reasonable human being. The contrasts in his character were getting more noticeable and it was only because of the depot's small contingent of personnel that his mood swings had not been subject to the need for a psychological assessment.

The major turned towards the mine entrance, his face lightening up once again in anticipation, his steps showing a deftness of movement. Luckily, he was far enough away in fairy explosiveland to even remotely notice the increasingly strange commotion, coming from the kennels over his left shoulder, which had earlier attracted Dickie's attention. It was Private Johnston rolling around the inside of Fluffy's compound with the recalcitrant Sheppy, attempting to wrestle Kenneth the killer whale from the beast's slobbery mouth. Fluffy was clearly enjoying the rough and tumble and showed Johnston who was boss with an orchestra of growling sounds and the occasional flash of teeth, all beautifully conducted by an energetic wagging tail. Fluffy had returned from an enjoyable afternoon's walk off base with his favourite cuddly toy for comfort but a reluctance to hand back Kenneth was giving Private Johnston cause for concern. Direct man-dog action was the only solution. The other guard dogs were out on patrol, but were due back any minute, and Johnston knew that extracting Kenneth was a must if he was to protect Fluffy's secret.

Dickie waited anxiously until the major had entered the mine before sprinting over to the compound to see what was going on. He spotted

Fluffy, who by now was standing on his hind legs with his front paws on Private Johnston's shoulders, Jimmy tugging frantically to extract Kenneth from his vice-like jaws. Cupping his hands to his mouth, Dickie whispered loudly: "Fluffy!" It did the trick: the dog immediately looked around and caught sight of Dickie, a friendly face and potential opportunity for more walkies. He instantly let go of Kenneth, causing Private Johnston's arms to fly upwards, one hand gripping Kenneth tightly as he proceeded to shoot backwards before finally losing his balance, falling on his back and rolling into a pile of unmentionable doggy stuff. Fluffy, now back on four legs, wandered over to Dickie, head down, tail and beam swooshing submissively as he put his nose to the compound mesh to lick Dickie's outstretched fingers.

Dickie looked over at the private, who was by now back on his feet, barely visible in a cloud of doggy dust and still trying to remove from his person the worst of the unmentionables that Fluffy's compound had to offer. "For Christ's sake, Johnston, get out of that cage now and bring that thing, that… Bring Kenneth with you. You're on borrowed time, Johnston."

"Yessir, sorry sir, sorry, sorry. Oh, I see you remembered Kenneth's name, sir. Not difficult to forget really… although you could have called it Ollie. Ollie the killer whale doesn't sound quite right though, does it, sir? Err, you won't tell anyone, will you, sir?"

"Shut up, Johnston. I'm thinking," Dickie said. The major was by now long gone and none the wiser. Dickie realised that he had left it so long to decide whether or not to report the recalcitrant private that he was probably now in as much trouble. In truth he also liked taking Fluffy for a walk to Trecarsick and somehow the lovable giant helped to foster the captain's ever closer relationship with Karensa. It also took his mind off what was to come with the Gooleys' public inquiry and what, if anything, his role might be at the inquiry in facing Karensa, her mum and most of the village.

***

The *Trecarsick Trumpet* was formally notified of the public inquiry and Trevedic Penhaligon got to work in his usual diligent way to make sure that he met his deadline for Thursday's edition, ready to grace Karensa's village shop.

It was a classic. "Government to Grapple with Gooleys over Ministry's ARCE."

Chapter 17:
Brigadiers, Briefs and Boxes of Joy

The news of the public inquiry didn't come as a complete surprise to Penelope or Johnny. They had been there before with other cases that had been referred to the Secretary of State for Planning. They knew the government tended to adopt a cautious approach in considering planning application referrals by airing potentially controversial schemes at public inquiries rather than having its decision challenged in the High Court by disgruntled protagonists. It became all the more important when another government department was involved, particularly one as powerful as the Ministry of Defence.

The public inquiry rules were strict and highly procedural and Johnny and Penelope agreed that it was important to get their strategy right as early as possible. Of course it was the council who would be in the spotlight, as it was its decision to approve the Gooleys' planning application but, as applicants, the Gooleys were entitled to participate too. Jim Stern knew that financial constraints precluded him from outsourcing expensive legal representation. Trefriggit district council's own legal team would just have to take up the cudgels, but he felt confident that the council's decision to approve Fred's development was robust and eminently defendable. He was nevertheless delighted to hear from Penelope that Fred had instructed her to lead his attack on the Ministry and in the process give the council all the support it needed. Her formal request for the Gooleys to be represented at the inquiry was soon accepted by PINS.

Johnny had already visited Fred and Grace to explain what the process entailed and they realised that despite the extra costs, there was no going back. This was a moral, spiritual and financial fight. Fred was used to making feathers fly despite the fact that he was now spitting feathers and was determined to see it through. He knew it wouldn't be long before his favourite bank manager, Dennis Blackstaff, would be back again rattling the sheep's head knocker, wanting the proverbial shirt off his large torso to keep head office's faceless number crunchers happy. The embattled turkey farmer knew he would just have to deal with whatever unsavoury proposal Dennis had this time for him but in another one of his imaginative moments seemingly reserved just for bank managers, Fred felt that Attila might just keep Dennis at bay long enough to see the matter to the end. He knew that, when it came to defending the Gooleys, the feisty fowl would be up for a scrap. He pondered for a while. Perhaps it wasn't such a bad idea.

On the upside Penelope was now armed with Johnny's excellent planning report, the one he'd prepared soon after his eventful day at the council planning office while ogling the pretty Kylie and her plotting sheets. This enabled her to diligently pursue Ashley's firm for compensation over the consequences of his bad advice. Penelope also had the clearest instructions from Fred to claim whatever compensation she could from the Ministry of Defence by whatever means necessary, but she knew that extracting any money from a government department wouldn't be easy and they still had to win the day at the public inquiry before any claim could realistically be made. But she knew that she had nothing to lose in going on the offensive by approaching the Ministry and threatening it with costs for its unreasonable delay in promoting what she and Jim Stern considered to be a flawed objection and, as far as she was concerned, the sooner the better.

The declining state of the economy was now well and truly beginning to affect property values. It was now a year since early signs of the recession had showed themselves. Feathers Farm was continuing to decline in value. The housing market – including the demand for second homes – was also continuing to weaken. There was simply nothing anyone could do about it.

Rising above it all, Fred stayed positive in the knowledge that, in Penelope and Johnny, he had a good team of advisors behind him.

Moreover, despite his antipathy towards the larger than life councillor Trevelyan 'Rely-on' Trelyon, a line of communication to the local MP Sir Michael Stride-Pecker had been established which Fred knew Trelyon was going to follow up.

But there was still one vital member of the team missing, one whom Penelope urged Fred to appoint for the public inquiry. A barrister. In Penelope's view, the council's in-house legal team were just not up to the job and she had no idea what big guns the major, who she assumed would be supported by the Ministry, would wheel out to defend its objection. It was too risky to call; Fred needed to fight fire with fire. In Penelope's eyes, there was only one man who could expose the major's obsessive but flawed defence of his beloved explosives: Christopher Hartlock-Naddertrout, Queen's Counsel, a silk affectionately known in the legal profession as CHN.

Hartlock-Naddertrout, a very successful barrister, was head of his chambers, No 1 Hangmans Buildings, Inner Temple, London and had been a QC for nearly thirty years. CHN was occasionally appointed to sit as a deputy high court judge in the planning division and was lauded for giving sound and well-reasoned judgements. He undertook this task willingly but his main love was the cut and thrust world of the public inquiry, where his noted planning advocacy prowess would continue to place his respected chambers at the forefront of the planning bar. Revered amongst his peers, CHN was one of, if not *the* best planning brief in the country. A fierce opponent and the ideal advocate to have on your side, yet his common touch endeared him with clients, whose often optimistic and sometimes unrealistic expectations of success he was extremely adept at managing. At six foot, the lean, silver-haired, softly spoken and well-dressed CHN struck quite a pose in any public inquiry room and his eloquence quickly gained him respect from all sides. This often endeared him to the one key individual in officialdom appointed to make the vital decision, a civil servant before him charged with being persuaded that he, CHN, was absolutely right in his arguments and his opponent was absolutely wrong in theirs: the public inquiry planning inspector.

CHN's style was more smiling assassin than the barrack room bully boy for which the planning bar had something of a reputation. In Major Fox-Thrasher's world, CHN's strategy was more search and destroy than Blitzkrieg. It was a style regularly used to good effect in the rarefied atmosphere of the public inquiry, where his razor sharp cross-examination technique would regularly extract precisely the answer he was looking for from an unsuspecting, and often far too relaxed, opponent's professional witness. There wasn't a lot of difference between CHN's incisive but somehow seemingly innocent cross-examination and hypnotism. Many a time an opponent's witness would return to his professional team after three hours of CHN's polite grilling believing that he had done a pretty good job, only to find his disconsolate and strangely suicidal brief head in hands, knowing that his client's case was unravelling as quickly and as badly as a politician's expenses claim form.

Penelope and Johnny had agreed to meet at Steel, Cash and Scamper's office in late November to discuss the division of their workload and the contents of CHN's brief. PINS had set down the mandatory timetable for the public inquiry, which required the district council, the Ministry of Defence and the Gooleys to each send their outline Statement of Case to the appointed PINS programme officer by early December. The officer would then circulate each Statement to all parties. The full Statement of Case would be required a month before the public inquiry was due to commence.

Penelope came down to meet Johnny in reception, barely noticing the wafts of acrid blue smoke circulating just outside the glass front doors like a deadly alien about to force entry and wreak havoc on its inhabitants. The brakes on Johnny's car were going through their recognisable blue haze phase as they slowly cooled down, passers-by covering their faces as the plume momentarily enveloped them. There was never any need for Penelope to ask reception to let her know when Johnny had arrived. She could always hear him coming.

Johnny could see the disapproving Penelope was about to launch into a lecture on road safety. He didn't give her the chance to comment. "Hello Pen. What have you done to your left arm?"

"Hello Johnny – it's Penelope, by the way. I fell down the stairs at home and twisted my elbow. Hence the sling." Penelope was looking for a little sympathy at yet another one of her mishaps but braced herself in anticipation that Johnny would probably say something outrageous.

"Well at least it's not your writing arm – which is good news – although I can see that pulling up your knickers might be a problem! You have got them on, haven't you? Who'd be a lawyer with no briefs!!"

"Yes, thank you Johnny and, no, it wasn't too difficult. Believe me, you'd be the last to know if I was struggling to get my knickers on."

"Well Pen, I am always here to help. You know me."

"I do, Johnny, and that's precisely why you'd be the last to know!!"

Penelope took Johnny upstairs to her office, past the glazed curved corridor of corporately-inspired meeting room suites which were familiar to Johnny . As they walked past Integrity and Honesty, Johnny could see that there was a meeting in the next suite. "What's going on in there, Pen?"

"Oh, we are having a lunchtime seminar for clients on conflict resolution," she said.

Johnny couldn't resist it. "Really? Why don't you rename it the 'Fuck Off, Loser' Suite?" Penny just smiled, quickened her pace towards her office and ushered Johnny in before he had the chance to make any more inappropriate quips. He headed for one of the uncomfortable-looking plastic chairs and sat down opposite her. "Like the see-through plastic chairs, Pen. Very trendy."

"Yes they are, aren't they, but to be honest I think the interior designers got a bit carried away. I think they are known as ghost chairs."

"I bet they come into their own at the office Christmas party, eh Pen? Makes a change from sitting on the photocopier!"

Penelope knew that when it came to dealing with Johnny on

professional matters, once he was focused on the job he was very good, but until that point anything was a candidate for another inappropriate quip. She knew Smidgen just didn't take life too seriously.

"Johnny, we have had an interesting development in Fred's case. We've been copied into a letter from PINS, sent from the inquiry inspector, who has taken an early lead and made his position very clear on what he is looking for." She produced the letter, which set out how he intended to run the inquiry and laid out the questions that all parties should consider, as they would form the basis for his report and recommendations to the decision maker, the Secretary of State for Planning.

One issue sought clarity on the council policy on barn conversions and house extensions, which Penelope knew was not controversial. The second issue, however, was going to be the main battleground. This was where the major was going to have to defend his objection with words and evidence, not bombs and bullets. The inspector was incisive in his questions, which Penelope read out: How was the safeguarding map prepared? What technical criteria was used for determining the Tredyedeath Depot explosives capability? How were agricultural operations assessed within the Tredyedeath Depot safeguarding area? What impact would Feathers Farm have on Tredyedeath Depot's explosives storage capability, either if it was to continue as a Christmas turkey business or if it was to be redeveloped in accordance with the Gooleys' planning application? The inspector also requested clarification of the Health and Safety Executive's position claimed by the major to have been issued verbally to him in support of his objection – which, to date, had not been clarified.

It was better than Penelope and Johnny could have hoped for. 'A hands on' inspector focused on issues he wanted answering gave them added impetus in their strategy to send an early salvo across the bows of the major. However, Penelope knew that, to date, the major had managed to control the whole issue himself, supported only by a sleepy and disinterested Division who had just been forwarding any PINS paperwork on the public inquiry to Tredyedeath. It was now time to wake them up. She agreed with Johnny that she would write directly to the head of the explosives section within Division, Brigadier Anthony Bloodworth, to express her concern and threaten a claim for costs against the Ministry. Her letter would be copied to Trevelyan Trelyon, who had already arranged to meet Sir Michael Stride-Pecker.

She would also brief CHN whilst Johnny would do some surreptitious research to satisfy the inspector's searching questions. CHN's clerk confirmed that although CHN would be on holiday in Cornwall in mid-December he would be happy to meet at Feathers Farm for a consultation, which would also give him the opportunity to look around the area – including Tredyedeath Depot. By then the much anticipated response to Penelope's letter to the division's brigadier and receipt of the Ministry's Statement of Case would give the Gooley camp plenty to talk about.

***

At Tredyedeath Depot, Captain Lovely was, as usual, opening the morning post. The inquisitorial letter from the planning inspector was on top of the pile. Dickie could see immediately from the inspector's questions that Fred Gooley's turkeys were coming home to roost. He walked down the hallway to the major's empty office and dropped the letter onto his desk like a hot potato – but not before making a copy of it for his blue file.

The captain had earlier heard a kind of chanting coming from the major's office, followed by the rapid clattering of footsteps along the wooden corridor as the major went down the stairs and through the office building's main entrance, leaving the doors swinging violently in his wake. Dickie wondered whether the major had eaten something disagreeable, necessitating his rapid exit, or had perhaps reacted badly to a power nap dream echoing his experiences in Northern Ireland during the Troubles, infamous for that IRA warning that had become a catchphrase: "You've got three minutes to get out." Whatever the reason, the major couldn't have arrived in the car park any quicker than if he'd jumped out of his office window.

But it wasn't long before Dickie realised that the Land Rover carrying the long awaited delivery of SSPHE had arrived at the gatehouse and it was the major, outside in gleeful mood, who had cause to make such a dramatic exit in his rush to welcome the cargo of death like a visit from royalty. This was the moment the major had been waiting for, almost yearning for, since the announcement had been made a few months earlier that the Tredyedeath Depot ARCE was to receive a supply of the experimental SSPHE. With the security barrier raised, the Land Rover driver was faced with what looked like a slightly demented military man performing a particularly poor interpretation of an Irish jig as the vehicle approached the car park. It was still reversing when the still skipping major, in his haste, started to unbuckle the neat row of webbing straps holding the green canvas cover in place only to catch his foot on a kerb, which sent him sprawling. As the vehicle came to a halt just short of the major's left leg, he quickly got up, dusted himself off and regained his composure to complete the task, flipping the rear cover onto the vehicle's roof. He looked inside, eyes wide. He was like a small child staring at the Christmas tree at some ungodly hour to see what Santa had delivered. As expected and in accordance with the all-important accompanying paperwork prepared in octuplicate, there were twelve boxes in total, two groups of six, each group containing the separated red and blue Jenga-like explosive sticks. The paperwork confirmed that these were the twelve hour explosive variant type. It wasn't particularly clear which box contained which colour explosive as much of the mass of stencilled writing on the side seemed to be in code. Still, as they were only being stored, it didn't really matter to anyone and it was probably intentional given that this was a secret experimental consignment.

Dickie looked out of the upstairs window to see the animated major touching the boxes in a sort of religious laying on of hands ceremony whilst a bemused warrant officer watched on, patiently waiting for instructions as to where in the mine they should be stored. Karensa's mischievous suggestion came to Dickie's mind once again. Maybe it was the final piece of the temple to the god of mass destruction waiting to be ceremoniously slotted into place by the slobbering major, who wouldn't have looked out of place in a cassock. Dickie knew that he had identified a special place for their storage well away from the other explosives because of their experimental nature, as required by the procurement boffins in Bromsgrove.

Dickie suddenly remembered the other security requirement: a dog patrol to guard the SSPHE. He had a brilliant idea. Fluffy could be transferred to special duties to guard the special explosives. It was perfect. He would be out of harm's way. He might even be able to take Ollie and Kenneth with him. Dickie would use the opportunity when he checked the paperwork to have a word with the major – after he'd calmed down, for Dickie knew that once the major saw the planning inspector's 'hot potato' sitting on the top of his desk, there would, in all probability, be a 'Blue Streak' moment. Over the time they had worked together, Dickie could read many of the major's habits, some of which involved a number of synchronized, chronological actions. To make light of it, Dickie and Karensa named the major's more common habits after post war British missiles – which also saved time in Dickie's regular phone calls to Karensa to talk about what sort of day they had both had. The major's most popular 'action' was 'Blue Streak'. This started with the muffled sound of uncontrolled anger contained within his office, the rapid flinging open of his office door, the clattering of footsteps along the corridor at pace, followed by a forceful opening of the captain's office door, without knocking, whereby the major would stand in the entrance with his arms crossed and stare at the captain, generally in silence, for a few seconds.

The major returned to his office and within seconds Dickie's prediction that there would indeed be a 'Blue Streak' moment was spot on. Standing in the shadow of the captain's doorway, the major finally came to life, frantically waving his arm around like a Chinese police traffic officer, his hand grasping the now crumpled letter. "Lovely, what the hell is this?"

"Well sir, the planning inspector clearly thought it would be helpful, before we issue our outline Statement of Case, to set out the issues he wants to consider at the inquiry on which we have to produce evidence. That's all really."

"More bloody paperwork, Lovely. Why doesn't he just read our objection? What Statement of Case? I have phoned my explosives colleague and he will explain everything at the inquiry." It was clear that the major hadn't read that helpful PINS booklet the captain had diligently placed on his desk.

Dickie reminded him that he would soon have to submit his outline Statement of Case. It was, after all, all in the rulebook and as the major knew, 'rules are rules'. The major turned and performed the 'Bloodhound' manoeuvre: a slow walk back to his office, leaving Dickie's door open, head down, shuffling and mumbling, followed by a firm office door closing and more mumbling inside. Inwardly, he knew from Dickie's constant reminding, now reiterated by the planning inspector, that he would have to wade through some procedural government treacle. Even worse, instead of reading the latest edition of *Bang!*, he would have to waste his time producing a statement for the bureaucrats to explain why the Gooleys' application should be stopped in its tracks. The total lack of necessity of it all remained at the forefront of his mind and he was damned sure that he was going to produce as little as he could get away with.

***

Sir Michael Stride-Pecker was at his Saturday morning constituency surgery in Bodmin, having arrived on his favourite Night Riviera train from London after a busy week in Parliament. He changed en route from his city suit and accompanying attire into one more befitting of a country

MP, one he knew would put his constituents at ease as they launched their woes onto the well-seasoned MP. He didn't have a permanent constituency office of his own but leased a small office in Bodmin town hall, an imposing nineteenth century granite-faced structure with a history as a former law court known for ruthlessly applying the rule of law to anyone who crossed its threshold. For some constituents the building still retained that imminent feeling of incarceration but, with no other office available, Stride-Pecker knew he had his work cut out to quell the malaise. To ease the strain and tension and brighten up the gloominess, his constituency secretary, Doris, worked hard to make sure that his office was adorned with plenty of scented flowers. In the spring she took great pride in showcasing a wonderful assortment of Cornwall's nationally renowned daffodils.

It was a busy morning as Stride-Pecker listened patiently to a range of constituent concerns. From genuine social problems to housing need, he worked hard to help but the morning was always interspersed with a few oddities: the removal of a dead rat from the roof of a local bus shelter, a recommendation for a good dating agency, advice to help a single mum move house and the bad smell coming from a local drain, a particularly recurrent theme. An MP's life, it seemed, was nothing if not varied.

The last knock on the door was typically thunderous. It was the ebullient Trevelyan 'Rely-on' Trelyon. "Thank you very much for coming to see me, Trevelyan," Sir Michael said. "So nice to see you again and glad to see that you are working as hard as ever. I am sorry to hear about Fred Gooley's plight and I do want to help if I can. Who hasn't had one of his turkeys? I certainly have and they were always delicious. We met earlier this year at the Cornwall Show in Wadebridge and spent some time chatting about his love of turkeys. It's so sad that what some see as progress has driven him out of business. But I'm afraid, Trevelyan, that the news for the moment is not good, but I must assure you that it's not to do with the strength of Fred's case. It's because I am powerless to intervene in a process which has not yet come to a natural conclusion."

"Bloody hell, Michael, can't you swing a few favours with the Secretary of State? I thought that's what you guys did."

"Trevelyan, my old chap. I know that is the approach which your antecedents used with gay abandon, in the old sense of the word, but not these days. We are in the world of 'transparency' and I am not talking about glasshouses. We MPs are always looking over our shoulders. The case will have to stand on its own two feet. Let's see what the planning inspector recommends first following the public inquiry."

"Oh! Really? Can't we…err … can't you do anything at all, Michael?"

"Well, Trevelyan," Sir Michael said, "I have had one thought. I am going to give the Right Honourable 'Gunpowder' Guy Gunston a ring at his Ministry of Defence office. We are friends and get on well. I am just going to tell him that, if it all goes tits up and he loses the inquiry, his Ministry is going to look pretty daft and it'll probably cost him as well. From what I have heard on the grapevine about that major at Tredyedeath Depot, it may just be that he is leading them all up the garden path, or should I say in this case, into a minefield. Ha ha. Guy's Ministry needs a reality check and I can certainly speak bluntly to him. I know him well enough to know that if he promises to get the message to his troops on the ground, he will."

It was all Trevelyan could realistically hope for and at least he could tell Fred that he had put some wheels in motion at the highest level. True to his word, Stride-Pecker took the opportunity to phone 'Gunpowder' Guy over that weekend, not at the Ministry but at his home where he knew he would be more accessible. Weekends were marginally quieter for a full time politician and it was the best time for the two of them to speak for a little longer than during the working day.

***

Division was based in Croydon, London, located in an anonymous four-storey post war office block whose days were numbered. It was a busy place. Rows of identical offices were hidden behind plain wooden doors, their strange numbering denoting a Chinese-style bureaucracy of departments and job titles all accessed off cream painted corridors. It was like a sanatorium. Its occupants, a mixture of civilians and military personnel, created a unique arrangement for a government department. The management of the Ministry's national vast estate required teams of civilian professionals from all disciplines whilst the military staff would bring to bear their practical experience when it came to considering the implications of decisions on operational activity. This led to friction from time to time as the uniformed staff had a natural and unsurprising tendency to protect their own regiment's reputation and role. From the Infantry to Logistics, from the Royal Engineers to the Royal Artillery, all the regiments were fiercely defended as having equal validity. This potentially fractious relationship continued at a higher political level in the Defence headquarters in Whitehall, with senior 'pips' battling with city-suited mandarins, the latter claiming greater objectivity in the battle to reduce the Ministry's vast and regularly uncontrolled annual expenditure as they danced to the tune of their Secretary of State, whose own head was not immune from the political guillotine.

Brigadier Anthony Bloodworth was at his desk at the Ministry's busy Division. He was an industrious man, well organised, well respected and at five foot six, shorter than the average male. Bloodworth was not to be messed with but he had a softer side as a pragmatist and was always open to constructive suggestion. A Sandhurst graduate with no family military background to speak of, the brigadier had science qualifications and soon specialised in explosives, taking the opportunity to become a bomb disposal officer, gaining practical experience after the Falklands conflict in helping to clear the islands of mines. This made him a decisive decision maker, a quality which never left him as he progressed through the ranks to the desk job he commanded as head of explosives storage within Division. His bomb disposal experience taught him one valuable life lesson: step away if you are not going to succeed and take any failure on the chin. For the brigadier, despite some close calls in the field, he remained ever thankful he still had a chin to take it on. An occasional wry sense of humour was put to good effect when he moved into the safer world of lecturing part time on bomb disposal techniques, as demonstrated by his opening address to new recruits which was intended to strike a poignant chord: "Only adopt a 'hands on' approach at the start of a job, if you can be sure you'll have hands on at the end of it."

Bloodworth's role as the head of explosives storage required an intimate knowledge of the workings of the legal direction and safeguarding maps that played such a pivotal role in managing capability. The future of Tredyedeath Depot ultimately fell under his command. He also knew his decisions required the application of political astuteness as his job landed him squarely between the uniformed high ranking 'pips', whom he saw as his natural bosses, and the besuited mandarins in Whitehall whose masters followed an altogether different agenda.

Much of the brigadier's current work programme was taken up with the preparation of a confidential report he had been instructed to prepare on the cutbacks in explosives storage required to meet the politically driven and wide ranging Defence Spending Review. Bloodworth's report would be one of many produced by different Ministry of Defence Divisions covering a variety of military disciplines. His role was to focus on all explosives depots, including the high ranking ARCE facilities, and Tredyedeath Depot would not escape his keen analytical skills. He was a realist. He knew that military and civilian cuts were going to be made right across the Ministry and whilst he would fight his corner to retain as much explosive capability as possible, the writing would almost certainly be on the wall for some locations. He was just going to have to do the best he could and hope that, higher up the chain of command, the role of explosives storage would be argued by the 'pips' as fundamental to the country's defence strategy and thus escape the knife.

His concentration was broken by a knock on his office door. It was his staff sergeant secretary. "Morning, sir. A couple of matters have come to light sir, both of which are, coincidentally, related. I have a letter here which is addressed to you. It's from a solicitor, Penelope Breakage from a Cornish law firm, Steal, Cash and Scamper. You'd better have a look at it. It's about a public inquiry relating to the Tredyedeath Depot ARCE. She's on the warpath."

"Bloody hell, it's not what I need right now. Thank you, Sergeant. What's the other matter about?"

"Sir, I took a phone call this morning from the office to Guy Gunston's Parliamentary Under Secretary in Whitehall. They wouldn't say in detail other than it was about Tredyedeath Depot. They want you to give them a ring."

Bloodworth was experienced enough to know that, when it came to military issues, coincidences were very rare. It was clear that something was going on at one of his more distant ARCE outposts and whatever it was, it wasn't on his radar. He quickly scanned over Penelope's letter to get the gist of her complaint and decided to make the phone call to Whitehall first. A mid ranking mandarin, charged with being the messenger, answered the phone and was economically abrupt. The brigadier picked up the threads to make sure he understood what turned out to be a short conversation.

"I see. So just to get this absolutely right, this is an off the record conversation we are having. Guy Gunston has been approached by Sir Michael Stride-Pecker MP who is concerned about a public inquiry on his patch in Cornwall in which my division is being represented by Tredyedeath Depot's commander, Major Fox-Thrasher. The major has objected to a planning application for residential development inside the area of the safeguarding map. Trefriggit district council wants to grant planning permission but the Secretary of State for Planning has called for a public inquiry, at the Ministry's, or more to the point Division's request, which is to be held in March. Guy's concern – and his message to me – is that when we are in the spotlight defending our objection, we don't cock it up and make the Ministry, with Guy as its leader, look like a bunch of amateurs. Ok. I've got the message."

Bloodworth occasionally got calls from Whitehall poking its nose into something military it knew precious little about and he wouldn't have been unduly concerned about just another 'moaning mandarin', had it not been for the threatening letter from Penelope which was too much of a coincidence. He decided to look into the background a little further as Fox-Thrasher would have needed some authority from Bloodworth's Division, both to agree that there was a need to object in the first place and also to force the public inquiry. Someone in Division was accountable. It was not long before a slightly nervous Wally Dinsmore was standing in the brigadier's doorway, having been tracked down to find out what was going on. The brigadier decided to give him enough rope in the hope that he wouldn't hang himself and quickly saw from his nervousness that, with everyone else in the office too busy, he had been given the short straw in dealing with the fractious major's demands. On the face of it Bloodworth could understand the legitimate concerns expressed to protect the integrity of the Tredyedeath Depot ARCE storage capability, particularly now that it had been chosen to store SSPHE and given also that, as he discovered, the Gooleys' application had been recommended for refusal by the district council's chief planning officer.

Although the brigadier had only met the major briefly, he had quickly formed the view, confirmed by other colleagues, that he was an officious and not particularly warm character, in fact not his type of officer at all. However, as long as the information in his objection was correct and above board, there was no need to intervene or chastise the nervous Wally, who was still trying to defend how he had been steamrollered by the major. After all, it wasn't a new town that was being proposed in the explosion zone and any military 'man on the ground' worth his salt should be able to deal with an 'attack' on his patch from a simple farmer. He could see why it was a civilian decision to let the major take the reins without needing to disturb him.

With the well-travelled message from 'Gunpowder' Guy's mandarins still in his mind and despite Wally Dinsmore's explanation, Bloodworth decided to give Fox-Thrasher a ring just to make sure there were no banana skins lying around. Bloodworth decided to approach the major by 'surprise attack', immediately opening the conversation using Penelope's threatening letter to see how the major would react.

The major's pre-programmed phone came alive to the familiar sound of Eric Coates's famous Dambusters March. "Morning Major, Brigadier Bloodworth here. I'm head of explosives storage at Division. I think we might have met once or twice before. Anyway, it's been brought to my attention that you are representing Division in defending an objection to a planning application at a public inquiry in March. I have received a threatening letter from the applicants' solicitor. I'll send you a copy. She says that your objection is a load of bollocks and the Ministry is going to have to pay for your nonsense if her clients win – which they confidently predict they will. She is demanding a copy of the minutes of a meeting you had with the council over your objection and a copy of an objection you say has been made by the Health and Safety Executive. What do you say about all that, Major? Got your troops armed and ready for battle, have you? Arguments sound, are they?"

The phone went silent for a moment. The major's attempt to keep everything locked up 'on camp' had well and truly escaped and was now on the doorstep of his immediate and straight-talking superior at Division. He felt flustered. Forgetting all the military strategy subtleties he could have called upon, he decided to launch a blunt, blame-led counter attack. "Absolutely, Brigadier. If we surrendered every time we got a threatening letter from some country woman solicitor, there wouldn't be an army, would there, sir? Bloody bureaucrats, solicitors, planners, consultants, inspectors, the lot of them. Poxy paper-producing, pen-pushing, fancy-suited legal layabouts. Poncy planners with big fancy words. They are all mumbo jumbo-talking wasters. Send it to me, sir and I'll sort it out."

"Thank you for the rhetoric, Major but that's not really the answer I was hoping for. I am doing some paper pushing myself at the moment. It's just part of the job. Look, I am very busy right now and I just need to know that this isn't going to erupt into something bigger, Major. I don't want your ARCE landing on my desk as a steaming pile of poo. On the face of it, it's a barn conversion and house extension and I am reliably informed it's within the explosion zone so you should be on safe ground. No mess-ups, Major. No mess-ups. Understood? I'll send you the letter and you deal with it. I'm afraid you will just have to get your pen out this time."

The brigadier took the measured decision from what he had heard to leave it to the major to sort out; he had more important matters to attend to, like dealing with his Defence Spending Review report. But the major hadn't quite given him the confident assurance he was looking for and doubt continued to linger in his mind.

***

A few days later, a copy of Penelope's letter arrived on Dickie's desk with a compliment slip from Division. He immediately headed to the photocopier before delivering it to the major, who was far too immersed in *Bang!* to acknowledge his presence, let alone the letter. However, just as he closed the major's office door behind him, Dickie heard what sounded like paper being screwed up and tossed into the waste bin. It was too much of a coincidence.

Chapter 18:
Big Slips and Slip Ups

The master bedroom at Feathers Farm was especially busy as Grace was preparing herself to receive royalty: the arrival of CHN, a proper Queen's Counsel from London, no less. A rather inviting dress, the latest of Gwenifer's creations, awaited its adornment onto Grace's well-built frame. Flossie was looking on with interest, her head poking out from the top drawer of a mahogany tallboy in the master bedroom which Grace had left ajar in her quest to find some fresh underwear for the event. 'Smalls' would have been a misnomer for the yardage of undergarment required to cover Grace's ample body, not that it made any difference to Flossie, who wasted no time in leaping straight into the drawer after a particularly successful night on the rampage in the undergrowth. She snuggled down for the day amongst the freshly washed cotton, purring loudly as she did so to make sure she wouldn't be accidentally shut in. At the risk of being decapitated, she watched in fascination as Grace began to take on the image of a large tent covered in gigantic green ferns. A pair of matching green shoes soon followed but a rather too hasty application of 'slap' had the effect of making Grace look not dissimilar to a ventriloquist's dummy. She quickly went downstairs to check progress in the oven. The homely smell of ginger biscuits wafted around the farmhouse, fortuitously replacing the distinctive but fortunately diminishing aroma of Burley Blend which Grace had extinguished a few hours earlier.

It was now mid-December and the Bodmin landscape was in hibernation mode, but no less dramatic. The once green moorland, granite drystone walls, blackthorn hedges and isolated copses dulled by the changeable climate remained equally beautiful in winter guise. It was a frosty morning and some distant snowy outcrops still littered the landscape from an earlier cold snap. Fred was well wrapped up and returning from one of his regular solitary walks around the eerily empty courtyard and paddocks beyond. His morning walks always gave him the opportunity to think clearly and reflect on his past life amongst his turkeys, which were never far from his thoughts. The sound of the farmhouse back door opening was the trigger for Attila to make an appearance from the barn home Fred had made for her, to accompany him on his daily constitution. Fred knew she was tuned into his habitual wanderings but he also knew that the stroll would keep her spirits up in her solitary life as they wandered into the paddocks, stopping occasionally to sit on an outcrop and take in the views over the harsh moorland.

Attila would often scramble onto his lap as he started talking to her in the vain hope that she might somehow understand his woes and take the weight of the world off his shoulders. How had something so simple all gone so wrong, at the wrong time, with months – maybe years – yet before there would be an end to it all? It was all costing him dear and his beloved Grace was spending increasing time in the comfort of her kitchen as she put on a brave face. He found it all so upsetting. All so unsettling. Attila would cock her head from time to time. She might not be able to speak but she could, like many animals, recognise human voice tones and read body language. Fred had grown to empathise with her simple yet responsive actions, which were enough to fantasize that she really did know what he was saying to her. He liked to think it was possible but ultimately it didn't really matter. Attila remained a rock and a comfort to him during these dark times.

It was a quiet moment that didn't last long. Fred's 'troops' were due at Feathers Farm at any time to discuss public inquiry tactics. As he headed back to the farmhouse with Attila, as always, proudly leading the way just ahead of him, he heard a wailing sound in the distance, its volume increasing by the second. Fred immediately recognised it as Johnny's car approaching as it hurtled between the narrow but solid stone and soil Cornish 'edges' leading up to the farm, the funnelled, straining sound of a thousand protesting mechanical parts all vainly pleading for a life of normality. In what seemed like a nano second later, the hot hatch slid to a halt outside the front door in a cloud of blue smoke and grey gravel dust. Johnny proudly emerged from the fog like an expectant Grand Prix winner awaiting adulation, and strode purposefully up to the front door. A disapproving-looking Fred had quickly arrived on the doorstep from the back of the farmhouse and, in welcoming Johnny, suggested, man to man, that he take it a little slower next time, particularly when he was leaving. Fred's beloved grandchildren were due at the farm soon for a sleepover. They would occasionally play football outside on the road – on Johnny's playground – and Fred didn't want to have the task of posting them back to his daughter in an envelope.

Penelope arrived in more sedate fashion not long after, joyous in missing out on another vomit-inducing rollercoaster trip with Johnny. She had already arranged to collect CHN from Bodmin and used her time in the car to good effect in bringing him up to speed on events.

An excited Grace was standing in the doorway just behind Fred, the flash of large green ferns on her dress dramatically appearing in the silk's view as she hopped expectantly from side to side, anxious to greet the elegant barrister. CHN had decided to break with protocol by wearing something 'smart rural'. He was, after all, on holiday and in the country. He immediately offered a welcoming outstretched hand to break the ice. "Well good afternoon, Mr and Mrs Gooley," he said. "Delighted to meet you both. It's Christopher. I have heard so much about you and all this nonsense from the Ministry. You must be under quite a lot of strain. Let's hope common sense will prevail. You have appointed a good team and we are all going to do the best we can for you."

Those few opening remarks meant a lot to Fred and Grace and the front room once again swung into action like a wartime operations room, with Fred, CHN, Johnny and Penelope, perched on the plush velvet sofa and matching chairs, gathering around the coffee table to map out the location of the incoming enemy and prepare for counter attack.

Grace rushed back to the kitchen to check out the ginger biscuits and dust off the best china. She quickly looked around to make sure Flossie and Attila hadn't crept inside for a dust up. It looked like the cosy attraction of the tallboy smalls drawer was just too much for the sleepy tortoiseshell, who was undoubtedly dreaming about making ever bigger conquests in the jungle outside. Attila was snoozing after her morning walk with Fred. The coast was clear.

Penelope's neck was in a brace, which didn't stop Johnny mischievously enquiring after the solicitor's health. Penelope replied hesitantly, unsure of what was to follow: "Oh that. It's just temporary. It was in bed. I just woke up this morning with a stiff neck."

"Nothing like waking up with a stiff one, eh Pen?" Johnny chortled. "Ha ha. Did it in bed, eh? Have you thought about trying the missionary position?" For Johnny, the anticipated response disappointingly didn't materialise. A few raised eyebrows and some frowning was enough for him to move on.

He took out his papers from an ancient brown leather satchel inherited from his father, which he liked to use from time to time. CHN confirmed that he had read Penelope's excellent briefing notes and background papers and had already contributed, via video link, to the outline Statement of Case she had prepared, with Johnny's input, for onward dispatch to PINS. CHN was completely up to speed and asked Penelope to bring him up to date on the response to her threatening letter to Brigadier Bloodworth, the content of the Ministry's outline Statement of Case and what Johnny had managed to uncover in respect of the practical operation of the Ministry's safeguarding map and associated direction.

"Well Christopher," Penelope said, "I have heard nothing whatsoever from the brigadier at all but I am reliably informed that he sent my letter to Major Fox-Thrasher at Tredyedeath Depot to sort out. In all likelihood it immediately ended up in the bin." Word had soon got back to Penelope from Karensa, who learnt about the letter and its likely demise from Dickie over a pie and pint at the Tinner's Whippet.

Penelope continued. "As for the Ministry's outline Statement of Case, which is being spearheaded directly by the major, it's appalling and, to be frank, little more than what was in his original objection to the planning application. It alleges that there is a net gain in persons within the explosion zone and states that it is inappropriate to compare Fred's Christmas turkey business with his proposed development because farming operations are exempt in the Safeguarding Area Direction. It then goes on to claim that the alleged net gain in persons will, de facto, reduce the Tredyedeath Depot explosive storage capability to the detriment of the national defence strategy. It also suggests that even if a comparison were to be made with the Christmas turkey business, there would be more people in the explosion zone anyway and this is based on the extent of each dwelling's occupation. However, it assumes both the barn conversion and the extended farmhouse would be permanently occupied to the maximum bedroom capacity of each dwelling all the time. By that I mean 24/7, where no one leaves either dwelling for work, shopping, holidays, social activity or any other purpose. The calculation distorts the result ridiculously to make it look like there will be more people in the explosion zone from the new development compared to Fred's turkey business – assuming, by the way, that he does not employ anyone other than himself and Grace, which of course is not true. I should also add that the outline Statement of Case has not answered the specific questions raised by the inquiry inspector's letter which was circulated by PINS to all parties. I don't think the inspector will be very pleased if this is to be the Ministry's response to his letter. Finally, the major also claims that Fred's turkey business is not an agricultural business but an illegal factory operation which needs planning permission which, if applied for, would not be granted as the Ministry would automatically object to any such application."

CHN interjected. "I think before I make any comment, perhaps Mr Smidgen should bring me up to date on what he's discovered about the safeguarding map and explosion zones."

Johnny was chomping at the bit. "Well, CHN, it's absolutely

fascinating. I have found a serious but simple anomaly in the government's Safeguarding Map Direction. You need to firstly understand the reason why agricultural operations are exempt in calculating an explosives depot's storage capability. All military explosive storage depots are naturally located in the countryside and are chosen where the living and working population is as low as possible within the five hundred metre explosion zone, as defined on the safeguarding map. It's all about public safety. An explosives storage depot's capability – that is, its capacity to store explosives – is calculated using a formula that counts the number of people within the explosion zone who would be at risk in the event of an explosion. However, as it would be impossible to find an explosion zone anywhere in the UK within which no one lives and works, those working in agriculture are not counted in calculating an explosives depot's storage capability. So in terms of risk therefore, agricultural workers are, in effect, treated as expendable in the event of a major explosion.

"Now, what the Ministry of Defence does not want to see are planning applications for new development within the five hundred metre explosion zone which would result in a net increase in the number of people within it. If that were to happen the Ministry would be forced to recalculate the risk, the result of which would require a reduction in explosives storage to keep within the same risk profile that existed previously. It also assumes that any planning application for agricultural use – and most of it does not require planning permission anyway – would not generate any additional workers, which is largely true."

"I see, Johnny, that's very interesting background information," CHN said. "So where is this anomaly you have unearthed?"

"CHN, the anomaly is this. Intensive agricultural operations, like turkey farms, are capable of employing a significant number of people which, depending on the scale of the operation, could be described as a factory style of business even though, in planning terms, it would still be defined as an agricultural use. The government's direction does not differentiate between different intensities of agriculture because it has always been assumed that, in calculating explosive storage capability, agriculture is a low level employer whatever the nature of the business. This assumption was undoubtedly a mistake when the direction was written. You see, it is therefore possible to replace an intensive type of agricultural operation within an explosion zone with new, non-agricultural development, like housing, which would generate fewer persons than the agricultural use it is replacing. Logically such new development would reduce the risk to humans but only if the intensive agricultural operation being replaced was taken into account. If the Ministry decides that it cannot – or, more to the point, will not – legitimately undertake that comparison because of the exempt nature of agriculture in the direction, it will always find that the new development represents a net increase in humans and consequently it would be obliged to object to protect explosive storage capability. Now, if it were to make an objective comparison of existing and proposed uses to meet its own desire to protect human safety, you could have a situation where a reduction in the number of humans within the explosion zone would not only be more acceptable but also, ironically, it could provide scope to actually increase explosives storage capability whilst keeping within the same risk profile."

Everyone looked aghast. They all turned to look at CHN. He slowly lifted his Mont Blanc pen, the equivalent of a modern day quill, and part of any respectable silk's trappings, to assert his immediate thoughts. "Well. Thank you very much. I have to say that the Ministry are clearly at fault in not looking at this in the round. Whatever the direction says about agricultural operations, it must be incumbent on the Ministry, on receipt of a planning application that Trefriggit district council requested it to comment on, and as required by the drection, to reasonably assess the risk to humans by looking at all the facts. The direction may say one thing but, in law, it is perfectly reasonable to take into account what in planning parlance are known as 'material considerations' in arriving at a sensible view which might influence the Ministry's response to the council. We have to expose the Ministry's failings and I understand from you, Fred, that you had a meeting with Major Fox-Thrasher and the council in which the nub of these arguments were explained by the chief planning officer, so the Ministry really has no excuse. Absolutely no excuse at all. The other objections about illegal factory operations are all rubbish – and as for Penelope's binned letter to the brigadier, the major has behaved outrageously. He will get his comeuppance."

Johnny leaned forward. "CHN, I think we have two problems here which may affect how the Ministry responds at the inquiry. The first is that we are dealing with the intransigent major, who has taken it upon himself to resist Fred's application with very little of the full facts of the case being known to his immediate superiors in Division. I think he has bullied them into letting him to do what he likes and he is clearly going to lead the charge at the public inquiry, so to speak. The second point is that we may have stumbled on a significantly more unpalatable issue for the Ministry at a national level. I think it could now be faced with having to review the risk to human habitation within all its explosion zones across the country if it finds that there are legitimate intensive agricultural businesses within them of a scale significantly in excess of the sort of operations it had assumed existed when it determined the risk and consequently the scale of explosive storage capacity. We might be setting a wider precedent for the Ministry which, when it finds out, it may not want to face. But I think we might be able to turn that to our advantage by threatening costs and a wider exposure of the issue, which the Ministry may be reluctant to have disclosed. This may put us in a very good negotiating situation."

Slowly, CHN put his Mont Blanc down again. "Johnny, I think that's a very pertinent point and one which I would like you, Penelope, to develop in putting the pressure on the Ministry. We need to follow up your letter to the brigadier".

It was an opportune time for Grace to appear with a pot of tea and some home-made ginger biscuits, all beautifully laid out using the Gooleys' best tea service. Grace was a little late in bringing in the tea as she had to rush back upstairs, having glanced at herself in a small mirror on the kitchen wall. A quick and more successful transformation soon emerged, as Flossie lay fast asleep, motionless amongst the smalls. It certainly made Grace more animated, if not still reminiscent of a buxom lady on a saucy seaside postcard. As she leaned forward and placed the tea service on the coffee table, large swathes of her green fern dress swung around and began to consume CHN like quicksand. Quite soon he had totally vanished from view behind a mass of bouncy cream and green fabric whilst she manoeuvred herself into position. She soon spotted the slightly embarrassed barrister fighting with the 'dress creature' to regain visibility and pivoted around to help, her arms urgently pressing down on the stiff material from which he finally reappeared to regain his composure. Johnny whispered to Penelope that it looked like Grace had put on just a little too much silk for the silk. Grace flashed her eyelids apologetically.

The discussions carried on for another hour and in sensitive recognition that Fred's resources were diminishing fast, it was agreed that the next meeting with CHN would be at the public inquiry itself, but that he would liaise with Penelope and Johnny in the meantime. The general feeling was that the Ministry was heading for the abyss and, on the basis of what Fred's professional team had seen to date, its full evidence would be woefully inadequate.

CHN felt it was the right time to explain some home truths. "Fred. I think you have a good case for compensation here but I must warn you that claiming it from the Ministry, a government department, will not be easy. I am afraid that the planning inspector at the inquiry will tell me that he has no jurisdiction to award costs against the Ministry even if it is found to have acted unreasonably. However, I think I should act a little naive and make the claim anyway, to see if we can get some sympathy from the inspector, which might help us later on. Ultimately I think we may have to promote any claim by threatening to issue a writ against the Ministry and underpin this by making a complaint to the Parliamentary

Ombudsman. He has wide jurisdiction to make an award of costs as his job is to deal with complaints against government departments. All I can say at the moment is that we need to keep the pressure on and manage how it will play out."

Fred looked a little dismayed about the prospect of funding yet more legal procedures but felt comforted that a compensation route was at least available to him. "Well Mr CHN, I have now heard it all and Grace, Attila and I remain resolute and very pleased that we have a strategy to make it ugly for the Ministry and that bastard at the mine. We keep the fight going. We must keep the fight going."

CHN nodded in full agreement and tilted his head slightly to raise a question.

"Attila? Who's Attila?"

Fred realised that, over the months since it all started, he had unwittingly confided in Attila more than he realised because he didn't want to burden Grace with all the processes and technicalities now required to get them out of the mire. He was spending more time with the lonely fowl and Attila, just like a member of the family, was beginning to unconsciously creep into his one sided conversations. That it happened to be a Wirral White turkey didn't seem strange at all to Fred but CHN's question was timely and Fred could see that it probably wouldn't have been good for CHN's excellent reputation at the bar to be tarnished by rumours from jealous competing chambers that the top silk was also representing a turkey.

"Oh, she's just a friend who I confide in from time to time. I sometimes include her in my conversations when she is not, for your purposes, your client so you will have to excuse me for mentioning her."

A quick trip around the farmyard and rear paddocks soon followed, which helped CHN understand the local scene, Fred's former business activity and the relatively small scale of the proposed barn conversion and farmhouse extension over which the Ministry were making such a fuss. Attila had been in her home when she heard all the activity going on outside. She quickly got to her feet and scrambled out to see what was happening and, immediately spotting CHN as a friendly face, wandered over to say hello. Fearing that the leather on his newly acquired Barker brogues was about to be subjected to some additional and unwelcome sporadic tooling from a rather sharp-looking beak, he quickly stepped back. He was just about to ask Fred what a solitary, inquisitive turkey was still doing on the farm, when the relative tranquility was disrupted by the joyful screams of Dan and Gordon Gooley, who ran out from the farmhouse back door, arms outstretched, to greet their favourite grandfather. Fred was slightly surprised to see them a little earlier than expected and missed the opportunity to see his daughter Rozen who, as always, was late for something and had to rush off. Grace had heard a long beep of the car horn and by the time she arrived at the front door, her daughter had already vanished in a cloud of blue exhaust smoke, having bundled her two boys unceremoniously out of the car. They stood on the doorstep with their rucksacks, looking up at Granny like two lost orphans from the workhouse in a scene from *Oliver Twist*.

With Attila watching on with interest, Grace looked up to see a worried-looking Fred introducing his grandchildren to CHN, fearing that his beloved turkey's true identity was about to be innocently revealed by one of the boys. As CHN stooped down to Dan's height, Attila wandered off in a huff, insulted that she was no longer the centre of attention.

"Hello Dan," CHN said. "My name's Mr Hartlock-Naddertrout. I'm a friend of your grandad's, and he tells me that you and Gordon are here for a sleepover. How exciting! Is that your handsome-looking pet turkey who's just wandered off? He's very white, isn't he? Do you know, I think you should show him off at the village fete! I am sure Trecarsick has a village fete. I bet it would win a prize. I am sure Grandad would love it. You would like to win a prize at the fete, wouldn't you, Dan?"

Dan stood to attention, hands by his sides as he listened attentively to a voice of authority. He couldn't contain himself any more. "Brilliant! That's a brilliant idea, Mr Troutynad. I'm sure Attila would love to win a prize.

I'll ask Grandad!" He rushed off, his short attention span having been consumed too quickly for the bewildered barrister to enquire about Attila, who to CHN was clearly an important member of Fred's family who could take Dan's pet white turkey to the village fete. Luckily mum still remained the word. The cat wasn't out of the bag.

To avoid any more close calls with the grandchildren taking his mind off matters for the rest of the day, Fred gently hastened the visit to a conclusion. With the public inquiry strategy and war chest primed for action, he politely corralled his team off the premises, thanking them for their diligence and guidance. Penelope was taking CHN back to Bodmin via Trecarsick and Tredyedeath Depot to allow him to get his bearings, and Fred had a quick word in her ear about keeping Attila's identity to herself. He managed to give the same message to Johnny, and as Johnny stripped off his jacket and rolled up his sleeves in preparation for another dice with death, Fred waved his finger sternly, his other hand pointing at Dan and Gordon who had come out, holding a football, to say goodbye. Johnny got the message and drove off sedately. A thousand mechanical parts had just got the afternoon off.

Chapter 19:
Mopeds, Managers and Ski Lifts

Christmas came and went. For Fred, it was a poignant reminder of times past, of the hustle and bustle of days gone by, as he and his employees rushed to prepare festive turkeys for sale and distribution to his loyal customers. Even the aggressive discounting tactics of the big supermarkets didn't dull that exciting and frenetic period of activity in the run up to Christmas, one where Fred always made sure that, despite the nature of his business, turkey welfare remained his priority. This year Rozen had decided that she, her husband and the boys would spent Christmas with Fred and Grace and this helped to take Fred's mind off matters as they rallied round to make it a joyous occasion. Attila was never far away and Flossie would always enlighten the dark nights by gleefully depositing something wild and unrecognisable in the hallway, usually half eaten and barely alive, as a reminder that she too was part of the family. With the public inquiry still months away and resources now being borrowed, Fred and Grace could only sit and wait whilst Penelope and Johnny kept them up to date.

Dan had spent the whole Christmas period tugging sharply at Fred's increasingly stretched tweed trousers in his quest to persuade his grandfather to enter Attila in the Trecarsick village fete. Dan would regularly remind his grandad that, if that 'Mr Troutynad' thought it was a good idea, it must be. Like all small demanding children, Dan just wouldn't leave it alone and the irritation began to show on Fred's face as he wandered around holding tightly onto his well-worn leather belt as Dan's tugging attacks became increasingly more frequent.

On Thursday morning, regular as clockwork, the *Trecarsick Trumpet* landed on the doormat and quickly found its way onto the breakfast table. Rozen, having a well-earned rest from keeping her quarrelling sons apart over something typically trivial, picked it up to see what was going on locally. It was a timely arrival for there, on the front page, was a leading article to lift the Christmas gloom: the parish council's plans for a revamped, bigger-than-ever summer village fete, to take place in early June. All the oddly English favourite village fete competitions would return once again including ones for best cakes, jam, knitted things and small horses along with stalls selling plants, truggs, bird boxes, strange-looking hats, ancient rusty garden tools and water saving devices. The local car club had offered to bring along a few old bangers and the parish were delighted that well known district councillor and steam fan Bert Sloggett had offered to fire up his rusty old traction engine, Betsy. The article quoted the joking Bert that Betsy's appearance would be on condition that everyone stood back a bit as she had failed her last boiler pressure test inspection, and that was twenty years ago. For those who knew Bert, he wasn't joking. The article went on to highlight the parish council's hard-working village fete sub-committee, who had worked tirelessly long into the winter nights in the back room of the Tinner's Whippet to plan new and exciting competitions. For this year, the sub-committee chairman was proud to announce competitions for the hairiest dog, most irritating mother-in-law, and even the scariest looking local, not in fancy dress. In reality, such distorted ideas were probably the result of too many pints of the pub's appropriately named Adit Ale, a strong brew created by Steve the landlord in his micro-brewery at the back of the Whippet to commemorate the tin mining of times gone by. The article suggested, rather bravely, that the sub-committee's overeager inventiveness might result in an additional unintended competition: the nastiest brawl. However, it was one of the saner competitions that caught Rozen's eye: the prettiest fowl.

The dedicated website address and contact number details were all there and in her quest to quieten Dan and put her father out of his misery, Rozen was soon grappling with her mobile technology. Before Fred had time to consult with the intended exhibit, Rozen had successfully tuned into the interactive website, completed the online competition entry form and quickly hit the send button. Attila was now a formal entrant in the prettiest fowl competition at the village fete, whether she liked it or not.

Rozen made sure for Dan's sake that Attila's entry in the village fete was Grandad's idea and he was soon rewarded with a big grandson kiss. Dan had got his way and there was no going back. At least Fred wouldn't have to keep pulling his trousers up any more. The family left on New Year's Day and a sense of quiet reigned again at Feathers Farm.

***

It was now early February and Division's postbox was, once again, graced by another well-crafted letter from the offices of Steal, Cash and Scamper about the impending public inquiry. Penelope had sharpened her pencil this time in the way only Penelope could and CHN had given her ten out of ten for effort. Severe criticisms of the Ministry flew out of her damning missive like missiles, targeted at the woeful failure to address the specific questions raised by the planning inspector, the lack of any credible support for its objection and the factual inaccuracies in its outline Statement of Case. Penelope also made it clear that her client was now seriously considering pursuing the Ministry for costs in whatever procedure was available to them. It was pretty trenchant stuff.

Brigadier Bloodworth was on leave and his staff sergeant recognised the respected law firm's logo and, from the letter's heading, the subject matter. Knowing how Penelope's last letter was dealt with and in view of the brigadier's absence, the sergeant quickly walked along the corridor to the relevant office, knocked once and entered sharply. Sensing a uniform and seemingly operating a code of honour, none of the four civil servants who shared the dingy office looked up so the sergeant walked a few paces towards the corner desk occupied by Wally Dinsmore. The sergeant leaned forward slightly and coughed deliberately to attract his attention. Wally's head rose slowly to focus on the smart uniform and the distinctive envelope which was about to be deposited squarely on his desk.

The staff sergeant's impending command came as no surprise. "It's another bolshie letter from that woman solicitor in Truro about the Tredyedeath Depot public inquiry. Bloodworth's on leave. You'd better deal with it like you did with all the others. It's in your hands. I'll tell the brigadier on his return."

With that, the staff sergeant swivelled on his steel-tipped heels and made a swift retreat, leaving Wally staring at the envelope whilst his disinterested colleagues remained motionless. Wally's careful, slow motion pick up, followed by the merest of peeps into the envelope at eyelevel, was textbook stuff for someone trained to open a suspect package – but not to deal with the sort of explosive material from Penelope that Wally knew inwardly it contained. He was still recovering from his last briefing with the brigadier but quickly decided that, for his own sanity and general health, it would be entirely consistent with the brigadier's previous instructions to send the letter of venom directly to the very depot to which it was, after all, targeted. An official internal envelope was duly produced into which the offending letter was deposited. Dinsmore's barely legible writing resembled an eerily authentic scrawl from the deceased brought back by an ouija board séance as his trembling hand scrawled 'Major Fox-Thrasher, Tredyedeath Depot' before juggling the package into the internal post tray.

A day later, Penelope's letter duly arrived on Dickie's desk and, from a quick perusal, its contents didn't really surprise him. The Gooley camp were on the offensive and the major hadn't done anything to help himself following the last letter from Penelope which, of course, Dickie suspected had been 'dispatched' by the major quicker than one of Fred's Christmas turkeys. A copy of her latest missive was, as always, duly made for the blue file before its onward passage to the major's empty office. Dickie knew that the time was approaching where the Ministry's full Statement of Case for the inquiry, the important proof of evidence, had to be lodged with PINS to comply with the mandatory six-week submission date. It was all set out in that handy little PINS booklet Dickie had given the major which, to date, seemed to be gathering dust.

The major was due back shortly from his visit to brief his colleague, his salvation, Major Augustus Blitherington, an explosives expert bar none who would be his star witness at the inquiry. He was sure Blitherington and his world class knowledge of explosives would save the day and put everything right.

It wasn't long before the sound of an army Land Rover pulled into the car park and came to an abrupt halt. The clicking of a handbrake and loose rattle of the driver's door was quickly followed by the officious sharp clicking sound of steel-tipped heels gracing the entrance hall and stairs of the office building. Fox-Thrasher had returned and, appearing to be in a reasonably good mood, was heading back to his office with the latest copy of *Bang!* tucked under his arm like a baton. Dickie felt that Blitherington must have said all the right things but knew that it could all change once the major had sight of Penelope's letter. Dickie waited patiently for the 'Blue Streak' moment, which he reckoned would be in about thirty seconds.

It took twenty. Dickie's door swung open, and the major walked in, foaming at the mouth. It was either incandescent rage or he had contracted a bad dose of rabies. He could barely speak. "What the, what, what the, what, what, what, what, what…"

Dickie looked down to avert his smile as he listened to an uncannily realistic impression of a 50cc moped he once owned as a teenager. He looked up, raised his eyebrows and cocked his head to one side, like an elocution teacher, enticing out those words which seem to have become firmly lodged in the major's throat.

The major tried again. "What the, what the…… bloody hell is this women trying to do? She can't threaten us like that. She has no right. No right at all. She's insisted we withdraw our objection. They're my explosives and her turkey shagging farmer client can go screw himself. When we get to the public inquiry, I am going to personally wrap some SSPHE round her insulting letter and stick it up her…"

"I think you'll find, sir, that she can, as you say, threaten us with reasoned argument. That's what the public inquiry is for. It's a democratic process. As for the SSPHE, I don't think that would be a good idea, sir. Anyway, we took delivery of the twelve hour sticks, so she would have plenty of time to extract them before they went off."

"Don't get smart with me, Lovely. It's all bollocks. Blitherington will sort it all out at the inquiry. They haven't got a case. Just you wait. Where's your waste bin?"

Dickie pointed to the side of his desk and ducked his head as, in one smooth manoeuvre, the major ceremoniously ripped the letter to shreds, screwed it up into a ball and impressively lobbed it over the captain's head straight into the army issue mesh bin. Dickie caught his attention as he turned to leave the office. "Sir, I ought to just remind you that you have about a week to submit your full Statement of Case, which, just to be clear, is your proof of evidence on which you will be cross-examined at the inquiry. It's all in the PINS booklet, which I am sure you have read. All parties have to produce one and they are swapped six weeks before the inquiry. If Major Blitherington is to appear, he will have to produce a full Statement of Case as well. I'll send you an email reminder just to be sure. I do think it's quite an important part of the process."

"Bollocks to all that, Lovely!" the major shouted. "I'll just resend the outline Statement of Case. That'll do. I've got more important things to do than pander to some stupid planning process, and the pathetic paper-pushing parasitic planners and their lawyer leeches. Blitherington and I will make mincemeat of that Breakage woman when she cross-examines me. I suppose the inspector will be some faceless civil servant jobsworth, filling in forms and ticking boxes. Another bloody waster. I'm going down the mine." Little did the major realise that it wouldn't be Penelope who would be cross-examining him but CHN, who had instructions from Fred to take no prisoners, an action which Fred, in a lighter moment, joked that the major should be entirely familiar with.

The major then performed a 'Thunderbird' manoeuvre: a swift exit from the office, descent of the stairs, followed by a rapid and purposeful walk across the car park and access road towards the mine, often interspersed with a 'happy hop'. Every now and then he swung the all-important mine alarm fob and key chain around with his right hand like a cheerleader. It only took about thirty seconds for the 'Thunderbird' manoeuvre to ensure that the major was fully out of sight and in the mine.

Dickie's growing concern for the major's demeanour led him to wonder where it would all end. His arrogant dismissal of the public inquiry process and its participants – except, of course, for himself and his secret weapon, Major Blitherington – seemed increasingly likely to lead the Ministry into shark-filled waters with an inflatable dinghy. To top it off, his increasingly lengthy periods inside the mine were – well, just inexplicable. Dickie would occasionally chuckle at the irony that a mine full of explosives should, for the major, be such a place of apparent solitude.

During the time they'd been together, Dickie and Karensa had become quite close and Dickie was now confiding in her about the major's irrational behaviour and how it might somehow shape his post army career – not to mention their possible life together. He felt instinctively that change was coming and drew comfort in Karensa's warm support for him in whatever direction it took. Their regular visits to the snug in the Whippet, which had become their confession box, were the source of much tittle tattle amongst the village womenfolk, who were hoping that the parish church bells would soon sing out again for a good old fashioned wedding.

***

A few days before the Statements of Case had to be submitted, Penelope and Johnny arranged a telephone conference with CHN in his London chambers. CHN's traditionally furnished office had a rare and welcome view from a sash window over the iconic Inner Temple's historic buildings, many having been rebuilt and restored after the Blitz. Despite the window's ample size, the courtyard configuration did a surprisingly good job of shielding most of the available sunlight from all but a small part of CHN's office. This, combined with its dark, Dickensian interior, contributed to a solemn yet somehow appropriate setting for a place of great thought and study. The dark panelled walls were graced with tall mahogany bookshelves consistent with the trappings of a barrister's cerebral existence. Rows of matching leather-bound volumes of court judgments, planning law encyclopedias and reference material lined the room awaiting their recall to feed another case. On one side lay a not inconsiderable number of new briefings, all neatly bound in pink ribbon – a centuries-old tradition – awaiting assessment by the master to extract the fundamental arguments which would win the day. A well-used modern coffee machine sat inconspicuously in a corner which, together with a laptop perched on CHN's well-worn, leather-topped nineteenth century desk, provided the merest of hints that this was indeed the twenty-first century.

The telephone conference was cost effective in managing Fred's diminishing resources at distance, and Johnny's proof of evidence, his full Statement of Case, for the inquiry had been sent to CHN in advance. This enabled him to comment and, if necessary, suggest additional evidence to reinforce the arguments which would unequivocally demonstrate that Fred's planning application should be granted. The phone technology came to life and it wasn't long before, subject to a few changes, CHN felt happy to sign off Johnny's evidence for onward submission to PINS.

"Well done, Johnny and Penelope," he said. "I think we have a very good case. I noted from a letter sent via PINS that Clifford Stump is the planning inspector. Perhaps I should have mentioned it earlier but that is excellent news. Stumpy's a no nonsense chap, a senior inspector with a reputation for cutting to the chase. I've been in front of him before and he gets on with it. I think the major's going to be in for a shock."

Johnny and Penelope had agreed they would meet in Penelope's office for the telephone conference, which took about an hour to complete. Once CHN was off the line, Johnny grabbed the opportunity to pass comment on a pair of crutches propped up in the corner. Penelope looked almost normal although he did recall catching a glimpse of a knee bandage when he'd been shown into her office by a secretary – which was in itself unusual, as Penelope normally came down to meet him in reception. He put his pen down and leaned back. Penelope braced herself. "Don't tell me, Pen, you lost your balance running? Were you chasing him, or was he chasing you?"

Penelope was a little surprised, almost relieved that the subject had not revolved around sex, though it was clearly heading in that direction. "It's Penelope, by the way, Johnny. Well actually, I was chasing him. In fact I was chasing a lot of 'hims'." Penelope had gone skiing with a gang of friends and in her clumsy attempt to manoeuvre onto a permanently moving ski chair, caught one ski on a handrail and was unceremoniously ejected face down after only a few yards. Luckily the faint outline of her body in the deep snow, with the back of her skis protruding vertically, helped the giggling staff to locate her presence for a quick extraction and ride to the medical centre.

"Oh, so it's back to the missionary position then, eh Pen? Surely you must have got some practice in after the neck brace incident? No leg over needed, eh? Ha ha!" Johnny giggled.

Sex had indeed reared its ugly head again. Penelope put on her 'sexist' expression, kept solely to deal with Johnny's politically incorrect banter. It showed both forgiveness and pity in equal measure but Penelope knew inwardly that the optimistic Johnny would probably read only forgiveness – which was why he was such a repeat offender. In truth, Penelope didn't mind that much as, whatever Johnny came up with, it somehow lightened her day and certainly made a momentary welcome change from wading through pages of heavy duty legal stuff. Not that she would give him any encouragement.

It was time to move on – literally. In one action Penelope, making no sound and completely expressionless, pointed at her office door, looking for all the world like she had crossed over to the dark side in a scene from *Invasion of the Body Snatchers*. Johnny could see that, in view of her incapacities, and with the work tasks completed, he was required to show himself off the premises.

***

The closing date for the submission of the full Statement of Case to PINS came and went and, as Penelope predicted, the Ministry's case had not been expanded on. It comprised a terse letter from the major accompanied by what amounted to a repackaged outline Statement of Case and an indication that Major Blitherington would attend to give evidence on the day. As all evidence was required to be submitted in advance of the inquiry, the major had clearly breached the rules, suggesting not only disrespect but an arrogance that his interpretation of them would be on his terms.

Following a further brief telephone conference with CHN and Johnny over the Ministry's approach, it was decided that another letter from Penelope to Division would make no difference and, like the others, would probably end up in the waste bin. She and Johnny had all the ammunition they needed and it would be left to CHN to pull the trigger. The Gooleys were ready for action.

***

Dickie had largely managed to escape the build-up to the public inquiry because of the major's insistence that he, and he alone, would handle it. Dickie's walks with Fluffy up to Trecarsick village shop to see Karensa in his spare time had now become so regular that they were almost part of the landscape and his relationship with Karensa continued to head unabated in the direction of the altar. It was also a relief for Dickie to be away from the increasingly unstable major.

***

Cordelia was determined to continue the fight for her old friends Fred and Grace and she had a secret plan to keep their plight in the local limelight. She commandeered the shop's *Trumpet* pavement display board to try some subliminal advertising. She knew from experience that Trevedic Penhaligon's infamous headlines had a shelf life of a couple of days – which provided her with five days of free space before it was needed again. This gave Cordelia the opportunity to insert marginally cleaner versions of the local placard material that had been used so effectively by locals on that now infamous day of the meeting at Tredyedeath Depot with Jim Stern et al. In addition, the placards, which had been used in support of the Gooleys' planning application at the district council's planning committee meeting, provided Cordelia with more than enough 'headlines' for her campaign in the run up to the start of the inquiry.

To ram home the message, Cordelia also made fliers for wide distribution around the village. They were on the counter at the village shop, where Karensa duly inserted one into every shopping bag, whilst others were dished out with drinks at the Tinner's Whippet. They were tied to lampposts, the bus shelter, garden gates, and the parish council noticeboard. One even made a fleeting appearance on the parish church noticeboard before it was quickly removed for being a little inappropriate. Cordelia was never going to win the war she had with the indignant vicar by conspicuously pinning a luminescent 'Get behind the Gooleys' flyer between the evensong programme and a notice for the service of Confirmation of six local schoolchildren.

It wasn't long before snappy sayings like 'Save the day: Support your Gooleys', 'Stand up for the Gooleys' and, rather inventively, 'Don't let the Gooleys get a kicking' quickly became the words on everyone's lips. Everyone was fired up and Cordelia had another couple of tricks up her sleeve for the day of the public inquiry. To bolster Fred and Grace's fight and to show that she was right behind them, she dropped off a set of all the campaign material at Feathers Farm.

***

Jim Stern was at his desk looking at a pile of paperwork which, despite the previous day's heavy workload, had got predictably taller. The chief planning officer had kept in regular contact with Penelope over the preceding months. He knew that the council's resources were limited and it therefore came as a welcome relief that Penelope's professional team included the use of a leading silk. He could prioritise his workload and resources particularly as, at his end of his telescope, the Gooleys' planning application wasn't the biggest fish in the sea. In any event it wasn't the council's battle to fight. It had already made its mind up to grant Fred's planning permission on the basis of a reasoned assessment, which had arrived at the same conclusion as Penelope's team that Fred's development proposals would have no adverse impact on public safety. It was the Ministry of Defence who had other ideas. It was the Ministry's decision to request a public inquiry and it was the Ministry's fight to have.

Jim's full Statement of Case had been lodged in accordance with the PINS rules and, as required in the regulations, it explained why the council were prepared to grant planning permission. It also contained a draft planning permission for the inspector to consider on a without prejudice basis as, ultimately, if the Secretary of State for Planning accepted his recommendation to grant permission, it would be the district council's responsibility to ensure that permission was correctly implemented. Jim had done his job.

Chapter 20:
Elevenses, Mischief and the Medieval

Two weeks before the inquiry, Fred received a phone call from Trevedic Penhaligon, who had decided to run an article in the *Trumpet* about the inquiry and wanted to get some background facts from Fred plus a few pictures of Fred and Grace at Feathers Farm. Trevedic had already contacted the major at Tredyedeath Depot for an official statement but, from what he knew about the major's arrogance, wasn't surprised when his calls weren't returned. Despite Trevedic's professional desire to maintain an even hand in his reporting, privately he wanted Fred to succeed and he knew inwardly that this would inevitably influence his article's slant, which could readily be defended by the major's unwillingness to give his side of the story. A date was arranged for the meeting with Fred which would give Trevedic enough time to meet his deadline for the edition of the *Trumpet* immediately prior to the opening of the public inquiry the following Tuesday. In his own mind, Trevedic was celebrating another classic headline which he had already crafted. Its launch on the locals and his long-harboured dreams of a call from Fleet Street was just a few days away.

Coincidentally, Fred had reluctantly agreed to meet his bank manager, Dennis Blackstaff, at the farm on the same morning as his meeting with Trevedic. Blackstaff had insisted on meeting urgently but he wouldn't say why. Fred was more than a little nervous. After all, he had signed everything he needed to give the bank's head office the blood transfusion it required. What could Blackstaff possibly want now? He decided to tell Grace that it was just a routine meeting. Nothing to worry about.

***

It was a typical morning at the farm. Grace was coming to the end of a self-imposed smoke and Flossie was fast asleep on some warm towels in the airing cupboard, all four paws and nose twitching in response to either a happy dream sequence or the result of the overnight consumption of something wild. Attila was outside walking with Fred, who had just been for his usual thoughtful stroll around the paddocks.

The sheep's head knocker rattled to announce the arrival of the first visitor. It was, as Fred preferred, Dennis Blackstaff. Fred answered the door, his large frame casting an overpowering shadow over the compact and smartly suited bank manager, their contrasting sizes exacerbated by his location on the bottom of the two front door steps. Fred ushered Blackstaff in, his 'bank issue' briefcase tucked tightly under his arm, but only as far as the hallway. He was anxious to have answers and didn't want the bank manager to use the comfort of Fred's front room as a tactical softener to break bad news. He wanted answers now.

Sensing Fred's desire to take control of the situation, the noticeably nervous Blackstaff decided to take the initiative. "Thank you for seeing me, Mr Gooley, at such short notice. I'll come straight to the point. Head Office has given me instructions to sell Feathers Farm now, as a distressed sale, because of your financial situation. However, I have discretion to make the final decision and I want to have a look around the farm."

Fred looked visibly shocked, his cheeks taking on the volcanic rouge of one of Grace's more flamboyant dresses. He heard Grace lumbering around upstairs in the front bedroom, which was fortuitous as he didn't want her involved in what he feared might follow. To be safe, and without saying a word, he grabbed the bank manager's arm and marched him down the corridor and through the back door like an errant schoolboy heading for dire punishment. Blackstaff briefly caught sight of one of Cordelia's posters, 'Hands off the Gooleys', on the hall table and wondered what was going to happen next. Once outside, Fred headed towards the slaughterhouse with Blackstaff still in his grip, only just managing to keep up. Fred finally came to an abrupt halt and swung the bank manager around so his back was facing the slaughterhouse's rickety door, which was propped open by an old wedge. The rare anger on Fred's volcanic face was very clear to Blackstaff as he hesitantly stepped back.

"That's not what we agreed when I completed the extra guarantees for you last year!" Fred raged. "You knew there would be a public inquiry into my planning application and that until that process was complete, I would not be able to repay my debt. All my resourses are tied up in Feathers Farm. I told you that the professional advice I received was that the chances of obtaining planning permission were good. You accepted that I was going to incur more costs in instructing professionals to act on my behalf and that your money-grabbing colleagues in head office would still be protected by the value of the Farm as it stood, even if planning permission was refused. That was the basis on which I agreed to sign more guarantees for you. It makes no sense for Head Office to take this stance now. The inquiry is in a matter of days and I am being represented. This is dishonest, absolutely bloody dishonest."

"Mr Gooley, I appreciate what you say, but we at the bank didn't anticipate the last time we last spoke that the national recession was going to get worse," Blackstaff reasoned. "It's not just you. The bank is now calling in all its debts, whatever the reason." Fred moved his large frame towards the bank manager, who stepped back further, only to find himself now standing in the open doorway to the slaughterhouse. "Look, Mr Gooley. I understand from the bank's advisors that it could take another six months for your planning application to be decided. So the public inquiry is not the end of the process, and your debt remains exposed and growing."

"Of course I know that, you stupid little man," Fred shouted, "but we will have a pretty good idea by then which way it is likely to go. Hasn't anyone advised you of that? Anyway, my debt isn't exposed, is it? It's not exposed at all. Well, is it?"

"Well, err, no, not exactly, but your costs are still rising and we don't want them to get out of hand. We are thinking of you."

"Bollocks. You're thinking of yourselves. You don't give a shit about me and Grace. I know exactly what my costs are and what they will be in six months' time. Believe me, they are never far from my mind every waking second. Now. Tell me exactly what is this discretion you claim to have that gives you the absolute power to ruin me? Or are you just the unfortunate messenger sent to screw me?"

Blackstaff had never before seen the normally patient Fred so angry and decided to stay cool as his increasingly heightened priority was to leave the farm in one piece. "Well, at the moment I have not been forced by Head Office to dispose of the farm but if I don't, I have to give a very good reason why. Mr Gooley, the time may come when I simply won't have that discretion. I have the planning application details here in my briefcase. I would just like to look around the farm to see how it relates to the buildings to be converted. It will give me a clearer idea of the investment value you want to extract and the bank's exposure to the risk. I can then take a decision."

Fred's head was spinning. He was beginning to lose all sense of rationality when the front door knocker rattled again. It was Trevedic. Fred looked at Blackstaff and sarcastically opened his arms to invite the embattled bank manager to look around but by now eye contact had gone and Blackstaff was too busy fumbling in his briefcase to extract the proposed development plans.

"Someone's at the front door," Fred said. "It's all yours. Take as long as you like. We wouldn't like your discretion to become an indiscretion, would we, Mr Blackstaff?"

Grace was still busy in the front bedroom and was oblivious to what was going on but Attila had heard the commotion and decided to take a look. She scrambled to her feet and wandered out of her barn home to see Fred walking purposefully back into the farmhouse. She could tell from his raised voice and body posture that whoever he was talking to was not a friend. Her eyes caught sight of the troubled Blackstaff, who was still fumbling in his briefcase. This must be the enemy, she thought; he deserved a closer look. The foreboding fowl picked up her pace and headed across the courtyard, head slightly down and eyes focused in readiness for a pre-emptive early strike if the need arose. Blackstaff heard the rapid sound of clawed feet heading his way and looked up to see wisps of dust now curling off the Wirral White's claws as she headed directly for him. He pulled his briefcase and partially extracted papers against his chest and started to reverse towards the dark innards of the slaughterhouse. Attila arrived in a cloud of dust to see the faint shadow of the bank manager standing just inside the doorway, looking around for an implement to defend his person from certain disembowelling. It was an opportune moment. Attila looked down at the old wedge propping the door open and with one sweeping action of her strong right claw, immediately flicked it backwards and stepped sharply out of the way. The slaughterhouse door gave an eerie creek and rapidly slammed shut with a loud bang, its external safety latch dropping firmly to incarcerate anyone unfortunate to be inside. That unfortunate person was Blackstaff, whose face escaped serious modification by just a few millimetres.

By this time Flossie had graced the courtyard with her presence, and was immediately distracted by the sight of something alive, edible and moving fast in the direction of a small opening in the side wall of the ancient slaughterhouse. With no time to lose, she took haste to see if it would do as elevenses and managed to squeeze through the opening to find herself in almost total darkness. She stopped to listen intently, taking no comfort from the faintest of daylight which permeated the building's innards through its sole grimy courtyard window.

Back in the farmhouse, the *Trumpet's* hack, with his long coat, fedora and camera in hand, struck a recognisable pose. Fred greeted him warmly. The front room beckoned and, hearing a friendly voice, Grace came downstairs to greet him.

Fred couldn't resist showing his anger. "My bloody bank manager's here and he's causing me grief. I better go and see what he's doing around the back. He's threatening to foreclose, you know. Bloody outrageous! He claims that as we are in a recession, the bank's calling in its loans but I provided all the financial guarantees they wanted. Trevedic, come with me. I may need your help if I can't control myself."

Fred and Trevedic had known each other for quite a few years and they always got on well although Fred felt that the hack never seemed to be off duty, which made him a little guarded. Fred was not the type to court publicity but Trevedic had come to his aid when he launched his campaign to stop the big supermarkets unfairly discounting and monopolising the Christmas turkey market. Although the campaign had ultimately failed, they had shared many nights and pints of Steve's Adit Ale in the Tinner's Whippet thinking up campaign slogans, 'Don't let the supermarkets ruin the Gooleys' being one of the more successful ones despite attracting the ire of the council's trading standards department.

Trevedic had been listening attentively. "Fred, if there is a story in it, I will be delighted to help. It might just make Blackstaff a bit more sensitive to your position if he knows who I am and what havoc I can wreak. The bank won't want any more bad publicity than they are already getting at the moment with this recession. Hang on a mo! I can see the headline: 'Bank bully boy Blackstaff squeezes the Gooleys'.

Fred let out a rare laugh. "I think we might have trading standards on our backs again, Trevedic."

Fred and Trevedic wandered out into the rear courtyard, only to hear a muffled voice coming from the slaughterhouse and the sight of Attila looking rather proud of herself in front of its now firmly closed door. Fred could hear the muffled sound getting louder and more desperate.

"Help, help. Can anyone hear me? I need to get out of this building now! Help, help!"

Fred called out, "Who's in there and what do you think you are doing?"

"Mr Gooley. It's Dennis. Dennis Blackstaff. The door slammed shut. A turkey did it. What is this place? It's dark but I can just see knives, chains, strange implements and overhead rails with big hooks – and a concrete trench." Dennis was of course describing the equipment for dispatching and the evisceration trench but Fred saw an opportunity for mischief making with the beleaguered bank manager and winked at Trevedic.

"Oh, all that stuff. Grace collects medieval instruments of torture, you know. It's her hobby. I think it's a bit weird myself and I don't allow it in the house. She's been collecting it for years. I didn't realise there were so many ways of torturing someone to death. I don't go in there myself as she says the equipment is haunted by those who died in excruciating pain. You say a turkey locked you in? That's a new one on me. Oh dear! I can see the door latch is jammed. Do you know, the last time that happened it took me two hours to open it. Bloody latch. Let me have a look."

A potential two-hour incarceration in the temple of doom was not what Dennis wanted to hear but he nevertheless thanked Fred for his efforts to extract him from the haunted torture chamber, his voice now trembling in fear, not helped by his phasmophobia: a fear of ghosts.

Just then Flossie, who had been biding her time in the darkness, heard her elevenses scurrying about in the dust and old feathers. It was too dark to see but it was time to strike. She hunkered down, stretched out her neck, wiggled her bum and back legs into launch position, and leapt forward towards the sound of the target. In one sense it was a spectacular miss but in another, it was perfectly timed. In her instinctive and failed quest for that snack, her right paw caught the side of a large spade, its precarious position fully exposed by the ensuing domino effect on a further four spades and a collection of nasty-looking spiky tools, all previously vertical and quite happily minding their own business. Any hard-up rural orchestra short of a few instruments would have been proud of the clattering crescendo that followed and, in coming so soon after Fred's illustrative description of Grace's hobby, the now trembling Dennis came to only one conclusion: medieval ghosts of the tortured dead were coming his way to vent their revenge. He looked around and in his quest to hide, caught his heel on the lip of the evisceration trench and started to fall backwards towards an uncertain outcome – but one that was a lot less certain than the many turkeys who had been there before him. Arms now flailing wildly, it was miraculous that certain back injury or worse was prevented by a large suspended hook which, fortuitously, caught the collar of Dennis' buttoned suit jacket, leaving him dangling helplessly from an overhead rail.

Dennis' attempt to emulate that cinematic masterpiece, the Arbogast stairs scene from *Psycho,* came just at the moment Fred managed to release the reluctant door latch and prise the door open. Dennis could have been forgiven for squinting had the sun been shining but it was Trevedic's flashgun frantically working like a nightclub strobe as it lit up the building's sinister innards in capturing the bank manager, dangling like a giant suited turkey awaiting its fate.

Trevedic had only one thing on his mind and it didn't take long for the headline to appear in his head as he pointed at his camera and looked over to Fred. "Thanks Fred. That was a great photo opportunity. I think I have got some great 'bankers' there. Ha ha. How about 'Turkey Traps Macabre Meddling Manager in Supernatural Slaughterhouse'?

Fred smiled in acknowledgement and poked his head around the door to observe Dennis' futile Houdini-esque shaking in a veiled attempt to release himself. He could see that, unlike Houdini, he wasn't going anywhere, anytime soon. "Hello, Dennis. Looks like you are in a spot of bother. Well you must at least be pleased that we got the door open? Do you know what? I think I might have trouble tying down Trevedic! He's got so many pictures of you – and a cracking headline to go with them. You know what journalists are like when they get a story. Goodness knows what your boss is going to think when he sees the pictures and reads all about it. Of course, I think it's way too small for the *Trecarsick Trumpet.* I think this is one of those stories for that interweb thing. What's it called? The social twitfacetube? Of course, if the bank were to stand by my financial arrangements, which we had agreed to, and let me carry on with my development proposals – the public inquiry and all that – I am sure I can persuade my friend Trevedic here to keep this all under wraps. Funnily enough, he is more interested in the public inquiry; he actually came here today to see me and Grace about running a story on it. If there is no inquiry because you have sucked all my assets from me, the only story he's got left is the one about you, Dennis. From where I am standing it's no contest. What do you think, Dennis? Oh, and as an added bonus I will even lift you off that unfortunate hook."

Dennis could see that his negotiating options were non-existent. There was no Plan B and explaining to his wife and bosses how he ended up being trapped on a hook in a haunted torture chamber by a turkey would be just a tad tricky. Social media would have a field day and his career path would start going downhill as fast as an out of control skiing Penelope. A few silent nods of agreement was all that was needed. Fred got his way and there was no more to be said. One large bear hug soon followed and the bank manager was off the hook and back on his feet. Trevedic's camera rattled off a few more 'bankers' for safe keeping just in case Dennis changed his mind. Dennis picked up his standard issue briefcase, pushed Fred's still unseen plans back inside and dusted himself off. Fred ushered the quiet and still shaking bank manager through the farmhouse and to the safety of his car.

An official letter from 'Mr Blackstaff' arrived on cue a few days later to confirm that, "having given the well designed proposals a lot of detailed consideration and in view of the bank's excellent relationship with the Gooleys, Head Office are happy to maintain their existing financial arrangements."

Flossie wandered back out of the darkness of the slaughterhouse with a mouse in her mouth. She was very surprised but delighted to find an extra bowl of warm creamy milk with that night's evening meal.

Chapter 21:
Stumpy, Scorn and Swinging Doors

It was the end of March. The day of the public inquiry. The day when Major Fox-Thrasher would finally have his opportunity to defend his beloved explosives depot, come hell or high water. PINS accepted the district council request to hold the inquiry in Trecarsick village hall because it concerned a local issue. It was nine o'clock in the morning, an hour before the inquiry was due to commence, when a guilty-looking Cordelia sneaked out of the village hall to meet the assembled but quizzical throng of grey-haired Gooley supporters, their well-used placards standing to attention ready to do battle. It was fine and dry but with the throng's average age matching that of the late 1940's village hall, it wasn't long before flasks of tea appeared accompanied by some very nice home-made lemon drizzle cake Grace had baked especially for the occasion. Just the sort of sustenance required for any old fashioned protest.

At 9.30, the inspector, Clifford Stump, aka Stumpy, arrived wearing an anonymous-looking civil service suit and carrying his standard issue PINS briefcase. A stocky, good-looking man of an age that showed experience in the lonely life of conducting public inquiries, his face and demeanor suggested that here was a man firm and fair. However, his grey, flowing Italian-style locks gave perhaps just a hint that his real passion was the Ferrari in his garage, waiting for him to come home and terrorise the neighbourhood. But you would never know it. He walked through the throng of aging protesters towards the village hall and as he gave a polite "Good morning," they scrambled to attention and raised their placards proudly in unison. He smiled and remained silent, knowing that under strict rules of engagement, making small talk with any 'side' might suggest a lack of impartiality. However, just a few minutes later he returned from the hall looking a little irritated and immediately enquired whether the throng's ringleader was present. Cordelia, having already given the commanding Stumpy the once over, gleefully took no time in proudly stepping forward to introduce herself in only the way a woman can.

Clifford felt justified to break his vow of silence – but not because of Cordelia's fluttering eyelashes. "Good morning, Mrs Craddock. It's a pleasure to meet you. As you will have probably guessed, I am the inspector appointed to conduct this public inquiry. I do of course recognise that in a democratic society, everyone has the right to protest and I have no problem with you and your colleagues making your point. However, I noticed on the walls of your lovely village hall that the framed pictures of eminent past parish council dignitaries have been, shall we say, doctored? My suspicions, not to mention some experience in the matter, tell me someone is attempting to influence my recommendation to the Secretary of State for Planning. I can tell you that I am immune from such subversions and my instincts tell me that the obvious culprit would, in fact, be you. Would I be right, Mrs Craddock?"

Having worked herself up into a lather to visually seduce Stumpy, Cordelia was now finding it difficult to look remotely insulted by his suggestion that something mischievous was going on. She wasn't helped by her troop, who had suddenly worked out what she had been up to. In full view of the inspector and in a classic regressive trait symptomatic of the elderly, they started giggling like school children at someone's misfortune. Cordelia straightened her back in a vain attempt to be affronted but the game was up.

Stumpy saved her the blushes. "You see, Mrs Craddock, I would be surprised if last year's chairman was in fact a large white turkey named Demelza Friggins as that rather nice brass name plaque underneath its picture suggests – or that her predecessor Treave Tregowan in the adjacent picture was prepared to be photographed with his pipe-smoking wife wearing a loud dress and holding up a brace of plucked turkeys. My guess, and please do correct me if I am wrong, is that the former is one of Mr Gooley's Christmas products and the latter is in fact a picture of the proud applicants themselves, Mr and Mrs Gooley. As to each of the remaining dozen pictures, you clearly ran out of photos and resorted to inserting some rather lewd posters that are remarkably similar to the messages on those placards being waved by your colleagues behind you. Now look, Mrs Craddock, I am sure you mean well but this is a public inquiry, not a theatre, and you certainly don't need those sort of props to make your case. You've got five minutes to restore the dignity of those former eminent parish councillors and make the hall the respectable place it should be for this inquiry."

Before Cordelia had time to say anything, the inspector leaned over, put his left hand on her shoulder and whispered in her right ear. In the forlorn hope that it might just be the offer of a dinner date at the Tinner's Whippet, she cocked her head in anticipation. "Oh, and by the way, please don't tell anyone but do you think I could have the poster that says 'Don't Stump on the Gooleys'? I thought that one was particularly clever and I have just the place to hang it in my downstairs toilet."

Cordelia smiled. At least Stumpy was human – but she could see it was futile to resist the good-looking inspector's demands. She nodded her head in acknowledgement and, waving her arms in the direction of the hall, beckoned her colleagues over for the rapid clean up whilst the inspector stood outside looking officiously at his watch. Cordelia returned in time and secretively smuggled Stump the rolled up poster, which he quietly slid inside his jacket before he returned to the hall to prepare for the inquiry. Cordelia's gang of protestors followed him in peacefully two by two, like a flock of choirboys, their placards held high like ceremonial crucifixes.

Shortly afterwards, all the main parties started arriving and it wasn't long before the village hall was busy with the sound of papers being shuffled in and out of plastic boxes, the clattering of chairs and tables being rearranged and the rattle of the occasional protest placard falling on the floor whilst some older protester dozed off. Groups huddled together and whispered, interrupted by the occasional knowing hand wave at someone recognisable across the hall. The inspector sat quietly at the head of two facing rows of tables with CHN, Penelope, Johnny, Fred and Grace on the left and Jim Stern and his council solicitor on the right. With five minutes to go, the rattling sound of an Army Land Rover pulled into the overcrowded car park. It was the majors, Fox-Thrasher and Blitherington, in their smartly pressed uniforms, normally reserved for ceremonial occasions. The chattering momentarily subsided as the assembled throng looked over to watch them confidently enter the hall and pull up their chairs to sit down beside the district council representatives. Johnny noticed that Fox-Thrasher was holding just the slimmest of files. He leaned over to Penelope and commented that perhaps he and his boffin colleague weren't expecting to stay very long. Penelope smiled and gave a knowing nod, her hair just concealing a small plaster on her head that Johnny hadn't spotted, the result of a nasty collision with a kitchen wall cupboard.

The quiet distraction of the majors' entrance was soon disrupted by the arrival of Trevelyan Trelyon, who swooped into the room and paused briefly to survey the audience, hoping for even a hint of global recognition, before he yanked out a chair from the neat front row of empty seats which for some reason the public never like to occupy at these types of events. This provided ample space for his rotund torso to perch unimpeded. The hiatus in activity was not followed by adornment, as 'Unrely-on' had confidently hoped. All eyes had been averted towards the rapidly swinging double doors caused by Trevelyan's theatrical entrance, their aged hinges squealing in protest from their strenuous workout.

Trevedic Penhaligon soon followed and quickly found his press desk, a standard issue for all public inquiries. His article in the previous week's *Trumpet* about the history of Fred and Grace at Feathers Farm and the upcoming inquiry was crafted after his visit to the farm on that unfortunate day in Dennis Blackstaff's life. Those 'temple of doom' photos of the unfortunate bank manager were well and truly under lock and key, at least for the time being, leaving Trevedic to concentrate on the human rather than sensational angle. By his standards the headline, though less sensational, was still characteristically 'Trevedic': 'The Future of Feathers Farm: By Fair Means or Fowl?'

Peace resumed. It was ten o'clock. In inquiry terms, it was the witching hour. The inspector came alive to rule with authority. As Stumpy got out his pre-prepared hymn sheet ready to speak to the congregation, Johnny warned Fred and Grace that it was initially going to be a bit procedural.

"Well good morning, ladies and gentlemen," Stump opened. "It is now ten o'clock and I formerly open this public inquiry. My name is Clifford Stump and I am the planning inspector appointed by the Secretary of State for Planning to hold this Section 77 Inquiry, under the 1990 Town and Country Planning Act. This is into a planning application by Mr and Mrs Fred Gooley, for proposed residential development at Feathers Farm, Trecarsick, the details of which I am sure all parties will be familiar with. The planning application has been resolved to be approved by Trefriggit district council, but it was referred to the Secretary of State for Planning as required under the Safeguarded Aerodromes, Technical Sites and Military Explosives Storage Areas Direction 2002. At the request of the Ministry of Defence, who I can see are here today, the Secretary of State has called in the application for his determination via this public inquiry. The inquiry will hear evidence from all parties and I will make my recommendation to the Secretary of State for Planning, who will then take it into account in determining this planning application. Who appears for the…"

The inspector carried on with the formal process of recording the names of each party, who was representing who, how he was going to run the inquiry, how long he thought it might take and who from the public wanted to say anything for or against the planning application and when they might be saying it. On finding out from the inspector's opening speech that Fred was being represented by a Queen's Counsel, and a senior one at that, Fox-Thrasher couldn't conceal a quiet gulp and looked decidedly flushed. The presence of a solicitor and planning consultant accompanied by large boxes of paper seemed to further prolong his inability to swallow. That was the least of his troubles.

The inspector continued. "Ladies and gentlemen, before we start, I have a few important housekeeping matters which I want to rehearse with all the main parties for their comment. As you know, after I was appointed to hold this public inquiry and having reviewed the planning application documents and the council's reasons for formally resolving to approve it, I wrote a letter to all parties very early in the process in which I set out, very clearly, a number of pertinent questions which seemed to me would form the basis on which this planning application should be determined. I requested that each of those questions be answered by each party in its evidence, to be submitted in the normal way in advance of this inquiry. This would help me clearly understand each party's position and of course it did not preclude the opportunity for any party to add additional evidence if it helped its case. It's my way of doing things and in my experience it normally speeds up the inquiry."

Johnny, CHN and Penelope looked at each other. Their experience told them what was coming next. The shit was about to hit the proverbial fan – and the poo wouldn't be heading in their direction. The inspector continued.

"Well. Within all the regulation deadlines, I have received evidence and responses to my questions from both Mr Stern at the district council and from Mr Gooley's consultants. However, I have received little to assist me from the Ministry of Defence. Furthermore, I note that a Major Fox-Thrasher has indicated that he will call a Major Blitherington to give evidence but to date I have not received any written evidence from him at all, as required by the regulations. I should also add that the evidence I have received from Major Fox-Thrasher on behalf of the Ministry of Defence is, to be frank, woeful, and little more than a regurgitation of its scant outline Statement of Case. As I am aware that it was the Ministry of Defence who precipitated this inquiry, I am at a loss to know why it has failed to meet even the minimum requirements as set out in the regulations."

Stumpy had barely finished when CHN, anticipating the inspector inviting the major to respond, jumped to his feet, buttoned his jacket and cupped his hands behind his back. "Sir, do forgive me for interrupting you but I am glad you raised this issue and with respect, it was something I also wanted to raise with you at the beginning of this inquiry. You will also have seen copies of two letters to the Ministry's Property and Protection Division written by my client's lawyers querying the veracity of the Ministry's concerns about my clients' application and urging it to withdraw its objection, which we consider to be based on spurious reasons – particularly bearing in mind the points you respectfully raised in your letter to all parties. I anticipate that you were about to ask Major Fox-Thrasher to address you on your points so do forgive me for jumping to my feet but I felt that if you were, perhaps the major could also deal with the matters which we raised in those letters."

"Thank you, Mr Hartlock-Naddertrout," Stump replied. "I have indeed received copies of those letters you refer to from your lawyers to the Ministry's Division in question and understand the points they make. Whilst I take your point entirely and will leave it to Major Fox-Thrasher to comment, I am just a little reluctant not to turn this matter into an ad-hoc debate as your witness can use the Ministry's lack of reply to your lawyer's letters in presenting his evidence in chief and of course you will have ample opportunity to cross-examine the Ministry's representatives on the matter in the normal way. The fact remains that it appears that my original letter to all parties was, metaphorically, binned by the Ministry of Defence and remains unanswered and it has also clearly failed to comply with the Inquiries Procedures Rules on the submission of evidence. I had formed an initial view that the parties at this inquiry may be prejudiced if we were to continue with the Ministry giving evidence, as it were, on the hoof, as we do not know what it is going to say. I think it is now appropriate for me to ask Major Fox-Thrasher what he has got to say for himself. Major?"

This was not the start the major had hoped for. The inspector was clearly a significantly weightier civil servant than the box-ticking jobsworth he was expecting. The formality of the whole process had taken him by surprise. He was beginning to wonder if perhaps he should have heeded Captain Lovely's advice after all and read that handy little PINS booklet. The room went quiet. Classically and mistakenly, the major decided to go on the offensive and, if necessary, die in battle. The alternative – a bureaucratic firing squad – was unpalatable and he wasn't prepared to get out his last cigarette just yet.

The major rose to his feet. "Thank you, sir. Well. I can just see you have the explosion zone map lying on the side of your desk. There is no dispute that Mr Gooley's farm is in the explosion zone. It's plain as a pikestaff. That being the case, Major Blitherington will explain to you the sort of explosives we store and why we need to protect our explosives capability. New houses in the explosion zone will reduce our effective explosives storage capability. I can't see why we have to produce reams of paper to show that. We can't have this sort of thing. You're an intelligent man, Mr Stump. It's not rocket science."

Stumpy was writing everything down, an inspector's absolute requirement in public inquiries in case the whole process ended up being challenged in a court of law. There was a momentary silence whilst he completed his written summary of the major's pathetic response. He put his pen down slowly, waited a moment to gather his thoughts and looked across at the major, the scorn clearly showing.

"Major Fox-Thrasher. I think you have missed the point. You haven't told me anything I didn't already know. Of course you may be right. It may be all very simple – but the evidence I have before me from your opponents argues cogently that the return to turkey farming at Feathers Farm will, as a matter of fact, have more impact on your explosives storage capacity than the housing proposed in Mr Gooley's application. I have no substantive evidence from you to the contrary and I don't even know what Major Blitherington is going to say. None of us does. This is about procedure and decision making, where all parties have an equal opportunity and an equal say based on evidence required to be submitted in advance. If I may say so, your approach seems to me to be saying, and I will be careful with my words here, 'I am right and everyone else is wrong, so I don't need to participate in this farce'. In the circumstances you leave me no choice but to adjourn this public inquiry to enable you to respond to the tasks I specifically requested in my original letter and to produce a properly constituted proof of evidence which can incorporate what you and or Major Blitherington are going to say. This will give me and all parties the opportunity to cross-examine you on the strength of your arguments compared to those already submitted by Mr Gooley's consultants and in the knowledge, of course, that the council wants to approve this planning application. Do you understand that, Major?"

The major decided to stay seated and nodded his head in agreement. Even he could see the situation worsening if he started to argue with the inspector, who was in no mood for excuses. The clearly irritated Stumpy averted his gaze from the major and directed his attention towards CHN, making sure that Jim Stern was not excluded from the dialogue.

"I am sorry, Mr Hartlock-Naddertrout, but as I suspected and, regrettably from what I have heard, I have been left with no choice but to adjourn this inquiry to allow for the Ministry to submit the information I requested and to comply with the rules. Would you like to address me about anything else before I formally adjourn and we all look at reconvened inquiry dates? Like, for example, a claim for costs against the Ministry? You realise of course that I am not inviting such a claim but it would be remiss of me to leave today without knowing what your client's position on costs might be when we reconvene. I don't need to remind you that the rules are clear in that I and any relevant parties should be notified of any such claim as early as possible and as we are all here, it seems to me to be a good opportunity to give it an airing if you so choose."

CHN was surprised at such a candid invitation as it was not something an inspector would normally lead on. It only reaffirmed CHN's opinion that the inspector was, deep down, hopping mad. He sprang to his feet and straightened up once again. "I'm obliged, sir. You have touched on an issue which I can say I have already discussed with my client and yes, I would like to put the Secretary of State for Planning on notice that we will be pursuing a costs claim against the Ministry of Defence, at the very least for the delay caused by this highly regrettable and totally avoidable adjournment. Quite frankly, sir, in all my years at the bar, I have not seen a government department act so willfully and so arrogantly. It's appalling. Furthermore I should add that this costs claim may be expanded, depending on what evidence Major Fox-Thrasher over there actually manages to scramble together, if we consider that the Ministry has acted unreasonably in calling for this inquiry – particularly when the district council were prepared to grant planning permission based on sound and well-reasoned judgement." CHN paused, a triumphant look on his face. "There is one final matter, sir, I would like to raise with you and it is this. We are concerned on this side of the hall that the Ministry's Property and Protection Division, to whom all correspondence on the matter from PINS has been addressed, has been kept 'in se mutuo separatus' throughout the entire process and we are not convinced that it fully knows what's going on. Sir, I am not a conspiracy theorist but I do think it would help if you could write to Division giving your reasons for the adjournment, together with an explanation as to what you now expect to receive prior to the reconvened inquiry. Of course such a letter would give you the opportunity to comment on the Ministry's behaviour and we would of course respect any decision you make on whether you feel it appropriate to do so at this time. For the record, we think you should. Thank you, sir." CHN sat down.

Stumpy looked at CHN and across to Fox-Thrasher. "Thank you, Mr Hartlock-Naddertrout. The costs claim comes as no surprise to me and no doubt you will furnish me with the full statement at the appropriate time when you have decided what the basis of the claim will be. Any retort to that, Major Fox-Thrasher?" The major shook his head. The inspector continued. "Ah yes, my limited Latin suggests that 'in se mutuo separatus' means 'in isolation'. I see, Mr Hartlock-Naddertrout, you are nodding in agreement. That does appear the situation to me too, given that there is no representative here today from the division. Of course, I have no way of knowing how the Ministry of Defence has prepared for this inquiry but I agree that further correspondence from me to the division, as you suggest, should keep us all on the straight and narrow. I will reserve judgement as to what I will say about its behaviour but I note and thank you for your comments."

Stumpy looked across at the major and, suspecting that it was actually he who was operating 'in se mutuo separatus', commented sarcastically: "Major. I am sure you are in daily and close contact with your division, like the well-oiled machine we all know the Ministry of Defence to be, but just in case there has been a rare occasion, or dare I say, occasions, when something might have conceivably slipped through the net, I am sure you have no problem with me writing directly to the division rather than you, as Mr Hartlock-Naddertrout has kindly and politely suggested. Happy with that, Major?"

The Major nodded despondently. The problem was not going away. It was now chasing him with a big stick. He turned pale and started to gather up the few papers he had brought with him. The quicker he could exit the hall and avoid any further procedural beatings, the better. He felt a yearning for the mine, to help him clear his head – but he couldn't leave before Stumpy had formally concluded proceedings. Blitherington just sat there bemused by the whole affair. It was clear that Fox-Thrasher had kept him in the dark as well. All he wanted to do was to talk about explosives and what an awful mess they make when they go off.

Jim Stern had watched it all with mild amusement, relieved that Stumpy had little quarrel with the district council: its position was clear as planning policy fully supported Fred's proposals and its further evidence was similar to Johnny Smidgen's. The chickens were coming home to roost for the major in a bad way, as Jim had predicted, but for Fred, his turkeys were coming home to roost in a good way. In his summing up

Stumpy had a few coded words to say to Jim, more in deference to the district council having been reluctantly dragged through the process when it probably had more important things to do with its scare resources and time. Fred picked up on it. The inspector was on his side.

More procedural discussions followed and a date for the reconvened inquiry was finally set for late July. Fred lowered his head to think. If the bank's head office found out, it might force Dennis to press the Feathers Farm distressed sale trigger despite the humiliating photos of him hanging in the temple of doom which remained safely under lock and key. Fred averted his thoughts to more positive scenarios and saw the adjournment as an opportunity to put more pressure on the beleaguered major.

He leaned over to Penelope, Johnny and CHN for a quiet conflab. "This is a right bugger, this is, but I sense a kill. I think the timing is right for another one of Penelope's excellent letters to Brigadier Bloodworth, which should land on his desk around the time he receives the inspector's letter. I think we can also make sure that both Stump's and Penelope's letters get to Trevelyan Trelyon and onward to Sir Michael Stride-Pecker and the Minister for Defence, Guy Gunston in Whitehall. The major's not going to survive this."

Stumpy concluded the adjourned proceedings by addressing the bemused supporters, at least those who were still awake after all the legal chit chat, to explain his decision to adjourn the inquiry, to thank everyone for coming along and to reinforce the point that they would have their day again when the inquiry reconvened. He looked over to Cordelia and commented how lovely the hall looked, and how appropriate it was for it to be bedecked with pictures of those who had given so much of their time to serving the local community. It brought a wry smile to Cordelia who, as she left the hall, attracted the inspector's attention by quickly flashing the hastily removed photo of Attila masquerading as Demelza Friggins.

The majors made a rapid exit, and made no attempt to look around or speak to anyone. CHN, Penelope, Johnny, Fred and Grace returned to Feathers Farm for a debrief and hearty casserole, which Grace had left simmering on the range.

Trevedic Penhaligon was the next to leave, having been frantically writing some copy which he just managed to email to HQ by the twelve o'clock deadline for Thursday's edition of the *Trumpet*. It was a cracker: 'Government Goof's Gaff leaves Gooleys hanging over Ministry's ARCE'.

The village hall fell silent once again – but only for a few seconds. Trevelyan's exit was as theatrical as his entrance, as one of the hall's swinging double doors, having suffered yet another pummelling, decided to make a final curtain call. It dropped off its hinges, pivoting on one corner like a spinning coin for a few seconds before crashing to the ground, the recently installed health and safety glass fortunately doing its job and remaining shattered but intact.

It wasn't the only thing that had come off its hinges.

Chapter 22:
Doo-Wops and Dodgy Directions

It was only a few days since the public inquiry and the Secretary of State for Defence, 'Gunpowder' Guy Gunston was in his plush Whitehall office at the Ministry of Defence mulling over another irritating internal memo from the Treasury moaning about continued out of control defence spending. The phone rang. It was Sir Michael Stride-Pecker MP with some important news he needed to share with his friend face to face. They arranged to meet in the House of Commons Strangers' Bar at the end of the day. Guy got there early, found a quiet corner in the dark, panelled room and lined up a couple of gin and tonics.

A few minutes later Sir Michael swung the bar door open and was confronted by a body lying spread-eagled on the floor, its partly concealed face just recognisable. It looked like a typical murder scene from a police training video. Sir Michael shook his head in displeasure, delicately stepped over the lifeless figure, looked around and spotted Guy quietly sipping his gin. "Good evening, Guy. It's a bit early for Jim Stoker, isn't it?" he said, gesticulating at the prostrate body on the floor. "The Irish MPs are normally off their face much later – or has that mad Scots SNP Conker McQueen thumped him again?"

Guy looked up and smiled. "Good guess, Michael. It was Conker. They were arguing about Catholicism. He'll come round."

It wasn't long before the pleasantries were over and Sir Michael cut to the chase. With the sort of concern in his voice reserved for raising constituent issues in the House, he explained that District Councillor Trevelyan Trelyon had called him that morning to bring him up to speed on the public inquiry and the enforced adjournment to enable the Ministry, or more to the point, Major Fox-Thrasher, to get his act together. He went on to explain that the inspector had reserved his venom for the Ministry in view of its shambolic behaviour, particularly given that it called for the inquiry in the first place. A letter from the inspector on the matter was on its way to Brigadier Bloodworth at Division and it wasn't going to make pleasant reading. It got worse. Sir Michael explained that Fred's QC made it clear he would be making a claim for costs against the Ministry due to the unnecessary and avoidable inquiry delay but that wouldn't be the end of it – a position which, he explained, the inspector had some sympathy with.

Guy was visibly shocked. "Christ! A claim for costs against the Ministry? A QC? Bloody hell. What the hell's going on down there? Michael, the last time we spoke, it was some backwater issue that we thought any sensible depot commanding officer could handle."

With a hint of sarcasm, Sir Michael pointed out that his Bodmin constituency wasn't a backwater. He continued. "Well Guy, the whole issue is turning out to be bigger and potentially more damaging to the Ministry than Division had clearly anticipated. I am just beginning to think that there is more to this than meets the eye. The Gooley camp are not going to go quietly. From what I have heard, I think their arguments have legitimacy."

Sir Michael went on to tell Guy that he had obtained some privileged information about the mismanagement of the whole process, which all pointed towards Major Fox-Thrasher, though he admitted he wasn't aware of the alleged reliable source – which was, of course, Captain Lovely. Dickie knew that pillow talk or a confession in the snug at the Whippet with his beloved Karensa would be passed on to Cordelia, then Fred and Grace, then Trevelyan and, if Trevelyan was worth his salt, Sir Michael himself.

It was time for Sir Michael to pass on some friendly advice, some home truths his friend from the Ministry would not want to hear. "Guy, of course it's not for me to say, but it seems to me that you need to put your senior mandarins on notice to establish what's been going on. Once Bloodworth gets the inspector's letter, I think you need to conduct an internal review of the matter. Make sure the review takes into account earlier letters which I know were sent to the brigadier from the applicants' lawyer, a Miss Breakage, which, I understand, set out what she believes to be a strong case for granting planning permission. Word on the street is she is going to send another one in a similar vein with the issue of costs thrown in. Most importantly, you need to exclude Major Fox-Thrasher from your review. I'm told he's been… well, you know the phrase from that old House of Commons Spycatcher episode? 'Economical with the truth'."

Still shocked, Guy had got the message. After a few more gins and some story swapping on who in the House had been caught, metaphorically or literally, with their pants down, Sir Michael departed. Guy immediately got onto his mobile phone to his Permanent Under Secretary of State for Defence who agreed that an internal review team within the corridors of power in Whitehall should be briefed. Guy wanted the truth, answers and recommendations fast. The Tredyedeath Depot ARCE was on the line. The Treasury wasn't to know, at least for the moment. Their involvement was the last thing he wanted in a recession where his department still had a reputation for buying twenty tanks when one would do. He knew that a costs claim against the Ministry at this time was just going to make some other cash-strapped squabbling government departments rub their hands with glee.

Something stirred in the corner. It was Jim Stoker. He had come round and, still dazed, started scrambling to his feet. Barely upright, he looked around sheepishly and wandered out of the bar. No one noticed except Conker McQueen, who quickly put his drink down and followed. The corridor echoed to some shouting about the Pope and choirboys followed by a thud. Stoker had gone down again.

Guy grimaced and shook his head in dismay.

***

The following morning, Brigadier Bloodworth was at his desk, his face showing all the strains of someone sitting on an unexploded bomb which had just started ticking. He had just finished reading Stump's letter, which had arrived that morning as a special delivery. It was indeed a bombshell. It was the first he knew that things had gone badly wrong at the public inquiry. The inspector had spelt it out in plain English. The brigadier's phone rang. It was timely. It was a Whitehall senior civil servant warning him that Guy Gunston, who had been lobbied by Sir Michael, was on the warpath. On the basis of reliable information, Guy's department had decided to hold an internal review into the Tredyedeath Depot public inquiry debacle. In true mandarin style, the conversation was abrupt. Whitehall wanted to see all the relevant paperwork and someone would be round that afternoon to collect it. They would be in touch once the review was complete.

The second post arrived containing Penelope's spectacularly well-timed 'stick the boot in' letter to the brigadier, together with copies of her unanswered two previous letters which had been forwarded to the major who, of course, had unceremoniously binned them. Penelope's latest missive had been copied to PINS, Jim Stern, Trevelyan, Sir Michael and Guy and formally put the Ministry on notice of a claim for costs and the threat of further costs if the inquiry was to continue with no substantive evidence which, she made clear, was the case thus far. The arguments already set out in Penelope's previous letters were reiterated which, on any analysis, concluded that the Ministry was on very thin ice if they were to persist with their objection. Bloodworth knew from those copied into Penelope's letter and the phone call from Whitehall that, with meddling politicians on the case, keeping it all under his control was now going to be difficult. The proverbial ticking seemed to be getting louder and faster.

It was clear to Bloodworth from the inspector's damning comments, reinforced by Penelope's letter, that the Ministry had looked like amateurs at the public inquiry, and it was all on his watch. Round two was coming up in July and the pressure was on. The buck was going to end up back on his desk after Gunston's bureaucrats had chewed it over and spat out its findings. The brigadier was not the type to play the blame game and reflected that giving the job to Wally Dinsmore might have been a mistake, partly because of his inexperience and partly because he should have been more forensic and robust in dealing with Fox-Thrasher's bullying.

He decided to pay Dinsmore a visit and wandered down to his office, firmly opening the door to find him sitting at his desk, minding his own business over a cup of tea. Typically, his office colleagues barely flinched as the brigadier, who couldn't hide his irritation, decided to get things off his chest. "The shit's hit the fan, Dinsmore. On my watch too. The Secretary of State for Defence is on the warpath. It's that bloody Tredyedeath Depot. The public inquiry inspector's blown up big time and we are being chased for costs. It's all gone tits up, Dinsmore. We should have managed this ourselves and not let Fox-Thrasher handle it. He's cocked up big time and we are all in line for the firing squad. There's going to be a Whitehall internal inquiry. The politicians have got involved." Dinsmore went to speak but the brigadier shouted over him: "Don't say anything in your defence. I am sure there is one somewhere, but now is not the time. Just reflect on what's happened and make a copy of all the papers by lunchtime. A sharp suited civvy from Whitehall is coming to collect them at one o'clock."

With that, the brigadier dropped the latest bundle of letters onto Dinsmore's desk, slammed the door and returned to his office. Wally's expressionless colleagues looked up momentarily, lowered their heads and went back to their tasks like automatons.

Dinsmore was shocked. Nervously, he started to shuffle papers about and fiddle with his computer as he slowly gathered his thoughts. He managed to access all the documents and copy everything before placing it in an official civil service box file. The box contained a printed form in quadruplicate which required completion before it moved anywhere. Head down, Wally started ticking, circling, crossing, highlighting and explaining in big blank boxes what each enclosure was all about. It took him half an hour. It was almost impossible to lose an official civil service box file although being left on a bus, tube or thrown on a rubbish tip seem to be the favoured exceptions.

On the strike of one o'clock, the box was whisked off Dinsmore's desk by Bloodworth's warrant officer secretary and into the hands of the waiting civil servant for onward dissection in Whitehall. Fox-Thrasher knew nothing.

***

It was now the beginning of May and a nervous three weeks had gone by. The brigadier's phone rang. He immediately recognised from their previous conversation that it was the same faceless Whitehall senior civil servant. He was even briefer than last time.

"We've completed the Gooley planning application internal review. A meeting has been arranged in Whitehall. We want you there. It's tomorrow morning at 10am, in room AAM/XRT/29357. Goodbye."

The phone went dead, leaving the brigadier to quickly check his diary to see what might have to be cancelled. It was lucky, he thought, that it wasn't on the day of a loved one's funeral.

***

The brigadier arrived early at HQ to try and find room AAM/XRT/29357. His fear of wandering helplessly for months, incarcerated within Whitehall's hallowed walls like many of the ghosts still there, was quickly quelled when he was met at reception and guided to the meeting room. The journey took him upstairs, downstairs, along one corridor and then another, through swinging doors and into yet another corridor. He felt like a giant pinball shooting from one corridor to the next but it was a momentary distraction for the apprehensive brigadier. He just hoped it wasn't going to be 'Game Over'. He finally arrived and was shown to his seat facing five identically-suited expressionless civil servants looking not dissimilar to a white 1950s Doo-Wop group. The introductions were all too brief for Bloodworth who, with pen in hand, was struggling to write down each name and hideously long suffix-ridden departmental post prior to the next introduction.

The coffee was still being poured when the most senior of the civil servants, the one with the biggest suffix, kicked off the meeting. For the Ministry and for Bloodworth it was the worst of all news. "Brigadier Bloodworth, we have a problem. A serious problem. There is an anomaly in the safeguarding direction which this Gooley planning application has exposed. We have never had this situation before but if it gets out, it could potentially prejudice the storage capability of all our ARCE depots across the country. We have been advised by our planning team that we will lose this public inquiry and if we do, it will create a precedent if similar planning applications are submitted within other explosion zones in the country on agricultural sites used for intensive farming."

The lead singer of the Doo-Wops continued. "Major Fox-Thrasher has, by his arrogance and actions, made the situation significantly worse for the Ministry than it could have been. We could have played this right down to buy us time in managing how we deal with the anomaly. He has also lied in his objections to the application – which Division gave him carte blanche to submit – and his preparation for and appearance at the public inquiry has been farcical. The inquiry inspector has made that very clear. We are facing having to pay costs at the very least. The minister is very unhappy. We are now into damage limitation. We have no choice but to withdraw the objection for fear of any more embarrassment – including further costs against the Ministry. We have come to the conclusion, and have recommended to the minister, that we will have to buy out the applicants. We will have to buy Feathers Farm to protect our explosives storage capability at Tredyedeath Depot. The Treasury will of course have to sanction this acquisition but we feel that they will have no choice if we are protect our explosive capability. You'd better read this."

A short report was handed to the brigadier for him to consider and deal with. It explained that, essentially, the Gooleys' advisors were correct in their calculations about the reduced danger to humans if the application for housing was to be successful compared with its continued use as a turkey rearing business. It recognised that all Penelope's letters to the Ministry had made the same arguments which, rather than being considered objectively, on which advice could have been sought, were flatly ignored by the major. It catalogued the major's 'untruths' including the now infamous and non-existent Health and Safety Executive objection. It explained that the anomaly was due to wrongful assumptions adopted in the explosives safeguarding direction that all farming operations in an explosion zone were small in scale, the limited loss of life in the event of an explosion being regrettable but acceptable. This was the basis on which development related to agricultural business was considered to be exempt. The direction had not assumed that labour intensive farming operations like the Gooleys', where much greater numbers of humans would be working compared to a typical farming business, might exist within an explosion zone. No assessment of risk to humans for this type of intensive farming had been taken for any explosives depot as this type of agricultural business was assumed not to exist. It was a major oversight in the direction in all senses of the word.

The report concluded it would be unacceptable not to assess the increased risk to human life where intensive farming existed within explosion zones and if this were to take place, it was quite possible that a number of explosive depots could have their explosive storage capability reduced. This would be unacceptable. The Ministry of Defence was in a difficult position. It was in a conundrum and in the short term Fox-Thrasher hadn't helped. There were a number of options the Ministry could adopt including changing the terms of the direction in the way agricultural operations were assessed, which could take years; closing Tredyedeath Depot; or revising Tredyedeath Depot's safeguarding map area; but all had wide ranging implications for the Ministry and none would deal with the Gooleys' immediate situation which had the capacity to, metaphorically, blow the Ministry's explosive storage strategy wide open. The Gooleys' application had to be dealt with now and the costs to the Ministry and its reputation protected. The bigger picture would have to be sorted out later.

After some general discussion about the report, it was made clear to the brigadier that 'Gunpowder' Guy Gunston wanted this problem off his plate fast and he didn't want his civil servants getting their hands dirty on a problem caused by a 'uniform'. If it was going to go tits up and the Treasury got involved, the 'uniforms' were going to take the blame for all the costs – which was, thankfully, consistent with their spendthrift reputation.

Bloodworth decided that he wasn't going to go that quietly, even though the bullets were heading his way and Fox-Thrasher was the culprit. He sat firm and decided to make a point blindingly obvious to him. "So. As I understand it, gentlemen, the flawed direction you have just so eloquently explained to me was drawn up here in the Ministry by the Civil Service. That's right, isn't it?"

The room went quiet and then, with heads down, the Doo-Wops shuffled some papers. The brigadier could have sworn that the lead singer's neck was starting to twitch. He continued, sarcasm now beginning to creep in. "And, as I recall from previous experience, when it comes to fancy worded directions like these, you guys just love to do them yourselves, don't you? They're your babies, aren't they? I mean, we tell you what explosives we want to store and what the explosives force is within 500 metres and then your magic formula determines storage capability, taking into account who is expendable and who isn't. So. You're the ones who identify how the risk is assessed, aren't you? On that basis, it looks awfully like your colleagues have forgotten to take an important factor into account in those risk assessments, haven't they? Or have I missed something?" He knew he wasn't going to get an answer but at least he'd pushed the blame firmly back into the Doo-Wops court.

The lead singer got up to leave, mumbling something about it being all a bit complicated. The rest of the Doo-Wops followed quietly, leaving Bloodworth alone with the hopeless task of finding his way out of the pinball machine. It didn't take long to get lost, as his accidental entry into room LAD/MJS/26683 demonstrated. It turned out to be the ladies' lavatory but fortunately a sympathetic and understanding cleaner helped to guide him out of the machine's innards.

The brigadier soon got back to Division and immediately called Dinsmore into his office. "Dinsmore. It's got worse. Read this report on the Gooley application and public inquiry and put a copy of it on file with all the documents you copied for Whitehall. I'm going to meet Major Fox-Thrasher at Tredyedeath Depot. We're withdrawing the Gooley objection."

***

Captain Lovely was in his office when the phone rang, its double ring indicating the call had been diverted as the intended recipient, the major, was out. Brigadier Bloodworth was on the other end of the line. "Captain Lovely, I'll be frank. I am concerned about the recent events surrounding the Gooley public inquiry. I am fully up to speed and I need to meet you and the major as soon as possible. The earliest I can do is early June, which still leaves plenty of time to deal with preparation of documents for the reopened inquiry in July. I would be grateful if you would just tell the major that I am doing a regular explosives audit."

Dickie suspected from the tone of the brigadier's voice that the major was going to be in for some stick, but the likelihood of a carrot coming with it seemed remote. To the army a 'carrot and stick' approach would be the equivalent of asking whether you wanted three people at your firing squad or six. Dickie made sure he was invited to the meeting. He didn't want to miss the fun.

***

On receipt of the internal review into the Gooley case, 'Gunpowder' Guy called his friend Sir Michael to bring him up to speed. "Michael, it's good news for your constituents – but at the moment I cannot reveal all. You were right. The application by the Gooleys has exposed us procedurally in relation to the storage of explosives. The safeguarding map direction is flawed. There is an anomaly. Our ARCE has been exposed. All I can say is watch this space – but if I tell you that I am due to meet the Treasury shortly and the head of explosives at Division is meeting Major Fox-Thrasher in a few weeks, you can draw your own conclusions about where this is all going. If the papers get to hear this, I will, of course, deny everything."

No sooner had Guy rung off than Sir Michael called Trevelyan with the cautiously good but confidential news. 'Rely-on' was beside himself with genuine delight and the message was with Fred and Grace moments later. The strain visibly fell from Fred's face. Grace baked a cake.

Chapter 23:
A Tale of Two 'Fetes'

It was early June and a sunny, warm Saturday, perfect weather for the Trecarsick village fete which was always held on the village green. In the distance Bodmin Moor was looking its best in the bright blue skies, its granite outcrops, derelict stone buildings and rugged dry stone walls contrasting with the multi-coloured ground covering, unique to moorland ecosystems. Dickie had the day off and offered to help Karensa and the locals prepare for the midday start. He knew that village fetes were always awash with dogs of every size and shape and, as the local children loved Fluffy, he decided to bring him along even though the hairy beast was still dozing in the back of the army Land Rover after a night on special SSPHE guard duty in the mine.

Karensa thought it would be a great idea for the village shop to have its own stand selling local produce, sweets, ice creams and cold drinks. She was looking particularly gorgeous in some noticeably tight, and probably too short, shorts and a loose fitting top which she hoped would have the same effect for her stall's turnover in the warm weather than it had done for the shop on Trumpet Thursday when the menfolk often returned home with two dozen bottles of bleach and fifteen packets of crisps. Here was an opportunity to sell something, anything, to the local menfolk who she knew would, like zombies, temporarily fall under her spell.

The stalls, marquees, stands and pitches were all positioned near the entrance, the idea being to capture the punters for some retail therapy as soon as they arrived and once again before they left. Weird and wonderful stalls started to appear. Sunglasses for cats, rude-looking balloons, holidays in former Iron Curtain countries no one had ever heard of, trendy garden sheds that looked like sputniks, novelty picture ironing board covers ranging from the semi naked to Paddington Bear. Yes, the summer village fete vendors' roadshow had certainly arrived at Trecarsick.

The avenue of local products tents made a stark and interesting contrast with Karensa's village shop leading the field amongst the ubiquitous stalls selling home-made cakes from the Women's Institute and plants from the gardening club. The community group stalls were always popular. Cubs and guides, the church choir, the football team and a rather dodgy-sounding men-only dominoes club plus many more, all running raffles, all looking for new members, all looking to do their bit for the community. There was always a lot to do in Trecarsick, particularly during the long dark Cornish winters.

The obligatory beer tent was provided by the Tinner's Whippet and, as always, Steve the landlord had worked tirelessly in his microbrewery to concoct a particularly dangerous-sounding brew just for the event. If last year's Whippet Wobble was anything to go by, this year's Tinner's Trembler suggested that it would probably have the effect of disturbing most, if not all, bodily functions. The adjoining marquee contained the school band, probably not the best location to have an audience but on the other hand it might raise extra revenue from the unsuspecting having had one Trembler too many. 'Dad dancing' couldn't be ruled out.

A marquee was reserved for the small animal and pet displays, beyond which the rest of the village green was laid out with bunting and brightly coloured tape around the arena, where all sorts of competitions and displays would take place. Dogs, goats, sheep, rabbits, Bodmin ponies, ferrets: they were all penned up close by and on show, eagerly awaiting their turn to compete in some way or other. There was even a falconer with some large raptors perched quietly in an open tent waiting for some exercise on the promise of a dead mouse or piece of raw chicken.

***

Down at Feathers Farm, Gordon, Dan and Rozen had arrived for the weekend, Dan eager as ever to remind his grandfather, on the threat of more trouser pulling, that Mum had entered Attila all those months ago in the fete's prettiest fowl competition. Just in case Fred had forgotten, Dan had borrowed a large Attila-sized cage from his school's hands-on mini-farm. It wasn't long before Fred, armed with the large cage, reluctantly approached Attila, who was sunning herself in a dust bath in the back courtyard. It was not something Fred really wanted to do. Turkeys weren't bred to be stared at, ridiculed, poked and compared for their beauty – although that may seem a tad more palatable than, with the exception of Attila, certain death. Attila looked up at the approaching Fred and outstretched her neck in disbelief at the sight of the cage, which Fred put down beside her.

The trusting but startled Attila stayed sitting and, suspecting something was up, shut her eyes as Fred put his hand under her frame, gently lifted her up a few inches and slipped her into the cage with her bottom pointing towards the quickly closing cage door. She opened one eye and then the other and, noticing her incarceration, started to cock her head from side to side, a sign Fred recognised as indicating her displeasure.

"Well my little beauty, if nothing else, it's going to be a change of scene for you this afternoon. We are going to the village fete," Fred said. "You are just going to have to put up with people gawping at you for a few hours. You have my permission to peck at anybody who sticks their fingers in your cage. Do a bit of flirting. Who knows, you might win a prize." He had a few more quiet words to calm her down as the grandchildren watched in awe at the obvious close relationship between Fred and his friendly fowl. Attila could hear the sound of Fred slowly lowering the simple cage door latch into place and she quickly turned around in the tight space to fix her gaze attentively on its mechanism.

As Fred turned to fetch some food for her, she put her beak on the catch and flicked up the lever. The cage door swung open with a noticeable squeak. It caught Fred's attention and he immediately turned around to shut it. "Bugger me. Not so fast, little one. I'm sure I just shut that door. Must be getting forgetful."

Fred had indeed shut it properly the first time. A pig couldn't open it but an intelligent turkey with a sharp beak could. Attila had already hatched a 'Great Escape' plan Steve McQueen would have been proud of – and it didn't involve any burrowing, dressing up or motor cycles.

***

It wasn't long before everyone was ready to go to the fete. Attila's cage was furnished with some straw, food and water and, with the grandchildren's help, lifted into the back of Fred's Land Rover and covered with a blanket. Grace had put on another bright Gwenifer dress for the day and was holding tightly to her chest a large plastic box of home-made coffee cake she had baked for the WI stall. She lifted her large frame into the front seat with Gordon, Dan and Rozen in the back. Dan occasionally leaned over to lift the blanket to placate Attila's complaining squawks. They soon arrived and Fred found a parking spot by the village green for entrants, next to Dickie's Land Rover. A few minutes later Fred placed Attila's cage inside the small animal and pet marquee at position fifty-seven alongside a host of significantly smaller, strange-looking feathered creatures. Attila used her physical dominance and 'death stare' to make sure that any inquisitiveness on the part of her neighbouring fowl wouldn't be tolerated. They all quickly decided to look the other way.

Trecarsick held one of the most popular village fetes in the area and by late morning queues had started to form. By 2.30 it was in full swing, with all the variety only an English village fete can muster on a sunny day. An errant display falcon had unfortunately whipped off a visiting tourist's toupee, mistaking the dark hairy mass for something edible; Karensa was doing a roaring ice cream trade, with some of the menfolk now on their sixth rather unfortunately named Choc Pocket Rocket; and the Tinner's Whippet had taken its first Trembler victim who fortunately just managed to deposit £10 in the school band collection tin on his way to a soft landing face down in something unpleasant. The dog agility competition was delayed for repair work when an out of control Irish setter managed to knock over all the jumps and stopped to do a poo in the tunnel. Dickie let Fluffy off the lead knowing he wouldn't go too far and it wasn't long before he was being chased by a gaggle of small happy children who were hanging onto his wagging tail and long coat as an evidently very pleased elderly lady walked past clutching a semi-naked Chippendales ironing board cover.

For Fred and Grace, it had been over a year since the whole stressful planning permission episode had started and this was the first time they had ventured out socially. They kept the news about the Ministry's emerging volte face – which Grace more appropriately pronounced as a 'volte farce' – to themselves but were really enjoying life after all the worry, and the frequent well-wishers made the day all the more perfect. Fred knew that Attila could look after herself and with Dan paying regular visits to keep her company, he left her alone until the competition results were due to be announced.

Fred could see in the distance the judges leaving the small animal and pet marquee, one of whom was clearly in pain and grasping his right forefinger. Attila's cynical portrayal of docility had seduced the errant judge's finger into the cage for a friendly pat on the head. Faster than a lynx's paw, her beak flicked around and clamped itself on the wayward finger so tightly that most if not all of the damage was done by the judge's attempts to extract it quickly from the cage, in fear that his piano playing days might have come to a premature end. For Attila, it was worth breaking the boredom, not to mention the endless, irritating gawping but she knew that any chance of winning a prize had long gone. The damaged judge probably had friends in high places and anyway, who was going to take the risk of tying a rosette to her cage and come away with all digits intact?

The public were barred during judging but once they had departed, the marquee went momentarily quiet. Attila's Steve McQueen moment had arrived. Noticing the emptiness, she quickly flicked the cage door latch up with her beak and with a squeak, the door swung open. In no time at all, she scampered to the edge of the cage and jumped to the ground. A ray of bright sunlight shone like a freedom beacon through a gap in the bottom of the marquee where the aging canvas wasn't quite joined. Attila headed for the opening and poked her head out. She could see Fred's Land Rover parked not far away; there was just the short distance across 'no man's land' to traverse once she had left the relative safety and quietness of the marquee. The coast looked clear. With her claws sinking into the soft turf for extra grip, she made a break for it, gathering momentum with head down and wings back as the Land Rover came ever closer, its green rear canvas fortunately rolled up to accept a direct assault into its innards. In a matter of seconds and with no one noticing, she made the last few feet airborne, her wings reversing at the last second to act as an air break. In a very unladylike manner, she dropped into the sanctity of the Land Rover, her feet scrambling in reverse for grip to slow her down on the shiny metal floor as her mass of white feathers cushioned the inevitable collision with the rear bulkhead. It was as perfect an escape could be and she was soon on her feet, all in one piece.

On hearing the tannoy announce that the impending results of the prettiest fowl competition would be held in the small animal and pet marquee, Fred, with Dan in hand, walked over expectantly. They both secretly hoped Attila had won something to make it all worthwhile. They soon entered the marquee and looked around to see rows of cages, all numbered, containing small creatures all waiting anxiously to be collected. Fred got his bearings from the morning's drop off and walked down the aisle, Dan's arm now outstreached as he slowed his grandfather to eye up a host of new pet opportunities. They eventually arrived at position fifty-seven. There was a momentary silence as they stared at the empty cage in horror, its swinging door still squeaking. Attila was nowhere to be seen.

Fred was trying hard to comfort Dan, who was close to tears, when a rather gleeful-looking judge with a bloodied bandaged finger wandered up to them. "Is this your cage? Number fifty-seven? The one containing a large Wirral White turkey? Well it's gone – and under the rules, if it's not in the cage when the results are announced, it will be disqualified. I'm now going to read out the results… so it's disqualified."

The short, insignificant-looking judge took a step back as Fred's Harris Tweed suit advanced into his personal space. Fred leaned over, grabbed the judge's arm and held up his hand to expose the blood-stained bandaged digit. "Disqualification, eh? Wouldn't be anything to do with your poor little finger, would it, little man? Just a bandage on it won't do any good, you know. I'm sorry to say that a turkey bite, particularly one from a Wirral White, normally starts with stiffness and then leads to total body paralysis within six hours. It's called Tighturkeytautellosus. Very nasty. Very nasty indeed. Oh, and if you are one of the very lucky ones to survive that, I'm afraid it's not good news. You will be doomed to be a petty little bureaucrat for the rest of your life. Still, on that score, you seem to have had quite a lot of practice."

A smiling Fred dropped the judge's arm and walked out of the marquee with a sobbing Dan in hand to look for Attila, leaving the worried judge hastening to unravel the bloodied bandage to see if he could feel any early signs of paralysis.

The afternoon was a great success. Even the winners of the 'most irritating mother in law' and 'scariest local' took it in good heart as all the money raised would be spent on local good causes.

***

Dickie spent most of the afternoon helping out on the village shop stall whilst Karensa fended off marriage proposals from those who'd had one too many Tremblers before their wives turned up to give them a dose of 'what for', particularly at their age. But it was time for Dickie to go as he had to prepare for some early deliveries of explosives the next morning and Brigadier Bloodworth from Division was coming to meet the major. After a few sharp whistles, Fluffy reappeared, now panting and looking decidedly dejected having just managed to escape the clutches of the same chasing, demanding gaggle of giggling children. Dickie opened the Land Rover driver's door and before he had the chance to get in, the large Alsatian launched himself across the driver's seat and squeezed into the passenger foot well to hide. The tired monster looked forlornly up at him as the children drew ever closer and Dickie could read the signs clearly in his drooping eyes: for Christ's sake, let's get out of here. They were soon off and it wasn't long before they were back parked outside Dickie's office at Tredyedeath Depot. Dickie had heard some squeaking noises coming from the back on the short journey which he hadn't heard before, but after all, it was a Land Rover and probably needed a service.

Back at the depot, a monosyllabic conversation with the major ended when Dickie reminded him of the explosives audit meeting with Brigadier Bloodworth the next morning. The irritated major immediately performed a 'Bloodhound' movement and shuffled, head down, back to his office, clearly upset at being usurped and muttering about there being no need for an explosives audit as he was in charge. A while later his demeanour perked up on his announcement that he was going to check out the explosives. To Dickie, the major's increasingly unhealthy mine obsession was by now almost out of control. Perhaps, he pondered, the brigadier's meeting might be a watershed in the major's role at Tredyedeath Depot.

***

Fred spent the rest of the afternoon and early evening looking for Attila whilst Grace, Rozen, Dan and Gordon got a lift back to Feathers Farm. The grandchildren had seen enough excitement for one day, the only disappointment for poor sobbing Dan being Attila's decision to go AWOL. Fred wandered around the village calling out Attila's name, causing most of the locals, who knew nothing of the missing fowl, to assume that he too had succumbed to one too many of Steve's Tinner's Trembler. With the light failing, Fred finally gave up. He climbed back into his Land Rover, totally forgetting to pick up the empty cage, which was still in the marquee. He soon arrived back at Feathers Farm and had to break the news to an optimistic Dan that Attila was nowhere to be seen. However, he said they would both return to the village green tomorrow for another search, and this just about kept further tears at bay.

***

It was beginning to get dark and Attila had now been hunkering down in the back of the Land Rover for some time, surprised that Fred hadn't come to take her back into her barn home. She poked her head out of the open back of the vehicle, blinked twice and gulped at the unfamiliar surroundings. This wasn't her farm but a strange place with fences, floodlights, tarmac and neatly mown lawns. She looked up to see light from a first floor room creating faint shapes over the car park.

Attila wasn't at Feathers Farm. She was at Tredyedeath Depot. To a turkey, even an intelligent one, all Land Rovers looked the same and her quiet comforting squawks, designed to let Fred know that she was happy to be returning home, had fallen on deaf ears.

Despite the fact that she had had enough Steve McQueen action for the day there was only one thing for it: she was going to have to make another run for it. Hastily, she cast her eyes around to find a temporary hiding place for the night. The tall metal fencing and gates a short distance across the car park immediately came into view to reveal what seemed to be a dimly lit cave beyond, which looked like an ideal hiding place. Suddenly, she heard someone coming and she crouched down just enough to allow one inquisitive eye to see who it was. The major, with a spring in his step, was heading in the direction of the mine, whirling his key fob lanyard around like a propeller.

Attila watched attentively as, once inside the gates, the major approached the adjacent security alarm master switch pad. With the security gates locked firmly behind him, he raised the key fob to the pad and in one swiping action turned off the security system which deactivated the alarm, cameras, lasers, floodlights and other detection devices. He then hung the fob's lanyard over the master switch pad for reactivation on his return. He only needed the emergency lighting for his inspection, which could take a couple of hours. Security for the experimental SSPHE storage area at the back of the mine relied solely on guard dog patrols, which normally started later. There was still some uncertainty over whether the hi-tech security systems could trigger the experimental Jenga-like explosive sticks into life so it was decided to use guard dogs instead. In any event the only access to the SSPHE was through the securely protected mine.

As the happy major wandered into the mine, it was clear to Attila that her passport for a safe entrance to somewhere to hide was that key fob and pad contraption thing. It certainly let the major in with no trouble so it should, she thought, do the same for her. After all, her ambidextrous beak had already had a workout in escaping from Fred's cage at the village fete; it couldn't be that difficult. She was on a roll. The major had now been inside the mine for half an hour. The coast was clear.

As Attila hopped out of the back of the Land Rover and onto the car park below, the nearby kennel's inmates immediately sensed something alien outside and started to growl. Angry barks soon followed and she quickly realised that this was no time to offer herself as a 'take away' for the hungry hounds. Time to get a move on. A quick flap of her infrequently used short wings freed a few dozing mites in a cloud of fine dust and showed that everything was in working order for the short flight. With head down and eyes focused, she headed at speed for the cave, the sound of her clawed feet scratching on the hard tarmac surface and her rapidly flapping wings now being drowned out by what had now become a cacophony of barking just as she cleared the tall razor wire-topped fence.

Dickie, still in his office, came to the window to see what all the fuss was about. He looked across the yard to the mine, but saw nothing.

Attila landed safely inside the fence, just underneath the security alarm master switch pad, resplendent with dangling lanyard and fob. Her arrival was soon followed by a few white bottom feathers which drifted down seconds later; evidence of her brush with the razor wire, which she felt was just a little too close for comfort.

Dickie turned, stopped and, thinking that something had caught his eye, looked back. Instinctively, Attila stayed motionless. The barking stopped. No, he thought, it was nothing.

Attila quickly looked up and, fully outstretching her neck, just managed to secure the fob firmly in her beak. A quick shake of the head dislodged the lanyard. It was now all down to timing. A rapid flap of her wings lifted her off the ground and in one sweeping action of her head, she flicked the fob across the pad. Exhausted by such deft co-ordination, she sank to the ground and dropped the fob, feeling relieved that she had had enough excitement for one day. The job done, she innocently entered the mine to find a quiet hiding place to rest.

***

At the army's surveillance headquarters in Bromsgrove, specifically set up to monitor security of all national ARCE facilities, it had been a peaceful night so far. Most nights were peaceful, except when a wayward bat or small animal triggered an alarm. Heat, movement, light, a fart: the security system could detect anything. The banks of monitors in the blacked-out operations room flicked incessantly as they switched between rows of motionless boxes of explosives, corridors, car parks, entrance gates, security gates, even the toilets, whilst a vaguely attentive security officer, coffee in hand, watched on in the vain hope that a real intruder might, just for once, break the monotony.

The security system was set up to sound in Bromsgrove a minute before an ARCE base would know about it. This would provide the opportunity to get a visual on the culprit, alert the base and plan his capture before he could hear the alarms, flashing lights and general bedlam which might otherwise hasten his escape before anyone arrived. It also allowed for false alarms to be reset without waking up the whole countryside with a sinister-sounding siren normally associated with the onset of an imminent nuclear war.

Suddenly the alarm sounded. The red warning light and buzzer showed it was at Tredyedeath Depot. The Controlling Officer, commonly referred to as CO, was called over immediately by the excited operative. "Look, CO. It's a bloody white turkey. How did he get in there?"

"Ok thanks, op," CO replied. "Christ knows. They probably shag turkeys in Cornwall. Funny place. False alarm. Do a camera sweep to make sure it's not got any friends or that it's one of a bunch of midget terrorists dressed as turkeys. Then phone Tredyedeath Depot to say we've had a falsie and we'll do an alarm reset once they've caught the turkey."

Twenty seconds went by as the operative started his security camera sweep. He quickly stopped, looked forward and frantically waggled the console's remote camera joystick to take another look at what he thought he had just seen. He couldn't be sure. He looked again, mouth open. "Bloody hell. CO! CO!! You'd better come and look at this. I've switched the cameras to high def."

The security camera swept back and zoomed in on a neatly folded army uniform lying on the ground, hat on top, what looked like underpants and a pair of highly polished black shoes adjacent. The camera slowly panned up the side of a five foot stack of explosive boxes and stopped when it reached the top. The next shift of operatives, who had been waiting quietly at the back of the operation room, moved forward slowly towards the bank of screens to join the CO. The room went quiet. Quiet in shock, quiet in amazement, quiet in horror, quiet in amusement. Gobsmackingly quiet. For there, horizontal, almost motionless and lying stark naked on his back, was Major Charles Fox-Thrasher, the depot commanding officer. The camera zoomed in further. He was smoking a joint. The operations room had uncharacteristically gone into shock. Protocol had been cast to the wind.

***

Five seconds later, Tredyedeath Depot came alive to the sound of alarm sirens and the glare of floodlights. It was bedlam.

All too aware that the alarm system had been triggered and knowing that he was being filmed in glorious technicolour, Fox-Thrasher quickly sat upright, like something from a Frankenstein horror flick. He threw his doobie on the ground and jumped down from the boxes, his right hand covering his nether regions whilst his left arm swept up his neatly folded uniform, underpants, hat and shiny shoes. Unfortunately for the major, his naked, drug-infused dreams of Nirvana didn't dull the pain resulting from his attempted extinguishment of the still smouldering spliff with his bare right foot. Any hope of a rapid escape now seemed doomed as he started to perform a very poor impression of The Riverdance.

The alarm bedlam shocked Attila out of her slumbers and in a blind panic she fled into the mine, wings flapping, head bobbing, claws scraping on the concrete floor. The terrified turkey had stopped momentarily to get her bearings when an eerie giant shadow of something hopping up and down appeared on the wall behind the stacked explosives. She flew onto the top of the boxes to get a better view and recognised that this was the person who had used that key fob thing to get into the mine. She was in no doubt. It was all his fault. She scowled. He looked up in amazement and shook his head violently in disbelief. He'd bought a box of spliffs on the promise that, in his nakedness, they would take him to a land of dancing maidens, a land where no one had a care in the world – not one where he would be disembowelled by a large white turkey.

Attila then made her presence all too real as she flew down off the boxes to express to the major her extreme displeasure. She had had enough stress for one day. Neck outstretched and legs and claws pointing backwards, she was ready to inflict some painful damage. Fearing the worst, the major immediately dropped everything and, with one leg still fully operational, started a sort of running hop, momentarily exposing what, to Attila, looked like a two-day-old turkey poult nestling between his legs. Attila immediately took up the challenge and followed the major in hot pursuit as they quickly carved out a gladiatorial circuit around and around the explosives boxes.

The banks of screens in Bromsgrove were now fully tuned in as the naked major, with Attila close on his heels, momentarily exposed himself about every three seconds as they flashed up on one security screen after another at full speed. The laughing congregation of operatives, on and off duty, were now fully engaged in watching the chase as their heads flicked in perfect timing from screen to screen to watch the action. It was like a Wimbledon final.

The CO came out of his trance and looked at his operative. "Shit. Get onto Tredyedeath Depot. Tell them what we have seen. We need some guidance. This guy is supposed to be in change. Shit. He's going to get pecked to death."

The alarm had already alerted Dickie, who was on his feet. From his window he could see that the dog handlers had already arived at the gates of the still locked mine. He took the phone call and, shocked at the CO's explanation, told him to keep the alarm and cameras running until he had established what was going on. He grabbed a spare set of mine keys, ran over to the entrance and opened the gate just wide enough to get in. The growling dogs were pulling at their leashes expectantly, awaiting that command which would trigggger everything they'd learnt in training: strike, strike strike.

It was good timing, as the speeding, naked major suddenly rounded a box of explosives and came into view. "Let me out of the bloody mine!" he yelled to Dickie, whilst the dog handlers watched on in shock and amazement. Blood was coming from his well-pecked heels and the squinting Attila, head down and neck outstretched, was only a few yards behind with no intention of giving up. The major was now on his tenth lap of the mine and was clearly beginning to tire.

Dickie saw an opportunity and swiftly opened the gate to channel the ignominious commander out of the mine. The dog handlers quickly recognised that it was their commander coming towards them and with just enough time to pull the dogs up and stand to attention, they managed to form a guard of honour and salute as the naked major shot past them, across the dark car park and back to the safety of his office.

Dickie slammed the gate shut in front of the advancing Attila, whose outstretched legs and claws scrambled for grip to prevent her from being shredded by the gate's metal bars. Dickie stood for a moment and stared inquisitively at the puffing Wirral White. Karensa had called Dickie earlier to warn him that Attila had escaped and how upset Dan and Fred were. He looked again as Attila made a few familiar squawks. The penny dropped. The Land Rover didn't need servicing after all. Dickie needed to call Fred straight away.

Seeing that Attila wasn't in the mood for any more dust ups, Dickie walked into the mine to collect the major's dusty clothes. Knowing it was her, he called repeatedly to indicate that he was a friendly face, hoping that she would recognise him from his previous visit to Feathers Farm. He quickly returned to the office building and, to save any more embarrassment, left the major's clothes outside his door and retired to his own office. Fox-Thrasher took no time to dress himself and, without saying a word, made a hasty exit from the depot.

Dickie kept Bromsgrove at bay for an hour to sort matters out, having found Attila a quiet place to sit. It wasn't long before Fred arrived in his Land Rover with an excited Dan in the front seat, in his pyjamas and dressing gown. Attila was delighted to see them both. A relieved Fred collected her up into his large arms and deposited her back into the cage, which he had collected from the marquee on his way to the depot. Home beckoned.

The Bromsgrove security protocol required all breaches of security to be reported to Division. A DVD of the unfortunate incident was waiting on Brigadier Bloodworth's desk when he arrived to prepare for his meeting with the major the following morning.

It had indeed been a day of two 'fetes'.

Chapter 24:
Shamed and Stumped

Brigadier Bloodworth had enough on his plate with preparing his report to form part of the Defence Spending Review. ARCE facilities were on the line for cutbacks yet each had logistical, security or operational advantages. It was going to be a tough decision recommending which ones were in line for the Ministry's guillotine. The last thing the brigadier wanted to interrupt his busy schedule was to travel all the way to Cornwall to meet the errant major, but it was a meeting he needed to have face to face. The politicians wanted it sorted. Anyway, as an ARCE facility, Tredyedeath Depot was by no means safe from the emerging cutbacks so the trip had other benefits in allowing him the opportunity to have a look around.

He opened his post. A DVD dropped out. It was from Bromsgrove. It had 'Urgent review required' written on it. He slotted it into his computer. Ten minutes later, the phone rang. It was the Bromsgrove operations room's CO. "Morning, Brigadier. Have you seen it yet?"

"I'm just looking at it now. What the...? Oh! Oh! Gross! Bloody hell."

"I assume you have had your breakfast, Brigadier? Sorry if you haven't. It's not a pretty sight. Not sure how high the major was expecting to get smoking that joint but if the mine had gone up, my guess is he would be in the Balkans by now. Christ knows where that turkey came from. The major always lets us know when he is on his mine inspection run because he switches off the alarms. We still can't work out how it was activated. Maybe he and the turkey had something going on when it tripped accidentally. Weird."

With the explanations and phone call over, the brigadier calmed himself. It was quite clear that things couldn't get any worse but he was going to keep that to himself for the moment. He now had the spliff-smoking naked major incident to deal with in their meeting. Armed with an official box file loaded by Wally Dinsmore and ready to take aim and fire, he was soon on his way to Tredyedeath Depot, arriving in good time to be met by Captain Lovely, who showed him to the meeting room. A moment later the corridor resounded to the major's irregular footsteps, Attila's pecking frenzy and the spliff extinguishment episode having put paid to his characteristic and perfectly timed regimental stride. On entry to the meeting room, the hobbling major still managed to keep a straight back and eye contact when he faced the brigadier. His strategy was to show authority tinged with civility: here was the depot commanding officer, fully in command of everything; an officer who could show to his officious Division chief that travelling five hours to undertake an audit of his depot and his beloved explosives was a complete waste of time. He couldn't have foreseen what was to follow.

Dickie's offer to write the minutes was immediately accepted by the brigadier, who decided to launch a surprise attack on the major. His strategy was to neutralise the enemy's firepower and prevent the possibility of a counter attack. They sat down facing each other. The brigadier took out a shiny brown envelope from his box file, which he flicked across the table towards the major. Bloodworth said nothing as the apprehensive Fox-Thrasher looked, first at the envelope coming his way and then when it stopped, at the brigadier. He slowly leaned forward, opened the envelope and slid out some photos. The silence was deafening. He closed his eyes, pursed his lips and lowered his head. The major was the philandering, cheating and unfaithful 'husband' to the brigadier's outraged and furious 'wife' and here, in black and white, was the damning evidence.

With piercing eyes, the brigadier stared at the major, preparing for an excuse, but the major's head remained submissively low with shame. "Major, as you can see, I know about last night. In fact I have a DVD of the whole sordid affair. These are just some extracts of the event. What have you got to say for yourself? I don't want excuses."

The room remained quiet. Very quiet. The major's anticipated counter attack had been neutralised. There were no bullets left in his armoury, no shells loaded in his cannon. Defeat was inevitable. It was only a matter of time before the white flag would come out.

The brigadier was not an insensitive man and after reviewing the DVD he had taken the trouble, before he left his office that morning, to discuss the episode with an old trauma psychologist friend in the medical corps he knew from his Falklands bomb disposal days. He had seen some of the symptoms before in a different theatre and suspected the cause may be deep-rooted. His friend explained that nakedness could be an escape, an opportunity to cast off deep-seated shackles of a past in which the uniform represented a form of obligated straightjacket. The use of drugs was not unusual in heightening the freedom nakedness could bring, but would only provide temporary relief from reality.

The brigadier soon suspected that the major's troubles, his unwillingness to capitulate, his intransigence and his arrogance, might be family related, given the Fox-Thrashers' well-known history of military service. Expectations to maintain that family tradition and an unloving relationship with a violent, dominating father also contributed to a truth the brigadier was closer to than he realised.

Whatever the reasons, the major's mine episode and his management of the Gooleys' planning application were enough for the brigadier to conclude that this was not a man fit to run an explosives depot. At even the most basic level of explosives management, and without delving into the major's troubles, smoking in a mine filled with enough explosive force to register an unexpected guest appearance on the Richter scale was, in any military man's eyes, a capital offence.

With the major's head even lower and Dickie looking decidedly uncomfortable, the brigadier continued. "Look, Major. Let's park all that stuff for the moment. Until last night, my main focus in coming here was to talk to you about your handling of the Gooleys' application." It didn't take long for the brigadier to spell out the catalogue of errors set out in the Ministry's internal report, commissioned at the highest level, into the major's handling of the whole affair. He tossed a copy of the report onto the table.

"In short, Major, if you had taken the trouble to understand the nature of Mr Gooley's business before you decided whether or not to object to his planning application you would have concluded that you didn't have a leg to stand on. You had plenty of opportunities to change your mind but you are not the 'charge of mind' type, are you, Major? You lied to one of my division managers over the facts of the application. What, Major, is really galling to me is that, paradoxically, the Ministry's civvies have cocked up too. They produced a safeguarding map direction without much input from my division with a bloody great hole in it bigger than the explosive effect of all our ARCEs put together. If you had taken some advice – a strange word, I know – we could have dealt with it differently. We are now faced with a perfectly reasonable claim for costs by Mr Gooley over this ridiculous inquiry – which you forced the stupid civvies in the Secretary of State for Planning's office to organise, and which you then treated with contempt. To make matters worse, I am also advised that we will have to buy out the Gooleys to protect Tredyedeath Depot's storage capability and its flawed safeguarding map direction.

"Major, you are relieved from dealing with the Gooleys' application any further. I will be personally withdrawing the Ministry's objection to it. And by the way, no more nakedness, no more drugs, and on the basis that you must have smuggled that turkey into the mine, no more turkey business either. In the mine or anywhere else for that matter. Disgusting! Finally, I will be retrieving the SSPHE as I can't risk you with it any longer than I have to. I will let you know when. I have still to make some recommendations about your position here and from where I'm sitting, your ARCE doesn't look good. Oh, and if I were you I would get some therapy."

In a state of abject denial, the major disengaged himself from the brigadier's dressing down by ostensibly looking through the report. The brigadier knew there wasn't much more he could say to the uncommunicative commander and he got up to leave. A warrant officer was waiting downstairs ready to conduct him on a tour of the depot before his return home back to Division. For Bloodworth – a man prepared to see the good in people, if good was there – it had been a particularly unpleasant day. He wasn't convinced that the institutionalised major was prepared to take any of his advice but at least for the time being he couldn't do any more damage.

The brigadier's assumptions were right. Dickie had only been back at his desk for a few moments when he felt rumblings coming from the major's office. It was a 'Blue Streak' movement and the corridor rattled with the major's hobbling, which was heading in Dickie's direction. The captain's door flung open. "You little shit. This is all your fault. I suppose you planted that turkey and recorded the DVD? Eh? I suppose you think it's funny? Well you're not getting away with it. You can take the bloody SSPHE back yourself when we get the go ahead from that officious git, Bloodworth."

As the major turned to hobble back to his office, Dickie, aghast at the major's pathetic rant, stood up and walked smartly up to him, their noses a few inches apart. He had had enough. "Sir. Was the turkey chasing you because she didn't like it or was she begging you for more? I would appreciate if you would tell me next time so I can decide whether or not to open the gates, let you out and retrieve your clothes, like the only friend you had in the world at that point. After all, I wouldn't want to interrupt your fantasies. Or is the nakedness and drug addiction altogether something quite different and the turkey was just an unwelcome intruder? I think we are well past the blame game, Major, don't you think? You need to get a grip if you don't want another guard of honour like last night. I am sure they will remember that for a long time. Would you like me to find you a therapist? I am sure the army's got one somewhere."

Shocked at the normally servile captain's response, the major, close to losing his rag, returned to the sanctity of his office. Dickie wondered where it would all lead. The major's future was now in Brigadier Bloodworth's hands.

***

It was now mid-June and Penelope was beavering away at her desk, her left hand in a bandage, the result of being trapped in a car door. The first post contained a letter from Brigadier Bloodworth.

"Dear Ms Breakage. After a thorough analysis of our procedures in relation to the safeguarding map and direction at Tredyedeath Depot, the Ministry has decided to withdraw its objection to the planning application submitted by Mr Gooley of Feathers Farm. We have today informed the Secretary of State for Planning of the Ministry's decision and a copy of this letter has also been sent to PINS. The Ministry will therefore not be appearing at the reopened public inquiry into the Gooleys' planning application, which is to be determined by the Secretary of State for Planning."

Bloodworth had been required to liaise directly with Whitehall on all matters to do with the public inquiry in order to protect the Ministry's tarnished reputation, particularly given the damage already wreaked by the major. It was a classic 'no fault' letter, having been subjected to the Whitehall 'Mandarin Mangle' to extract any hint of liability on the part of the Ministry.

Bloodworth had been given no authority by the Treasury to acquiesce on the issue of any costs that were going to have to be squeezed out of them. Dickie received a copy of Bloodworth's letter by email and reported its contents to the major who, like a spoilt child, showed total disinterest. It was judiciously slipped into Dickie's blue file for safe keeping.

Penelope soon circulated the letter to Johnny, CHN and a delighted Fred, who immediately phoned Trevelyan to give him the good news. A quick call from Penelope to Jim Stern at the council confirmed that he too had received a copy of the letter. Fred was delighted but warned Penelope that the value of Feathers Farm was now significantly less than it had been when his development proposals should originally have been approved, never mind all his costs in having to pursue the application at the public inquiry, which had sent him stratospherically into overdraft.

Penelope's experience told her that the brevity of Bloodworth's letter and its total lack of explanation for the volte face was a sure sign that the Ministry knew it was culpable – but it wasn't going to admit it. Any admission of guilt could have wider implications for the Ministry's flawed safeguarding map and direction and its other ARCE facilities if it were too willing to throw in the costs towel at this stage. Keeping everything under wraps was a priority and if there was to be a fight on costs and compensation, it would have to be particular to Tredyedeath Depot. Penelope had no doubt that Fred had a good claim and she briefed CHN for the reopened inquiry.

***

'Gunpowder' Guy sent a courtesy copy of Bloodworth's sanitised Ministry letter to Sir Michael Stride-Pecker MP to underline his pro-activeness on the case and it wasn't long before Sir Michael lined up a few gin and tonics in the Strangers' Bar to repay his friend for his diligence in helping one of his constituents. Guy was grateful but saw it quite differently. Sir Michael had done him a favour. The internal review had unearthed an anomaly in the safeguarding map and direction process which his department clearly needed to deal with, notwithstanding the cock ups caused by the major at Tredyedeath Depot.

Sir Michael had one other issue to raise. "Guy. What are you going to do about the issue of the costs claim against the Ministry? They are coming your way, you know. Of that I have no doubt."

"I thought you would mention that, Michael," Guy said. "All I can say is if you think back to the problems you had with the Treasury over keeping that bloody personal train of yours going – what's it called, the Night Riviera? – I would imagine the Treasury will want me to resist any costs claimed by your Mr Gooley. I mean, he'll get his planning permission, won't he? What more does he want?"

"He wants his bloody costs back because the Ministry has cocked up. That's what he wants, Guy. Wouldn't you?"

"Probably, but right now I'm not him!"

"Ok but if he decides to make a claim to the Parliamentary Ombudsman, I will be happy to back it," Sir Michael said. "I can't do otherwise because actually, I think he's right. He could go bust over this episode, you know. If he did, it would be a hollow victory and that would be awful. There would be no winners. If I have to ask questions in the House about this, I will."

"I fully understand, Michael. You have a job to do – but my hands are tied. Let's see where it goes. If it comes to it and we can't thrash out a deal, you have my word that I will personally make sure he gets his money fast if the Ombudsman gives us a bloody nose. If you are going to ask a question in the House about it, just give me some warning first, won't you? And not two minutes before you ask it!"

They agreed to keep in close contact. The distinctive sound of the Strangers' Bar door opening caught Guy and Sir Michael's attention and they both looked over in surprise to see Jim Stoker and Conker McQueen engaged in light-hearted banter about Protestants – but then, it was only five o'clock. Jim ordered the first round. Guy and Sir Michael decided to leave.

***

Late July soon came round and Planning Inspector Clifford Stump arrived back in Trecarsick the night before the reopened public inquiry. With the Cornish tourist industry in full swing, the only accommodation available in the locality was in the Tinner's Whippet. Stump arrived late and, after a quick freshen up, found a quiet corner of the pub for something to eat. The men-only dominoes team were having their weekly meeting which, judging by the smirks and suggestive arm movements, seemed to be playing 'dirty dominoes'.

Dickie and Karensa were on a date and were cuddled up chatting in the snug, when she recognised the inspector from his light-hearted contretemps with Cordelia over her village hall guerrilla tactics a few months earlier. Like her mother, she couldn't resist a bit of banter so she got up and walked over to the inspector. Loosening her top a little, she leaned forwards. "Would you like a Trembler?" she asked. The timing was a little unfortunate as a small piece of chicken goujon had just taken centre stage in the inspector's open mouth, and the shock of Karensa's suggestion caused him to almost choke. Karensa had had her fun. Time for her to retrieve the situation before Stumpy was able to make a sound. "You don't seem to have a drink and there is still some Tinner's Trembler left from the village fete. It's a lovely drop, you know. Hello, I am Karensa, Cordelia Craddock's daughter. You met my mother at the inquiry. I am sure you remember."

The inspector, having stopped spluttering, looked visibly relieved as he composed himself. "Ah yes. Hello. How could I forget your mother? I'm afraid I am going to have to decline both the drink and any further dialogue with you because I have to remain, and be seen to remain, impartial."

Karensa smiled and nodded knowingly. She wished the inspector a pleasant stay and returned to her beloved Dickie.

***

The next day soon arrived. It was quiet outside the village hall. No sign of the pensioner protestors or Cordelia. Word had got round about the Ministry's withdrawal from the inquiry and everyone had already gathered inside the hall to discuss the turn of events. Trevedic Penhaligon had arrived early for once and was sitting patiently, concocting his latest *Trumpet* headline. Just before proceedings were due to start the village hall double doors swung open to announce the characteristic arrival of Trevelyan. Everyone looked over and held their breath in the hope that the door repair after his last destructive entrance was good enough. The doors closed gracefully. They passed the 'extreme Trelyon' test with flying colours.

"Well good morning, ladies and gentlemen, it is ten o'clock. My name is Clifford Stump and I am the planning inspector. Today I am re-opening this inquiry into the planning application for Feathers Farm." The procedures started once again as the inspector explained the position from his hymn sheet and brought everyone up to speed.

"Ladies and gentlemen, as you will be aware this public inquiry has been called by the Secretary of State for Planning and I will be making my conclusions and recommendations for him to make the decision. Although the Ministry of Defence has now withdrawn its objection to this planning application and has decided not to appear today, I am still required to consider the application on its merits. However, I see no point in hearing evidence from the parties here today who are, shall we say, on the same side. I therefore intend to take the evidence already submitted as read – but first I have a few questions."

A further hour was taken up with some detailed questions from the inspector, which Johnny and Jim answered from their seats, ensuring that Stumpy had everything he needed. Cordelia was given the opportunity to make some comments on behalf of her throng of supporters, but she could see from the inspector's questions that she would only be repeating things and anyway, his body language suggested that he didn't want to continue with the inquiry any longer than absolutely necessary.

"Mrs Craddock, I am grateful for your brevity in the matter and of course I have read all your supporters' letters, which I will take into account when reaching my recommendations. Now. Mr Hartlock-Naddertrout, I would like to turn to the issue of costs, which, as you can appreciate, I am not permitted to invite, but it would not surprise me if you had prepared a costs submission, particularly given that you already put me on notice, when I opened the inquiry a few months ago, of your clients' intention to make a claim again the Ministry of Defence on the grounds of its unreasonableness."

CHN rose to his feet. "I am obliged, sir."

CHN immediately sat down again to allow Stumpy a further interjection. "Oh. Mr Hartlock-Naddertrout, I do need to say something, which perhaps I should have said earlier. As you had already put me on notice at the inquiry, I took the trouble during the adjournment period to refresh my memory by reference to the government's guidance on costs claims. I am afraid to say that, from my reading of the circular, it is not possible for you to make a claim for costs against the Ministry of Defence at this inquiry as government departments are specifically excluded from that process. I suspect that you may have been aware of this but I do need to remind you. However, you are of course more than welcome to make your submission anyway – which I can see you have there in writing for me – but it's simply not within my jurisdiction in this forum to deal with such a claim. Having said that, I see no reason why I cannot make reference to your submission in my report and recommendations, if I feel that the Ministry of Defence has been unreasonable. In that context your submission may be helpful to me and the Secretary of State as an aide memoire in relation to the chronology of events. To complete the point, and for your assistance, I would suggest that, to seek recompense, you take up the matter directly with the Ministry itself or failing that, I am sure you are aware that there is of course the Parliamentary Ombudsman who has specific jurisdiction to consider complaints against government departments and scope to award costs against that department if appropriate."

The inspector's comments came as no surprise to Penelope and CHN, who had advised Fred that his costs battle may yet be one still to have. However, it was clear that the inspector was sympathetic to the cause and his earlier questions suggested that he was also sympathetic to Fred's development proposals. They had nothing to lose.

Having sat down to allow Stumpy to make his comments, CHN rose to his feet once again and adopted his respectful stance. "I'm obliged and grateful, sir. I was aware of the circular's terms but your incisive summary, practical understanding and clarification of the costs position is very helpful. This inquiry is perhaps one instance when one wonders why it is not possible to seek costs against a government department as it seems to me to invite unreasonableness with no immediate sanction. However, sir, I am not on my soap box today and as you rightly say, the Parliamentary Ombudsman route is available as a failsafe."

CHN looked around at his team to see Penelope and Johnny nodding furiously in agreement. He continued. "Sir, my client feels very strongly that costs against the Ministry is something he wants to pursue. Even more so given that you had to adjourn the public inquiry specifically to allow time for the Ministry to, as it were, get its act together. Now that the Ministry has withdrawn altogether and is bunkered down somewhere, nowhere to be seen, my client is even more determined to pursue his claim, particularly as we have been given no substantive reasons as to its sudden volte-face. I am therefore grateful that you are nevertheless prepared to hear my submission which, if nothing else, will provide you with, as you say, a chronological aide memoire in the preparation of your report to the Secretary of State for Planning."

CHN then waded in with his incisively prepared costs claim, which he knew would probably end up in front of the Parliamentary Ombudsman but it was a good opportunity to give it a dry run. "Never in thirty years at the bar have I experienced such intransigence on the part of the Ministry of Defence, or indeed any other government department," CHN began. "It has shown a wilful disregard for any reasonable objective assessment of my client's application, despite being invited to do so on numerous occasions." CHN then catalogued the sad chronology of events, mistakes, lies, and total failure of the Ministry to meet any of the legal procedures and timetables required of it. Even CHN was getting a little hot under the collar in having to spell out the sorry tale of events, which he finally completed after twenty-five minutes on his feet. It was a measured and well delivered performance tinged with just a hint of controlled anger to indicate the seriousness the Gooley camp felt about how it had been treated.

The diminutive Cordelia had been mesmerised by CHN's performance and took the opportunity at the close of the inquiry to elbow Trevelyan Trelyon out of the way in her rush to congratulate the statuesque QC. Stumpy, it seemed was history in her eyes. It was only a pity, she commented to the flattered barrister, that Major Fox-Thrasher and his cohort Major Blitherington hadn't been put through CHN's cross-examination mill to expose their atrocious behaviour.

The inspector wound up the inquiry just before lunch and confirmed that his report and recommendation would be with the Secretary of State for Planning within a month. The completion of his duties required a mandatory visit to the planning application site at Feathers Farm, which was arranged to start at 2pm. Penelope and CHN left the team to discuss a strategy for pursuing costs against the Ministry given the inspector's acknowledged lack of jurisdiction over the matter and they were soon on their way to the offices of Steel, Cash and Scamper.

The inspector arrived at Feathers Farm on time and was met by Jim Stern, Johnny and Fred. Grace was ready and waiting with some tea and cake. The sound of footsteps in the courtyard soon stirred Attila from her early afternoon nap and she rushed out to see what was going on. Her nodding soon revealed to Fred that she detected no enemies in the camp but he picked her up anyway just to be sure she didn't change her mind. Now was definitely not the time to make enemies. The inspector accepted Grace's tea and cakes on the basis that everyone else had exactly the same in equal measure and, following a thorough walk around the farm, made his formal goodbyes.

Trevedic Penhaligon decided to stay on in the village hall and use the time and quietness to prepare his next article, capped off with a suitable *Trumpet* headline. Fred had made his friend aware of the withdrawal of the Ministry's objection but the inquiry and CHN's costs claim really brought it all home. A particularly incisive headline beckoned and by the following Thursday, the village store pavement board said it all: "Ministry Made a Mockery by Meddling Major over Military Magazine".

Chapter 25:
Good Things Come in Threes

With the inquiry over, Penelope and Johnny wasted no time in preparing, with CHN's guidance, a letter to the Ministry setting out Fred's claim for substantive costs. Stumpy's confirmation that he had no jurisdiction in the matter had been clear and Penelope had drafted a writ to accompany the letter seeking recompense by other processes. It demanded repayment of all costs associated with the inquiry. Compensation was also sought for the drop in value of Feathers Farm caused by the unjustified and unnecessary delay. Whilst planning permission had yet to be granted, she made it clear that the Ministry's withdrawal of its objection was likely, in her view, to lead to a positive outcome and that permission would be forthcoming.

It wasn't long before a hard-hitting letter arrived on Brigadier Bloodworth's desk giving the Ministry two weeks to respond or else. It soon found its way to Whitehall and, inevitably, on to the Treasury. The time bomb was still ticking and firmly in the Ministry's court.

Bloodworth's phone rang. The brigadier immediately recognised the voice of the Ministry's Whitehall mandarin, who was a little more animated than usual. "Morning, Brigadier. Thank you for the letter from Steel, Cash and Scamper. We need to delay. We need to buy time. I suggest that you respond by offering hope. You need to suggest that the Ministry is considering purchasing Feathers Farm but it cannot justify this expense to the Treasury until the Secretary of State for Planning has received the inquiry inspector's recommendations and issued his decision on the planning application. There's an outside chance that it could be refused and the Ministry needs to be clear on property values. Of course, I appreciate that we are weak in unnecessarily calling for the public inquiry, which has legitimacy in a costs claim whatever the outcome. We are likely to lose if we try to resist that, but our approach is to make any decisions on any claims for compensation all at the same time. The carrot of an outright purchase of the farm might just buy us some time."

Whitehall had cunningly worked out that property values were falling faster than Penelope from a ski lift so any delay it could buy wouldn't do it any harm. Bloodworth soon responded to Penelope by email.

The message failed miserably. Penelope immediately saw through the subterfuge as a delaying tactic and, by return, her acidulous email pointed out that, whilst the Ministry's consideration of the purchase of Feathers Farm was a new, encouraging, and indeed welcome gesture, it was not the granting of planning permission the Ministry should consider to be the determining factor. If its acquisition was a way to protect explosives storage capability at Tredyedeath Depot because of the flawed safeguarding map direction, then they should buy it now. The issue of values was of course important to her client but this could be determined later once the planning application had been decided by the Secretary of State. There was therefore no reason why acquisition, along with the rest of the compensation claim, could not commence straight away. By the tone of Bloodworth's response Penelope concluded that either the Ministry did not appear to have a clear picture of its own priorities or someone was pulling its strings or, more to the point, its purse strings. She reiterated that her clients' costs claim was entirely independent of the decision on the planning application. There was, therefore, absolutely no reason to delay resolution of the matter any longer in view of the considerable hardship the Ministry had unnecessarily put her clients to. An immediate response was requested, failing which her clients would adopt the 'nuclear option', one she was sure would be totally recognisable to the Ministry of Defence, the resulting fallout being particularly unpleasant.

Bloodworth knew he had a worthy adversary in Penelope and was increasingly beginning to feel like he was carrying Whitehall's messages on its dirty laundry. But he had little option but to fire the next salvo. Time for Plan B. Whitehall suggested that, if all else failed, a meeting at Division with all parties could buy time in seeking a solution.

Penelope, having put down a marker, reluctantly agreed but only on the basis that the meeting would make real progress. She made it clear that any sniff of prevarication would result in an immediate commencement of proceedings against the Ministry via the offices of the Parliamentary Ombudsman, for which she already had the requisite and willing sponsor in local MP Sir Michael Stride-Pecker.

Penelope soon reported to Fred and Grace the Ministry's idea of purchasing Feathers Farm outright and a delighted Fred agreed that there could be significant benefits in a deal with the Ministry if they could agree on values, including his costs. It was all beginning to go Fred's way – and about time too, for his portly frame was rapidly expanding as Grace's industrial scale cake output was becoming inversely proportional to her drop in blood pressure.

Penelope then received further good news and was soon on the phone again. Ashley Sweet's insurers, who had been kept regularly up to date with events, had confirmed that it would compensate Fred for loss of anticipated income from his Christmas turkey business, ceased unnecessarily on Ashley's advice. The award recognised, in coded language, that the location of Feathers Farm within the Tredyedeath Depot explosion zone was a major risk that Ashley should have assessed as a possible delaying factor in his management of the planning application which, in turn, should have made him more circumspect. The insurers also accepted that, in any event, it was not absolutely critical to close the business simply to demonstrate its commercial unviability and Fred was therefore put to undue hardship by Ashley's advice. Penelope knew Ashley from her local Truro contacts and she gave him some friendly advice that, in future, he stick to his core business and to come and see her or Johnny if there was a planning problem.

The years were beginning to fall from Fred and Grace and the insurance cheque was quickly banked, though a lot of it was swallowed up by their overdraft, the costs of the inquiry, interest and now the ongoing costs claim against the resistant Ministry. It wasn't long before the payment pinged up on Dennis Blackstaff's computer in the bank and he soon picked up the phone to congratulate Fred on the much needed injection of funds. To Fred, the call was not because of Dennis' genuine personal concern for his financial well-being, like it might have been in the old days. It was all about Dennis saving his scalp by avoiding having to fend off draconian demands from head office to reduce Fred's overdraft, whatever the personal implications for the Gooleys.

It wasn't long before Dennis homed in on the real reason for his congratulatory phone call. "Oh, and as an aside, Mr Gooley, just before I go, I wonder whether I could have those photos back now. You remember, the ones of me in the slaughterhouse?"

Fred played it cool. "Well Dennis, I am not quite out of the woods yet and I still have more expenditure to come. Of course, I know the bank will have our best interests at heart if I need some more resources during the recession but I wouldn't want your head office colleagues to get cold feet at this critical time. I am sure you understand. Sorry Dennis, I'm afraid I am going to have to keep you dangling a little longer. It shouldn't be a problem, should it? After all, you are used to dangling, aren't you, Dennis?"

Dennis played it down as just a passing request of no consequence but this wasn't what he wanted to hear at all. It was a big deal to him. The lingering threat of ignominy had made him remarkably adept at keeping Head Office at bay and his inventiveness was more than Fred could have hoped for. For Fred and Grace their insurance card – a merciless *Trumpet* expose: 'Turkey Traps Macabre Meddling Manager in Supernatural Slaughterhouse' – remained on the launchpad but hopefully they wouldn't have to press the 'fire' button.

***

The day of the meeting at Division arrived. It was the end of August and Penelope and Johnny sat patiently in the foyer rehearsing their party line.

Penelope was going to take the lead and Johnny would write the minutes. Johnny was about to comment happily that she appeared to be devoid of any medical apparel when she put her hand up to flick her long brown hair behind her ear, forgetting that she was still holding her biro. Fortunately her right eye just escaped a direct hit but as her ballpoint swept across her forehead a second blue eyebrow appeared just above the real one. She hurriedly licked a tissue and, holding a compact, started to frantically wipe it off, rejecting Johnny's flippant suggestion that if she drew a similar one on the other side of her head, the Coco the Clown look might just catch on. Normality had just returned when Brigadier Bloodworth appeared to escort them to the meeting room, where two senior Whitehall Doo-Wops with long suffix job titles and matching suits introduced themselves.

With the pleasantries over, Penelope set out the basis of her clients' costs claim but, with Bloodworth staying silent during the discussions, it wasn't long before Penelope and Johnny could see from the blank faces staring back at them that there was a total failure to accept any sort of responsibility whatsoever for what had happened. The Ministry mantra was fired back over and over again: "The Ministry had a duty to protect its explosive storage capability at Tredyedeath Depot and had, in all respects, acted responsibly in the best interests of defending this important national facility…"

It was clear that, if nothing else, the meeting demonstrated the Ministry's consistency with its previous delaying tactics. After rejecting absolutely the Ministry's position, Penelope rose purposefully to her feet and, packing her briefcase, made a short 'see you in court' statement. Having read the runes, Johnny stopped writing and he too started frantically packing his briefcase. The brigadier's smart uniform somehow gave more authority to the meeting and he could see the need to use his recognised adept communication skills. He leaned forward in an attempt to retrieve the situation. As his colleagues were clearly not used to negotiating anything, let alone a compromise, Bloodworth started prompting the Doo-Wops, still glued to their seats with their arms folded, by hinting with coded references at the private discussions he had had with them about how the matter might just be taken forward to everyone's benefit. As he reminded them, that was, after all, the purpose of the meeting.

For fear of being the only ones left in the room, the suits got the message and suddenly sprang back into life. "Ah, yes. Thank you, Brigadier. However, Miss Breakage, in these exceptional circumstances, and without accepting responsibility for any blame whatsoever, the Ministry of Defence is prepared, on this rare occasion, to acquire Feathers Farm from your client. However, this very generous concession would be at a value decided once the Secretary of State for Planning has determined the planning application and would represent a full and final settlement including any costs incurred by your client arising out of the inquiry."

Still on her feet, Penelope carried on packing up and then, looking particularly angry at the arrogance of the offer, she leaned forward over the table and stared at both of them. "The only conceivable way that your pathetic offer would be acceptable to my clients is that it would be on a without prejudice basis to any claim we may continue to make to the Parliamentary Ombudsman over the Ministry's shambolic handling of the affair, together with the effect this has had on the depreciating value of my clients' property. The Ministry will have to buy this farm anyway to protect Tredyedeath Depot – so don't think you are going to get it cheap. In my book, culpability costs – and the Ministry is culpable."

With the situation going backwards for the Ministry, Bloodworth butted in. It was uncharacteristically ill timed. "Of course, Miss Breakage, I can say confidentially that I am currently reviewing Tredyedeath Depot ARCE for possible closure under the Defence Spending Review and it's possible that we may not need to buy the farm at all if we close the base."

Penelope quickly retorted: "Brigadier, that seems to me to be a veiled threat suggesting that if we don't accept your colleague's ridiculous offer now, you won't be obliged to compensate my client at all if the depot is closed. Nothing could be further from the truth. Whether or not you pull out of the purchase is your affair. It doesn't absolve the Ministry of its appalling behaviour. Good day."

With that, Penelope, with Johnny in tow, walked defiantly out of the meeting room and were soon on their way back to Cornwall and straight to Feathers Farm. Whilst Fred and Grace had a buyer for the farm in the Ministry, and even with Ashley's compensation claim in the bank, they were still a long way short of where they needed to be financially. It was agreed that the complaint to the Parliamentary Ombudsman should commence immediately in the hope that it would galvanise the Ministry into action in purchasing Feathers Farm.

***

It was now late September. Penelope and Johnny had worked tirelessly with CHN in preparing Fred's complaint and costs submission prior to onward submission to the Parliamentary Ombudsman. The formal process required the claim to demonstrate maladministration and that all reasonable avenues to resolve the issue had been taken without success. It also had to be sponsored by a Member of Parliament and Sir Michael Stride-Pecker had, through Trevelyan Trelyon, offered to take up the cudgels on Fred's behalf.

Sir Michael's next Saturday morning surgery in Bodmin town hall soon came around and he was delighted to meet Fred, Grace, Penelope and Johnny. It made a welcome relief from another dose of constituent troubles: a complaint about the smell of a neighbour's rubbish bins; a distraught constituent wanting a full scale police search for her grandson's lost guinea pig.

Penelope proudly handed over a box file containing her costs claim report, supported by numerous accompanying appendices all in chronological order, all numbered, all neatly tied up by CHN's clerk with a pink ribbon ready for Sir Michael to lodge on his return to London.

A few days later, Penelope was standing by her desk when the first post arrived. She noticed a brown envelope conspicuously poking out of the usual white and cream pile and she flicked it out purposefully to reveal the standard PINS logo on the front. She knew immediately that this had to be the formal decision on Fred's planning application. Opening it quickly, she slid out the Secretary of State for Planning's formal decision letter and Stumpy's accompanying detailed report. After a momentary focus on the letter's front page where the all-important words could be found, she let out an uncharacteristic yelp. "Yes... yes! The planning application is granted!"

This was the approval that Ashley had told Fred eighteen months earlier would be a forgone conclusion. It was a major success – but with the Ministry still fighting Penelope's costs claim and a recession in full swing, she knew Fred might see it as a hollow victory until and unless the Ministry paid its dues. She sat down and focused again to see if there were any nuggets that might help with the compensation claim against the Ministry. Time to read the whole decision and Stumpy's report and recommendations carefully. It was damning. Stumpy had clearly been irritated by the whole affair and only he, as a senior planning inspector, could get away with his candid comments knowing that the Secretary of State would, unsurprisingly, make no comment other than to acknowledge that any claim against the Ministry for costs was not a matter which fell within his jurisdiction. CHN's incisive costs claim had indeed been carefully and subtly used by him as a chronological aide memoire in his report. Stumpy couldn't resist it.

"I find it regrettable that the Ministry ... The actions of the Ministry were wholly unjustified ... The evidence from the report to the planning committee was plainly one which highlighted a potential weakness in the safeguarding map direction as worded, yet the Ministry's failure to reflect on this ... Significant time could have been saved if the Ministry..."

He nevertheless made sure that in his findings and recommendation to the Secretary of State that permission be granted, Fred's proposals had merit irrespective of the Ministry's behaviour. This was all the Secretary of

State needed.

***

The news spread fast to all corners of the Trecarsick community and beyond. An elated Fred and Grace saw it as another nail in the Ministry's coffin and despite the battles still to come, felt that right would prevail over wrong. Good over evil. It was now only a matter of time. Fred's daily discussions with Attila now took on a new level of optimism, one where he could look to the future with hope. She detected tones of joy in his voice and confidence in his swagger; laughter had returned, as had extra portions of turkey feed, which started to appear at all times of the day. Attila studied Fred carefully as he filled her bowl. In a DNA moment, it briefly crossed her mind that perhaps she was being fattened up for Christmas – but she decided to give Fred the benefit of the doubt.

The timing was perfect too for Trevedic, who had just enough time to keep Fred's plight at the forefront of local issues as Thursday's *Trumpet* deadline loomed. The village shop pavement board once again proudly carried the message all his supporters had hoped for. This time Trevedic was getting personal: 'Government's Gaff is Gooleys' Gain. Defeated Depot Dictator Dished a Drubbing by Development Decision'.

***

A copy of the Secretary of State for Planning's decision letter and Stumpy's report landed on Dickie's desk, coincidentally at the same time as an altogether darker letter from Brigadier Bloodworth. The major was required to attend a hearing at Division in the New Year. In the meantime he could continue to fulfil all his duties to the best of his ability and should he have any issues, the brigadier would be more than happy to discuss these with him. The brigadier's letter suggested that, on his way to the hearing, the major return the boxes of SSPHE to the Ministry's explosives depot near Reading. To make matters worse, Dickie's late morning second post contained a copy of the Parliamentary Ombudsman's acknowledgement letter of the Gooleys' complaint together with a compliment slip from the brigadier containing a short message. In anticipation that the Ombudsman would leave no stone unturned, the brigadier requested Dickie send him forthwith copies of all paperwork relating to any aspect of the Gooley case, no matter how insignificant. Dickie's blue file beckoned. He pondered all the letters with mild amusement. It seemed that good things really did come in threes.

By this time Dickie's relationship with the major was non-existent. The naked spliff-smoking incident had driven the depot commander to adopt a denial-infused siege mentality. He placed the blame squarely, but not fairly, on the innocent captain's doorstep and to the major, Dickie's continued rejection of the accusations only appeared to confirm his duplicity.

Fox-Thrasher had become so unpredictable that Dickie suspected that sight of Fred's official planning permission, the brigadier's hearing 'invitation' and the Parliamentary Ombudsman's complaint acknowledgement, all relating to matters directly the result of the major's actions, might have the effect equivalent to lighting a dodgy Chinese firework: there was a good chance it would go off before you blew the match out. The major's mine episodes had stopped but he had started taking longer lunch breaks a few times a week and coincidentally the three letters had arrived on one of those days. It was a good time, Dickie thought, to deposit them on the major's desk during his extended lunch break. This gave the captain enough time to light the blue touch paper and retire to a safe distance – though he suspected that his office wouldn't be anything like far enough.

Lunch was an anxious time for Dickie but it wasn't long before the jocular major's arrival back at the depot confirmed Dickie's suspicions: the naked spliff smoking had probably continued unabated somewhere else, probably in the major's cottage on Bodmin Moor. However, Dickie's visions of the major returning in his Land Rover wearing only his army peaked cap were fortunately dispelled. The upside was that he was in a marginally better mood than normal, no doubt caused by the effect of the illegal substances. The danger of an explosive 'Blue Streak' occurring once he had digested the contents of the damning letters seemed to have waned and Dickie waited to see if the Chinese firework turned out to be just a damp squib.

The major's calm demeanour and quiet arrival at Dickie's open door caught the captain by surprise. As he turned to face the major, he could see from his slightly contorted expression that the calming effect of the drugs was just beginning to wear off. With the three letters grasped in his right hand, it was soon clear that the major had taken only a cursory look at them.

"Lovely. You deal with all that," he said, throwing the letters from the Secretary of State and the Parliamentary Ombudsman on the floor at Dickie's feet. "I don't care. It's history. Bloody farmers, bureaucrats, the lot of them." Then he waved the third letter at Dickie. "But what's this letter from Bloodworth all about? A hearing? I bet it's all your doing."

No drugs could soften the impact of the brigadier's command and the major knew that any impending hearing would cast a dark shadow over his standing in his family, who would have to bear the disgrace that one of their own, from a long line of distinguished military forefathers, was about to face the firing squad. To them, even stealing a regimental ashtray would be the same as inviting the enemy for afternoon tea and any hearing, whatever the reason, was likely to spell doom and dishonour.

Dickie picked up the screwed-up letters from the floor and, showing the hand of friendship, quietly suggested to the major that he properly read the letter still in his grasp. The first few lines requested his attendance at the hearing, but the brigadier then adopted a conciliatory tone, one in which the suggestion of help formed part of the hearing brief. Although there was clearly a disciplinary element to it, Dickie pointed out, this wasn't so much a dressing down as an offer of assistance from Division to help the major rebalance his life – if he was prepared to receive it.

But he was too arrogant to see it, too arrogant to accept help – and certainly not from his second in command. The return of the SSPHE, his babies, which he had felt so privileged to babysit, just made it a lot worse. They were now being adopted because he wasn't trusted to look after them. He looked at Dickie and shook his fist. "I bet you had a hand in this. You and bloody Bloodworth are trying to send me to the loony bin. I'm not going. You can take the bloody SSPHE back in the Land Rover yourself."

Bravely, Dickie followed the major back to his office, hoping to explain his interpretation of the brigadier's letter, but the door was resolutely slammed in his face. The siege mentality was well and truly rooted in the major's head. The shutters had come down.

Dickie packed up his infamous blue file on the Gooley application, which contained all his emails to the major, the uncirculated minutes of the meeting with Jim Stern, Ashley and Fred all those months ago, and records of conversations with Division. It was soon on its way to Division, and on to the Parliamentary Ombudsman.

Chapter 26:
Completed and Deleted

It was now early December. Fred's complaint and claim for compensation, sponsored by Sir Michael Stride-Pecker, had now been with the Parliamentary Ombudsman for nearly three months. The man appointed for the task was Norman Stronghold, another no nonsense, common sense civil servant in the Stumpy mould, with an independent brain and a seniority that kept him immune to criticism from mealy-mouthed politicians driven by ulterior motives. Both sides had been afforded limited additional time to add to their case, having read the other's submissions. The Ministry made veiled attempts to reject claims of maladministration over its handling of the affair but Penelope and Johnny, with CHN's assistance, were able to provide damning evidence at every turn to robustly reject the Ministry's counter attack. The Gooley camp felt confident.

Penelope received a phone call. It was Brigadier Bloodworth. The Ministry wanted to do a deal. It would purchase Feathers Farm on the basis of its current value with planning permission for conversion to housing, as approved following the inquiry. That would be its full and final offer. No other payments would be made. It was clear to Penelope that Whitehall's tail was being wagged by the Treasury's dog. She made it clear that any purchase would have to include all her clients' costs otherwise the complaint to the Ombudsman would continue. Bloodworth conceded that his 'wriggle room' was limited but he eventually offered a compromise in allowing the purchase to proceed unconditionally and that the Ministry would agree to comply with all of the Ombudsman's recommendations.

Whitehall's thinking behind the offer was that a purchase now might just show the Ombudsman that the Ministry was taking Fred's claim for compensation seriously, showing contrition. Cynically, it believed that a purchase now might also help to reduce the level of possible compensation, if it were to lose. Penelope took the opposite view. To her it showed a sign of weakness, and at this stage of the process, a sign of desperation. The fact that the Ministry were not prepared to pay any other compensation also suggested that they were trying to steal the farm now, maintaining explosives storage capacity whilst benefiting from the development value of the farm when the recession subsided. It wanted to have its cake and eat it. As far as she was concerned, in the eyes of any reasonable person this would make the Ministry's position worse.

Bloodworth reiterated to Penelope the possibility that Tredyedeath Depot may close anyway under the Defence Spending Review, obviating the need for the Ministry to do anything at all but she quickly pointed out that the Ministry's 'do nothing' scenario assumed that the Ombudsman would ignore its behaviour in the whole affair, which she doubted. As far as she was concerned, it was and remained an insulting gesture.

Nevertheless, the offer was a step in the right direction and she and Johnny travelled to Feathers Farm to go through the purchase details with Fred and Grace. It was a warm day and Fred was on the doorstep as usual to greet them. Penelope's recommendation was to accept the deal and keep going with the Ombudsman complaint. It was a big decision for Fred and Grace, whose front room had seen so many strategies discussed with every twist and turn over the previous eighteen months. Fred needed space to think and he got up to leave whilst Grace dutifully poured another cup of tea and offered an unusually large variety of cakes. WI sales of Grace's cakes couldn't match her speed of production as a stress reliever, which had been on such a prolific scale that even Flossie and Attila were now in on the act, regularly finding pudding to supplement their daily dish of Mog-o-Munch or Fuller Fowl.

Fred knew it was right to accept the offer but he wanted some free time to roam around the courtyard and paddocks, just to be sure. Even in the darkest days of the recession, the planning permission for his development had created more value than the farm's use as a Christmas turkey business ever could, but it was nevertheless a seminal moment for both their farm and their future. Attila had joined him for comfort and, sensing a man deep in thought and reflection, kept her distance.

Fred soon returned and agreed that he would accept the offer on two conditions. First, that he would be allowed to stay rent free for up to a year to allow time for some renovations to their retirement cottage in Bodmin. Second, that it would be made clear to the Ombudsman that the offer was accepted reluctantly and represented no acquiescence on the Gooleys' part in their claim for rightful and fair compensation.

With the ball back in the brigadier's court and with his encouragement to settle, the Treasury advised the Ministry that it would accept Fred's terms. Penelope worked tirelessly to put Fred back in the black after nearly two years and the sale was completed by Christmas. But his retirement fund had taken a beating – and it was not over by a long way.

***

It was now Christmas time, and Dennis Blackstaff had decided to take a few extra days off work to spend at home with his loving wife, Dorothy. It was breakfast time and the kitchen stove was spitting and crackling with the sound of an unhealthy Full English when the letterbox rattled. Dennis scooped up the typical selection of variable-sized Christmas cards. He noticed one envelope thicker than the others and sat down to open it, just as Dorothy guided the last sausage into position. It was from Fred and Grace Gooley. A pretty, home-made Christmas card painted, as it was every year, by Grace's artist friend Christine, featuring a smiling Fred, wearing his tweed suit and matching flat hat, his faithful, pipe-smoking Grace by his side in a loud floral dress. Their cards would never be complete without Attila, proudly cradled in Fred arms, and an inquisitive Flossie around his feet. Dennis opened the card and a small brown envelope dropped out onto the breakfast table. He picked it up and peeked inside, immediately recognising six photos from his Feathers Farm incarceration.

Dorothy looked over Dennis' shoulder. "What's that, love? Who's it from?"

"Oh … It's er, it's from Fred and Grace Gooley, farmers from Trecarsick. They bank with us. He forgot to sign something before the Christmas break so I told him to send it to me here. He's put it in that brown envelope. I'll just put it in my briefcase."

"What's that other signature on the card, love? Who is Trevedic Deleted? That's a funny name!"

"Oh. Oh! I see. Yes, he's one of Fred's employees. Nice guy. Yes. Strange surname, Deleted. Still, it takes all sorts. Could I have a cup of tea, love?"

Dennis rushed out to hide the evidence in his bank issue briefcase – one Dorothy never looked in. He was flushed with relief that Fred's new found liquidity had enabled him to instruct that strange person 'Trevedic Deleted' to meet his side of the bargain and banish to the ether the electronic evidence of Dennis' unfortunate trip to the slaughterhouse, as confirmed by the cryptic Christmas card signature. Dorothy was none the wiser, and Dennis finally got his life back – albeit shortened a little by Dorothy's 'heart attack on a plate'. He smiled, tucked in and had a very happy Christmas with the family.

***

With Christmas now a distant memory, normality reigned as all parties got on with life whilst they were waiting for Norman Stronghold to deliver his findings into the Gooleys' complaint. For the previous eighteen months there had barely been a moment where one party or another was not grappling with the fallout of Fred's perfectly innocent planning application to convert his farm buildings.

At Tredyedeath Depot, the major had made it clear he wasn't going to make an appearance at his hearing, and Dickie was trying to work out what to do about it. The time had come around quickly since the brigadier's letter in September. In truth the hearing probably should have happened earlier as, by now, the major had almost totally barricaded himself in his office, only surfacing for food, water, coffee and those extended drug-infused lunchbreaks. Contrary to what the major believed, the captain hadn't blown the whistle on his unstable state of mind and he wasn't disposed to change that now. It would be up to the major to face the more draconian consequences of his absence when those appointed to conduct his hearing would find it to be a one-sided affair.

The major had ordered Dickie to take the SSPHE back to Reading. He and Karensa were going to London for a romantic weekend; they were leaving the next day so it was no real hardship to drop it off on the way. Dickie had worked out that if they left at one o'clock, they would be there in good time.

There was a knock on Dickie's door. Dickie lowered his voice in view of the visitor. "Ah. Private Johnston. I see you have been keeping out of my way with that guard dog of yours," he said. "What can I do for you? Nothing that's going to put us both in the brig, I hope?"

"Well sir, I am of course very grateful that you've allowed us to patrol the unalarmed part of the mine reserved for the SSPHE," Johnston replied. "Fluffy has enjoyed taking Kenneth and Ollie with him. He's been good as gold, you know. We've kept well out of trouble."

"I am glad to hear that, Johnston. But if you remember, once you spilt the beans to me, I don't think I had any choice in the matter. Go on."

"Well sir, Fluffy's just getting a bit bored and Kenneth and Ollie have seen better days now. Could I take a Frisbee into the mine tonight? There's plenty of space in there and he could do with some extra mental stimulation. There's only twelve boxes of SSPHE; they won't be in the way."

"All right, Johnston, but just mind how you go. We have had enough excitement down here to last a lifetime, what with the major's unannounced streaking event. Division is watching our every move."

***

The delighted Private Johnston's night shift soon arrived and he unlocked Fluffy's kennel to let the excited canine out for the overnight eleven to four patrol. It was normal practice to switch off the alarm, walk past the corridor of stacked boxes of explosives which the major had temporarily turned into a gladiatorial circuit and, once inside the SSPHE storage area, turn the alarm back on again. There was still some concern about what extraneous forces might trigger the experimental explosive, so its storage area remained unalarmed and out of influence of any alarm systems. The Bromsgrove operations room knew the protocol and the times when the alarm would be switched off and on for dog patrols to access the SSPHE storage area.

It was now 12.30am and with three and a half hours to go, Private Johnston slipped a yellow Frisbee out of his uniform. Fluffy looked up in the dim light and, recognising the yellow saucer, excitedly dropped a very damp and semi-shredded Ollie in anticipation. Time for some fun. Fluffy had become adept at catching a Frisbee in mid-air but Private Johnston knew that he hadn't yet reached his limits and here was the space to try him out. Throw after throw, they edged further into the mine as the yellow projectile was hurtled higher and longer. Distracted by the game, neither of them noticed that they were slowly advancing on the two stacks of SSPHE boxes. There was no reason for a guard dog patrolman like Johnston to know about the unique properties of the experimental explosive: how it worked, how it was detonated or its variable pre-detonation period. To him, they were just boxes with lots of meaningless army writing on the side.

"OK Fluffs," Johnston said, wearily. "These are the last few throws. Anyway, you look a bit pooped and I need a rest too."

Fifteen minutes passed and Fluffy, sensing that this might be the last throw, started to crab-walk backwards, his eyes remaining focused on the projectile firmly held in Private Johnston's right hand in preparedness for the final fling and Olympic-style mid-air catch. Johnston drew the projectile across his chest and, in a flash of yellow, flicked it off his wrist, sending it hurtling towards the mine's ceiling. Fluffy, now crabbing as fast as he could, picked up his pace as the saucer flew over his head and gained height before it slowed. Just as it started a gentle curling descent, the chasing canine detected it to be within range. He flicked round and extended his back legs fully to launch himself at the drifting disc, grasping it firmly in his flashing teeth. It was a brilliant, spectacular mid-air catch and timed to perfection. His best yet.

Unfortunately, over the course of the fun, 'Frisbee creep' had brought Fluffy and Private Johnston perilously close to the SSPHE and the inevitable happened. In one almighty crash, Fluffy, still with the Frisbee clamped tightly in his mouth, landed backwards with such force that both piles of boxes crashed to the ground, two of the boxes' lids springing open to scatter the red and blue explosive 'Jenga' sticks everywhere. A worried and shocked Johnston rushed over, his only concern to make sure his beloved dog's legs were still all pointing in the right direction and that his Frisbee catching days hadn't come to a premature end. He was about to crouch down to comfort his dazed companion when the shocked Sheppy suddenly rose to his feet. With a quick shake of each leg, followed by neck, back and a swoosh of his beam and tail to confirm that everything was in working order, Fluffy dropped the Frisbee at the private's feet, his teeth marks a visible reminder of the extra grip required during his destructive descent onto the offending boxes.

Johnston, now relieved, gathered his senses, surveyed the carnage and scratched his head. He could see Fluffy looking intently at the sea of scattered explosive sticks which, only moments earlier, were sitting safely in the security of their strictly organised home. To Fluffy, here was another game, one which he learnt when he was a pup. Jenga! These were Jenga sticks – and who better to put them back in their box than him? After all, he had had enough practice. Frisbee was history. He pricked his ears up, looked at Johnston for 'permission to Jenga' and wandered over to the red and blue sticks for a quick sniff. He looked over at Johnston again and then turned around to find an empty box still upright. Carefully and without any prompt, he picked up a stick and dropped it into the box, pushing it with his nose into the corner ready to place the next one alongside.

Johnston got the message. "Good boy, good boy, Fluffs. Well done. It's Jenga! It's Jenga! God knows what all that writing is on the side. Typical of the army. Everything's got meaningless writing on it."

Fluffy gave a few excited wags of his tail in recognition that he was onto a winner whilst Johnston righted the other box in readiness for the new game before he sat down to watch. This was a good opportunity for Johnston to test Fluffy's colour recognition skills and, enticed with a few treats he always kept in his pocket, Fluffy started to stack the sticks in alternate colours, one blue, one red until both boxes were full again. The top layers glinted like seaside rock before the shadow of each lid came down, sealing them back into darkness. Johnston clouted the lids' protruding nails with a piece of granite to make sure they were firmly secure once again. He looked very pleased with Fluffy who, with a few more treats, clearly felt that he had passed the doggy colour recognition test.

"OK Fluffs, all we have to do now, my boy, is to stack them like they were before. Christ, look at all that writing," Johnston said. "Wait a minute … Look Fluffs, some boxes have got one set of numbers on the side and some have another set. Let's stack them by their matching numbers. It's the best we can do."

In a stroke of pure luck, Private Johnston had managed to stack the twelve boxes exactly as they were stored: six red in one stack, and six blue in another. No one would notice. There was only one problem. The coloured sticks had all been paired in two of the boxes. They were now lying side by side. Blue next to red. The twelve hour chemically timed proximity detonation process had started. It was now one o'clock in the morning.

***

The Tredyedeath Depot gatehouse security men knew Karensa well from her regular trips to the base to see the love of her life. Wrapped up in a winter coat, she decided to walk from Trecarsick in the fresh, cold January air to meet Dickie at the depot, leaving Cordelia to look after the village shop. Dickie had been at work since the early hours to give him more time to clear his desk so they could leave for London straight from the depot. It was 12.30. After a quick chat with the security guards at the gatehouse, Karensa approached the office block to see Dickie poking his head out of the window, directing two guards who had just finished manhandling the SSPHE boxes into the back of his Land Rover. They tied down its green rear canvas cover with those webbing straps which the major, in his excitement, had been so eager to undo on its arrival all those months ago.

The off-duty Private Johnston had been watching events. There were too many uniforms around so any gratitude to the captain for a successful Frisbee evening in the mine needed to be in code. "I see that you are taking those boxes away, sir. Well, sir, Bismarck and I had a very good night last night guarding them. He was very alert, sir. Very alert, he was. Untouched they are, sir. Safe in your hands, they are, sir. Whilst I'm here I'll flick off the Land Rover immobiliser for you." Johnston opened the driver's door and reached under the driver's seat to deactivate the Land Rover's engine immobiliser – not that army vehicles were a particular target for thieves, but Land Rovers of all ages did have a geek following so the immobiliser was a token gesture to security.

Dickie went back to his desk and, on hearing Karensa coming up the stairs, went out to greet her just as the major surfaced from his office grasping a copy of the latest *Bang!* magazine. He looked at Dickie, grunted about having to take a long lunch hour and brushed past Karensa on his way down the stairs. It was 12.40. Karensa just shrugged her shoulders and joined Dickie in his office to warm up and chat excitedly about their London soiree. It wasn't long before they were distracted by a sporadic whirring sound coming from outside, followed by a lot of banging.

A few minutes later, the office stairs rattled with the major's distinctive footsteps. The door swung open. "Bloody Land Rover. Won't start. Bloody Land Rover. Can't wait. Can't wait any longer. Need yours."

With that, the major snatched Dickie's Land Rover keys, which were hanging by the door, and marched, head down, out of his office towards the stairs.

Dickie took chase. "Sir. I need the Land Rover. I'm leaving in a few minutes to deliver the SSPHE back to Reading and then on to London. The boxes are in the back. They have to be there today. I have the afternoon off. I've been here since five this morning."

"Too bad. Need Land Rover. Can't wait. Must go. You will just have to wait until I get back. Get mine repaired, would you? Bloody Land Rovers." The major was clearly on a mission. The drugs were waiting at home. It was now 12.50. There was nothing Dickie could do about it. Reading was expecting the SSPHE that afternoon, in accordance with the brigadier's strict instructions, but he was just going to have to wait until the major returned.

The major fired up Dickie's Land Rover and drove out of the base and into the wide open landscape. As he drove further away from the depot, his demeanour started to change in anticipation of the impending but temporary relief from his woes. The inherited family cottage on Bodmin Moor, like the mine, was one place, with or without drugs, that provided solitude, time to reflect. The drone of the engine became part of his reverie as the Land Rover bounced along the winding road, jostling its dangerous cargo. The major, relieved to be heading for a dose of heaven, allowed his mind to drift. Injustices he had suffered, but also those he had so unnecessarily inflicted on others and buried under mounds of denial, began to bubble to the surface. Any lack of remorse only confirmed that he was a product of a complex past, which had forged a personality driven by suspicion and rejection. He wasn't going to stand in front of any army hearing. They could whistle as far as he was concerned.

A strange smell wafted into the front of the Land Rover. One o'clock arrived. His dose of heaven was nearer than he realised…

The experimental SSPHE twelve-hour detonation cycle proved to be remarkably accurate. A large black mushroom cloud soon appeared on the horizon and seconds later the sinister sound of a huge explosion rumbled through Trecarsick, Tredyedeath Depot and the surrounding valleys. Windows rattled, pint mugs hanging in the Tinner's Whippet tinkled in unison, the picture of Demelza Friggins in the village hall crashed to the floor, the *Trumpet* headline board outside the village shop moved a few inches sideways and, to Cordelia's delight, her dodgy-looking Men-an-Tol long service award fell off its high shelf in the shop and smashed irreparably on the floor.

Dickie looked out of his office window and spotted the pall of black smoke coming from the direction of the major's departure. He told Karensa to stay put and ran downstairs to the car park. He looked at the major's recalcitrant Land Rover, its keys still in the ignition, and jumped in, hoping there might just be some life left in the battery. He slipped his hand under the driver's seat to reach for the immobiliser. It was still on. In his haste to leave, the major had simply forgotten to switch it off. Dickie paused and collected his thoughts. With a large lump in his throat and hands shaking at the realisation of what might have been for him and Karensa, he flicked the immobiliser switch and turned the ignition key. With a large puff of blue smoke, the Land Rover fired up and the captain roared out of the depot in the direction of the sinister black column, yelling at the security gate guards to alert the emergency services as he shot past.

After two miles of winding roads, Dickie rounded the next bend to find his worst fears realised. He slowed the Land Rover to a walking pace as he picked his way around fragments of hot smoking metal, rubber and canvas scattered indiscriminately over the road and hedges. There in front of him was utter carnage and a large, perfectly formed hole in the road any explosives expert would have been proud of. From the twisted metal scattered around, there was no indication that this was once a military Land Rover, though Dickie recognised enough of the green fragments to know that here, and over a large part of Bodmin Moor, was the major's final resting place. Confirmation came in the form of a steaming engine block lying on its side, a recognisable 'Property of the British Army – Report any damage' plate still fixed to it.

The emergency vehicles soon arrived to clear up the mess and as Dickie solemnly drove back to the depot, he spotted something smouldering on the top of the 'Trecarsick. Please Drive Carefully' road sign. He pulled over to have a look and immediately recognised it as the major's still smoking peaked cap, a charred fragment from his favourite periodical, *Bang!*, fused into the fabric just above the peak. The major, it seemed, had consumed his own smoke in more ways than one and was now finally out of his misery – and Dickie's too.

The weekend trip to London with Karensa was cancelled as Dickie had to file his report into the incident immediately. Despite his antipathy towards the major, he just wasn't in the mood to give Karensa the loving attention she deserved. His report quickly concluded that the experimental, prototype SSPHE, which had been stored strictly in accordance with the Ministry's instructions, must somehow have become unstable. He recommended more research into its storage environment and further tests to take place immediately on the other batches stored in other depots around the country to establish possible failings in their properties.

Something told Dickie not to interview Private Johnston about the previous night's Frisbee patrol just in case he was able to extract some unpleasant truth from the honest dog handler, a truth which just might be too unpalatable to bear. Anyway, he felt comforted by the thought that no one in authority would conceivably believe that there was a pet Sheppy on the base, masquerading as a guard dog, whose Frisbee jaunts amongst the SSPHE might have somehow been instrumental in the demise of the depot commander. It was so fanciful a scenario that he decided to let sleeping dogs lie. Literally.

Dickie was soon put in charge of Tredyedeath Depot. A sense of normality reigned for the first time in many years.

Chapter 27:
Explosive Stuff

With the major's demise and what had gone on before, Dickie could feel that Tredyedeath Depot was beginning to look like a backwater to Division, despite his very able management style. Despite scientific tests the instability of SSPHE had not been proven and questions lingered about what really happened in the days leading up to the explosion. The Treasury had to shell out in buying Feathers Farm, which it didn't want to do, and the Ministry didn't need any more damning events that might put another nail in the depot's coffin.

It was now March and 'Gunpowder' Guy Gunston called Sir Michael Stride-Pecker to let him know that his spies were telling him that the Parliamentary Ombudsman's report was imminent and word on the street was that the Ministry was going to get a pasting. The news soon travelled through the grapevine via Trevelyan Trelyon, eventually reaching Grace and Fred. Everyone was braced for its arrival.

Guy's spies were spot on. Norman Stronghold's confidential twenty page report was issued a few days later directly to its sponsor, Sir Michael, who took no time in distributing it to those entitled to see it. He started to prepare his question for the House, which Guy Gunston knew wouldn't be long in coming.

***

Penelope and Johnny had arranged to meet Fred and Grace at Feathers Farm as soon as the report was issued but managed to squeeze in a short briefing lunch in advance. They knew the report might need some explanation and despite the thought of being force fed more cakes and tea by Grace, there was no better place to share the news and the implications for the Gooleys' future than at Feathers Farm.

The narrow Cornish lanes to Feathers Farm echoed once again to the sound of Johnny's protesting hot hatch, its engine and gearbox sounding like the dying throes of a wild animal. Fred had learnt to recognise his planning consultants' mechanically assisted arrival and despite his disapproval, this was probably not a day for road safety recriminations. It was surprising to see that Penelope had let Johnny drive her but it soon became apparent why, as her exit from the car revealed her walking, slightly bent and assisted by a stick, the result of a twisted back and related pulled muscles which prevented her from driving. Her condition had caused her to spend most of the journey doubled up with her head too low in the car either to be carsick or to observe Johnny's dodgem-like skills in negotiating his way to the farm. On her collection, Penelope wasted no time in warning Johnny to avoid making any crude suggestion that the causes of her physical state might have been due to her attendance at some form of all night orgy. He obliged but she could see from the expression on his face that he was deriving much enjoyment from the imagery alone. This glee was unfortunately supplemented by Johnny's execution of a sharp left hand bend at such speed that the G-force caused Penelope's face to end up in Johnny's lap.

The front room beckoned and Penelope could see that Fred was past making small talk. She decided to cut to the end of the report – its findings and recommendations – first. "Well, Mr Gooley, Johnny and I are very pleased to say that you have won the day. The Ombudsman, Mr Norman Stronghold has found in your favour and has awarded you significant compensation to be paid by the Ministry of Defence. This is made up of the loss in the value of the farm since you first submitted the application, interest on that lost income caused by the unnecessary and unjustified delay and all your costs associated with the public inquiry and pursuing this claim against the Ministry. It's a major victory. I should warn you that the recommendation is not legally binding but, to make sure you get it, I would lobby your MP to put pressure on the Secretary of State for Defence. My understanding from having spoken to Trevelyan

Trelyon is that Guy Gunston has confirmed to Sir Michael Stride-Pecker that he will be as good as his word but we need him now to deliver. He is, after all, a politician."

It was indeed a major success and the substantial award ensured that Fred and Grace's retirement plans were back on track. It had been two years since the whole process started and it had taken its toll on Fred and Grace through worry and, at one point, the prospect of bankruptcy.

Penelope started to go through the report but could see that it wouldn't be long before Fred and Grace glazed over in the euphoria. The news had been overwhelming. She decided to keep it short by highlighting just some of the Ombudsman's disturbing findings. The plethora of internal memos and briefings from within different departments in the Ministry and the Treasury, which Penelope had never been privy to, had exposed a catalogue of intrigue and agendas which had conspired against Fred from the beginning. Their exposure to the Ombudsman's forensic scrutiny led him to only one stark conclusion: the Gooleys had been badly treated and it was payback time.

Penelope started to highlight some of the shocking findings. It was explosive stuff. "...I quote from that internal Ministry memo which referred to the inquiry inspector's perceptive questions on the Ministry's attitude to risk with regard to people employed in buildings used for agricultural purposes. The memo is telling and states: 'Sir, regrettably, I have to report that our regulations on this aspect of our guidance are at best unscientific and therefore, as you can appreciate, their exposure at the resumed inquiry would show the Ministry's systems in a poor light...

"...It was very early in the consultation process that the Ministry was fully aware of the Gooleys' application, as the comprehensive Tredyedeath Depot file containing a newspaper cutting about the scheme reveals. That file also contains the minutes of a meeting with the chief planning officer, who explained to the Tredyedeath Depot commander the inconsistencies in the Ministry's objection given the number of employees employed in the Gooleys' business. Yet for some reason the Ministry maintained its ill-advised objection despite being informed that operation of the turkey business did not require planning permission even if it was to intensify its business, increasing staff numbers in the process. It is telling that the Ministry blindly maintained its view that Mr Gooley's business was an illegal activity despite being told to the contrary early in the process by the chief planning officer. It also argued that the application breached Health and Safety Executive (HSE) statutory regulations. This was incorrect and – forgive me for using military parlance – something of a smokescreen. The HSE quite simply has no jurisdiction in the matter. It is clear to me that the Ministry's representatives were ill equipped properly to comply with public inquiry procedures, and its failure to provide all the proofs of evidence, which ultimately would have revealed its weaknesses, drew particular criticism from the planning inspector. I therefore have come to the conclusion from the Ministry's own files that it was motivated – indeed, obliged – to withdraw its flawed objection as it had clearly come to the view that its defective safeguarding map regime would have been exposed at the reopened inquiry. In withdrawing its objection, I note that the Ministry was at pains to make clear that it had adopted a conciliatory stance in accepting a reduction in operational efficiency at Tredyedeath Depot but to my mind this was a disingenuous offer. The truth was, it had no choice…

"…The Ministry's management of the Gooleys' compensation claim was also flawed. In reality, it cannot defend a claim that it belatedly knew of the case because its own files tell us to the contrary, as I set out above. It simply does not stand up to scrutiny. It took far too long to recognise that there was no justification and no substance to support its allegations against the Gooleys' application in defence of its explosives depot. The inquiry inspector had no jurisdiction to award costs against the Ministry for its behaviour but I note that he made his frustrations very clear on that matter. I share those frustrations. The Ministry's feeble acceptance that recompense was due is demonstrated by its acquisition of Feathers Farm, albeit at recessionary values. But its offer was made on the basis of the threat that Tredyedeath Depot may close and within any claim for compensation, and left the Gooleys with little choice. In my opinion this approach lacked a proper sense of equity and natural justice. The Gooleys' representatives were right to adopt a trenchant view on the matter and I agree that the reluctant acceptance of purchase, though a step in the right direction, was not the end of the matter…"

By this time Fred and Grace had gained a second wind – and it wasn't due to Grace's cakes. Penelope, still struggling with her back, rejected Johnny's mischievously innocent suggestion that sitting on his knee would have a miraculously beneficial effect. She pointedly suggested that it wouldn't be her who would be getting all the benefit and quickly steered Johnny, Fred and Grace back to what she felt was the seminal part of Norman's report.

"…In my communication with the Permanent Under-Secretary, he expressed his regret that his department had not handled the matter well and for that he wished to convey his apologies to Mr and Mrs Gooley. He accepted that Mr and Mrs Gooley had, through no fault of their own, been deprived of fair treatment at the hands of the Ministry and hoped that the Ministry's unconditional purchase of their property had, in some small way, brought them short term relief. My suggestion that the Ministry makes a substantial ex gratia payment over and above the purchase price of the farm was accepted without hesitation. This would include interest on the purchase price and lost value from the time when Mr and Mrs Gooley could reasonably have been expected to receive planning permission. It would also include all the costs incurred through the public inquiry and pursuing this claim. To my mind, this represents a satisfactory response to a wholly justified complaint…"

It was a momentous occasion and Grace rushed into the kitchen to dust off some ancient home-made dandelion and burdock wine she'd been experimenting with for some time, awaiting its grand opening at a special occasion. Its slow exit from the bottle to reveal what looked like treacle suggested that Grace hadn't got it quite right and, fearing that its consumption might require the immediate assistance of a life support system, Penelope and Johnny declined on the basis that Fred and Grace needed time to absorb the full implications of the damning report. They made their excuses and headed for the front door. Their job was done and with Penelope accepting Johnny's offer to drive very slowly on the promise of a celebratory drink at a wine bar close to her office, they parted company knowing that another planning problem would probably see them working together again one day.

Trecarsick was rumbling at the news of Fred's successful compensation claim and its timing was perfect for Trevedic Penhaligon to produce what he knew would be his last *Trumpet* headline on the Gooley saga. It would soon be old news, just chip paper, and he needed to give Fred the sort of send-off he thought his grandchildren would appreciate for their scrapbook in years to come. Karensa slid the header into the pavement board outside the shop and, wearing her tantalizing Trumpet Thursday attire, prepared herself to sell another twenty balls of string, ten packets of Elastoplast – in fact, multiples of anything – along, of course, with that week's copy of the local paper.

'Mandarin Mauls Meddling Ministry over Mine Maltreatment.'

***

Two months had passed and the Ministry had gone to ground over the fallout from the Ombudsman's report but Penelope continued to keep the pressure on with endless emails to the brigadier, all of which had been copied to Trevelyan Trelyon and onwards to Sir Michael. The MP soon brought the matter to the House of Commons, as he promised Guy he would. The question had been circulated to Guy and his mandarins in advance, in accordance with the traditional rules of the House.

It was question time and the Speaker looked over to Sir Michael. "Sir Michael Stride-Pecker MP. Your question to the Secretary of State for Defence, The Right Honourable Guy Gunston, please."

"Thank you, Mr Speaker. Would my Right Honourable friend confirm that the Ministry diligently are prosecuting the award of costs to my constituents, Mr and Mrs Gooley of Feathers Farm, Trecarsick, which has been awarded by the Parliamentary Ombudsman on which I had received assurances that he would honour? I know he will be familiar with the specifics of this case."

"Mr Speaker," Gunston replied, "I can assure my friend for Bodmin Central that the Ministry expeditiously will be handling this compensation claim in the diligent manner for which this Ministry is held in high regard. It is working closely with the Treasury to ensure that his constituents are not put to any ongoing hardship."

Nothing could have been further from the truth. The Treasury had made it clear to Guy's mandarins that, whilst it was alright for him to grovel at the feet of the Ombudsman to retrieve some semblance of respectability, it wasn't going to be at the Treasury's expense. The best the Ministry of Defence could hope for was a Treasury loan to pay off the Gooleys – but it would have to be repaid from the ever decreasing defence budget. The loan was eventually agreed.

With Feathers Farm sold and the monies from Ashley Sweet's insurers and eventually the Ministry now in the bank, Fred and Grace started to think about their future. Their retirement.

Chapter 28:
A Watershed Moment

Dickie decided not to relocate his office into the major's for fear, superstitiously, that he might somehow take on the major's Jekyll and Hyde persona. His warrant officer cleared it out and it remained an empty, eerie space behind its firmly closed door. In the Ministry's cutbacks, the major's post was not replaced and Tredyedeath Depot was slowly reverting to a backwater explosive storage facility.

The internal post arrived and Dickie recognised a letter from Division. His efficient and pragmatic management of the depot was such that he had been left largely to his own devices since the major's demise so when he did receive a letter from Division he knew it was something quite important. His suspicions were right.

It was from the brigadier. It was short and sharp. Bloodworth had completed his review of all the explosive storage areas across the country as part of his Defence Spending Review and would be recommending the immediate closure and disposal of Tredyedeath Depot. Captain Lovely's job would be protected, possibly in line with promotion to run another depot, as would the other military personnel.

The brigadier, not one to hide behind paperwork, soon followed up the letter with a phone call to explain his reasoning. Ironically, the sale of the depot would help to fund the Gooleys' compensation claim and with the Ministry now owning Feathers Farm, which it didn't really want in the first place, the sale of that too, with the planning permission Fred had fought for, would help to recoup some much needed income.

For Dickie, the closure of Tredyedeath Depot was the timely trigger for him to decide on his future. It was a watershed. The time was right for him to move on and he rejected the offer of promotion, which the brigadier fully respected. The captain had met the love of his life in Karensa and he was going to make Trecarsick their home. Had it not been for the major's unfortunate end, he had planned to propose to Karensa that weekend in London. It was taking time for them both to recover from the 'what might have been' nightmare scenario if the major had just flicked that immobiliser switch under the seat of his Land Rover.

For Private Johnston the news fitted well with his plans and the end of his current army contract, which he soon confirmed he would not be renewing. His girlfriend in Wadebride was not only still in tow but she'd bought a companion for Fluffy. The private had accepted a job at an animal rescue centre in the Camel Valley only a few miles from Wadebridge and he was looking forward to his new career. It wasn't that difficult to persuade Dickie to explain to his masters in Division that, if Johnston was going to leave the army, so too would 'Bismarck', whose bond with the private was such that he would be useless as a guard dog with any other handler. That of course was true, but for entirely different reasons. This suited Division perfectly, as its agenda was focused on cost saving.

Within a few months the de-commissioning was almost complete and all the personnel now transferred to other military locations. As retiring incumbents, Dickie, Private Johnston and Fluffy were left to take one more walk around the empty mine before locking up. With no one around, Johnston had brought the infamous yellow Frisbee with him for one last fling. With all the explosives gone and the alarm systems removed, it wasn't long before the flying saucer was being hurled around with impunity. Now well into the mine with no evidence of any military equipment remaining, Johnston made one final throw before he and Dickie both turned around to walk back. Fluffy shot off down the mine like a rocket after the swerving Frisbee and soon vanished around a promontory of rock. It went quiet and in that moment Johnston instinctively turned around, fearing that his canine friend had vanished down an old mine shaft. He ran through the mine, frantically calling his name as Dickie looked on, finding himself to be surprisingly worried for his walking companion. Johnston arrived and breathed a sigh of relief as there, in the dim emergency lighting, he could see a pair of back legs and a vigorously wagging tail. A few seconds later, a head appeared with something in his mouth. Fluffy looked very pleased.

"What have you got there, you silly old thing. Drop that now!" Johnston ordered. Fluffy walked over submissively to the private, who by now had been joined by Dickie, wanting to see what was going on. The dog looked up at them and dropped something on the ground between them. It was a red SSPHE 'Jenga' stick. Dickie was speechless. He looked inquisitively at Johnston but, try as he may, he was unable to say anything.

Johnston decided to break the silence. "Well, sir, we did accidentally knock over a couple of those special boxes of coloured explosives when we were playing Frisbee the night before it was taken off the depot. I thought we put it all back but we must have missed this one. Nice colours, don't you think? Red and blue they were, sir. I put the lids back on good and proper and nobody noticed. Not to worry. Why don't I just chuck it down the mine shaft over there, the one that's not been concreted over properly? Back in a minute, sir."

There was nothing Dickie could do. Johnston and Fluffy had been unaware of the enormity of their actions and anything he reported now would only send all three of them to a fate probably worst than the major's. Private Johnston and Fluffy, he thought, had probably done the major a favour – but it could easily have been him and Karensa.

***

It was dusk. Fred wandered into the empty yard, which had been home to thousands of turkeys over the years. Its eerie silence still played tricks on his senses. After a year preparing their Bodmin cottage, it was the Gooleys' last night at the farm. It was the end of an era. He sat precariously on the edge of the feeder he had filled up hundreds of times before and stared over at the emptiness of the Cornish stone barns, stone walls and increasingly dilapidated fencing that he and his father had once toiled over. He still half expected the daily cloud of white feathers, dust and a cacophony of whooping to come jostling towards him in eager anticipation at feeding and bed time but only the ghosts of past flocks were left to play tricks on his imagination. Only Attila remained and she was tucked up in her barn home.

Something stirred beyond the courtyard wall. At first it was a little chortle, the faint sound of scratching and what sounded distinctly like the movement of outstretched wings. Fred thought nothing of it. Why would he? All his birds were long gone. He must have been dreaming. Just then, a small single white feather drifted into the air above the courtyard wall and slowly the top of a white head appeared in view, followed by one eye and then the other and finally a beak. Fred jumped to his feet, his heart racing just like the first time he grappled with the ample Grace with youthful enthusiasm amongst the turkeys all those years ago. It was Attila. Her neck rose like a snake charmer's cobra and in one movement she hopped onto the wall and stood majestically in front of him, her chest protruding proudly in characteristic defiance. Fred strode purposefully forwards and scooped her into his arms, holding her firmly like a new born baby. Her eyes closed and her neck sank slowly onto his shoulder.

He looked at her like a long lost friend. "You're coming home to Bodmin with me," he said.

He turned his back on the yard for the last time. She was indeed. Attila was coming home.

The end

A Note from the Author

Like many debut authors, I am sure that I'm not the only one to have been taken, in my head, to places I never thought existed as I proudly and diligently crafted away at the storyline in the solitude of my office. New thoughts would come into my head as the twists and turns of the plot very quickly took on a life of their own only weeks into the 'journey'. I soon felt I was becoming the messenger. The idea of a parallel story within the novel, in this case based on a wise turkey, had been fascinating me for some time and developing its character was just another part of my amazing journey. It was of course pure fiction. At least that's what I thought until, three months after I completed the novel, we decided to take a holiday in America, the home of the turkey. The spirituality of the Native American culture fascinated my wife Gail, and it wasn't long before the weight of our luggage was heading dangerously towards airline health and safety limits as more and more books on the subject were acquired and knowledge absorbed.

"You'd better read this," Gail said as she thrust into my hands a copy of 'Spirits of the Earth: a guide to Native American nature symbols, stories, and ceremonies' by Bobby Lake-Thom. There, in the chapter called 'Bird signs and omens', was a page about turkeys. I picked up the book with trepidation.

"*The turkey is a good sign, but its character is arrogant, colourful, sneaky, quick minded and tricky. Turkeys can warn of people's personality. If you happen to see a turkey just before a visitor comes, it is an indication that your visitor is nervous, arrogant, fickle in decision-making and unreliable...*"

It seems, in novel writing, you really are just the messenger!

About the Author

After forty years working as a planning consultant, Martyn Smith turned his hand to writing to create this debut novel, Spitting Feathers.

Martyn is married to Gail and lives in the Cotswolds. In his spare time he enjoys music, travelling and photography.

Acknowledgements

With so much thanks to the following people, who helped to make Spitting Feathers a reality.

Gail, my wife, for putting up with my solitude and obsession.

Alison Thompson, aka the Proof Fairy, for so much help and guidance, editing, formatting, doing all the technical stuff, helping to make it all happen and her continuing support during promotion.

Christine Southworth, for taking my vague idea for a cover and turning it into a beautiful piece of art.

The oh so helpful Beta Reader Group for keeping me on the straight and narrow – Angela Clarkson, Nikki Morrow-Brown, Judith Aram, Sheila and Les Jones, Su McLaughlin, Eileen Grout, Jonathan Beech and Ian Ashworth.

Christopher Lockhart-Mummery QC for being a good sport.

Lou Thomas, Office Manager at Pegasus Planning in Cirencester, for helping to format numerous drafts for me, Alison and the Beta Readers.

All my friends at Pegasus Planning Ltd and the company for their support.

All my family and friends, particularly Ann and Chris Conroy and Sian and Nick Salter, who have given such invaluable support and feedback.

Made in the USA
Charleston, SC
13 December 2015